RUNNING CRAZY

RUNNING CRAZY

A THRILLER

BASED ON THE CASE FILES OF A CRIME-SOLVING CLAIRVOYANT

D.J. ADAMS

ALSO BY D.J. ADAMS
SCENTING EVIL

CAPITAL BOOKS, INC.

CAPITAL BOOKS, INC.
22841 Quicksilver Drive
Sterling, Virginia

CAPITAL BOOKS, INC.
P.O. Box 605
Herndon, Virginia 20172-0605

Library of Congress Cataloging-in-Publication Data

Adams, D. J.
Running crazy : a thriller based on the case files of the
crime-solving clairvoyant / D.J. Adams.-- 1st ed.
p. cm.
ISBN 1-892123-99-1 (alk. paper)
1. Clairvoyants--Fiction. I. Title.
PS3601.D37R865 2003
813'.6--dc21 2003001677

Printed in the United States of America on acid-free paper that meets the American National Standards Institute Z39-48 Standard.

First Edition

10 9 8 7 6 5 4 3 2 1

For my mother,

who endured having a clairvoyant child and

maintained not only her sanity but mine as well.

Thank you for your love, my life,

my education, and your patience.

For my brother, who fought

the war on drugs and lost.

For my children, all four of them,

who have brought me so much joy

and helped to ease the loss

of my childhood family.

I love you with all my heart.

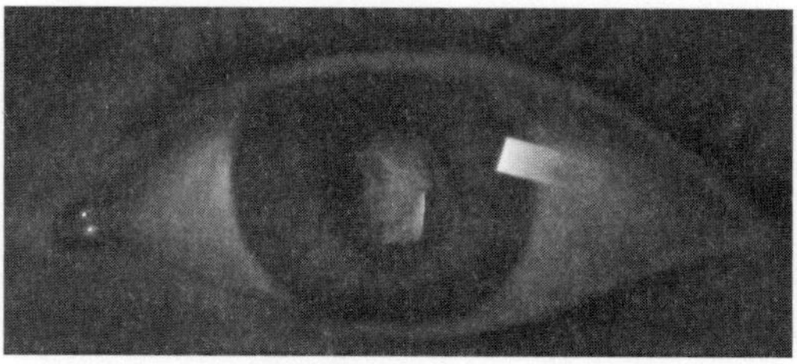

PROLOGUE

"Woohooo! Yeah!" Mike Hennessey yelled as he leaned out the window of the '69 Chevy van and beat his hand against the door. He looked over at his partner Tony Garrison and yelled again, "Yahoooo!" as he toked on the joint in his other hand and then handed it to Tony. Tony took it but it wasn't his drug of choice. He preferred the bottle of tequila he held tightly in his free hand.

With the joint held between his first two fingers Tony tipped the bottle of amber-colored liquor back and pulled long and hard on it. He grimaced and swallowed hard. The liquor burned going down, but it gave him the fortitude to keep up with Mike. With a shake of his head Tony slammed his foot down on the accelerator and floored it. Terror drove through the beautiful northern countryside. Mike Hennessey and Tony Garrison were on a rampage that would take them across some of the most beautiful country in the United States. In their path of destruction lay a busy city filled with Ripney High School students getting ready for senior prom.

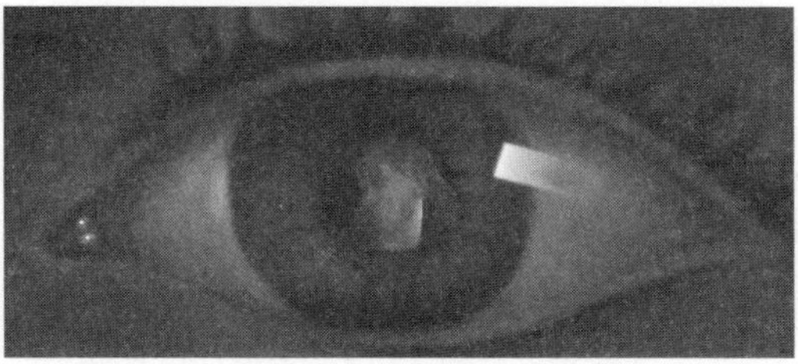

CHAPTER 1

Lindsay walked into Room 5436 and flipped on the overhead light. The television was still on and turned up loud, so she reached over to the bedside control and eased the volume down.

"Lindsay, is that you?"

"Yes, Mr. O'Reilly, it's me. Rest easy, I just came in to say goodnight," Lindsay said as she tenderly laid her hand on his forehead. Henry O'Reilly thought the touch was for gentleness, but Lindsay was also assessing his temperature. He was warm to the touch.

"I'm going to have the night nurse check your temperature first," she said as she eased the pillows under his broken leg. "Are you in pain, can I get you something before I leave?" Lindsay watched his face for signs of discomfort.

"No, Missy, you go on home. Your young son must be wondering where his momma is. I'll be fine till morning. Then you can come in and fuss over me some more."

Lindsay looked lovingly into the blind eyes of the man lying in the bed. She knew he must be in great pain, but he would never complain. Besides, he hated the drowsy feeling from the pain medication. He was afraid he would miss something going on in the hallway outside his room.

"Take the meds and get some rest, Mr. O'Reilly. You know nothing ever happens around here unless I say so," Lindsay joked. "You know this place needs my permission in order to function."

Henry chuckled. "Ah, Lindsay girl, you're a good nurse and a loving child. Kiss my forehead and ease on out of here and leave an old man to his dreams."

Lindsay leaned forward and gently kissed his brow. "Sweet dreams. I'll see you in the morning."

Lindsay gathered her things from the nursing station and headed for the parking lot. As she let herself out the emergency entrance she gazed up at the stars.

"What a beautiful night this is going to be." She inhaled deeply, and the sweet smell of rain-freshened air filled her lungs and brought a smile to her lips. She reveled in the feeling of the cool summer evening. As she felt release from the day's stress, she let out a sigh. She squared her shoulders and walked toward her Jeep Cherokee. The fading sun cast an eerie glow over the cars and the wet pavement of the parking garage. But the rain had washed everything clean and fresh. Lindsay let her mind wander. She always kept a tight rein on her emotions until she was outside the hospital. Then she welcomed the freedom. Her thoughts ran this way and that, touching on things that mattered in varying degrees.

Suddenly a chill swept up her spine. Glancing around, she scanned the parking area. The feeling of freedom and comfort had left her. The hair stood up on the back of her neck as she hurriedly made her way to the left side of the car. Goosebumps spread over her skin, and every sense in her body came alive. Struggling with her bag, books, and keys, she let herself into the car. She quickly slammed the locks into place. For some reason she still didn't feel safe. She started the car and eased it out of the parking lot. Turning left toward home, she turned on the radio and listened as music filled the air. Lindsay let the moment wrap itself around her. Her throat tightened as fear crept up her spine.

"Someone's in trouble," Lindsay whispered out loud. As she drove the two short miles home, she let the feelings dwell within her.

Pulling into her driveway, she looked at the house. "Everything here seems okay," she said to no one but herself. As she walked up the front steps and opened the door, the uneasy feelings vanished.

"Mom!" Jackie yelled, as he catapulted himself in her direction. "Can we go for ice cream, can we?" He was jumping up and down.

"Whoa, I just got home, give me a minute. Let me put my things down and let's see what you've been up to," Lindsay said as she kissed his cheek.

Lindsay glanced around the house. "Everything okay here?" she asked.

"Yeah, things are fine, Ms. Lindsay," Melly Carpenter said as she came from the kitchen. "I'm gonna go so I can get dinner at my house. He was good today. No temper tantrum, so ice cream might be a good idea."

"Have you had dinner?" Lindsay said as she looked into Jackie's bright blue eyes.

"Yes ma'am, and I ate it all. Can we go for ice cream, Mom?"

Lindsay was still fighting off the uneasy feeling that had come over her. "Is everything okay, Melly?" she asked.

"Yeah, you okay?"

"I just had a creepy feeling in the hospital parking lot. That feeling that someone was watching me, you know?"

"Oh, yeah, I know that feeling. I always check the back seat of my car when I get that feeling. Of course I don't check it till I get in. Now, does that make any sense? Must be a blonde moment." Melly laughed.

Lindsay felt somewhat better, but still not completely over her strange feeling. "Come on, Jackie, let's go get ice cream."

"Whoopee!" Jackie hollered as he ran out the front door. Lindsay looked around one more time.

Melly smiled as she reached out and touched Lindsay's arm, "You okay, Lindsay?" she asked.

"Yeah, I'm just tired. I'll see you tomorrow, Mel." They walked out the door together.

"It's gonna be a pretty night," Melly said. "Not bad, huh? That and an ice cream will get you twenty pounds."

Lindsay laughed. "Better a pretty night like this, ice cream, and twenty pounds. A man and a night like this, ice cream or none, will get you nine months and twenty pounds."

They both laughed. "Good night, Jackie, enjoy your ice cream. Lindsay, rest that clairvoyant brain of yours," Melly said.

CHAPTER 2

Amanda Wiggins stood in her bedroom and gazed into the full-length oval mirror that she'd gotten for her seventeenth birthday just a few weeks before. She turned slightly to the left and then to the right, tucking her chin provocatively as she stared at her reflection.

"Cammy, when you look at me what do you see?" Amanda asked her best friend as she gently guided the golden letter A that hung on a chain around her neck to the front. It settled between her breasts.

Camilla Burke shrugged her shoulders and said, "I see you, silly. Why, what do you see?"

"You know what I mean; do I look older to you, more grown up?" Amanda said, turning to her friend.

"Mandy, you look like you, like you've always looked. I mean—you're older now than we were in kindergarten, but you still look like the Mandy I've always known."

"Cammy, what I mean is... well, prom is coming up, and I want Jared to ask me, and he hasn't yet. I'm afraid he's going to ask Melody Parker. Cammy, I would just die," Mandy said dramatically.

Cammy sat up, suddenly interested. "Amanda Schlanda Panda, with Jared Sinclair's reputation, do you really think your dad is going to let you go anywhere with him, especially to prom? Your dad would shoot him on the front porch," Cammy said, leaning forward and propping her chin on her hands. She stared at Amanda as she cuddled the toy panda bear she had given Mandy for her birthday, gently blowing its fur away from her nose to avoid its tickling.

"I have that all worked out," Mandy said in her typically animated style. "Billy from next door is gonna pick me up and drop me off at Jared's house. That is, if I can get him to ask me."

"What! You're gonna use poor Billy again? Gosh, he's such a nerd for letting you do that to him, not to mention all the other reasons. He's really got it bad for you," Cammy said, shaking her head and making a face.

"Cammers, you just don't understand. Billy's a sweetheart, but he's kind of dopey. I know he would do anything for me, and I really do like him, just not the way he likes me. Besides, you have Jeremy; he's crazy about you. So there's no way you can understand how I feel. I mean, you guys are probably gonna get married after college and have a trizillion kids and live happily ever after. That's how you two are. I'm not like that, Cammers, I wanna live and have some fun before I get tied down to the old ball and chain routine. I wanna do fun stuff with fun people. I just want to go out with Jared Sinclair one time before we graduate so I can say I did it." Mandy was busy putting her hair up in a ponytail and tying it with a pink ribbon that matched her sweater, but not so busy that she didn't notice her best friend's silence. She turned to look at her.

"What?" Mandy asked as she saw the hurt look on Cammy's face.

"I'm not fun?" Cammy asked, the pain on her face very real.

"Of course you are. It's just that we do the same thing all the time, hang out with the same kids. Nothing different or exciting ever happens here. No one famous ever comes to this town. We never go anywhere famous. I love you, you're my bestest friend in the whole wide world, and I wouldn't have it any other way. But I know there's something more out there. I wanna be somebody, Cammy."

Cammy smiled. "Yeah—and if your dad finds out Jared Sinclair is that something more, your butt is gonna be in the meat grinder. You'll have to tell everyone that you wore a chastity belt and your dad swallowed the key once they see you at the prom with Mr. Hot-to-Trot," Cammy said, bursting into laughter.

"Well, who's to say that I'm not ready to, uh, you know, with Jared?" Amanda asked, as she turned back to her reflection in the mirror. She ran her hands over her pastel pink angora sweater and turned from left to right again.

"That's the only way he's gonna ask you to the prom. He always gets what he wants, and we all know what that is, Mandy. He'll ruin your reputation. Don't do it, not with someone like him. He's a worm," Cammy said. She giggled and made a gesture with her index finger like a wiggling worm; then she popped a chip into her mouth.

Mandy laughed too. "Well, I'm getting old, and I don't want to die a virgin, ya know?" They both giggled with glee as Cammy threw the empty plastic chip bowl at Mandy.

"Hey, let's go to the mall. I want to get stockings and a garter for my dress at that new lingerie shop that opened last week. Jeremy just loves stockings and a garter," Cammy said, with a giggle in her voice as she got to her feet.

"Let me tell my mom. Maybe we can take her car," Mandy said, as she headed for the door.

"Okay, I'm gonna call Jeremy and have him meet us there. We can get some pizza later. Is that cool with you?"

"Yeah, sure, one of us might as well have a guy on her arm. Tell him to bring money," Mandy hollered as she ran down the stairs.

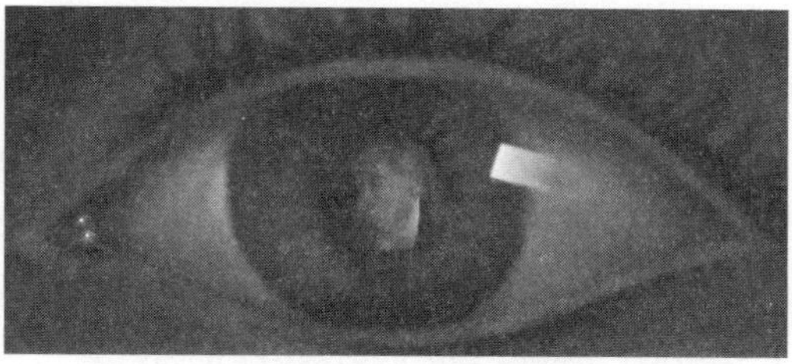

CHAPTER 3

The girls drove to the new mall in the center of town. Everyone was talking about the Grecian-looking architectural style, with its red brick and white trim, its large windows already dressed in the latest fashions. Designers from the city had come in to give everything a modern appearance. The landscaping was still in progress, but already you could tell that it was going to be luxurious all year round. The blue spruce trees and English ivy hedges curved gracefully around the two-mile perimeter. Rosebushes flowered in pink and white, adding to the look of a northern spring. The designers of the mall were said to be foreigners, and its artistic design suggested that this was true.

The mall had large windows inside, as well, trimmed with white framework that allowed you to see inside the stores. Designers were busy dressing mannequins behind screens. Beautifully tiled floor pathways led to many different stores. Sears was the one most frequented, but there was a J.C. Penney and even a Carson Pirie Scott. An enclosed mall was a new concept for the area, a place where you could shop inside, out of the elements—a blessing in the northern states. On this busy Saturday afternoon, juniors and seniors from the area high schools were busy shopping for prom paraphernalia, everything from accessories to clothing.

Mandy and Cammy greeted friends as they walked through the wide hallways, peering left and right into store windows. Shoes, clothing, house wares, card shops and even a trinket shop or two filled the large building. A few of the stores hadn't actually opened for business yet, but you could see people inside getting things ready. The mall was filled with people. Prom was the biggest event at present, but there were also a lot of June weddings coming up. Brides, their mothers, and their bridesmaids hurried in and out of The Bridal Shop.

Cammy and Amanda stopped to watch. "I want a long, flowing, off-white gown with dozens of silk tea roses on it when I get married," Cammy said dreamily.

"Not me. I want bright white and short, ultra-modern. That's for me," Amanda stated determinedly.

"Yeah, right, you in a bright white wedding dress after a date with Jared Sinclair. That's a laugh," Cammy said, as both girls headed towards the lingerie shop.

"Gosh Cammers, way to be brutal," Mandy said, as she playfully shoved Cammy.

Mandy laughed as she followed Cammy into the lingerie shop and looked at all the lacy, feathered, peek-a-boo things the store had to offer. Cammy made her purchase and the two of them left the shop in peals of laughter. Cammy felt self-conscious as she carried the pink and white bag. She was in the process of hiding it behind her back in mock modesty as Mandy accidentally bumped into a group of guys. As she turned to say she was sorry, her apologies died in her throat. There before her was Jared Sinclair, smiling in all his football hero glory. Mandy stopped dead in her tracks and stared at him.

"Hi," she whispered.

"Hi yourself. What are you doing, shopping for prom? You got a date?" Jared asked in his slow, soft voice. That was the voice that had helped him through school. Actually it had gotten him everything he'd ever wanted since he had acquired it at the age of fourteen. Puberty had been good, very good, to Jared Sinclair.

Mandy blushed under his stare and involuntarily stepped closer to him. "No, just going with Cammy to get some things that she needs. How about you, do you have a date yet?" Mandy held her breath and waited.

Somehow she knew he was going to tell her that he was going to take Melody Parker.

"Yeah, I think I do. Hey Cammy, what's in the bag?" Jared asked, as he leaned forward and pulled the bag his way with his index finger.

"None of your business, Jared Sinclair, and don't try to sweet-talk me, I'm immune!" declared Cammy.

Jared laughed. "Yeah, sure you are."

"Who are you taking to the prom, Jared?" Mandy asked softly. Cammy could see that her friend's heart was breaking.

"Come on, Mandy, let's go," she said, pulling on Mandy's arm.

"You," said Jared.

Mandy and Cammy both looked at him. Jared loved the drama of this moment, and you could see that he was polished at it. He had dropped his little bomb subtly, then stood back and watched the reaction.

"You are?" Mandy stammered.

"Yeah, didn't you know that? I heard you wanted me to ask you, so I'm asking. Now if you want to go with me, turn around and go back in that store and get yourself a little pink and white bag just like Cammer's here."

Jared knew that no one but Camilla Burke would ever turn him down. She had lived next door to him all her life, and she'd hated him since second grade. But Amanda—well, now, that was a different story. The fact that she wanted him was all over school. Jared's sister had brought home a note that Amanda had passed in study hall. Jared thought ahead to the night he had planned. He was really looking forward to it. Not just for his own selfish reasons, but because he found himself actually liking Amanda. She was a pretty girl, but she was also really nice.

Jared smiled, and Amanda almost melted right there in the hallway of the shopping mall. Cammy made a face at both of them.

"Call me later, and we can discuss the particulars," Amanda said as she leaned forward and scribbled her number on his arm. She boldly kissed his cheek and said, "See you in school on Monday."

Cammy and Mandy wandered through the stores looking for the perfect dress for Mandy, just as they had the week before for Cammy. Mandy wanted something both daring and feminine. Cammy had chosen a satin creation in Jeremy's favorite color, royal blue. Mandy found a deep red dress with lace, sequins, a bare back, and a trumpet skirt made of red chiffon. It hugged her figure and looked very feminine. She was thrilled with the look. Clutching her own pink and white bag along with her other purchases, Mandy walked with Cammy toward the pizza parlor.

Guido's Pizzeria was the hottest spot for the teens to hang out in the mall. The owners catered to the younger crowd, and most adults steered clear of it when shopping without their teenagers. It had all the right Italian décor. Red and white checked tablecloths, dripping candles in Chianti bottles, and wicker bread baskets. The east and west walls of the pizzeria were filled with windows. The east side of the pizzeria opened into the parking lot, bringing in the sunlight from outside, while the windows on the west side of the room opened into the mall hallway. There were also two doors for access to the restaurant, one outside, off the main parking area, and another in the hallway that led to the mall central court. Music played on the jukebox—the Temptations, singing a love song. The place was packed in typical Saturday afternoon fashion. Shopping bags filled the aisles and the smell of pizza and fresh bread filled the air.

The girls approached Jeremy where he was sitting at a window table. Jeremy had been Cammy's boyfriend since their junior year. No other two people at Ripney High fit together as well as they did. He was one of those guys everyone liked. A track star, a football player, and a journalist for the high school newspaper, he was intensely loyal to Cammy. His eyes always lit up when she walked into a room, just as they were doing now. He stood to greet them and kissed Cammy lightly.

After lunch they all started for the parking lot. Jeremy joked about being the pack mule for the Female Olympic Shopping Team. Cammy pinched him on his blue-jeaned bottom and told him she would take care of his sore muscles later.

"Yeah, you always promise and you never deliver," Jeremy pouted.

"Put the ring on my finger, Baby, and I'm all yours." Cammy laughed out loud as Mandy and Jeremy giggled.

"Blackmailed! I'm being blackmailed by the tightest wench at Ripney," Jeremy sighed. Amanda laughed at him as he performed for them in mock exasperation. As the three walked across the parking lot, they heard the loud screech of tires and turned in the direction of the sound. They all saw it at the same time, but none of them could react fast enough. The pale tan 69 Chevy van was heading toward them. The two men inside leaned out the windows and pounded on the doors, shouting and yelling as the van careened through the parking lot.

The man on the passenger's side looked at the three kids in their path and pointed at Amanda. "Hey, baby, you wanna go for a ride? We can take you for the ride of your life," he yelled out the window. He disappeared, only to reappear seconds later in the side door as he pulled it back and leaned out.

Amanda looked at Jeremy and Cammy and realized that somehow they had gotten about ten feet ahead of her. She turned toward the van again, looking frightened. Jeremy started toward her as the van sped at them. Amanda turned to run, putting even more distance between herself and Cammy and Jeremy. In what seemed the blink of an eye the van was upon her. The man leaning out the passenger-side door grabbed Mandy by her ponytail and dragged her into the moving vehicle. The van never slowed down, and Mandy's body slammed against the outside of it. The man pulled Mandy inside as the van sped off.

Jeremy immediately took off on foot, chasing the van with everything he had. Screaming, Cammy stood in the parking lot with packages lying at her feet where Jeremy had dropped them. Her body started to run forward as her mind realized the futility of it. She fell to her knees and screamed out in anguish, "MANDY!"

Jeremy chased the van out of the parking lot and down Muerll Avenue. He ran until his chest hurt, until his body burned with pain, and then he pushed it harder. He could hear Mandy screaming inside the van as the driver stopped behind another car at the stop light.

Jeremy ran to the back of the van and pulled on the handle, but the doors were locked. He raced around to the side door, where Mandy had disappeared earlier. He pulled the handle back, opening the side door and exposing a horrible sight. He could see Mandy lying on her back, her face bleeding profusely and her arms flailing against her attacker.

She looked in his direction and screamed his name as the man leaning over her hollered, "Go!" to the driver, throwing the torn pink angora sweater at Jeremy. The sweater hit him full in the face and momentarily blocked his view. The van lurched to the left and shot around the other cars, dragging Jeremy as he held onto the door handle. He was forced to let go as he grappled with the sweater. The van careened around other cars, running the red light as shocked and angry drivers blasted their horns. Mandy had disappeared from his sight.

Jeremy gave chase again, only to watch in horror as the van turned left, climbed onto the expressway, and sped off. He collapsed to the pavement at the junction of the interstate and Muerll Avenue, clutching the pink angora sweater to his chest, screaming out his pain. He had been able to chase the van more than two miles.

CHAPTER 4

A gaping crowd gathered around Jeremy as he lay on the pavement crying, clutching at his chest and gasping for breath. Many people had seen bits and pieces of what had happened, but one couple had accidentally followed the van as it had left the mall parking area. They had been leaving the mall at the same time and had simply gotten in line to exit the parking lot when Jeremy had run up behind the van in front of them. They watched as the van swerved among the traffic with Jeremy running as fast as he could to catch it. They'd pulled up in time to see Jeremy fall first to his knees and then roll to his side, but later, when asked, they couldn't say where the van had gone. They didn't know why Jeremy had been chasing it.

"When we saw him fall to the ground and clutch his chest, we ran to his side and my wife tried to take the sweater that he was holding, but he held it tighter and screamed, 'No!'"

"I just want to lay it under your head, son," she had tried to tell him.

"No, please. It's Mandy's. It's all we have left of Mandy," Jeremy had sobbed. The gentle woman had nodded and placed her own sweater beneath his head. She glanced at her husband and said, "You'd better call the police and get an ambulance.

Jeremy drew in all the oxygen he could and screamed, "Mandy!" as loudly as his wounded chest would allow. He rolled from side to side as he lay there on the pavement struggling with the pain. Although he seemed to be in intense physical pain, the emotional suffering was just as agonizing.

An ambulance took Jeremy Wright to Mt. Sinai Hospital, where he was diagnosed with heart strain, something like a heart attack, but not as serious. His legs were wrapped in support bandages for shin splints. He lay deathly still on the bright white sheet as the tubes pumped lifesaving drugs through his body and the oxygen mask delivered the air he needed.

Jeremy's parents were allowed to sit with him for a few moments. He rolled his head to one side as they entered and his mother took his hand. "Mom, two guys in a van took Mandy while we were walking through the mall parking lot. I tried to save her but I couldn't," Jeremy croaked out in an emotion-strained voice as his shoulders shook with the sobs that wracked his body. "I couldn't save her, Mom. Oh God, I couldn't save her."

"Shhhh, be still, son, the police are doing all they can and you did what you could. You tried, and that's all that anyone can ask of you," Jeremy's mother, Leslie, said, as she tried in vain to comfort him. She stroked his face and laid her hand on his chest. She could feel it tremble beneath her fingers.

"They're going to rape her, Mom. I have the sweater she was wearing. Oh God, she screamed my name, she counted on me to help her, but I let her down." The desperation Jeremy felt made his voice tremble as he struggled with the memories of the afternoon. He looked from his mother to his father. Tears rolled down his mother's face.

His father stood as he always had, silent and strong. Finally he walked to the bed and took his son's hand. "Jeremy, no one could have done more. You were caught off guard and reacted the best way you could in the situation. These men seem to have had a plan long before they got to you and your friends. I'm so very proud of you. Words aren't enough to tell you just how I feel, but I can say this, you showed more courage, more fortitude than I have ever shown in my life. But now you have to be calm and clearheaded so you can help in the investigation. The police are here; they've been waiting to talk to you. Try to remember everything so you can help them. Your memory must be on target. If

Mandy can be saved, it's up to you, son, only you. You're the link. Does that make sense? You've seen these guys up close and you're the only one who has so far," Jeremy's dad said.

"What about Cammy, has anyone heard from her?" Jeremy asked.

"The last we heard she was still at the mall with the police and Mandy's parents. I'm sure she'll be here as soon as she can."

The door to the intensive care room opened and a nurse entered with a syringe in her hand. "Okay, folks, it's time for him to rest. You can both come back in an hour, but only for fifteen minutes at a time."

His parents kissed his forehead and gently trailed their fingers across his face as they left. Jeremy felt the tears come again as he relived the last moments when he had seen Mandy. Her screams haunted his ears, but images of Cammy floated through his mind as he faded off to a fitful sleep.

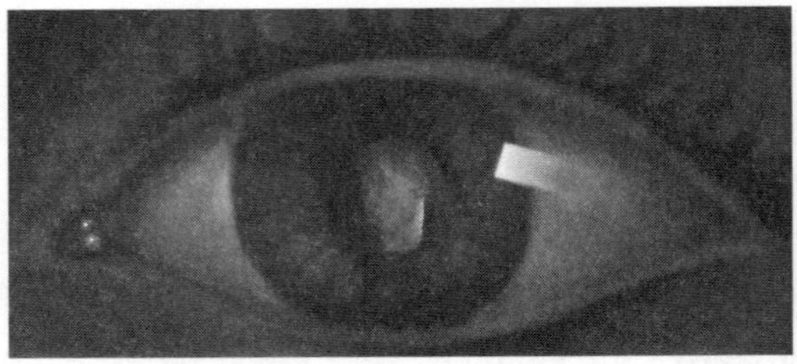

CHAPTER 5

At the mall, people gathered around Cammy as she knelt screaming. She appeared to be in shock as she rocked back and forth. It was clear from the look on her face that she couldn't fathom what had happened. Many people in the crowd were stunned, and a few were not sure what they had seen. They had witnessed the abduction but initially thought it was a hoax, a game played by rambunctious teens.

"Call the police, call Mandy's dad," Cammy screamed to Kellie Conroe, a fellow classmate who knelt at her side. "Oh my God, call someone, please!" Kellie ran for a phone inside the pizza parlor. As she turned and looked over her shoulder, she could see the crowd gathered around Cammy. Somehow it just didn't seem real, but the fact that Mandy was gone gave evidence to the contrary. She ran harder with her destination in sight.

Jerking open the door, Kellie screamed, "We need the police. Please, can I use your phone? A girl's been taken, kidnapped from the parking lot." Kellie's heart seemed to stop as the words she'd spoken sunk in. "Oh my God, Mandy's been kidnapped."

The man at the counter handed her the phone. She dialed zero for the police. "I need the police to come to the mall, my friend's been kidnapped by some men in a van. We need help, please!" Kellie was crying and shaking now, as the police promised to send someone right away. She looked out the window. In the distance she could see the crowd gathered around Cammy Burke. She knew it was real. She also had a feeling it wasn't going to end well. Walking back towards the crowd, she spotted the bags littering the parking area, not twenty feet from where Cammy said Mandy had been taken. She knelt and gathered them to her. A red satin shoe slipped from its box and lay on the ground like a bleak omen. Stooping instantly to collect it, she looked directly into the eyes of Cammy Burke. "Oh, Cammy, they're coming. I called them, and they're coming."

CHAPTER 6

Two police officers lifted Cammy Burke from the pavement of the parking lot. As she struggled to stand, someone brushed away the pebbles that had become embedded in the soft flesh of her legs. Her things were handed to an officer as the crowd dispersed. All those present gave their names, phone numbers, and addresses for later use. The crowd watched with heavy hearts as Cammy was led away—it almost seemed that the tragedy had happened to her, instead of to Mandy.

Cammy was taken into the mall security office, where a policewoman sat with her. She sobbed out her story and gave as much detail as she could. Suddenly her mind fixed on Jeremy. "Oh God, my boyfriend chased the van. He ran after them. I don't know where he is. Can I call my mom, please?" Cammy was sobbing, shredding the tissue she held into tiny pieces that fell to the tiled floor.

"Sure you can, sweetie. Let's get her on the phone."

Within twenty minutes, Cammy's mother burst through the security office door. Cammy ran into her arms as she sobbed out the story one more time. Each time she told it she remembered more and was able to tell it without breaking down completely. "We need to call the Wigginses," Mrs. Burke said to the officer sitting on the other side of Cammy.

"They've been notified and are on their way," replied the policewoman.

Mrs. Burke ran her hand over her daughter's cheek as the gravity of the situation lodged itself deep in her heart. It could have been her child. Instantly she felt horrible for the feeling of relief. She loved Mandy as her own daughter. She said a silent prayer as the door to the mall security office opened and Cammy's father, along with Mr. and Mrs. Wiggins, stepped into the room. Cammy looked up and ran to her dad. "Oh, Daddy, it was horrible. They took Mandy, Dad. Jeremy chased them. They took Mandy, Daddy," Cammy cried as she looked up at him through her tears. "You'll fix this, right? I mean, don't you know someone who can fix this?" He held her close and whispered the same prayer her mother had uttered silently only moments before. He glanced over her head at the Wigginses.

Aletha Wiggins's hand covered her mouth as she realized that her child had not yet been found. Rake Wiggins looked at the police. "What are you doing? What's happening to find my daughter?"

"We're gathering information at this time, trying to get a detailed story." The officer told them all he knew. They talked at great length and went over the story again and again. Mandy's and Cammy's packages lay on the floor of the security office. The person who had turned them in was long since gone. As Cammy spotted them, she quietly stood and walked over to them. Everyone in the room watched her. Gently she knelt next to the beige Lerner's bag and untied the knot. She slowly removed the red sequined dress and held it to her heart. Rocking back and forth, she started to moan—a long, deep, sad sound that came from her heart. The police were mesmerized; her parents and Mandy's were all horrified. Everyone's heart ached for her and Mandy.

Rake and Aletha wiped their eyes and seemed visibly to steel themselves for the days to come. Aletha knelt next to Cammy. "Cammy, come on, sweetie. Don't worry now; Mandy will be home by dinner. You'll see."

The officer behind them cleared his throat, "Folks, why don't you all go home and let us get this investigation underway. This little girl needs some medical attention, and she's not going to get it here. We'll call you when we know something. Mrs. Wiggins, you're probably right, she'll be home by dinner" He stood and showed them to the door.

At first they all just sat and watched him. Then one by one they stood and started to leave. "What about Jeremy?" Cammy asked.

"We'll check on him. He's fine, I'm sure, but right now we just don't know. It's one more thing we need to work on quickly. So please, let us get started. They will want to see Cammy at the police station so she can give them a detailed description of the van and the men in it. It's not much, but believe me, it's important, and we need it as soon as possible. Let me make a phone call to see if I can get some information about Jeremy and his whereabouts." Everyone held their breaths as he dialed the phone on the desk. "Jeremy Wright has been taken to Mt. Sinai in stable condition," he said as he hung up.

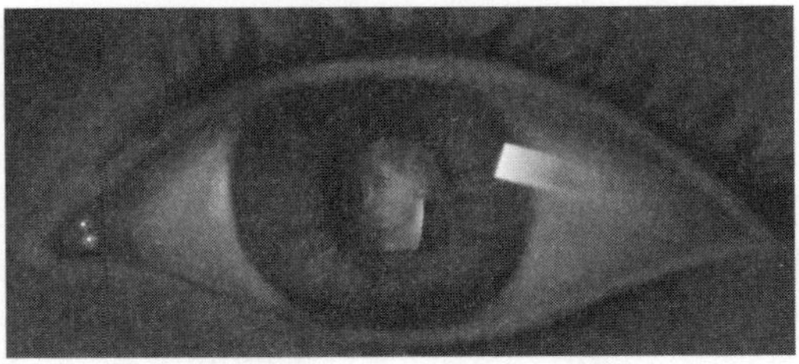

CHAPTER 7

It was hours before Cammy could be with Jeremy. She'd spent the majority of the time after Mandy's kidnapping at the mall security office. Then she'd been taken to the local police department. Papers had been filled out and questions had been answered, time and again. All four parents stood at her side listening over and over to the events of a day that had started out so normally. They listened as Cammy described the van, the man she'd seen driving, and the man who had taken Mandy. It was almost like a bad dream, but none of them could wake up.

Aletha Wiggins had produced a recent picture of Mandy, the one that would be in the graduating class picture extravaganza. Her hand trembled as she turned it over to Officer Scott Brandon, who was sitting behind the desk. A tear slipped from her eye and landed on the picture. Quickly she rubbed the wet spot with her thumb as she let it go. She looked into his eyes and saw the sympathy there. "I want this back, please."

"Yes ma'am. However, I think it will be awhile," the officer said.

"That's okay, I just want it back."

A sketch artist arrived to do a drawing of the man Cammy described. Working with a grease pencil and lots of paper as well as some artist's renderings of noses, chins, eyes, and mouths, he put together two pictures that were similar to what Cammy could remember.

"I'm not sure. I mean, it all happened so fast, I'm just not sure. This is what my mind tells me is right, but something seems off. Maybe it's the light, maybe my mind just can't remember," Cammy said, pointing to the drawings. The faces that stared back at her were almost scary but not nearly enough so. The feeling was missing.

"That's okay, sometimes we remember as time goes by, sometimes not. Sometimes the mind shuts down so as not to remember something so traumatic that it can't handle it," the artist said. "Let's just let this lie here for a bit. Tell me what you bought at the mall."

"What?" Cammy stammered. "No, I want you to work on this. I want all of you to work on Mandy. Mom, Dad, make them find Mandy," Cammy cried out.

"Cammy," Scott Brandon said in a soothing voice, "What the artist is trying to do is jog your memory. He's getting you to remember other things, bringing you visually back to the moment. That way you'll see everything with a clearer vision, so that you can describe these men better."

Cammy starting crying again, "I'm sorry. I'm not much help am I?"

"Cammy, you listen to me. Because of you and Jeremy we have a chance here, a real chance to get Mandy back. Without your description, whoever took her would be long gone, and we would have no clues. All those people standing around the parking lot, trying to be helpful, gave us conflicting stories. You, sweetheart, and only you, have been believable. What you've been through is terrible, but you have a chance here to help. Your memory is incredible in spite of the trauma you've suffered. We would be lost without you." Scott Brandon grabbed Cammy's hand for emphasis.

Cammy couldn't do much more than shake her head in understanding. She dabbed at her eyes again with the tissue in her right hand. Pointing at the drawing, she said, "His chin was more pointed, and his hair was longer." Officer Brandon squeezed her hand again and nodded at the artist.

As time passed, the composite image of Mike Hennessey came to life in the hands of the police artist. Looking at Cammy he raised a questioning eyebrow. "Is that it; does that look like one of the men who took your friend?"

"Oh my God," Cammy gasped, "that's him. That's one of them, the man who stood in the door of the van and grabbed Mandy." Suddenly, she looked at Mandy's parents.

"We tried to stop them, honest we did, but it all happened so fast," Cammy sobbed out. "He took her, oh my God, those men took her," Cammy said as she pointed to the picture. She was crying uncontrollably again.

Mandy's mother folded her arms around her and laid her head against Cammy's. "Cammy, hush now honey, we'll get her back. Won't we, Rake?"

Rake Wiggins cleared his throat. "We're gonna do our damnedest." He looked at Officer Brandon as he said, "What do we do now? I mean, now that we know what he looks like, isn't there something that you guys do? Like put out some sort of warning so people in the area can be looking for them? We need a plan, something that we can do too. I for one can't just sit and wait." Aletha stood and took her husband's arm. She gripped his sleeve as she nodded her agreement.

Captain Morris, who had been sitting quietly by, said, "Go home, or better yet, go to the hospital. Be with Jeremy and talk to each other. Look around Mandy's room. See if there is any indication that she may have known these men somehow. Try to figure out why they singled her out. In the meantime, we'll do what we do in instances like this. We'll run a profile of this face through the computers and see if anything comes up. Usually someone like this has a record. Or they knew the person, and all of this could be a hoax or a personal vendetta. Mandy may very well be home in no time at all, madder than a wet hornet, but home nonetheless. Is anyone at your house now?"

Everyone stared at him. Cammy was the first to react. "Do you really think this is a joke?" she said as she stood. The eyes that were still red and swollen from crying now burned with anger. "Do you really think that we know the kind of people that would or could do this sort of thing? Have you lost your mind? This is no joke. A man grabbed my best friend and pulled her by her ponytail into a moving van. Her body hit the side of the van as it drove off. My boyfriend chased the van. Her parents are frantic, and you can stand there and say, after all we've been through this afternoon, that you think this could be a hoax? Oh my God, I can't believe this is happening. We need to find out where Mandy is." Cammy sobbed and bent forward to lay her head in her hands.

"Folks, please, you misunderstand me. So many times in the past someone has come up missing and frantic parents or neighbors call. Then the child turns up sleeping in her own bed. Now, I'm not saying this is what's happened here, but what I am saying is we need to cover all the bases. On the surface, this seems to be something altogether different. But until we know all the facts we have to keep an open mind. We're gonna do our part and investigate every lead. We'll keep you informed, but it's gonna take time. In the meantime, let us know if you hear anything or if Mandy comes home on her own. We'll assign a special unit to this. Two detectives will work on Mandy's case until it's solved."

Once again the group stood to be ushered out of a law enforcement office. Turning back, Cammy said, "She didn't know them." Then she closed the door.

CHAPTER 8

The Burkes drove toward the hospital to see about Jeremy after a tearful goodbye and promises on both sides to call if there was any news about Mandy. It was hard to believe that four hours had already gone by, hard for everyone but Cammy. To her it seemed as if a lifetime had slipped away. Sitting in the backseat she stared out the window as her folks drove through town. Silently, she prayed, "Please, Lord, don't let her suffer." A tear slipped freely down her face. The tracks left behind by previous tears made a graceful groove and it fell in line as if it knew the way or had a mind of its own.

A cold chill settled over Cammy as her mind called up the images and set them before her. She embraced the feeling that had plagued her all day; what was it? Suddenly she knew—it was guilt, she felt guilty because it hadn't been her, guilty but relieved and then guilty again because she was relieved. The cycle played over and over in her mind, and she caught her breath and sobbed quietly until they reached the hospital.

As Cammy walked down the long corridor toward the room the nursing staff had pointed to, she took a deep breath. Her chest shuddered as the air filled her lungs, and she shivered deep inside. As she placed her hand on the door and pushed it open, she braced herself for what she would see. There, in a bed that seemed too small for him, lay Jeremy. A cry caught in her throat. She saw all the tubes and heard the beep of the monitors as she moved toward him. "Oh God, Jeremy," Cammy whispered as she slipped into the chair by his bed.

But Jeremy was sound asleep, and her murmurs went unheard. She laid her head on the bed near his arm. Gently she took his hand in hers as she let the tears fall softly onto the white sheet. Her shoulders shook, but no sound came from her throat. Instinctively, Jeremy folded his hand around hers. As Cammy cried herself to sleep she heard him mumble, "They're going to rape her, Mom. I couldn't stop them."

Fifteen minutes later the nurse opened the door to tell Cammy it was time to go. She saw them there, holding onto one another tenderly. Jeremy's large hand was wrapped around Cammy's small one, and they were both sound asleep. She didn't have the heart to wake them, so she let the door close and for once disregarded hospital protocol.

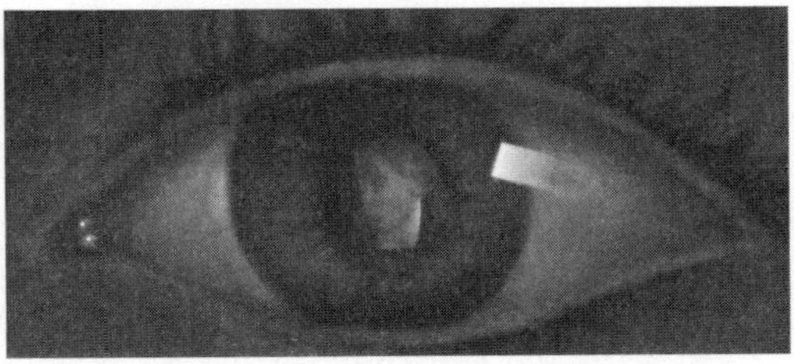

CHAPTER 9

The investigation began as soon as everyone had left the police department. Mandy's parents went in two different directions. Using the keys that had been taken from Mandy's purse, found in the parking lot exactly where Mandy had disappeared, Aletha drove her car to the hospital to see Jeremy's parents and find out how he was. It felt strange to be driving the car. It responded the way it always had, it felt absolutely familiar, but somehow something was wrong. She could feel the presence of her beautiful daughter. Looking behind her into the back seat and then to the floorboards, she felt a blanket of sadness envelop her.

Rake Wiggins drove around the mall. He wanted to talk to people and hear other views of what had happened. As he pulled into the mall parking area, he saw several officers gathered together and yellow tape being stretched across the parking spaces in an odd shape. He watched from a distance. Then he realized that this was where his daughter had been kidnapped. Tears filled his eyes and he wiped them away. He drove in the direction of the officers.

Rake Wiggins was a big man, strong and capable of protecting his family and property. He rarely let things weaken him, and even when they did he rarely showed that weakness. Today he couldn't help himself. Suddenly he realized that the connection he had shared with his daughter since her birth no longer existed. Shaking his head to rid himself of fear and depression, he steeled himself to see this thing through.

"Please let this just be a teenage hoax, some kids goofing off and not realizing how far out of hand this has gotten," Rake whispered to himself.

He knew in his heart that wasn't the case, but he couldn't give up hope. He drove to the spot where the abduction had taken place. People were milling about, still amazed and horrified by the day's events. Rake parked his car and got out. Standing there, looking around, he could almost see what had happened. Shaking himself, he took note of the people there. Then he headed in their direction, hoping against the odds that maybe someone remembered seeing something that would quell the shaking in the pit of his stomach.

As he approached, a uniformed officer stepped away from the group and waved him off. He walked up to the officer and said, "I'm Rake Wiggins, my daughter is Amanda Wiggins. I believe all this is about her." The officer nodded, "Yes sir. You can talk to the man in the dark suit, standing over there, if you want to."

Rake looked around and realized how out in the open they were. Surely someone had seen something, a license plate, anything that would help them. For just that instant he felt a spark of hope. He put his hands in his pockets and walked toward the man the young officer had pointed out. As he approached, he stuck his hand out. "I'm Rake Wiggins, Mandy's father."

"Mandy?" the officer asked, as he took Rake's hand and looked him in the eye.

"Are you investigating Mandy Wiggins's disappearance?"

"Ah, yes, yes sir, Amanda Wiggins, right?"

"Yes, Amanda, we call her Mandy. I'm her father."

"Mr. Wiggins, I'm Lieutenant Ray Strider and the man coming up behind you is Detective Will Halpin. We'll be working on your daughter's case. Hopefully, with some good witnesses, she'll be home soon. Is there anything you can tell us that might help?"

"I don't know much really, just what I heard from Cammy—Camilla—Burke. Cammy and Jeremy Wright were with Mandy when she was kidnapped."

"Kidnapped? Have you received something that leads you to believe this is a kidnapping?" Lieutenant Strider asked.

"Well, just what the kids say. What else could this be? I mean, my daughter was pulled roughly into a moving van and spirited away by someone that we don't know. I would call that a kidnapping, wouldn't you?"

"Well sir, usually a kidnapping is for ransom or some other form of personal gain for the kidnapper. That's why I asked you if you had received anything that could be considered a demand for her return."

"No, not yet. Can I ask what you're doing here? Is there anything that I can do to help in any way? I feel so useless."

"Right now we're canvassing the mall, trying to find someone who may know something or have seen something that would help. There are officers inside talking to customers and officers out here looking at tire tracks and talking to people as they come out. We need to do a re-enactment to get a feel for what took place. Can you fill me in on what you've heard so far?"

For the next hour, Rake told Lieutenant Strider and Detective Halpin all that he knew. He reminded them that what he had was not firsthand information, but the hysterical ramblings of Camilla Burke.

Eventually there was nothing else to talk about. Feeling depressed and helpless, Rake headed for the hospital. Prayers fell from his lips as the tears from his eyes rolled down his cheeks. He drove around in silent and absolute misery, yet he couldn't bring himself to go home. He just couldn't face the empty house. He sat in the parking lot of the hospital and stared at the building. Inside was the young man who had tried to save his daughter. Rake wasn't sure he could stand to hear what Jeremy had to say. He wasn't ready yet to admit they might not get Mandy back. "Seventeen, Lord, she's just seventeen. Her life has been too short. Please bring her home," he prayed.

He arrived at the third-floor Intensive Care Unit and saw everyone gathered together. People he had known for years. The Wrights and the Burkes were there. Cammy and Jeremy had dated for at least two years that he knew of; hell, for all he knew about these kids it could have been more than that. He saw his wife standing with Mark and Carla Burke. As he approached the group, they all turned to look at him.

"Any news?" his wife asked.

"No, not yet, but it's still early. They'll find her."

Jeremy's dad shook his hand, "Our prayers are with you, Rake."

"And ours with you. How's your boy?"

"He's holding his own. His heart has taken quite a beating, but he's strong, so time should heal him. Emotionally, he seems pretty shaken. He tried, he really did. He seems to be struggling with his memories. The nurse gave him something to help him sleep, so he'll be out for some time. Cammy is being allowed to sit by his bedside for fifteen minutes. Right now that's all the hospital will allow, although it seems as if she's been in there longer."

"When you see him, tell him thank you for me. I know he gave it all he had. A witness said he had the side door to the van open before it took off and dragged him down the street."

"Yeah, but his lacerations are the least of our concern. That's just skin. Right now his heart and his mental status are the big issues." Jeremy's father rubbed his hand over his eyes.

"Well, tell him that I can't thank him enough for trying. What the witnesses saw could be our only lead." Rake Wiggins rubbed his eyes, too.

The two men shook hands again, and Mark patted Rake on the back as they turned back to the group. The door to Jeremy's room opened and Cammy stepped out, smoothing her hair. "He's sleeping. He looks so peaceful, but then he cries out. It breaks my heart to be in there with him."

Jeremy's mom reached for her hand. "I'll go in, sweetie. Go home with your parents, get some rest and we'll call you when we hear something new."

Cammy nodded, "Give him my love, and tell him that if he needs me I'll come right back."

As they drove home, Cammy cried softly in the backseat. Her heart was broken by the words she'd heard Jeremy whisper in his sleep, "They're gonna rape her, Mom, we have to help her. They're gonna rape her." She prayed quietly for a speedy resolution to this situation. It was a prayer that would not go unanswered.

CHAPTER 10

Three days later, on a beautiful Tuesday morning, the phone rang at a police station forty miles from the mall. "Station forty-one, Michelle Hunter. May I help you?"

"Oh my Lord in Heaven, we need the police out here right away. My name is Terry Michels; my boys found a lady's body near the fishing hole."

"Sir, can you repeat that please, and give me your name again?" The dispatcher had been trained to speak slowly and get all the facts.

"I already told you, my name is Terry Michels, we need the cops out here."

"Where is here, Mr. Michels?"

"We live on Rickters Road near the Pine Ambly fishing hole. My boys were fishing and they found a lady's body. Are you gonna send someone?"

"Yes sir, I have an officer in route. Can you wait outside for him and show him the way?"

"You betcha, we'll meet him by the main road. It's tricky getting back here if you don't know the way. You guys better bring a blanket or something. She doesn't have any clothes on."

"Yes sir, someone's on the way."

Detective William Halpin was a hard-nosed Texas cop. Now he was, and felt like, a rebel transplant. Fifteen years ago he'd met, fallen head over heels in love with, and married Betty Luke, and darned if she didn't go and change his whole life for him without ever asking him if he had other plans. To her credit they had a good marriage and great kids. It wasn't easy being married to a Texan, or a cop, either, for that matter. The only thing missing was the warm Texas summers and the Civil War attitude. He was farther north than he cared to admit to his buddies from the academy. This was Betty's hometown. She had roots here. How did he ever let himself fall in love with a damn Yankee? Nope! Wait, she wasn't a damn Yankee, those were the ones who came south and stayed. Betty had just been a damn Yankee back then, one with fire and sass. He was the damn transplanted rebel. This was their land. Gosh, he loved her still. But he hated the cold weather. Somehow he had let Betty talk in him into coming all this way and taking this job as a detective for some huge town that was growing faster than a weed in the yard.

Will longed for the familiar southern drawl. He wanted to go home, but each time he brought the subject up to Betty she reminded him that the kids were still in school and that her parents needed them. He thought about all of this as he drove around looking for clues to mysteries that didn't seem to be forthcoming. He was working homicide now, and he was good at it. He was well-respected in his department and had just received a commendation.

He felt alone, lost in this world of northerners that didn't understand him more than half the time. They were always picking at him, saying "Y'all" and stuff like that. It was all in good clean fun, and he knew it. His partner, Jerry Leeme, was a Yankee. Will took more slack from him than anyone else. But he liked him, he trusted him, and that was more than he could say for any other human being that he knew. They'd been partners for three years since he'd come north and begun working homicide. He liked homicide. He was willing to admit that to himself, but he hated murder cases that had no rhyme or reason.

Will realized he was grumbling to himself. He looked over at Jerry and saw a smile on his face. Will was already in a foul mood and the day had just gotten started.

"What are you lookin' at?"

"I'm just watching you. Any reason you look like someone put a burr under your saddle?"

"I'm pissed off. You got a problem with that?"

"No, you can ride around all day with that damn rebel scowl on your face, or you can smile and show off all that new dental work. Either way, makes no difference to me. We got work to do no matter what mood you're in. What are you mad about anyway?"

"Aww, shit. I heard from my brother last night. They're all going to Rayburn Lake for the bass fishing tournament and I can't go. Gosh, I love to go up there and breathe in all that clean air, fish, lay back, drink a few beers, and shoot the shit with the boys."

"We got fishing here. Good fishing, too. I bet you never caught a bass the size of your foot," Jerry teased.

"Hey bud, this is Texas we're talkin' about. Everything's bigger in Texas. Don't you know your history?"

Jerry laughed at his partner. It was easy to pull him out of a funk. Not that he needed pulling often, but when he did Jerry was the one to do it.

"Look let's get this case behind us and I'll take you to one of the best fishing holes in this area. Deal?"

"Deal," Will said. He looked at Jerry and smiled, "Thanks, man."

"Sure, anytime, you'd do the same for me." They were good together. They thought alike, worked the angles together well, and when push came to shove they had each other's back.

Jerry had been raised to do things a certain way. Not the Texas way, but he was good, thorough, and always on time. He'd cut his teeth on the law enforcement manual—his daddy and granddaddy had both been cops. He'd made it to detective in record time, something no one else in his family had ever aspired to, because his mind was built that way.

Will was the first cop in his family. He didn't have experience or family members guiding him. He had raw instinct, and he loved to read. In fact, he read everything he could get his hands on about law enforcement and homicide. Being a cop was never good enough for him. He had to be the best at what he did, no matter what that was at the time. Now he was a detective, and in his department he was one of the best.

The radio in the car crackled. "All cars in the area of Rickters Road please respond. We have a D.B. near Pine Ambly fishing hole. See the man there, Mr. Terry Michels."

Will and Jerry exchanged a look. Will grabbed for the mike. "This is Detective Halpin. We can respond to that call with uniform."

A DB was a dead body. That was homicide. "I guess we're going to get to see that fishing hole sooner than we thought," Jerry said.

"No shit, just what we need, another dead body," Will said, as he turned the car in the direction Jerry was pointing.

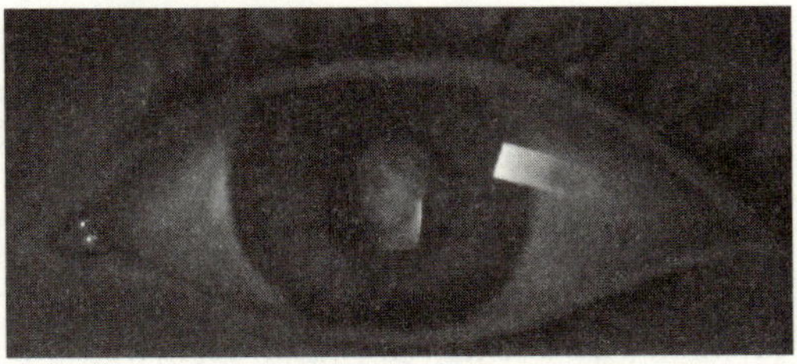

CHAPTER 11

In front of them, Will and Jerry saw Terry Michels standing in the road waving his arms wildly over his head; behind them was a black and white squad car with flashing lights. Looking again at Terry Michels, Will laughed out loud. He looked like he was doing jumping jacks. "Over here," he shouted. "Over here."

They turned in his direction, and both could feel the tension in the air. Call it gut instinct, call it cop intuition, call it whatever you want, but they both had it going.

"It took you guys long enough. We called fifteen minutes ago. My boys found a lady's body in the Pine Ambly Fishing hole."

"We came as soon as we could get here but we were clear across town. My name is Detective Will Halpin, and this is my partner, Detective Jerry Leeme. We're with Homicide. Can you show us the way?" Will said as he and Jerry got out of the car.

Terry Michels looked at both men. "You better bring a blanket or something. She ain't got any clothes on."

Jerry grabbed a blanket from the trunk. "What time did you find her?"

"Like I said, my boys found her. It must have been about 10:15 or so, this morning. She looks pretty bad. You might want to get your stomachs ready for it."

"We've seen it before. Just show us the way," Jerry said.

Five minutes later they stood over the badly bruised and battered body of a young woman. Even though these were well-seasoned detectives with more than twenty years on the force, they grimaced. Each took a handkerchief from his pocket and placed it over his mouth and nose. Will spoke into a hand-held recorder first. The professional in him had to take over even as tears came to his eyes. Everyone present looked away as Jerry knelt on one knee to get closer and dictate notes.

"The victim is an approximately seventeen-year-old white female with blonde hair, eye-color undeterminable at this time. She is nude, with several abrasions about her body and a puncture wound approximately one inch to one-and-a-half inches in width in her mid-thoracic area. She is lying in a supine position with her lower extremities, from the hips down, in Pine Ambly Fishing Hole," Will said into the recorder.

"Sir, has anyone touched the body or walked around this area?" Jerry asked Mr. Michels.

"Well my boys found her. She was lying there like that. They did go up and touch her on the shoulder to see if she was okay. But I don't think they did anything other than that."

"Where are your boys, Mr. Michels?"

"They're up at the house. Both of them are pretty upset about finding this lady like this. They ain't never seen a naked woman before."

"Not to mention a dead one," Will whispered under his breath. It was pretty obvious that Mr. Michels's main concern was that the young woman was nude.

Will went back to his dictation, and Mr. Michels took Jerry up to speak to the boys. The uniforms had arrived and were heading in Will's direction.

"Mind the crime scene," he said as they approached. "Tape us off and find out if anyone else has any more information about who she might be and where she came from. How she got here would also be a good question to ask. Get a camera going, too, if you have one."

"The victim appears to have a gold chain around her neck and will have to be turned over to see what might be attached to it. She has yellow, seemingly nylon, rope around her wrists and ankles with deep, wide lacerations, approximately two inches wide, as well. There is also a piece of the same material around her neck. She was found at a local fishing place, popular with fishermen in this area. She is lying in the mud and up to seven inches of water. There are several footprints in and about this area, but the two Michels boys admit to being near her. There are also some large bootprints that may belong to Mr. Michels and some gym shoe prints in a man's size. We will have the lab make molds of these for comparison."

Jerry was back with the two boys. Will was surprised to see the spots that covered both of them. "We got chicken pox," the smallest one said, "But our mom says we ain't 'tagious no more." Will was glad to hear it, never having had chicken pox himself.

"Can you boys tell us what you saw?" Will asked.

"Yes sir. We found her right there, mister, and we didn't see nothing, honest, 'cept maybe her butt. We just touched her shoulder, nothing else." Both boys looked scared to death. Will and Jerry chuckled to themselves.

"Did you see anyone else around her?" Jerry asked.

"No sir, she was there all by herself, just lying there with the water going up her nose like that. We was gonna get her a blanket 'cause she feels cold, but my dad said she had gone on to meet her maker and didn't need a blanket. Is she dead, sir?"

"Yeah, son, she's dead. Do you know who she is?" Will asked.

"Nope, she ain't from around here. Girls from around here don't swim with no clothes on like that," the smallest boy answered. He had more spots than the other one, and he was still scratching. Will took a step back. Will and Jerry looked at both boys.

"Our mom wants us back at the house when you're done talkin' to us. Can we go?"

"Sure, run along. Thanks for your help," Jerry said with a smile. He looked back at the dead young woman lying in the water. "Somewhere, someone loves her and will be grateful to you both."

"Yeah, and we didn't even give her the chicken pox neither!" they said as they ran off.

Yellow tape that said "Police, Do Not Cross," was strung up between the trees and the area surrounding the dead body. Pictures were taken of the crime scene. The lab guys had come and were pouring the molds of all the footprints and tire tracks. Better to be safe than sorry, since this crime scene couldn't be preserved.

"Okay guys, she's all yours," said Dave Matthews from the lab. It had only been two hours.

"You guys wrapped that up in record time. Thanks again," Jerry yelled as he watched them gather their gear. Jerry and Will bent over the body. With gloves on they gently lifted her out of the water. The sucking sound the shore made as it gave up its latest victim made everyone wince. They all knew it would happen, it did every time, but it still made you sick to your stomach. As they turned her over the golden letter A hanging from her chain sparkled in the sunlight, even though it was partially covered in mud. Pretty blue eyes stared blankly toward the sky.

Will took the photo of Amanda Wiggins from his shirt pocket and studied it. Then he reached down to smooth the hair from her face and said, "Hello, Miss Mandy."

Will whispered more to himself than to Mandy or the others gathered there. "I'm sorry I didn't find you sooner, but you have my word that we will find out who did this to you and make him pay." The vengeance in his voice was unmistakable as he laid her gently on the stretcher. "Let's get you out of here, little lady."

He nodded at the attendants to take her to the shore. He stood in the shallow water and looked up and down the shoreline. "Someone has to have seen something. I mean, look at all these people. Dave, how long do you think she's been out here?"

"I would say no longer than five or six hours. But that's just a guess till we get back to the lab. Another thing, this isn't the place of death," Dave said.

"No shit? I can see that for myself," Will said. His temper was getting the better of him. Jerry placed a hand on his arm. "He's just trying to help. No one knows what to say at a time like this. Cut him some slack, Will."

Will stood with his fists clenched at his side. As Will stepped over to where Mandy was lying on the stretcher, he studied the marks on her body, making notes as he went. Again he spoke into his recorder.

"The victim has several puncture wounds around her chest and stomach area that match the pattern of the puncture wound on her back." The fact that her hands and feet were still bound was a good thing. It gave them the rope to work with, but it was apparent the ropes hadn't caused all the damage to her wrists and ankles, since the lacerations were wider than the rope. Will studied them for a few minutes and then looked up at Jerry.

"What do you make of these marks around her wrists and ankles?"

"I saw that. They look like cuff marks. You know how the tight cuff of a shirt sleeve can sometimes leave a wide mark like that? That's what it looks like to me, but worse, of course. And the ropes did some of the damage, but that seems to be more about being tied and pulled along." Skin was missing from her body in patterns that suggested she had been dragged for some distance. Her hair was matted and dirty, like the rest of her body. She was lying on the white sheet of the stretcher, and the attendants were waiting to cover her with the sheet.

Will and Jerry finished their preliminary examination of Amanda Wiggins and nodded to the attendants. "Take her away, but take good care of her. She's been abused enough. Now our abuse starts. We get to go inform the family."

CHAPTER 12

Jerry and Will left the crime scene to the criminologist. Their job was just beginning. They walked toward their car as they talked about what they had seen.

"What do you think, Jerry?"

"I agree this is Amanda Wiggins. The chain and charm give it away. I also don't want to be the one to tell that father that we found his little girl all beat up, probably raped repeatedly and who knows what else. I don't want to go and look into the eyes of family and friends and stand at another fucking funeral and look around for some homicidal maniac and hope that he comes to witness his handiwork. I don't want to, but I will because I want to see justice done, and if it were my little girl, I would want you and me to handle it."

Will nodded at his partner as each pulled a dry pair of sneakers from the car's trunk. This was another thing time and experience had taught them—carry spare everything, and keep it light.

As they pulled into the driveway of the Wiggins home the exterior porch light radiated a warm welcome. The daylight had faded in the time it had taken to find, examine, and move Amanda Wiggins's body and then drive the forty miles to her parent's home. It was a nice, single-family home, surrounded by plants and flowers. The pinks and deep reds of the carnations, pansies, and roses enhanced the pink in the brick. It looked like a house that would be filled with love and laughter. Will and Jerry felt terrible in their roles as bearers of bad news.

They both got out and walked along the paved path to the front door. Will pressed the doorbell. They both shifted uncomfortably as they stood there waiting, with their hands folded in front of them, and listened to the chimes echoing through the house. This was the hardest part of being a homicide detective.

Mr. Wiggins opened the door slowly. One look at the faces of the detectives told him what he didn't want to hear.

"Mr. Wiggins, may we come in?" Will asked, looking down at his shoes.

"Yes, please do. Can we get you something to drink?" Rake said as his wife came into the room to stand by his side.

"No, thank you. Ah, Mr. and Mrs. Wiggins, there's no easy way to say this. Would you both please sit down?"

Aletha started to cry softly, clutching a handkerchief to her mouth. Rake put his arm around his wife and held her close. They sank to the sofa in unison.

"You've found our daughter, haven't you, officer?" Aletha asked.

"Detective, sweetheart, these men are detectives. I guess it really doesn't make any difference at this point, though, does it?" Rake said.

"No sir, it doesn't." Jerry said, swallowing uncomfortably. He felt worse than terrible. "I'm sorry, a young woman has been found who matches the description of your daughter. We have every reason to believe it's her."

"Is she dead?" Rake asked in a shaky voice.

"Yes sir, I'm afraid she is." Will and Jerry said.

"Oh my God in heaven, my baby, my beautiful sweet baby girl," Aletha cried out in pain. Rake covered his face with his free hand, the other one clutching his wife's shoulder.

"I knew it. You know, somehow I just knew she was never coming home." He cried softly. "You know, I wasn't there when Mandy was born. She came early and I was out of town on business, but I knew the moment she came into this world. We have a connection, she and I. We always have had. The other day when everyone was looking for her, I lost that connection, I knew then that she was gone." He seemed to be speaking to himself, but his wife nodded.

"I remember, sweetheart."

"What do we do now?" Rake wanted to know.

"One of you needs to come down and identify her. You still have some time if you'd like to do it tomorrow. Everyone will understand." Jerry said.

"No, we don't want her lying in some cold morgue somewhere. I want to bring her home." Aletha said. Everyone turned to look at her. It seemed that she didn't understand what had happened.

"Mrs. Wiggins, your daughter can't come home. The police can only release her body to a licensed mortuary after the medical examiner is finished. What we need now is for someone to come and positively identify her," Will explained. Aletha started to cry again.

"I'll come with you, detective," Rake said. "Let me get a neighbor to sit with my wife." Aletha's sobs could be heard even though her fist was stuffed in her mouth. Her wailing was getting louder and louder.

"Mr. Wiggins, perhaps a doctor and a minister would be a good idea too, for your wife." Jerry offered. Rake nodded and reached for the phone.

As plans were made and assistance started to arrive, Aletha seemed better. She had something to do. Nellie Cord from next door sat at her side. As Rake, Will, and Jerry left she actually smiled a tiny smile. "Rake?" she asked quietly. Her husband turned to look at her, "Yes, dear?"

"Call me, just in case it's not Mandy. I mean, it might not be, so call me. Would you, please?"

He walked back over to where she was sitting. "Aletha, if the girl in the morgue isn't our Mandy, I will call you, okay?" With raised eyebrows, as if to make a point, he nodded at her and smiled.

She clutched his shirtsleeve. "I'll wait right here." She placed her hand on the princess phone for emphasis. Rake understood her meaning and nodded as he walked out the door behind the two detectives.

Aletha sat with her hand on the phone. Fifteen minutes went by, then thirty, then thirty-five. "Oh Nellie," Aletha said as she rubbed the phone, willing it to ring, "He's not gonna call. Oh Nellie, my baby girl is dead. What are we going to do?"

Nellie Cord held her friend and neighbor's hand. "Aletha, honey, we're gonna pray. That's all I know to do, just pray."

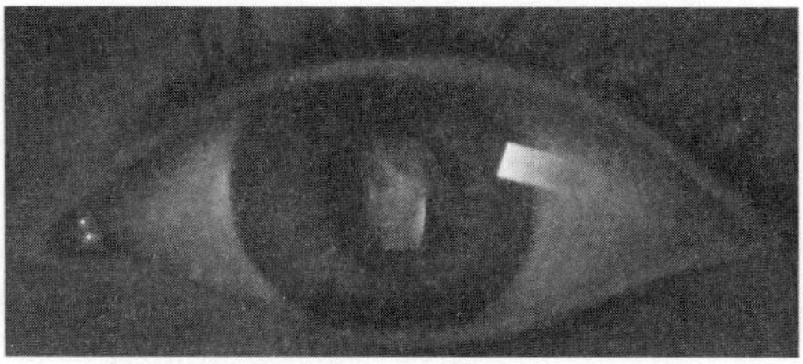

CHAPTER 13

Rake cried out loudly as he stared down at his daughter's badly beaten and battered body. Even though the county examiner had pulled back the sheet only enough to show her face, Rake Wiggins knew that his daughter had suffered. Her face was battered. Her wet hair was matted and tangled. Grasping the edge of the cotton sheet, he started to ease it back.

"Sir, we can only allow you to see the face," the examiner said.

"I'll have you know this is my only daughter. I love this child more than my own life, and I want to know what happened to her. I don't want to hear some half truth now and then find out the rest in a crowded courtroom."

The medical examiner looked at the detectives for permission. They both nodded, and the sheet was pulled back further. A gasp and then a sigh escaped from Rake's throat as he looked down at the lifeless body of his beautiful daughter. Then a low deep moan of intense emotional pain slipped from him. This is the one thing life never prepares you for, identifying your baby in a cold metal room as she lies there broken and still.

The bruises bore evidence to the fact that she had suffered greatly—bodies don't bruise after death. The skin abrasions, the lacerations, the missing hair, and the puncture wounds bore witness to the trauma she had endured before dying.

"What kind of monster does this to a person? This is my daughter. She's an innocent young woman. She hasn't even had time to live, and some kind of animal has cut her life short," Rake cried out as he sank to the cold floor of the morgue.

"What am I going to do, what am I going to tell her mother? What words can I say?" Rake was beyond consoling. His strength was gone, and something in his eyes died as he knelt there.

Amanda had actually been cleaned up quite a bit before her father saw her. Will and Jerry knew it and were grateful. They helped the suffering father to his feet.

"Mr. Wiggins, let's step outside," Jerry said. As he led the way to the corridor outside the morgue, Rake turned one more time to look at his daughter. Mandy lay on the cold metal slab, so still, her body ghastly white after enduring its death throes. "When will her body be released?"

"It's hard to say, but I think it will take at least three days for the medical examiner to complete his work. However, you can make arrangements, plan a funeral and service if you want to."

"You know, this is one thing you can never be prepared for. I never thought this would happen. I could never have dreamed that I would bury Mandy. Her mother and I both have living wills; we both have burial plots and plans made. But we never planned to bury one of our children."

Three days later, true to his word, Will sat reading the autopsy report and signing the forms to release Amanda's body. What the medical jargon boiled down to was that Amanda had been raped repeatedly. Her system had been flooded with drugs and alcohol. Her feet and hands had been bound, and evidently she had suffered greatly before she died. Bruises and black eyes, bloody nose and broken bones were all that was left of her. She was her parent's oldest child and the apple of her father's eye. Someone had killed all the hopes and dreams of this beautiful young woman.

Will wondered who Mandy had really been. He knew a lot about her because of the investigation, but he wondered who she was, really. What did her voice sound like, what was her favorite color? He picked up the phone and dialed the number of the funeral home the Wigginses had chosen.

CHAPTER 14

Amanda's funeral was crowded with family and friends. The whole senior class attended; in fact, most of the Ripney High School student body was there. They huddled close to each other for comfort, crying and sniffling and holding on to one another.

The shock on their young faces was evident. Cammy sat between Jeremy in his wheelchair and her parents. The Wrights were behind Jeremy. Mandy's family was seated in the front row. Her parents, Aletha and Rake, wept softly as they watched the pink casket lowered into the ground as their only daughter was laid to rest. Mandy's brothers, Kyle and Steven, looked stunned. They had been very quiet during the investigation, never saying much or asking questions. Today was no different.

The police were everywhere, standing with their hands folded politely in front of them. They were there because it was a well-known fact that killers often attended the victim's funeral. But so far no one had appeared who didn't know someone in the family. No one stood out among the mourners.

The pastor prayed, offering up to heaven the soul of Amanda Wiggins, a beautiful young woman cut down too early. Amanda couldn't really be called a woman; she hadn't lived long enough. She was young, innocent, lovely—and now dead. The mourners stood close together, and occasionally one or two of them scanned the surrounding area as if looking for the perpetrators.

Jeremy sat silently by Cammy, holding her hand. He had been hospitalized since Mandy's abduction and allowed out only for the funeral. His doctors had felt it might help him recover and accept the death of his girlfriend's best friend. They understood that Jeremy felt like a failure because he hadn't been able to save Mandy. Both Jeremy and Cammy were seeing the hospital social worker.

Jeremy covered his face with his free hand. He thought of Mandy and the last time he had seen her alive and smiling. Her face swam before him. She had once been so beautiful, but now the image was of her battered face as she tried to fight off the man crouching over her on the van's floor. Jeremy swayed in his chair, stamping his feet in frustration. Cammy reached out her arm as if to steady him, and he smiled up at her through his tears. She sank to her knees at Mandy's gravesite and laid her head in Jeremy's lap. Looking at Cammy made him feel worse. But her hand in his made him feel better. They held on to one another and buried their friend.

Jared Sinclair was there, too. He cried softly as the preacher asked God for strength and understanding. One by one the mourners filed past the open grave and tossed in the pink roses that had come from the graduating class of Ripney High School.

The minister handed Mandy's parents a white bible. "I'm terribly sorry for your loss. If you need anything, please call me."

"Thank you for your kindness," the Wigginses said in unison. It was becoming an automatic response.

Will and Jerry stood nearby and watched. There was so much trauma, so much pain on the faces of those present.

"You see anyone that doesn't fit, Jerry?" Will asked.

"Nope, you?"

"No, but somehow I didn't think we would. You ready to go?"

"Yeah, let's get the hell out of here," said Jerry as he started walking toward the parking area.

"I feel like we can get more by going back out to Ambly. Maybe take a walk in the woods. Are you up for a little nature study?" Will asked

"Yeah, I think I am. I have this burning desire to do something constructive, like find this bastard and cut his balls off. I wonder what he's doing right now. I sure hope this is a one-time thrill for him," Jerry said.

As Jerry and Will walked away, they heard the wavering notes of young voices singing a last hymn. Each felt a chill creep up his spine, and both darted a quick look around.

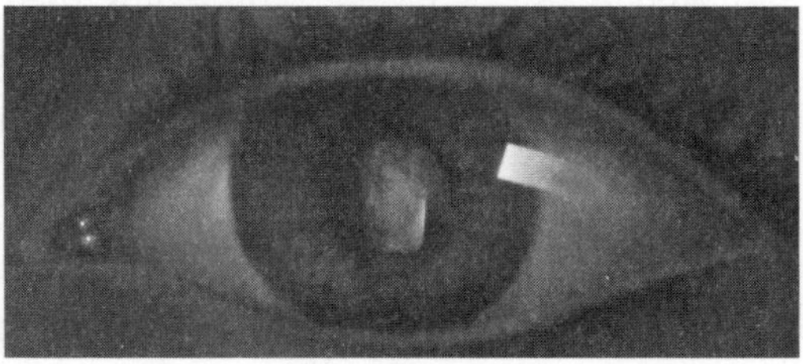

CHAPTER 15

Mike Hennessey and Tony Garrison had grown up in the same Wisconsin neighborhood. They had played stickball with the other kids and stayed out late, getting picked up for curfew violations countless times. Tony came from a strong Catholic background. His mother had tried to beat religion into him. She cried and prayed for him on bended knee, hoping to impress upon him the importance of salvation and the hereafter. At the age of thirteen he was considered the black sheep of the family. When he was sixteen, Tony ran away.

Occasionally over the last few years he had called his mother, just to let her know he was still alive. They would tell each other how much they loved each other, but it was better from a distance. Tony would wipe the tears from his eyes, and he always felt better after calling. Tony did keep in closer touch with one of his brothers. Gilbert, or "Gil," actually spent time with him once or twice a year.

In the first year after Tony ran away, Gil often slipped him food out his bedroom window late at night. But he always warned Tony about Mike. "That boy ain't nothing but trouble, Tony," he would say. "Nothing but trouble and someday you're gonna be the one to pay for what he does. He's got a mean streak in him. You watch your backside, Tony."

Tony would always laugh and say, "Don't worry, bro; we're partners, Mike and me. We cover each other's backs."

Mike had grown up on the street. His dad had raised him, if you could call it that, after his mom had taken off. Mike did have a mean streak in him—his father had made sure of it. He took one beating after another, and each beating seemed to be worse than the one before it. Some nights Mike went home, some nights he stayed at Tony's, and some nights he just stayed on the street. Mike's dad never bothered to look for him.

When Mike took off one day, Tony just went with him. They had been together most of the time since that day. Mike actually did some time in jail for breaking and entering and then again for robbing a convenience store. During those times Tony hung out, got a job, and just waited. Gil, who didn't like being around Mike, would visit his brother during those times.

Mike's mean streak was always the reason he got caught. He wanted to slap people around, prove that he was stronger and in control. Doing that took time, all the time that was needed for the law to show up, but Mike never learned from his mistakes.

They finally made it upstate and just hung around. Now they were in God's country, enjoying the scenery and taking advantage of all the sights and pleasures this state had to offer. Pretty countryside, lush state parks, gentle summer weather, cool at night and warm during the day. And the women, aah, the women, there were so many. It seemed like there were two women to every one man.

They took advantage of the trusting nature of the inhabitants. Doors were left unlocked, purses on kitchen tables next to open windows. Most men left their wallets in the glove compartments of their unlocked cars. Money was easy to come by, if you didn't mind stealing and you were quick on your feet.

While her family and friends, and a few police offers, buried Amanda Wiggins, Tony Garrison and Mike Hennessey played in the sunlight—just not in the same vicinity. It had never occurred to them to go to Mandy's funeral. They weren't even aware that her body had been found. Nor did they care. For them the time with Mandy was over, gone and forgotten.

Forty-five miles away from the funeral they sat around a campfire, laughing about the day's events as Tony's clothes dried. The clothes were stretched out on the ground, baking in the brilliant sunlight. The only thing he wore was the delicate pair of pink stretch lace panties that had belonged to Mandy until a short time ago. Tony had fallen into the Hudson River while scrambling around in the dirt and imitating Mandy begging for help. Mike had let the current carry him for a while as he ran along the bank and kept an eye on him. He enjoyed Tony's fear and had a good laugh before he reached in and pulled him out.

Tony was inwardly furious, but he would never let Mike know it. Nervously, he laughed along with him as he splashed and struggled to get a foothold or grab the branch of a passing tree. Many times Tony had wanted to cry out for help, but he knew that would only spur Mike on. Mike would have left him in the water even longer, gasping for breath and fighting to survive.

Mike was known for playing on the fears of others, and Tony knew that he would be Mike's next victim if his fears were ever discovered. He couldn't swim well and had always been afraid of the water, something he was trying to overcome. His strongest childhood nightmare had been about drowning, and each encounter with the water was sure to bring that nightmare back for weeks. Tony needed to let the moment go. It had been hours since Mike had pulled him from the water. His clothing should be dry and his anger should have abated. The trouble was that Tony was having a hard time forgiving Mike this time. He knew that eventually he would, he always did. Ever since they had been kids, Mike had done all the bullying, and Tony had done all the forgiving.

Tony tipped the bottle back and swallowed hard. He took the joint Mike passed to him and drew the smoke deep into his lungs. As he held it there and let the effect of the drug embrace him, he felt better. As he released the smoke, he let his anger at Mike go with it.

"We need some grub, man. I'm starving," Mike said.

"Yeah, let's go get some munchies, some more tequila and maybe a pizza," Tony said animatedly, as he struggled into his clothes and kicked dirt on the fire. His anger was forgotten. Tony was like a little kid in that regard, you could just give him something else to think about and send his mind in a different direction. Feed him and he was like a dog that forgot the beating he had just suffered.

They headed for the two cars parked side by side. One was a station wagon they had recently stolen in the neighboring state, the other was Tony's old truck. They had gone on what they called a "run" to ditch the van. As they'd been dumping Mandy's body in the water, they spotted a man putting his car in the garage for the night. Mike saw an opportunity. "Hey, man, I got an idea," he said. "Let's trade the van for that car."

"You mean steal his car, don't ya, Mike?"

"Well, it ain't like it's stealing. We can trade him. He has that car, we have this van. And you know we have to get rid of this. I mean this is what the cops are going to be looking for when they start looking—if they ain't already started," Mike argued.

Tony thought about it, "Yeah, yeah, Mike, that's a great idea. If we leave them this car and hide it in that garage, chances are they won't find it for a long time."

"Yeah, sure, kid," Mike said sarcastically, knowing full well that the van would be discovered in the morning. But by then, Mike thought, they would be back across the state line and in their little hideaway, safe in the woods.

They had watched the man close the double doors of the garage. It actually looked more like a barn than a garage. As he'd walked into the house he'd glanced around him almost as if he could feel someone watching him. Mike and Tony had driven past for the second time just in time to see him disappear inside. Mike had parked the van out near the road, a short distance from the garage. They'd waited until darkness fell and the barn-like structure was wrapped in the cover of night. Mike crept forward and eased the door open. As he tried the door of the car, he wasn't even mildly surprised to find it unlocked.

"I love this state," he said with a chuckle. Motioning Tony to come on, Mike walked around to the rear of the station wagon. Bending down, he removed a screwdriver and a license plate from where he had stashed them in the back of his pants waistband. He replaced the station wagon's plates with some he'd stolen from another car. Snickering to himself he said, "That should give Johnny Law something to confuse the shit out of him." He'd opened the garage doors wide and looked around for Tony. "Asshole," Mike whispered as he signaled angrily for Tony to come and give him a hand. "Come on, chickenshit," he'd said in a hushed whisper. He and Tony had pushed the car out into the yard.

"How we gonna get it started Mike?" Tony had asked.

Mike held up the keys in his left hand, "Country folks always hide their keys in the visor, and their wallets in the glove box," Mike said as he held up the man's wallet with his other hand.

"Wow, pretty stupid, huh?"

Mike just looked at him. Tony should have seen the disgust in his face, but he never did. "Yeah, it was pretty stupid of him, but damn lucky for us. Put the van in the garage, and be quiet about it, will ya?" Mike whispered.

Tony had quietly trotted over to the van and eased it into the garage. He came out and closed the doors. They had pushed the station wagon far enough from the house to muffle the sound of it starting, and then had gotten in and simply driven off. Now it had been their get-around car for two days.

Mike watched Tony struggle into his clothes and kick dirt on the fire.

"Are they still wet?" Mike asked.

"Yeah, but it's okay, they're just wet in the crotch, and that part of me is still smokin'," Tony said with a laugh in a voice that was clearly not his own. "They should be dry in no time at all." Tony lightly punched Mike in the arm. Mike laughed too.

"Come on, let's go get something to eat. Hey, maybe we can scout the mall again for some fun!"

Tony jumped up and down in imitation of an Irish jig. "Yeah, sounds good. But let's get some grub first. I'm hungry."

Mike drove to a town about 45 miles from where they were camped out. He tried to explain why to Tony, but Tony just didn't have a criminal mind. "You're stupid. If I left everything up to you we'd have the law on us in no time flat. You gotta start thinking, Tony, use that noodle of yours," Mike said as he poked Tony in the temple. "If we shop near where we're staying we're gonna get seen. Being seen means being caught. Don't you think Johnny Law is looking for us for what we did to that girl?"

Tony looked down. He didn't feel guilty for what had happened to

Amanda Wiggins because he really hadn't done much to her. Mike had done most of the damage. That was another thing that pissed Tony off. Mike always got the girl first.

"You coming in?" Mike asked as he got out at the little mom and pop store.

"What?" Tony said, coming back to the moment.

"I said are you coming in?"

"Yeah, I'm coming."

Mike looked around the store, walking up and down the aisles. Getting familiar with the store layout was important for any future business that he might have with them. Money had been getting tight before he had found that old man's wallet in his station wagon. He never knew where the next meal would come from, but somehow he had always managed.

Mike cased the store as he made his purchases; but he knew he would have to come back alone, without Tony. Tony always wanted to know what the take was, how much did they get. Then he would hold out his hand, and Mike would have to count his share into his palm right then and there or Tony would start acting stupid. Mike hated it when Tony acted stupid. He'd tried time and again to explain to him that some things were better done privately, but Tony would have none of that; he wanted his share, and he wouldn't leave the store without it. The first time Tony had done that Mike almost fell on the floor laughing. But Tony had been dead serious.

They made their selections and paid for them, smiling as they left. It was better to be friendly with the hired help than to get on their bad side and have them watch you the whole time you were in the store. Tony was munching even before they got out the door. He had a ravenous appetite that did no damage at all to his skinny physique. As he wiped his greasy mouth on his shirtsleeve he looked at Mike.

"Where are we going, Mike?"

"Remember, we talked about going to the mall again. That was a fine place to have some laughs and meet some women. Although you ain't gonna get no pussy with that greasy face," Mike said, laughing and punching Tony in the shoulder.

"The way you do things, I probably ain't gonna get any anyway," Tony said, beginning to pout.

"Aw, come on Tony. Shit, I didn't mean it. I told you I didn't mean it. That bitch was just plain mean. She wasn't gonna give it up without a fight anyway, and you know you ain't gonna fight for it. Now me, that's more my style. I like a tussle."

"You make me sick sometimes, Mike. Sometimes you make me just plain old-fashioned sick to my stomach. You always gotta be so radical. Why are you like that?"

Mike could see that Tony was serious. "Hey man, I thought we was bros. I thought we was tight. You sayin' you're sick of me now?"

"Not all the time, only when you're mean like that. Let's go get some girls, but be nice to them tonight, okay? Hey, there's a carnival over by that big open field, the one with the church on it about a mile out of town. You wanna go to the carnival? There's always chicks lookin' around for guys at them things."

"Okay, egghead," Mike said, ruffling Tony's hair. "We'll go to the carnival and I'll be nice. You got money?"

"Yeah, I got money, ain't you got no money?" Tony looked guardedly at Mike.

"Yeah, I got money for me. But you get your own money all the time, so you gotta pay your own way. And you gotta pay the way for any pussy you pick up," Mike said. "Deal?"

"Deal," Tony said, as he dug into his bag of chips and his beer.

Mike concentrated on the road. It secretly hurt his feelings that Tony was sick of him. Tony was the only person in his whole life who had always liked, even loved him. Mike glanced at him as he sat there happily munching on chips and sucking on the beer can. For Tony, the moment was forgotten. He was simple that way. Easygoing and easy paced. Mike realized that Tony was long past the feeling of being sick of him. Mike smiled and tucked the memory away.

CHAPTER 16

The ride back to town was short. It was finding a place to park at the packed event that took time. Families walked around pulling wagons filled with kids or food for picnics; people were shuffling livestock for the Friday evening judging. The state fair had started the weekend before, and livestock judging was a main event. But the food, the rides, and the funhouses brought children and young adults out in droves every weekend night. People of all ages came to have a good time. The scheduled events took two weeks to complete, and the fair was just getting started.

As Mike and Tony got out of the car and started walking towards the lights and crowds, Mike jabbed Tony playfully in the ribs. "Even you should be able to get laid here. Look at all these women."

Tony shot him a look over his shoulder as he wiped his mouth on his shirtsleeve. "Yeah, and look at those shorts. My momma would kill my sister for wearing shorts that short. Her butt's hanging out the bottom. I like that, don't you, Mike?" Tony asked excitedly.

"Naaah, I'm a boob man. Look at the hooters on that one over there," Mike said, pointing boldly at a girl coming their way.

"Touch 'em Mike," Tony giggled. "When she comes by reach out and grab you a handful."

"Are you stupid or what? We'd get kicked out of here in a minute, and that big dude walking with her would kick your ass, and I would have to save you again!"

"Why would he kick my ass if you touched her, stupid?" Tony drawled.

"Cause he could see by my face that I ain't that stupid and figure you must have been the one that told me to do it!" Mike howled with laughter. Tony laughed too as he fell forward from the waist down and stumbled into Mike. Mike slapped him on the back as the couple blended into the crowd. "Let's get a beer first, then we can get some grub and check out the chicks."

The two spent the evening walking around the fair. The lights, the rides, and the smell of food were like a drug. Smiling people ran from one source of entertainment to the next in almost frantic anticipation. Mike and Tony were caught up in the moment just like the others, enjoying the feeling of a high, just as they would have with any drug.

Mike wiped his mouth on his sleeve just as Tony had done earlier. He nodded in the direction of a nearby tent. "Let's check out the music. There should be babes in there for sure." As they walked toward the tent Tony burped out loud. He laughed as two passing girls cast him a look of disgust. He opened his mouth and let out an even louder belch as he bent towards them. Jumping away, they headed in a different direction.

Mike and Tony laughed as they walked inside. The band was playing a loud rendition of the Beatles' "A Hard Day's Night." Mike and Tony sang along as they danced in place. Soon everyone in the tent was dancing and singing. Two girls had joined Mike and Tony as they drank beer, sang the latest songs, and danced the night away.

As the fair closed, the two girls walked with Mike and Tony to the parking area in the field. "Come on, ride with us," Tony argued as the girls tried to explain that they had their own car and a curfew.

"Really, we can't. My dad will skin me alive if I'm not home by midnight. My mom and dad are divorced and I can work 'em sometimes, but I have to be real careful. I'll meet you right here tomorrow night at seven o'clock," Wanda said, pointing to the ground at her feet.

"Okay, but give me your phone number, and I'll call you," Mike countered.

Wanda took a pen from her purse and wrote her number on his hand. Lilly Williams did the same thing for Tony. The two guys read the numbers and both leaned in for a kiss. After getting what they wanted, they said their goodnights and shut the car doors for the girls. Walking in the direction of their own car the two guys looked at each other and shouted, "We're gettin' laid tomorrow!"

Wanda and Lilly had no idea until much later how close they had come to death that night. Close is an understatement—in fact, they had both kissed it!

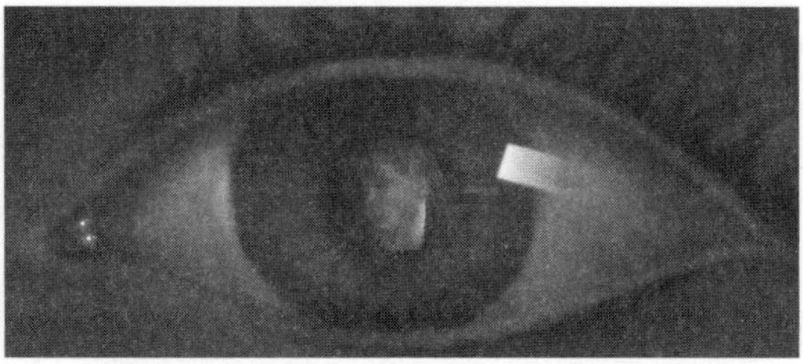

CHAPTER 17

Lindsay Freeman rolled to her side, clutching the damp rag to her forehead. The dark room and the cool rag did little to ease the pain in her head. She rolled back and forth on the soft bed; finally reaching in the darkness for the bottle of pain medication that she knew was on the bedside table. She hated taking it, but this migraine had been tormenting her for the last three days. Soon Jackie would be home and she would have to go back to work. She struggled with the child-resistant lid.

"Damn, where's Jackie when I need him? I can never get these caps off. An eight-year-old kid can do this and I can't. What's wrong with this picture?"

Eventually the lid let go. With a moan, she lifted her head just far enough off the pillow to sip some water and let the pill slide down her throat. She lay back and breathed hard as if she had just run up a flight of stairs. The pain was very real, the throbbing intense. The pill couldn't work fast enough for her, she thought, as its effects began to take hold. As she drifted off to sleep, the phone rang.

"What day is this?" she said out loud. "Is it Thursday or Friday?" She struggled to remember, then let the pill win. She barely heard her recorder pick up the call. "Lindsay, this is Marcus. Did I get the day of our date wrong? Call me back." She didn't want to go on the damn date anyway. In the last moments of wakefulness Lindsay thought to herself, "I'm glad that wasn't someone important."

CHAPTER 18

"I love you too. See you soon, baby. Hurry, I'm waiting," Georgia Amando said breathlessly into the phone. She gently set the receiver back in the cradle. Turning back to her dresser mirror, she studied her reflection.

"I wonder if anyone can tell," she said as she ran her hand over her still-flat stomach. The queasiness she'd had for days now started again. Telling Joey had been the best thing to do. She had actually slept last night. Her stomach grumbled and rolled as she jumped up and ran, with her hand over her mouth, to the bathroom down the hall.

"Georgia," her momma called from downstairs. "Is that you honey? You want some breakfast?"

Georgia hung her head and let go. She took a deep breath and wiped her mouth. "No momma," she whispered. "Breakfast is the last thing I want." She stood on shaky legs and walked slowly back to her room. "No thanks," she hollered down the stairs on her way by.

Back in the privacy of her own room she again caressed her tummy. Tears filled her eyes as she thought about Joey and how wonderful he'd been when she had turned to him and said, "I'm pregnant."

Joey had sat back in shock. "Are you sure? I mean, could there be something else wrong?"

"No, I'm sure," she had sobbed out. "I had a pregnancy test at the clinic at Barlow, and it came back positive. Oh Joey, I'm so sorry. I thought we were careful. I don't know what to do." Georgia had collapsed, sobbing, as Joey had wrapped his arms around her.

"Shhh, baby. Don't cry. We'll think of something," Joey had said.

"It's gonna ruin all your plans for medical school if we keep it. But I just can't do anything else. Joey, this is our baby."

"Georgie, stop crying," said Joey. "This is gonna be okay. I'll think of something. I would rather have waited a few years, had a house and all; but we'll think of something. I mean, when you think about it, who better to have a baby than a man who wants to be a pediatrician? Let's find out what the university says about married couples. I have a full scholarship, so if we both work we should be able to make ends meet. You'll have to work until the baby gets here, but I think we can figure this out," Joey said, holding Georgia's face in his hands.

Georgia, had stopped crying. She couldn't believe what she had heard then, and she still couldn't believe it now. Joey had gotten on one knee and said the sweetest words in the world to her. "Marry me, Georgia Lucinda Amando. Make my life complete." All she had been able to do was nod her head and dab at her nose with the tissue. It wasn't really how she had pictured her wedding, walking down the aisle in a maternity dress, but Joey couldn't have proposed in a more romantic way. He was her knight in shining armor.

"Georgia, you're gonna be late for school. You aren't a graduate yet, better get a move on," her dad hollered in his Italian accent. It always warmed Georgia's heart to hear him speak passionately. That was the only time you could hear his background in his voice. He had taken classes to become an American citizen and he was darned proud of it.

"Coming, daddy."

As she came to the table her parents looked up at her. "Honey, you don't look so good. Are you okay?" her mother asked.

"Yeah momma, I'm fine. I have to go straight to work today after school. Lisa needs someone to work for her today so she can shop for her prom stuff. So I won't be home until late tonight."

"Oh my God, she doesn't have her prom stuff yet? Goodness, you young girls always wait till the last minute, then it's rush, rush, rush to get everything done. Speaking of getting things done, you need to bring that pretty blue dress of yours home so I can get the hem and the bodice right. It seems to be too tight in the bust," Lucinda Amando said.

"I will, momma, and I need to drop my shoes off to be dyed at the shoe shop. Joey is coming in my car to pick me up, so I don't have time for breakfast. I'll grab something on the way."

"What is Joey wearing, Georgia, what color?" her dad asked.

"He's wearing baby blue, papa. You know that. And a navy blue cummerbund."

"A man shouldn't wear baby blue. It's not manly. Real men don't wear baby blue."

"Papa, Joey is a real man, and I'll have you know it's the most popular color this year, according to the tuxedo rental place. Momma, he looks wonderful in his tux. I can't wait for you to see it. Papa, will you get some film for the camera?"

"I already have it, princess," her father said with a smile. He loved teasing her about Joey. From his red hair to his dirty fingernails and now his baby blue tuxedo, George Amando loved to pick on Joey Mercer. If the truth be known, he liked the boy. The kid worked hard for a living, and he studied even harder. He was gonna be a fine husband someday, someday when he got out of medical school and could afford a wife. But that someday wasn't now, because now he was just a grease monkey who worked on hotrods and read every book in the library. Still, George liked him.

A horn sounded out front. Lucinda looked out the window over the kitchen sink. "Joey's here, Georgia."

Georgia kissed her momma and poppa goodbye and ran out the door. "Don't wait up for me, momma. I'll be late. I love you both." And then the door slammed.

Georgia ran down the front steps and stopped. There sat Joey in her car. He had washed and waxed it. The paint gleamed in the morning sun. "Oh gosh, it looks great!"

"You like?" Joey asked. "I like," Georgia said and she leaned over for her morning kiss.

"Should you be running like that, young lady?" Joey asked playfully.

"Well, doctor, I only ran a short distance, and I promise never to do it again," Georgia countered as she crossed her heart with two crossed fingers.

"Well, my dear, I think I can let this slide and promise not to punish you if you come along quietly," Joey said in his best spy voice.

"Oh really, dear sir, what do you have in mind?" Georgia giggled, loving the banter.

"Seriously, Georgia, spend the day with me. Just one day. I really need to be with you today to talk, make plans and just be alone together." Georgia could see in his eyes that Joey meant what he said. "Okay, what do you want to do? I have to be at work at one o'clock to cover for Lisa, but we could have the rest of the day. What are they gonna do, flunk us at this late date?"

Joey kissed her and pulled her to him. They drove to a spot where they often went to be alone. This is probably where their baby was conceived, Joey thought to himself. He had a picnic basket and a blanket in the back. Georgia looked at him and smiled. "You had this all planned out, didn't you?"

"Uh huh!"

"How did you know I would say yes?"

"You love me. How could you say no?" Joey grinned at her. "Come on babe, time's a wastin'."

They spent the morning on the blanket together, feeding one another and talking about their future. "Georgia, I know we agreed to wait for another two weeks till after graduation, but I just couldn't. I want the whole world to know." He reached into his pocket and pulled out a tiny black box. His eyes shone with tears as he reached for her hand. He laid the box in her palm and folded her fingers around it. Then he raised her hand to his lips and kissed her knuckles. "I love you, Georgia, please say yes." Joey whispered.

Georgia carefully opened her fist. She held her breath and opened the little box. Nestled in black velvet was a tiny diamond. Tears fell from her eyes. She looked up at him and whispered, "Yes."

Joey took the ring from its velvet bed and carefully slipped it on her finger. It was a perfect fit. The diamond was small, but so important. "It's not much, babe, but someday we'll get you a bigger one."

"No! This one's perfect; in fact it couldn't be more perfect. I love you, Joey." Georgia whispered through her tears as she gazed at the ring.

They rode slowly toward the auto body shop where Joey worked after school, neither of them in any hurry to be separated. "I'll see you tonight after you get off. Come by my house before you go home," Joey said as he got out of the car. His car was still in the parking area where he had left it the day before. Walking around the car, he kissed Georgia gently, and then with a wink he turned and went inside.

Georgia drove toward the mall, looking down at her finger at every stop sign and red light. The little ring sparkled on her finger. Her heart fluttered in excitement. She hurried, so she could stop by the drugstore and buy the newest bride magazine. She pictured the dress she would have and the explanation she would give her parents about going with Joey when he left in the fall. Georgia felt terrible about ruining all her parents' plans for her and college. But she would go one day. She had promised her dying grandmother that she would be the first Amando to graduate from college, and her grandmother had left a provision in her will for Georgia's education. Georgia looked to the sky, "I'm going, grandma, I promise. Someday I'll go."

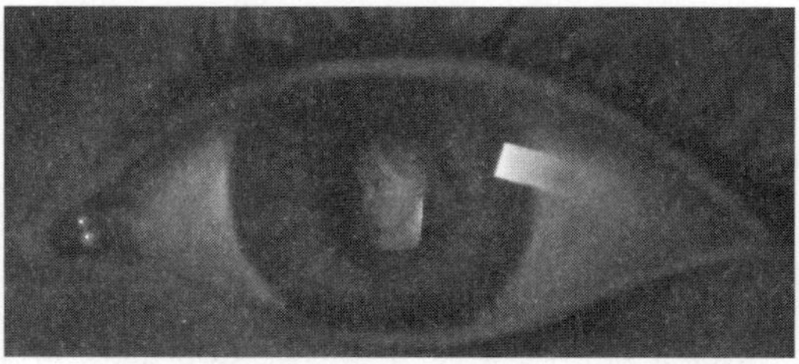

CHAPTER 19

Georgia sat at the counter in the shoe department at Carson's where she worked three afternoons a week and doodled on a scratch pad: "Mrs. Joey Mercer, Mrs. Georgia Mercer, Mr. & Mrs. Joseph Mercer." She loved the way it looked. She envisioned Joey at work. She could see him standing at the counter of the shop where he worked after school and sometimes on weekends, and she smiled at the mental image. If the university would only let them live together they would have the world by the tail. Georgia crossed her fingers and said a prayer, "Grandma, if you're listening, please let this go right for us."

"Hey, girl, what are you daydreaming about? It's just about time to go. Count your bank, and let's get the heck out of here," Melissa said, leaning over her shoulder.

"Oh my God, what is that?" Melissa gasped in shock as she grabbed Georgia's left hand. "Are you engaged?" Georgia nodded.

"When?" asked Melissa.

"This morning. Joey took me on a picnic. That's why we weren't in school."

"Oh Georgia, I'm so happy for you. Are you going to go to Illinois with him?"

"We don't know yet. But the plan is to get married right after graduation." Georgia said as she looked down.

"Georgia, are you P.G.?" Melissa asked in an exaggerated whisper.

Georgia looked up. "Oh Melissa, please don't tell anyone. We wanted to do this the right way, it's just that's not how it worked out. My mom and dad don't know yet and they would never forgive us. Please keep our secret and be happy for us."

"Oh girl, that's exciting. Mum's the word. My lips are sealed, and I'll never say a word," Melissa promised as they both giggled.

"Well, come on then. You really do need to get out of here and go home to rest. Don't forget your dress and shoes," Melissa said as she walked away.

Georgia closed out her drawer. Then, with the bank bag tucked under her arm she walked into the back room and took her beautiful prom dress down from the shelf. She couldn't wait to try it on again. "What if it doesn't fit?" she thought.

She walked to the office. Putting the bag on the counter for a recount she said, "I'm signed out, and here's the bank. We balanced to the penny." As Alvin Keller counted her bank and handed her a receipt that she tucked into her purse, Georgia said, "I'll see you tomorrow."

Alvin put the bank bag in the safe beneath his chair. "See you tomorrow, Miss Georgia. You want me to walk you to your car?"

"No thanks Alvin. I'm parked just outside, under the street lamp. Thanks anyway," Georgia said as she wrestled with her packages.

She dug in her purse for her car keys as she walked out the big glass doors, scanning the parking lot before going too far. From where she stood she could see her car. There were several others parked around hers—lately, everyone wanted to park under the light.

The death of Amanda Wiggins came to her mind. Georgia hadn't known Mandy well, but they had had a class together. She remembered her as a pretty blonde, kind of sexy and flirty.

Somehow, Georgia felt it before she actually heard it, a tingling in the air that felt and smelled like danger. She looked around tentatively. There they were, just to her right. She knew them in an instant, even though they weren't in the famous beige van that had been sketched on the front page of the newspaper for a week now.

"Hey baby. Come on, momma, you wanna go for a ride? Maybe have a little fun." Georgia kept her head down as she walked nervously toward her car, which seemed further away than she had thought. She refused to look at the men taunting her, just in case it might fuel their fire. Alvin Keller's offer of an escort to her car came back to her, and she wished she had taken him up on it. But it was too late to turn back. The men were between her and the store entrance.

"Hey baby, yeah, I'm talkin' to you," Mike yelled out the window.

"Yeah, baby, come go for a ride with us. We'll treat you real good," Tony said as he blew kisses out the window. The car turned down one row of parked cars and then came back up another. The wheels on the old station wagon seemed to rotate in slow motion. She could see one of the men hanging his head out the passenger window, pointing to her. "Run," her mind told her, "go back inside, scream!" Then it was too late. The car turned in her direction. She tried not to look at the faces of the men in the car. She just kept her head down and walked as fast as she could in the direction of the streetlight.

Her car was parked just beneath it, a sanctuary of peace and safety. As she reached the car, she shifted her packages to her other hand again and put the key in the lock. A hand closed roughly over hers. She tried to turn and look for help, but she never got the chance.

Her body was slammed viciously against the door of her car, knocking the breath out of her. Georgia opened her mouth to scream as a hand clamped hard over it. The man's mouth was on her neck, and she could feel him grinding his hips against her.

"I'm going to be raped," she thought to herself in desperation. She turned her head just enough to draw a breath. "Please, please don't do this. I'm pregnant, please," Georgia said as she started to cry.

"Good, baby, then we don't have that to worry about. I hate practicing safe sex," Mike growled into her ear.

Georgia drew a ragged breath as deep as her lungs and the hand over her mouth would allow and screamed, "Joey!"

"No, baby, it's Mike, but you can call me Joey if you want to," Mike laughed. A car screeched to a stop behind them. For just the briefest of seconds Georgia felt relief at the thought of rescue. But then her body was being dragged backward and her head was hitting the doorframe. As her body was pulled into the car the hand over her mouth loosened one more time and Georgia screamed, "Help me!"

"Go, go!" Mike yelled to Tony.

She could see her beautiful, baby-blue prom dress and her satin shoes lying on the pavement as she lost sight of her car. She could see the light she had thought would provide so much safety, and she could see the confused, horrified faces of the witnesses to her abduction. Georgia struggled to sit up as Mike struggled to keep her down. He grabbed her face and forced her to look out the back window of the car as his other hand crawled across her body.

"Say goodbye, baby, 'cause you ain't never gonna see this place again. That's the way it is, it's the way it has to be."

Georgia sobbed hysterically as she watched her life disappear. Why hadn't she let Joey pick her up? He'd wanted to... why hadn't she let him? Georgia whispered, "Joey, I need you."

CHAPTER 20

Within minutes the police were all over the mall. Both Will Halpin and Jerry Leeme had been called at home. Their responses were the same—they would be there immediately. Will had just gone to bed after a long, hard day, but he dragged on his pants, shoes, and a shirt, and then headed out the door. Within ten minutes he was standing with other officers where Georgia had stood and screamed for help only twenty minutes earlier. He reached out and shook his partner's hand as Jerry arrived.

"Good to see you, it's been what, maybe two hours?"

Jerry was trying to be funny, but Will wasn't laughing. "What have we got?"

Will pointed to the items lying on the gray pavement. The blue satin prom dress and the small white satin shoes with the sparkles on the toes lay there. A brown leather purse and some keys with the initials G and J in gold metal lay next to them.

"Are we getting witness statements from anyone?" Will asked.

The officer to his left nodded. "Yes sir, as many as we can. Some of the folks are pretty upset and have gone into the mall office. Security has them and they're recording as fast as possible. They've promised to make all the tapes available to us. There are plenty of people in there. Someone has to have seen something that may be helpful."

Turning to the officer, Jerry looked for his name. "Brandon, sir," the officer said.

"Okay, Brandon. Do you have a copy of that sketch that went out last week at roll call?"

"Yes sir, in my car."

"Good. Get it and show it to everyone here. Make sure they all take a good look and see if these are the same guys who took Amanda Wiggins." Jerry and Will raised their eyebrows for emphasis.

"Yes sir," Officer Brandon said as he started toward his patrol car. Turning, he spoke again, "Sir, I was the reporting officer for the Wiggins case. I just thought you should know."

"Thank you, Brandon, that's good to know," Will said as he went back to his paperwork. Scott Brandon started again for his car, grateful to have something to do other than wait for these two hotshots to think this thing through.

Suddenly there was a great commotion as the crowd parted to make way for a man and woman speaking in rapid Italian. The two rushed forward, their eyes scanning the crowd for someone.

"Our daughter, our Georgia, where you say she is?" George Amando demanded in a panic. "Where our daughter?" he asked again as he grabbed Officer Brandon's shirtfront. "The man inside that work with my Georgia say some man come and take her, he grab her and take her. You tell me?"

Officer Brandon pointed to Will and Jerry. "Those men over there can help you."

Lucinda and George Amando hurried in their direction. Will and Jerry saw them coming and steeled themselves for the onslaught of questions.

As they approached, Will stuck out his hand. "Hello, I'm Detective Will Halpin, and this is my partner Detective Jerry Leeme. We know you must be very upset, but please work with us."

George held onto his wife as she cried. "I just wanna know what has happened to my Georgia."

"Sir, at this point all we know is that your daughter was abducted by two men in a station wagon. There are conflicting reports as to its color, make, and model, but it's still really early. Let's go inside so we can talk in private. I know you're upset, but please try to be calm so we can gather all the information as quickly as possible."

George and Lucinda nodded and allowed themselves to be ushered into the mall security office. Alvin Keller took their hands as they came in. "I tried to get her to let me walk her. She wouldn't hear of it. Oh God, she said she was parked under the street lamp." Keller was crying, his grief overwhelming.

Lucinda reached out her hand to him, "Its okay. I know my daughter; she would never want to put you out."

Alvin nodded, "Yes she was that way."

"You mean, she is that way," Will Halpin said.

"Yes sir, she is that way," Alvin corrected himself. He looked at the floor in uncomfortable silence.

Officer Brandon entered the mall office through the outside door. "Sir." He motioned to Will. Will saw a young man standing on the other side of the police barricade. "That man is the young woman's boyfriend. He wants to talk to someone. Also, the crime scene guys are done and say we can take her things along with her car if we need to. They don't want it left there."

"Send someone to collect her things, and bring them in here. Also, have that young man leave his name with you, and send him our way, too."

"Yes sir," Brandon said as he turned to go. "Sir?"

"Yes?" Will said.

"Do you think this is the same guys that took Amanda Wiggins? None of the witnesses here saw them good enough to say whether it is or not."

"We don't know. It sure looks like it. Keep that under your hat for now, though, okay?"

"Yes sir," Scott Brandon said as he walked away.

Within minutes he was back with Joey Mercer in tow. He also had Georgia's things with him, draped over his arm. Lucinda Amando took them lovingly in her arms as George stepped up to Joey.

"Joey, someone take my Georgie," he said in his emotional broken English. It was the first time Joey had ever heard him speak that way. He realized then that it must take great control to speak the good English he normally did. Somehow it made him respect the man all the more.

"Tell me what happened," Joey said to the detectives, as he put his hand on Mr. Amando's back. Lucinda was crying quietly as she leaned against the wall. Joey could see her rubbing the soft fabric of Georgia's dress against her cheek.

"We don't know much yet. What we do know is that two men in a dark-colored station wagon were seen driving around the parking area yelling at women as they drove by. One couple saw one of the men get out of the car and sneak up behind Miss Amando and drag her into the car that came up behind them. It was the same station wagon. They were sure she didn't want to go—she put up a good struggle."

Joey covered his face with his hand. "Didn't anyone see which way they went?" Tears filled his eyes as he listened.

"So far there are conflicting reports. People panic, and their memories aren't very good until they get a chance to calm down." Jerry said. Joey nodded.

"Joey, you go and find our Georgie. She trusts you to come, and I know she'll be waiting for you," Lucinda Amando said as she clutched Joey's arm. Joey was trembling under her hand. She could see in his eyes the barely contained emotion he too was going through.

"I'll go and look for her. But first I need to hear everything they have to say. I promise you I won't stop 'til I find her." Joey patted her hand and hugged her. "Go home; wait by the phone just in case someone calls. Tell them we'll give them anything they want if they will just give her back," Joey said to George Amando, the fear and frustration starting to show.

George nodded. "Folks, we still have things to go over here. I need you to wait just a bit," Detective Halpin said.

"Sir, can't you talk to them at home, away from here?" Joey asked as he gestured around the office.

"Sure, sure we can. We'll see you there in less than an hour." Will said as he held the door open for them.

As the Amandos walked out the door, the curious faces of the crowd met them. They could see both sympathy and curiosity there. The latter made George angry, and he gestured with his hand. "Get away from here. They took my daughter, please leave us alone."

The crowd let them through as Joey walked them to their car. In the background he could hear people discussing the incident. One man shouted out, "They headed to the highway. Don't let them cops tell you nothing different. They headed to the highway with that poor girl kicking and screaming in the back seat." Joey looked in his direction and nodded as he continued toward the Amandos' car. Lucinda handed him Georgia's keys, "Bring her car home, Joey."

Joey nodded, "I will, Mrs. Amando."

He watched them drive off, and then sought out the man who had shouted. "Sir, did you see what happened?"

"Yeah, I saw it. I told them cops in there what I saw, but they don't believe me. I saw the man with the light hair grab her and pull her into the station wagon. It was a panel wagon with wood-grain sides. She was fighting and kicking, trying to get away when that one dragged her inside. Those are some mean men that got that little girl. Is that your sister or something?" the man asked.

Joey trembled with emotion and unreleased rage. "No sir, she's my fiancée. Did you see which way the car went?"

"I already told you, it went to the highway. Down that road right over there." The man gestured with a crooked finger. "Then they turned right and got on the highway. Took off like a shot. I hope you get that little girl back. It sure is a sad thing. I ain't never seen anything like that in all my sixty-seven years. No, I sure ain't," the man said, shaking his head.

Joey thanked him and ran back inside. "I want to help. I don't want to sit around and do nothing. I want to help you find her, and I have a feeling we don't have long."

"Joey, go home. Let us do our jobs," Jerry Leeme said. "This is a police investigation, and it really requires someone that understands police business. You would be in the way. Please go home and let us do our jobs."

"No. I want to help. She's my fiancée and I want to help find her." Joey's stance said he would take no argument.

"Your fiancée?" Will asked.

"Yes sir, we got engaged earlier today. Her parents don't know yet. We haven't had time to tell them, but we were engaged this morning. Also—I think you should know that Georgia is pregnant. It's not something that we planned, but it happened. We're happy about it," Joey said defiantly. He was challenging them, waiting for them to say something negative about the situation.

"Okay Joey, where would you look if we let you help?" Will asked.

"I would start with the outlying areas. Someplace outside of town, possibly near the water somewhere. In the dark it should be easy to find them. I have a feeling they would build a fire or have lanterns for light. We should drive around," Joey said, looking from one officer to the other. Will and Jerry looked at each other.

"Good idea. Brandon, go with Joey Mercer in an unmarked car and drive around the lake areas. See if you can find anything that looks like a campsite or an abandoned house, somewhere that seems to have unnatural light. I'd keep my eyes open for that station wagon, whatever it looks like."

It was clear to everyone that the detectives were patronizing Joey and that they wanted him out of the way. They didn't really believe that Joey would find her, but they also realized he wouldn't be put off. And he might get lucky. This seemed like a pretty good time to take a chance.

Officer Scott Brandon nodded as he and Joey left. "Yes, sir."

As they reached the parking area, Joey said, "Let's take Georgia's car. It's a car she would recognize if she somehow manages to escape."

Brandon nodded as they got in the car. "Have you ever had the feeling you were getting the bum's rush?"

"Yeah, I just got real familiar with it again, too," Joey said. "It doesn't make any difference to me; I just want to look for her. I know these are the same two guys who took Amanda Wiggins. I can feel it in my heart. I know they aren't around here, or someone would have seen them. But they must be fairly close, because this is the second girl to be taken from the mall. They aren't going to get my girl and have me sit and do nothing." Joey was rambling, not really paying attention to Scott Brandon. When he did finally look at him he saw the young officer staring at him. "What?" Joey asked as he stared back at him.

"You've given this a lot of thought, haven't you?"

"Not really. I mean, most of us have thought about it some since Mandy Wiggins was kidnapped and then found dead; but for the kids who didn't know her well, it was scary, but not something personal. I mean, we were kind of isolated from it. Now it's me, Georgia, and her parents. I just want her back, and I don't want to wait till they find her dead body in some pond somewhere. I don't want to bury her. God, I don't want to bury her," Joey said as he started to cry.

Scott patted him on the shoulder. "Then let's go find her, I'm out here till you say when." Joey turned right and headed for the edge of town as he wiped his tears away with his sleeve. They drove through the night, talking as if they were old friends, brought together by the night's events.

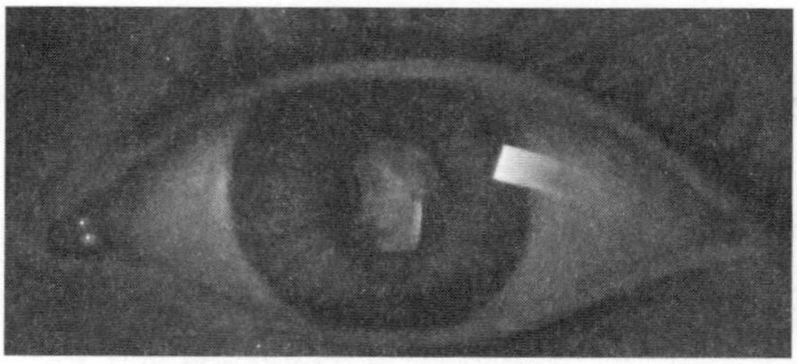

CHAPTER 21

Lindsay slowly tested the waters. Raising her head off the pillow just slightly, she waited for the pain. "So far, so good," she thought, letting the fog lift as she sat up. Again, she moved cautiously. She'd been down for more than twenty-four hours with the headache. The pain medication was the real culprit, but the headache created the need for it. "Shit, I feel like I've been through a tornado and everything in the house hit me twice."

She stumbled into the bathroom and splashed water on her face. Edgar, her tabby cat, rubbed his large body against her leg. "Ah, the bed hog came to make amends, did you?" Lindsay smiled as she rubbed the big cat. "Are ya hungry, big guy?"

Heading to the kitchen she paused to look at the light on the recorder. "Ugh, seven calls. I must have really been out of it." Hitting the button, she let the messages play as she made coffee. "Message one," the machine said. "Hello, Lindsay, this is Marcus." Lindsay hit the button and heard the beep. "Message two. Hi, Lindsay, this is Marcus."

Again Lindsay hit the button. Looking down at Edgar she said, "This guy is becoming a pest." "Meow," Edgar said in response. "Don't try to kid me, young man. I know all you want is something to eat and for me to come back to bed and keep you warm."

The last message caught Lindsay's attention. "Hi, Lin, this is Susan. We're having a girl's night at my house on Saturday. Come if you can and bring whatever you want. No kids, just us girls. We all hope to see you there. So far everyone is coming but you." Lindsay grabbed the phone and dialed.

"Hiya, I'm coming," she said into the phone. Susan giggled on the other end. "Where have you been? I've been calling you for two days. I bet you're avoiding that new guy, right?"

"Nope—well, yes—but I've had a migraine, and you know how I get."

"Are you feeling better?"

"Yeah, I'm better, but I had to take something and it really knocked me out this time. So what time should I be there?" Lindsay was eager for an evening with friends.

"Say around seven or so. Max is going to her dad's, and we'll have the house to ourselves. We're gonna watch chick movies, tell fortunes, and drink great wine."

"Sounds wonderful to me. Jack is at his dad's this weekend, so I'll have to see if Marie or one of the girls will keep him Saturday. But God willing and the creek don't rise, I'll be there."

Susan laughed. "Okay. Hey, what about that guy?"

"UGH!" Lindsay said into the phone. "I'm just not into dating, Suse. He keeps calling, but so far I haven't met anyone who really knocks my socks off. The thing is, I don't want to hurt his feelings, but I'm just not interested."

"Lindsay, go out one time with him. Just give it a chance and see. You're so turned off because of Jackie's dad that you won't give anyone a chance. Try one date, just one, and if it doesn't work then tell him no thanks after that."

"Oh, and you're such a pro. When's the last time you dated anyone?" Lindsay laughed as Susan made a funny sound into the phone. "Okay, fair's fair. We'll see you Saturday. Love ya."

Lindsay hung up and poured herself some coffee. Looking at the clock, she headed for the shower just as the phone rang. "Hi, there. I thought you fell off the face of the earth," Marcus said.

Lindsay rolled her eyes heavenward. "Hi Marcus, how are you? I've been down with a migraine, and I have to work later today. I'm sorry about our date. I really was out of it when you called."

"It's okay. I'm sorry to hear you were feeling bad. I have them too, and sometimes it takes days to get over a good one. How's your week look, or maybe this coming weekend?"

"That could work. Let me see what the schedule at the hospital looks like."

"Lin, I don't want to be a pest. I mean, if you'd rather not go out. just tell me," Marcus said. Here was her chance. Finally she had an out, and all she had to do was take it.

"No, Marcus, really, I'd love to go. I just haven't been feeling well, and I have to work and being the supervisor and all, I'm responsible for the shift. Let's try for Wednesday if that works for you." Darn, Lindsay thought to herself. "Coward," she muttered inaudibly.

"Okay, let's leave it open. Call me when you know, and we can do whatever you want. Sound good?" Marcus was trying. He really wanted to go out with her just one time.

"Sounds good. I'll call ya." Lindsay said, crossing her fingers.

Lindsay headed for the shower one more time. "I hate dating," she said to Edgar. He was stretched out on the bed, fast asleep. "Lazy cat!" Lindsay chuckled.

CHAPTER 22

Hugh Brandt woke up early. He stretched, sitting on the side of the bed that he shared with Amy, his wife of thirty-three years. He looked toward the dark window. "Time to get up," he said. "Amy, come on, babe, I'll get the coffee." He shook her shoulder gently.

"I'm coming. Just plug the percolator in, the grounds are already set up. What do you want for breakfast?" she asked, as she stood and slid into her robe.

"Just some toast and an egg or two. I got trouble with a fence over on the east side of the field and I need to get up there early. Someone tore that fence down two days in a row, and I need to get it fixed and find out what the heck is going on before fall. Wilson called, said he thought he saw someone camped out there. He put the fence up day before yesterday, but last night he called and said it was down again. Damn hippies, I suppose."

"Well, take Marvin with you then. I don't want you going up there in the dark and surprising anyone. Tell him to come on in for breakfast when you go to get the eggs." Amy liked Marvin. He was the best farm hand they'd ever had. He lived in one of the little bungalows out back, and he would eat just about anything you put in front of him.

Pulling a brush through her thick, graying hair and pushing her natural curls into place she yelled over her shoulder, "Hugh, set the butter out, will ya, so it won't be so hard."

"Got it!" Hugh yelled. He opened the back door and almost hollered out Marvin's name when the man stepped into his line of sight.

"Shit, Marvin, you just about scared me out of my remaining years. What are you doing up here on the porch?"

I was coming to get ya, Hugh. Something bad is going on up on the hill. I seen firelight from there most of the night. I heared them a hollerin' and a whoopin' up there, carryin' on something fierce." Marvin sounded agitated.

"Come on in here and have some breakfast and tell me what you saw. Then we'll go up there."

"Maybe you ought to call the police and have them go up with us," Marvin said as he put eggs from his shirt pocket on the table.

"Call the police, why?" Amy asked as she came around the doorway. "Morning, Marvin, thanks for the eggs."

Amy made breakfast as the two men sat and sipped coffee. "Are we gonna take the law up there with us, Hugh?" Marvin asked.

"No, I don't really see any reason to call them out this early unless something illegal really is going on up there. Chances are it's just some hippies camped out on my property. Let's go take a look after we eat."

"Why don't the two of you wait till after sunup, at least?" Amy asked with worry in her voice and on her face.

"It's going to be okay Amy, really. Probably nothing more than hippies camped out on the lake. I'll ask them nicely to leave and clean up after themselves. Don't worry, honey." Amy wasn't convinced, but she knew nothing would change Hugh's mind once he had it set on something.

"Marvin, get the truck and meet me out in front," Hugh said as they finished breakfast. He stood to kiss Amy goodbye. "I'll see you in awhile. Amy, stay near the house till I get back, please, just 'til I get a chance to check this out. It's probably no big deal, but I want to be sure. If it's just some campers I'll tell them they're on private property and run 'em off."

"Do you think they might be dangerous, Hugh?" Amy looked concerned.

"No, but we might as well be cautious. Just hang out around here till I check them out, okay?

"Okay. Lord knows I have plenty to do. I'll see you in a while," Amy said. The horn honked out front.

"Lord have mercy," Hugh whispered as he peered through the bushes. "Marvin, get back to the house, make sure Amy's okay. Then call the police and have them come here right away. You stay there until they get back and bring them up here. Be quiet, and don't burn the tires when you drive off."

"No way, I'm not leaving you here. Those are some rough looking guys. I ain't leaving you." Marvin said, sticking his chin out.

"Do you think she's still alive?" Marvin asked as he crossed himself. Hugh saw the movement and thought to himself, "If ever there was a God we really need Him now."

"No, I don't think so. No one could take that kind of abuse without moving if they were alive." Both men felt sick.

"What are we gonna do?" Marvin asked.

"I'm not sure. We need to watch for a few minutes and see what they're gonna do. Then we can come up with a plan of attack. We need to get that girl away from them even if she is dead. Damn, I never would have thought this could happen around here." Hugh wiped his hand over his face. Marvin knelt by his side there in the dark and waited. His heart was pounding, and his fingers and toes tingled in anticipation and fear.

It had all started out so innocently. They had driven up the hill on the east side of Hugh Brandt's property with the intention of running off a bunch of trespassers. "Let's sneak up on 'em, Hugh," Marvin had said. "We can scare the bejesus out of 'em." Marvin had laughed. Hugh had parked the big Chevy truck and they had walked around until they found human tracks in the soft soil near the water's edge. They followed the tracks into the deepest brush on Hugh's property near the lake.

The sun was starting to crest a soft coral in the sky, suffusing everything with a beautiful pink glow. As they parted the brush Marvin heard something. "Shhh, listen," he said, holding his finger to his lips. At that point both men were still smiling.

"What, what did you hear?" Hugh stopped walking and listened.

"I heard someone laughing. I'm pretty sure it was a man. Listen," said Marvin. What Hugh heard made the hair stand up on the back of his neck.

"Come on, baby, wake up and play with Mikey. Don't ya wanna play no more? Don't ya wanna scream no more? You can't scream no more, can ya?"

Hugh and Marvin had crept closer as quietly as possible. They had pushed the brush aside to witness a horrible scene. Mike was holding Georgia's hair and had her head twisted sideways, as if she could look into his face at that angle. She was slumped over a sawed-off tree stump. Hugh had cut that stump just last year. He had intended to clear this land and build something, like a cabin for fishing or retreating to when Amy was mad at him. The stream nearby offered some sweet bass. Hugh realized that this place would never seem sweet to him again.

Georgia's face was badly battered, with blood running from the mouth and nose. She was naked, and her wrists and ankles were wrapped in some sort of cuff-like object with buckles that were chained to shackles and then to the ground on stakes hammered into the earth. There was blood on both her ankles and her wrists, indicating that she had struggled to get free. Hugh and Marvin guessed that she had been raped.

Near the water's edge stood a tent, with two shotguns leaning against it. These guys could have been campers out for a weekend of fishing. Except what Hugh and Marvin saw proved they weren't normal campers.

The tall, skinny man was dancing wildly around the fire, spinning in circles as he jumped into and out of the flames. He sucked occasionally on a bottle of liquor as he scooped up burning embers with his bare hand and threw them at Georgia. She never flinched as the burning coals flicked her body.

The husky one was doing as much damage to the girl as he could, pulling her hair roughly as he banged her head into the stump and screamed, "Wake up!" Then he kicked at her, and dust from the dry ground flew up into her face.

"That poor thing, what are we gonna do?" Marvin asked. Hugh quickly held his finger to his lips again. The men were so close that Hugh and Marvin could hear Mike snicker. Both of them could see the sheen of sweat on Mike's back, and they were grateful for the cover of the thick brush around them.

"Hey Mike, we're out of booze, and I got a dry throat," Tony yelled, turning the bottle upside down. Mike looked at Tony across the campsite. Hugh and Marvin couldn't see his face but they guessed he still had that wild look in his eyes.

Tony must have seen it, too, because he stopped smiling and took a step backwards. "Yeah," Mike said, and laughed. "Let's go get something to drink. This bitch ain't no fun. She died right away."

"Woo-hoo!" yelled Tony. He flung the bottle at Georgia, striking her in the back. She never moved. Tony visibly relaxed. "Cover the bitch up, Tony," Mike said as he staggered toward one of the cars.

"No, you cover up your own dirty work. I didn't even get to have any fun with her. You want her covered up—you do it," Tony said, pushing past Mike. Mike fell to the ground, and Tony laughed. Hugh and Marvin watched as Mike jumped up, stumbling as he tried to gain his footing. He lunged at Tony, and both of them fell to the ground, rolling into the fire. The fight took less than two minutes. In the end Tony lay on his back with his hands on either side of his head, "I give, I give," he said breathlessly.

Mike staggered to his feet and kicked dirt at him. "You better give. I've been kicking your ass for twenty years, today ain't no different. I might be drunk, I might've had enough sex to take out an entire football team before the big game, but I can still kick your ass, and don't you forget it."

Marvin drew a breath and held it as he nudged Hugh. "Look, look at the girl" he whispered.

"What?" Hugh asked.

"She ain't dead. She just shivered or something. But she ain't dead."

"Marv, man, she's dead." No one could take that. No one could play dead that convincingly. Tony threw a blue plastic tarp over her, and the two men in the bushes stood perfectly still as Tony passed within a breath of them.

"Come on, asshole," Mike yelled from the car.

Tony looked up as he flipped Mike the bird. "Fuck you, I'm coming," Tony said, as he tucked the tarp around Georgia's body. He slapped her on the butt and staggered to the car. "Stay put, baby," he said.

As the car sped off dust flew up around the campfire creating a haze that added to the eeriness of the scene. The sun was almost completely up now, and the campsite was a grisly vision. Georgia's clothing lay scattered around. Liquor bottles and food wrappings were everywhere, along with men's clothing and trash. Two more shotguns lay on the ground next to the tent. A trail of toilet paper led into the woods.

Hugh and Marvin waited for a few minutes and then began crawling slowly out of the brush, keeping an eye on the dirt road. Suddenly the body under the tarp began to shake as if convulsing. Soft crying could be heard. Hugh ran to the tarp and pulled it roughly back. Georgia flinched and tried to pull away. "Oh my good Lord, you're alive!" Hugh gasped. "Marvin, come here, come help me."

Georgia was crying uncontrollably now. Her shoulders shook as she gasped for breath through swollen throat and nasal passages. "Marvin, quick, get her hands and feet free. We have to get her out of here before they come back."

"Sweet Mother of God," Marvin whispered as he hurriedly unbuckled the straps that held Georgia. Her ankles and wrists started bleeding again as the cuffs were pulled away. Spinning around, looking desperately in different directions, Hugh looked around for clothing, anything to cover her with. Grabbing some clothes from the various piles and a blanket from the tent, he wrapped Georgia up and lifted her gently in his arms.

She cried out, but settled down some as Marvin whispered, "Shhh, sweet girl. Were gonna take you out of here, but you have to be quiet. We ain't gonna hurt you, we're God-fearing men. You can trust us." Georgia laid her head against Hugh's chest. Her shivering continued but her sobs were the only sound she made.

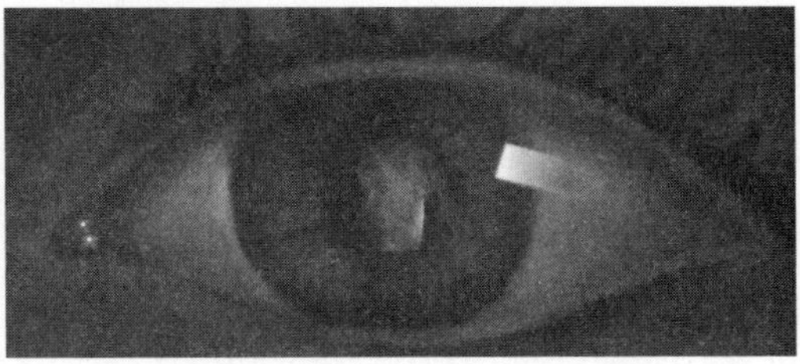

CHAPTER 23

Hugh held her as gently as he could while Marvin jostled the truck over the rough terrain. Just a short time ago they had come this way with the intention of running off a bunch of hippies camped out on Brandt land. Squatters! That's what they were called, and farmers and ranchers in this area worried about them all the time. Marvin didn't remember the road being this bumpy when they had come up this way earlier.

"Shit, I hate this road. I don't recall it being this rough. Damn, I'm sorry, Hugh, but there ain't nothin' I can do."

"Don't worry about it, she's out cold. She might have some broken bones, but I can't be sure. We need a doctor, Marvin, she needs a doctor real bad."

"What do you want to do? Should I head straight into town or take her to the farm?"

"Go to the farm. Amy can handle her better than we can till an ambulance gets to her. Shit, I'm scared to death to touch her for fear of hurting her more. Step on it, will ya? She doesn't look so good." Hugh was sweating even in the morning chill. He looked over at Marvin and could see beads of sweat on his face, too.

Marvin pushed down harder on the gas pedal, but it only made the truck bounce more. He looked over at the girl lying bundled haphazardly in Hugh's arms. She wasn't moving, and her breathing was so shallow that every now and then Hugh would lean in to listen. Marvin raised a questioning eyebrow. "Yeah, she's still breathing, but just barely."

"What do you think happened to her?" Marvin asked.

"I don't know, but she didn't go with them willingly, that's for sure." Hugh moved the hair back from her face as gently as he could. "I bet she was a pretty thing before this happened to her." Marvin nodded without looking.

"Say Hugh, those men, do you know them, ever seen them before?"

"I don't think they're from around here. What I'm worried about is what they're gonna do when they come back and she's not there. They're bound to come looking for her, and since we're the closest farm I bet our house is the first place they look. And you can bet your bottom dollar those two took the time to scout out the area before they set to doing something like this. This sort of thing takes privacy."

"I think they're gonna pack their gear and haul ass. They'd be foolish to come looking for her. What do you want to do? Should we get things ready just in case?" Marvin looked worried.

"Let's get her back to the house. I'll call the police while you get the barn and smokehouse closed up. We need to be ready to protect ourselves, just in case. We can't let them get her again—not to mention Amy." Hugh shifted Georgia in his arms and she moaned in protest. "Shh, little one. We're gonna get some help, hold on."

"Joey," Georgia moaned softly, but the word came out of her battered mouth as "Shoey."

Hugh and Marvin looked at each other. "What, honey, what did you say?" Hugh whispered in her ear.

But no sound came from Georgia; she had faded out again.

"Marvin, did you see anyone else there? Anyone else tied up or dead?" Hugh whispered.

"No sir, but the water's right there. They could have ditched a body in the water. With a weight it would be a long time before it was ever found. I wonder if those two bastards found some kids camping, killed the boy and left the girl for fun and games. We gotta go back and look, Hugh.

I didn't see anyone, but that doesn't mean no one was there. They could have him tied to a tree somewhere waiting till they finished with the girl."

Hugh wiped his free hand across his face. "We can't yet. We have to get her to a hospital and protect Amy. When the police get here we'll take them back to the campsite. Then we'll all look for another one. It's hard, but it's better this way." Hugh tried to convince himself that there had been no one else at the camp. He hadn't seen anyone, but of course Marvin was right—that didn't mean there was no one there.

"We'll get her to the house where Amy can take care of her and then we'll get things ready just in case they come. Then when the police come we'll go back and do a thorough search. Okay?" said Hugh.

Marvin nodded. "I just hope it's the right choice."

"It's our only choice, Marvin," Hugh said. Again he shifted Georgia in his arms, and again she moaned, "Joey."

CHAPTER 24

When they pulled into the yard, Amy came to the front door with a dish-towel in her hands. "Find anything?" she asked as she closed the door behind her. Hugh and Marvin scrambled from the truck with their battered bundle.

"Oh my word, what have you got there?" Amy asked as she ran to her husband.

"Get the door, Amy. This little one needs help."

Amy stood beside the bed as Hugh gently laid Georgia down on the soft mattress. "Amy, get some bandages," Hugh said.

"Oh God, Hugh, what happened to her?"

"Not now Amy. Get some whiskey, water, and bandages. We have to help her first. Then I'll answer your questions." Amy headed for the door. A sudden cry from Georgia stalled her footsteps. Georgia was looking at her desperately from the bed, fear screaming from her eyes. A drop of blood dripped on to the white linen as she tried to hold her battered hand out. The fear in her eyes touched Amy's heart and she turned and went back to the bed.

Taking Georgia's hand, she said, "You go, Hugh. I'll stay here with her." Hugh nodded and left the room. As he walked into the hallway Marvin was coming up the stairs.

"I called the police, they're sending someone," he said as he handed Hugh the bottle of Jack Daniels. "I thought this might help. They said a girl was kidnapped from that new shopping mall in town last night around ten o'clock. They said her name is Georgia Amando and we should try to call this girl by that name. They're also sending an ambulance for her." He spoke in hushed tones, as if someone might be eavesdropping. Hugh twisted the cap off the bottle and took a short drink. Shuddering, he handed the bottle to Marvin.

"Usually I'd say no, but today I need a belt."

"That's a good idea. She's hanging on to Amy for dear life. I'm gonna get some bandages and some ointment. Will you get some hot water so we can clean her up a bit? Man, I couldn't have taken the punishment she did and stayed still through it all. That is one tough little thing in there."

Marvin and Hugh returned to the room at the same time. Holding the glass of whiskey in one hand and the hot water pitcher in the other, Marvin stepped up to the bed. Georgia lay there, her pallor showing under the purple, red, and blue bruises on her swollen face. Bruises covered almost every inch of her. Her wrists and ankles were covered with blood that Amy was gently trying to wash away. "The police say a girl by the name of Georgia Amando was taken from the mall, Amy. They said we should call this poor thing by that name and see if we get any response from her."

"Not now, Hugh, can't you see she's in shock? She needs medical attention. Did you two call an ambulance?"

"Yes, ma'am," Marvin said from the foot of the bed. Worry was etched across his face.

Amy took the bandages and the whiskey and sent the men out of the room. Working quickly, she washed Georgia's face and body, asking for more warm water twice. "Georgia, is that your name, sweetie? I'm not gonna hurt you. You've been through so much. Is that your name, honey? Are you Georgia Amando?" Amy dribbled a few drops of the whiskey onto Georgia's lips. "Just a sip, honey. It'll help some," Amy said as Georgia grimaced.

Amy's gentle words seemed to soothe Georgia somewhat. She

wasn't sure if Georgia could understand her, but she kept talking anyway. "I wonder if your momma talks to you like this. Maybe that's why it comforts you so."

Amy was busy washing Georgia's feet and ankles, but a sudden intake of breath caught her attention. The young woman was sobbing softly. "Oh dear, did I hurt you? I'm so sorry. I'll be gentler, I promise."

"Sheorgia," came the soft whisper.

"What, honey? Did you say something?" Amy quickly moved to the head of the bed and bent toward the tiny figure. She watched as the girl tried to move her tongue around just right. Suddenly, out of her mouth popped a gold ring with a single small diamond. Amy reached for it and took it between her fingers. "Land sakes, there's just one surprise after another today."

"Sheorgia," she heard again.

"Oh, my word, you're Georgia?" Amy gasped.

"Shoey, I need Shoey," Georgia whispered again in a shaky voice.

"Oh honey, hold on. Someone's coming. Be still now, sweet Georgia. I'm gonna get you all cleaned up. The ambulance is on the way, and I'll take good care of your ring."

"Hugh!" Amy yelled from the room.

The door burst open, "What?"

"Hugh, she's Georgia Amando."

"How do you know?"

"Listen, say it again honey. Say it for Hugh," Amy whispered in Georgia's ear.

"Sheorgia," the battered girl whispered through swollen, cracked, and bleeding lips.

"Jesus help us. Marvin, get the rifle and the extra ammunition from the garage, and lock the doors. We have to be ready just in case those two come looking for her." Hugh himself ran downstairs to the kitchen. "Stay up here, Amy, stay with her and don't you come downstairs until I tell you it's safe."

Amy nodded and placed her hand on Georgia's forehead to steady and comfort her.

The men sat in the stairwell, armed and waiting. They hoped they were waiting for the ambulance and the police, but they were ready for anyone.

The police came first. Hugh and Marvin heard them pull into the yard and went to the door to meet them. Detective Jerry Leeme and his partner Detective Will Halpin followed a uniformed police officer into the Brandt's home. Seeing the rifles, he motioned for a uniformed officer to secure the weapons. Shaking hands and making introductions didn't seem to take much time. Hugh motioned them toward the table and they all sat. "I'm Hugh Brandt. This is my place, and this is my foreman, Marvin Hiller. We're the ones that found Georgia Amando."

"Tell us what happened and what you saw, please," Jerry said.

Hugh and Marvin went over the day until they got to the part about bringing Georgia back to the house. "She's here?" Jerry and Will said in unison, sitting forward in their chairs, clearly shocked at the news.

"Yes sir, she's upstairs with my wife right now, and to be honest she's not in good shape, so I hope that ambulance isn't far behind you. That's why we have the guns, just in case those guys come this way looking for her," Marvin explained.

"Wait, you mean to tell us you have Georgia Amando upstairs and she's alive and you're sure that it's her?" Will asked his questions slowly because he wanted to be sure of what he heard.

"Yes sir, that's what I'm saying," Hugh said, a bit exasperated. Standing up quickly, Jerry and Will exchanged looks. Seeing the stairs off to the left, they both headed for them.

"Detectives, wait!" Hugh said.

"What? We want to see her. We need to question her." Both Jerry and Will stood poised to go upstairs.

"I'm afraid you won't be able to do that. She's only whispered her name so far, but she can't speak much. She needs medical attention fast. She certainly won't let a strange man get near her."

"You got near her," Jerry pointed out.

"She was pretty much unconscious at the time. She struggled all she could when she came to. But there isn't much fight left in her," said Hugh.

"She's in no condition, trust us." Hugh and Marvin spoke at the same time.

Will and Jerry walked up the stairs as quietly and quickly as possible. As they carefully opened the door, they were shocked to see Amy Brandt standing at the foot of the bed holding a chair over her head. Just as she made a move to throw it at them Hugh put his hand up. "Wait, babe, these men are detectives from town. They won't hurt her. They're investigating her kidnapping." Hugh eased the chair to the floor. It landed with a bit of a thud.

Amy looked at the lowered chair as she stepped aside. Will and Jerry drew in their breath simultaneously. "Lord above, have mercy," Will said as he looked at Georgia, lying so still on the bed. He made the sign of the cross over his chest.

Jerry grabbed his hand-held radio from his belt. "This is detective Jerry Leeme; we need an ambulance dispatched to the Brandt farm out here on Route 135 and Cole Road, the big white house on the left with the blue shutters."

"Ten-four, detective. An ambulance is already in route," the dispatcher said.

"I called them," Marvin said. "Right after I called the police."

"Can I use your phone?" Will asked.

"Sure, it's in the kitchen." Hugh led the way.

Turning at the door, Will said to Jerry, "See if you can get Brandon on the radio. He and Joey Mercer must still be out looking for her."

At the mention of Joey's name Georgia stirred and cried out softly. Rushing to her side, Amy sat tenderly on the bed. "Shh, Georgia, he's coming, sweetheart. He's gonna be here."

Georgia settled back into a semi-conscious state.

Jerry and Will went downstairs with Hugh and Marvin.

Hugh looked at Jerry, "Sir, do you know who Joey is?"

"Yeah, that's her fiancé; he's been out looking for her with one of our officers all night. He'll be real glad to have her back. Man, she looks terrible. Can you two tell us more about what you saw, and where you saw it?" Jerry and Will walked over to the windows in the front of the house and peered out.

Hugh started explaining that Georgia had mumbled Joey's name. "We thought maybe someone was left back there in the woods. We made a quick search, looking for a blanket or something to cover her with, but we never saw anyone else. We thought maybe they had been camping, and maybe the boy was dead and had been thrown in the water. We sure are glad to hear that he's alive and well."

"I don't know how well he is. Last night he was in pretty bad shape. As a matter of fact, we let him go with a uniformed officer just to keep him out of the way. He thought he could find her near the edge of town or near water somewhere. I guess we should have listened to him," Will said.

"Yeah, considering that's where we found her," Hugh said quietly. "Do you think he had something to do with her kidnapping? I mean, since he knew where she might be found and all."

Marvin shifted in his chair. Hugh could tell that something was on his mind. "Marvin, what's up? You look really nervous."

"Well, I was just thinking that if we want to catch those guys we should get up that way. They've had time to come get their stuff and haul ass. I don't think it's the fiancé, since she seems to want him. I have a feeling someone she didn't know took her, and now they're up there on your land, Hugh, and they're gonna get away."

Jerry held up a hand. "We're gonna go up there, but we need to know what we're walking into. They may not even be back from wherever it was they went. You said they thought she was dead, right?"

"Yes sir, one of them said something about her dying too easy."

"Good, then they won't be in a big hurry to get back. How long ago did you find her?" Jerry looked at his watch.

"About an hour ago," Marvin said.

"Gosh, that long? What took you so long to call us?" Will asked.

"Uh, that ain't it, it's what took you so long to get here?" Hugh said with frustration in his voice. "Every time we need help up here it takes way too long to get it. We did have that long drive back over that bumpy road, too. It took us a while to get down from that side of the farm."

Will and Jerry were watching the two men as Hugh spoke. Something in their manner convinced the two detectives that nothing sinister was going on. They knew how long it took to get to this side of town, and depending on how far that lakeside was from here, the trip back with Georgia could have taken quite a while.

Again they went over what had happened, and what had attracted Marvin's attention in the first place. Jerry finally got Officer Brandon's home phone number and started calling.

"Jerry, we need to get to that campsite and see if we can't find these guys," Will said. Jerry nodded and handed the phone number to the uniformed officer, "Can you keep calling this number? That's where you should be able to find Officer Brandon and possibly Joey Mercer. They were together last night and were going to travel the roads for any possible leads. Someone will have to show us the way to the campsite, and I want the uniforms to stay here with the women just in case those two men come looking for the girl."

"I'll stay, sir," offered one of the uniformed officers.

"Okay, keep your eyes and ears open. These guys are armed and dangerous. Don't let anyone in unless you know exactly who they are. Also, we're waiting for an ambulance for the girl. Protect her, and ride inside the ambulance with her. Understand?"

"Yes, sir," said the officer.

"Okay, let's go." Will and Jerry turned to Hugh and Marvin.

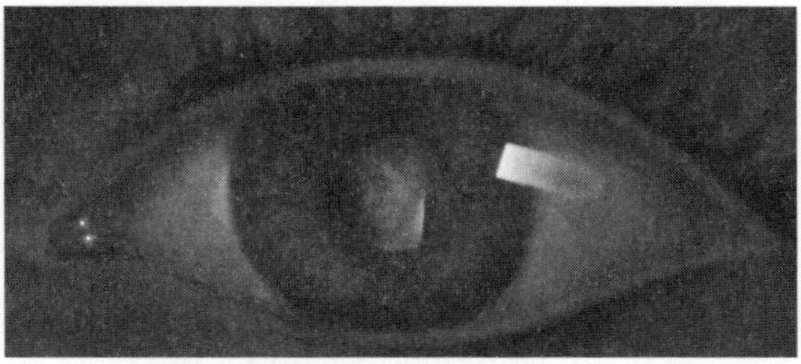

CHAPTER 25

Mike and Tony staggered out of the car as it came to a screeching halt at the campsite. Laughing and stumbling, they fell to the ground near the smoldering campfire. "Hey, asshole, light the fire," Mike yelled at Tony.

Tony looked around, too drunk to see much of anything in the dim light of approaching day. The night had been a long one for them. Time with Georgia, drinking and smoking pot all night had worn them both out. If the truth be known Tony wasn't as high as he pretended to be, but he would never let Mike know that. He just didn't like pot the same way Mike did. When the joint was passed to him, he would suck the smoke into his mouth so that the embers at the end glowed red, but he tried never to let it go into his lungs.

Now he struggled to his feet and staggered in the direction of the table. It was a crude excuse for a table, made of two pieces of tree trunk with a board laid over it, but it worked for them. Getting the matches and some lighter pine from the stash, he walked to the fire. Looking at Mike, lying in the dirt near the fire pit, Tony said, "Better move if you don't want to get burned." With that he tossed the embers and poked at them with the lighter pine. As the flames caught, the campsite lit up. Tony added more wood to the fire and blew gently on it.

Mike was sitting up now, and as the campfire light flickered across his face, Tony saw panic. "What? What's the matter?" Tony slurred.

"The bitch is gone—get your stuff. We have to get out of here."

Tony spun in the direction of the tree trunk. Sure enough, the blue tarp lay on the ground in a heap, and Georgia was gone. Tony dragged the tarp aside. "Shit, shit!" Tony said. "How do you think she did that?"

Mike looked at him. "She didn't, you dumb asshole, someone found her. She couldn't move. She was dead, remember?"

"I remember you said she was dead. I ain't so sure she was. Maybe you were wrong. Maybe she was knocked out or something. Maybe she came to and ran away." Tony started to cry and hiccup, scared out of his wits.

"She was dead," said Mike. "I know she was because I made sure of it. The bitch was dead, and dead people don't untie themselves and run away. Someone's been here, and we can be sure they're gonna be back with the law. Get your stuff, grab all that you can and get in the car."

Mike was racing around, grabbing stuff himself, heading in the direction of the car.

Tony stood there looking at him in complete terror. "Mike, wait, wait for me." He turned first in one direction and then the other, not picking up a single thing as he turned.

"No, I ain't waiting. Get your stuff or stay here, either way I'm leaving before they find us and take us to jail. Are you coming or not?"

Tony saw Mike walking towards the car and catapulted into action. He started to pull up the tent stakes.

Mike saw him and yelled from the car. "Leave it Tony; we don't have time for it. Leave it here and maybe once we've found some place to hide out we can come back for it. Come on!"

Tony picked up clothing and papers as he walked to the car. He was barely inside when Mike gunned the engine and spun the wheels, with Tony looking out the window at the things they were leaving behind.

"What are we gonna do without a tent and stuff?"

"We're not gonna be in jail, that's what we're gonna do. Shut up, I need to think about where to go. We need to be far away from here as fast as possible, and we don't need you sitting there blubbering like a girl." Mike was scared, and when he was scared he got mad.

Tony sniffled. "I should have listened to my brother. You ain't gonna take care of us like you promised, are ya, Mike?"

"I'm gonna take good care of us, don't you worry. We're gonna get out of here and find us a place to stay," Mike said. Even though Tony was a drag on him, Mike needed him. Tony offered the only companionship Mike ever allowed, giving but not taking much, allowing Mike to be who he was.

They drove all day, looking for a place to stay around the lake areas until Mike had a brainstorm. "We can't camp near the lake anymore. That's where they'll look for us. We need to be in the next town over, and we need to find us some shelter. Tony, remember that old farm where we took this car from?"

Tony nodded, "Yeah, what about it?"

"We can use that old house out near the end of that dirt road. Remember the one that we stopped at that night before going to the carnival?"

Tony was starting to get excited too. "Yeah, the one that had the cots in it, and that old chair on the front porch. But Mike, someone will see us."

"No they won't. No one goes down that road because of all the mud. If you paid attention you'd know that too. There wasn't no ruts in the mud! Damn, do I have to do all the thinking for us? You stupid asshole."

Tony stared down at his folded hands. "I'm not stupid. I was busy doing something else. But if you think that would be a good place, let's go there. I just want someplace to sleep for awhile." Tony's feelings were hurt, and Mike knew it was his fault. Tony might be simple, but he was willing to be Mike's friend.

"I'm sorry, I didn't mean to talk to you like that, Tony. We're partners, right?"

"Yeah, we're partners," Tony echoed sullenly.

Mike drove forty miles out of town in the direction of the only place he could think of that would offer privacy and safety. He knew it was Tony's fault they'd been found out, because of all the noise he had made the night before. Mike would have to find a way to keep Tony quiet. Maybe he should let him have more time with the girls. That usually kept him busy and quiet. Thing was, Mike had a need, a big need, and he didn't really like to share. Well, things had to change, and Mike knew it.

Quietly they crept down the dirt road. Mike realized how foolish it was to have brought the station wagon past the farmer's house in broad daylight. "Tony, get out and walk up the road some, see if that farmer is outside and looking this way. We need to be sure we can get past him with his car."

Tony got out and walked through the wooded area along the side of the road. He could see the farmer on a tractor on the other side of his house. Motioning to Mike, he had him ease the car forward. Tony ran to catch up as Mike passed him. But Mike never slowed down, he kept his foot easy on the gas and moved forward. He could see Tony in the rear view mirror, trotting behind him. Tony knew Mike was laughing at him, but there was nothing he could do but follow. He couldn't yell, for fear the farmer would hear him, so he just ran after the car.

Finally the car came to a stop in the front of the old house. The porch was dilapidated and falling down. Mike could tell by looking at it that the house had a roof leak, but he figured he could get Tony to fix it. Looking in the rearview mirror he saw Tony come trotting around the bend. "Asshole," Tony hissed, as he leaned breathlessly against the trunk of the car. Mike got out, laughing quietly as he gently shut the car door.

"I'm sorry, man, I just couldn't help it. We had to have a good laugh after the morning we've had. Didn't we?"

"Yeah, I guess so. But why does it always have to be because of me?" Tony pouted.

"Come on, dufus. Let's get the car in the back and covered up. Then we can get our stuff inside, and come nightfall we can get this place cleaned up some and ditch this car. I need some grub and a nap first." Mike picked up a box of powdered donuts from the back seat, and then put the car in neutral. Together they pushed it behind the house and covered it with branches from the nearby woods.

Walking in through the back door, Mike realized the house would need more fixing up than he had thought. Tony eased the door back on its hinges as he closed it behind him. "This place is a real dump. We're gonna have to keep the outside like it is so we don't draw attention to it, but tonight we clean this mess up," Mike said as he stuffed donuts into his mouth.

Tony nodded as he righted a fallen chair. He sat down and promptly fell to the floor, in a jumble of dust and broken pieces of wood. Mike burst out laughing, and Tony joined him once the shock wore off. Mike reached out a hand and pulled Tony up.

"Come on, let's eat and take a nap. If you get the blankets and stuff from the car I'll make us something to eat," Mike said. Tony brushed off his pants and walked out the back door. He started hauling their meager belongings into the house as Mike opened a can of beef stew. It smelled good cold, and hot would be even better. Mike grabbed the camp stove from Tony and used it to heat lunch, as Tony continued bringing things in.

Within an hour lunch was over, and things had been stowed away. Mike and Tony were sacked out on the cots left by the previous tenants.

Neither ever gave a thought to Georgia or mentioned her again that day.

CHAPTER 26

Upstairs at the Brandt's, Georgia was getting restless. She tossed and turned in her sleep, crying out occasionally.

"Shh, honey. Be still now, or you'll start the bleeding all over again."

"My baby," whispered Georgia.

"What, honey?" Amy whispered as she knelt by the bed.

"Did I lose the baby? Please help me, please." Georgia was crying again. Her lips were oozing blood and her nose bled outright every time she moved her facial muscles. Tears ran continually from her eyes.

"Oh, dear God," Amy said. Lifting the sheet, she examined Georgia lightly, looking for signs of bleeding that would indicate a miscarriage. There was none.

"I don't know, sweetie," she said to Georgia. "I can't really tell, but it doesn't look like it. Just rest now, and get your strength back. You have to heal, and time will take care of that."

Amy heard an ambulance siren and looked out the window. "They're here, Georgia. This is almost over, sweetie."

"Stay with me," Georgia whispered. "Please."

"Of course I will," Amy said, gently squeezing her hand.

The two paramedics immobilized Georgia's head and neck and moved her carefully onto the stretcher they had brought. She was strapped down and gently lifted.

As Georgia was being loaded into the ambulance, one officer stood in the yard with his rifle in clear view. The other officer was speaking on the phone in the kitchen. After hanging up, he walked outside and leaned in to say something to Georgia. "Joey's on his way. He'll meet you at the hospital." She squeezed his hand in understanding. Amy, the uniformed officer, and the ambulance attendant rode in the back with Georgia.

She slipped in and out of consciousness as the paramedic struggled to find a vein in her swollen and bruised arm, so he could establish an IV.

If Georgia had been awake, it would have hurt like the dickens. Life-sustaining fluids slowly dripped into her body. Just as the attendant was about to adjust the straps over Georgia's abdomen, Amy said quietly into his ear, "She might be pregnant."

The attendant looked at her and thought better of tightening the straps. Smiling, he patted Amy's hand. "Thank you."

An oxygen mask was fitted over her face, but Georgia never moved. Checking her pulse, blood pressure, and heart rate the attendant wrote everything on a chart and then reached for the radio, "Unit thirty-nine, to base."

"Go ahead, unit thirty-nine," came back over the speaker.

"We are in route to your facility with a young female, age unknown, in obvious shock condition with multiple lacerations and contusions. She has been immobilized on a backboard and C collar. We have established an IV line, administered O_2 at two liters and are monitoring her vitals. Pulse is one hundred and twenty, blood pressure is eighty-four over fifty-six. She is semi-responsive. She has severe lacerations and possible fractures. Her wrists and ankles have been cleaned and bandaged. What are your orders?"

"Stand by, unit thirty-nine."

"Unit thirty-nine, raise her oxygen to four liters."

"Ten-four, base. We're running thirty-three traffic and our ETA to your facility is about twenty minutes."

"Ten-four. Keep us advised on her condition. Room one on arrival. Base out."

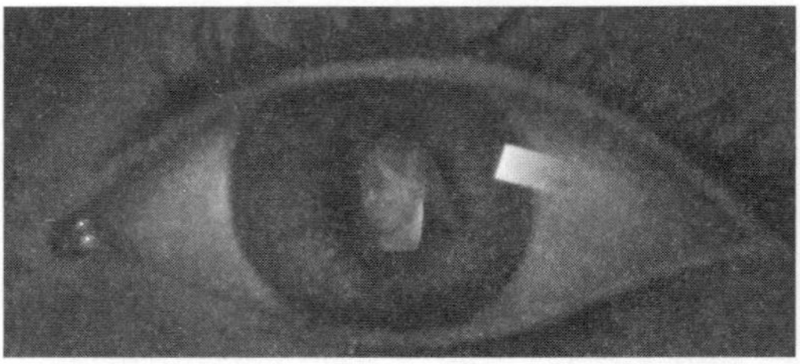

CHAPTER 27

Joey Mercer and Scott Brandon had driven around all night, down one dirt road after another. They'd talked of life and love, but eventually silence had claimed them as Joey drove around the outskirts of town. They had found a kinship in that silence. Scott understood Joey's tears and frustration, and Joey tried to understand Scott's problems with his career issues. They had stopped a few times for something to eat and a cup of coffee. Eventually, they'd pulled over to the side of the road for an hour of sleep that Scott had convinced Joey he needed. While they were sleeping in the early morning hours, Hugh and Marvin were waiting in the bushes to rescue Georgia.

Joey woke first and stretched his arms over his head. Banging his hands against the roof of the car he yawned, and then cried out in frustration. Scott looked over at him. "What?"

"I'm pissed off. I wanna know where Georgia is. I don't want to bury her, and I'm so scared that's all that's gonna be left of her, just something to bury. That's all Amanda's parents got back, a body. I took Mandy out once in our freshman year, did you know that?"

"No, I didn't. What was she like?" Scott asked.

"She was nice enough. In a hurry to grow up, and she really liked the guys. She was beautiful, with that blonde hair and all. I liked her, but then summer came and I went to camp to help out as a counselor. When I came back we just sort of drifted apart. We saw each other at school, but she was on to other things by then. A year later I met Georgia. I mean, I knew her, but that's when I noticed her. She is so pretty, dark hair, dark eyes, a tiny little thing. She's not big and strong but her heart is so good. She's a sweet girl. She didn't deserve this, she doesn't deserve this." Joey laid his head on the steering wheel and cried.

Scott didn't know what to do. He didn't like dealing with emotions. "Joey, you gotta have faith, buddy. You have to believe that she's gonna make it. There's still time. Have faith and be strong until you're sure there's no reason to. Come on—let's go home and take a shower, get some grub, and then start looking again. Today's my day off, so I can help you look all day. I won't give up till you do."

Joey nodded. "Can I use your shower? I can't face my house yet, not without Georgia. My mom and dad will want to know something, and I don't have anything to tell them. I don't have anything to tell anyone yet."

As Scott unlocked the door he heard the answering machine cut off. Tossing his keys onto the sofa, he reached over and pushed the play button. As the tape rewound and prepared to play, he said, "The shower's upstairs on the right. There are clean towels in the cabinet in the hallway just before you go in the bathroom." Joey nodded and started for the stairs. When he was halfway up, he heard the recording. Slowly he made his way back down the stairs, and both men stood absolutely still as the message played: "Scott, this is Mike Williams. Georgia Amando has been found. An ambulance is taking her to Mount Sinai Hospital. I don't have much information about her condition other than she is alive. We are looking for you and Joey Mercer. When you get this message, meet us there."

"Let's take my patrol car. It will be faster," said Scott, grabbing his keys. Joey nodded as they ran out the door.

The trip to the hospital was a quiet one. Both men were tense and lost in thought. Scott gripped the steering wheel with white-knuckle concentration. Joey poured out his pain and fatigue in tears. Scott looked over in Joey's direction. "Joe, you need to get hold of yourself. We're almost there, and you don't want her to see you like this."

Joey wiped his eyes and nose on his sleeve. "Yeah, I know. I guess I'm just tired."

"The guy that called was a friend of mine. He didn't give us many details but she's alive, that's all he knows. We're gonna see her for ourselves in just a few minutes. Let's get some coffee and wash up some before we go in."

"No," Joey said shaking his head, "I wanna see her. I'll get some coffee later. I need to see her face, Scott." The look in Joey's eyes told Scott not to bother arguing with him.

"Okay, buddy, we're going."

The hospital loomed in front of them just as Scott spoke. Joey rubbed his gritty eyes, sat up straighter, and put his hand on the door handle. "Go to the emergency department," Joey said. "That's where they're gonna take her."

Scott was already turning his cruiser in the direction of the emergency room parking area. An ambulance with siren wailing pulled in front of them. The bay doors of the emergency department opened, and nurses and doctors rushed out. Joey jumped from the car and ran to the ambulance. A man on a stretcher was being wheeled in. Joey looked inside the ambulance as if waiting for Georgia to be taken out, too. His heart just couldn't believe she wasn't in there. Looking in Scott's direction, he held his hands out. "Where is she?"

Scott grabbed his radio. "Dispatch, this is Officer Scott Brandon. What is the status of the transport of Georgia Amando to the hospital?"

"Officer Brandon, Ms. Amando is in route to that destination with an ETA of two minutes."

"Thank you, dispatch. Please notify her parents at their home phone of that situation if that hasn't already been done."

"Ten-four, sir, her parents are in route to that destination as well."

"Thank you, dispatch. Over and out."

"She's coming, Joey, and her parents are coming too. They'll be here in two minutes. Now can we go in and get some coffee?" Scott was dying for a cup of java.

"No, I'm not leaving. You can go, but I'm waiting right here. I want to see her face, Scott. I want my face to be here when she comes out of that ambulance. She needs to see me here. Please try to understand. I just need to see her."

Scott could see the fatigue in Joey—hell, he felt it in himself. "You really love her, don't you?" Scott had never felt that kind of love himself. His friends teased him about being a confirmed bachelor. Now he thought that they might just be right. Could he ever love anyone the way Joey loved Georgia?

"More than life itself," Joey said. "We're getting married after graduation. Georgia's pregnant, and I never realized just how happy I was about it till all this happened."

Joey saw the look on Scott's face. "What?"

"Joey, man, I mean she's been through a lot. There's a chance—well, I mean, I'm not a doctor or anything, but there's a chance that she may have miscarried. We don't know what all she's been through. It's gonna take some time for her to heal. I just want you to be prepared, that's all." Scott looked down at the ground.

Joey stood there, looking defeated. Suddenly he straightened up and said, "I don't care. We'll have another baby. It won't matter to me."

A siren split the air just as Scott started to say something. Joey watched it ease into the hospital parking area and then pull forward under the covered carport that housed the bay doors. Joey ran to the door as the ambulance came to a stop. Pulling it open, he saw her for the first time. "Oh my God, Georgia," he whispered as he stepped back. He grabbed his stomach and bent forward, trying to catch his breath.

Looking at Amy and the uniformed officer, he registered shock and disbelief. He hadn't been prepared for this. He hadn't given her appearance any thought. His mind's eye had seen her as he remembered her, her hair blowing in the breeze as she had driven off. Now he could barely recognize her. She was so badly beaten that her face held little resemblance to the girl he loved. Amy held her finger to her lips and shook her head at him. "She's resting, finally. The attendant gave her something to quiet her for the drive here."

Taking his arm, she gently led him back a few steps as the medical people took Georgia into the emergency room. Joey just let himself be led. His eyes never left Georgia; as she rode by on the stretcher he reached a hand out to her. "She's been through a lot, young man, and if you're Joey, then you're the only one she's asked for. My name is Amy Brandt—my husband and our foreman found her on our property." Amy reached into her jeans pocket and pulled out the ring. "She had this hidden in her mouth when they found her. She gave it to me when I was cleaning her up. I thought I should give it to you. You are Joey, aren't you?"

"Yes ma'am. I'm Joey. What happened to her? Oh, my God, Georgia." Joey started crying again as he slowly followed everyone into the hospital. Scott took his arm, steadying him. "Joey, come on, buddy. You have her back. Think of Amanda Wiggins's family. They buried their daughter. Be glad you got her back alive."

Joey nodded as Georgia disappeared into Treatment Room One. Clearly, he hadn't been ready for this. Turning to Amy Brandt, Joey held out his hand." I can never thank you or your husband enough for your kindness. Did she say anything to you? Is she gonna be okay?"

"She just said her name and asked for you. My husband didn't tell me much, but I know she must be afraid of the men that had her. The detectives, my husband Hugh, and Marvin, our foreman, have gone back to the place where they found her to look for those men. I did what I could—washed her up a bit and bandaged her," Amy said as gently as she could. "She's going to need you, young man. You need to get something to eat and some sleep."

"No, I'm not leaving her. I'm gonna stay right here and wait. I want her to know I'm here. She can't feel alone. It's my fault they got her. I should have made her let me pick her up from work, but I was tired. Damn, just because I was tired." Joey leaned dejectedly against the counter at the information desk.

"Sir, are you a relative of the young woman just brought in? We need a treatment form signed and some information," the woman behind the desk asked.

"Yes, I'm her fiancé," Joey said.

"Sir, if you're not a blood relative or a husband I can't let you give consent. Do you know her family; do you know where we can reach someone for permission to treat her?"

Joey stared dumbfounded at the young woman behind the desk. "Her family, uh, her mom and dad should be here. I mean they have to come so you can treat her, don't they? But you're gonna do something for her right now, I mean you're not gonna let her die, are you?"

"No, no, we aren't going to let her die. When her family gets here please ask them to come to admitting so that we can process her and get her into the system. The doctors are with her now. But we still need those treatment forms."

Joey nodded and followed Amy and Scott toward the door of Treatment Room One. He could hear voices and movement in the room. Joey paced back and forth with his hands in his pockets. Worry, guilt, and grief were etched across his young face.

CHAPTER 28

Voices behind him caught his attention as the doors to the emergency room swung open. Turning around, Joey saw George and Lucinda Amando running in his direction. Mrs. Amando had on a dark colored dress with stockings and flat, sensible shoes, as always. George Amando had on his suit. He wore that suit or one just like it every day, no matter what. Georgia hated it, but today it comforted Joey—at least something was the same. Mrs. Amando stretched out her hands to Joey.

"Joey, my Georgie, where is she?"

George Amando gently patted her back, "Mama, give him a chance to tell us."

Joey looked bewildered. He didn't know where to begin. Amy Brandt stepped forward and introduced herself. She told Georgia's parents the story of her rescue. When she finished speaking, Joey told the Amandos that they had to go to Admitting to sign consent forms so that Georgia could be treated. Thanking Amy, they headed in that direction.

Within the hour they were back. Still no one came from Georgia's room to tell them anything. Medical personnel came and went with carts of medical equipment and trays of medications. Everyone waited, some staring at the door, the rest pacing back and forth.

Finally, three hours later, the door opened as the sun outside rode high in the sky. "Mr. and Mrs. Amando, I'm Dr. Fells. We're treating your daughter," the doctor said as he shook hands with the Amandos.

"Thank you, doctor. And this young man is Joey Mercer," said Mr. Amando.

Dr. Fells shook hands with Joey. "Yes, I've heard your name several times over the last few hours. Let's sit down and talk."

Amy and Scott walked further down the hallway to allow the family some privacy. Turning around they could see the trauma Georgia had gone through on the faces of those who loved her. Lucinda cried softly into the white handkerchief she clutched tightly in one hand; her other hand held her rosary. Joey paced back and forth, and George cried into his hands. The doctor leaned forward and said something quietly. Sobs could be heard coming from the family. Amy Brandt covered her mouth with her hand, fearing that the worst had happened. Dr. Fells nodded and stood to go. Amy and Scott turned away again.

"Can we see her?" George asked.

"Yes, but I must warn you, she's had a severe shock. She has been badly beaten and there are severe injuries to her body and face. You must not show shock or emotion. She must remain calm if she wakes at all. It's imperative that she rest. That's the only hope we have, that and God. Each of you can have fifteen minutes with her. Joey, I'll let her parents go first—I need to speak with you." Joey nodded. He heard Lucinda's sharp intake of breath as she saw Georgia for the first time, and then the door closed.

Dr. Fells led Joey to a room off the hallway. "Sit down, young man. I have to say I have seen a body go through some horrific things. I've seen just about the worst of it. I want to know if you can stand by that young woman in there and be a man. I want to know if you love her as much as your face says you do. Because I have a very wounded young lady in there, and all she seems to want is to hear your voice. She hasn't even once asked for her parents."

Joey looked down at his folded hands.

"Do you love her, son?"

"Yes, sir," Joey said looking up suddenly.

"You know she's pregnant, don't you, son?"

"Yes sir. I'm aware of it. Is the baby okay, I mean with all she's been through? " Joey looked down at his hands. He wasn't sure what this doctor wanted him to say. He feared that he would say the wrong thing and not get to sit with Georgia.

"I don't know how, but so far everything with her pregnancy is okay. Her parents don't know, do they, Joey?"

"No sir, we were waiting to tell them until after prom. I've been accepted into college, a pre-med program, we were gonna get married. Georgia was gonna work for a while, just till the baby got here. I guess that's all changed now." Joey was crying again. He hung his head and sobbed out his pain.

"Son, you know she's been raped repeatedly. There's a lot of damage, mental and physical. She has broken bones, and she is going to have some scars. Can you live with that?"

"I don't care. This isn't about what Georgia did; this is about what someone did to her. I don't care about that. I want her and I want my baby. I want my life back, and I'll do whatever I have to do to get it." Joey looked Dr. Fells in the eye. His direct stare said all he couldn't find the words to say.

"Okay, young man, come with me. This looks bad, and it is. I won't lie to you. I want you to be aware that she is critical. She'll be critical for some time. She won't get up and go home anytime soon. Be patient with her. Give her love and support, and don't ask her any questions. Later, we'll send a therapist in to help her work through what happened. Just sit there, hold her hand, and listen if she says anything."

"I can do that," Joey said.

A commotion in the hallway drew their attention. Opening the door, Dr. Fells and Joey came face to face with four men. Hugh, Marvin, Jerry, and Will were in the hallway. A nurse was trying to explain that Ms. Amando was not able to receive visitors. The detectives were trying to explain that they just wanted to talk to Joey Mercer and Georgia's doctor. All eyes turned in the direction of the opening door. Dr. Fells stepped out with his hands held in the air. "Gentlemen, listen to me. Ms. Amando is not going to answer any questions. She can't, she's unconscious, and while we expect her to recover it is still too soon to say for sure. So you see she can't help you. You have to do your police work all by yourself this time."

"No sir, you don't understand. We're looking for Joey Mercer, and we'd like to get an update on Georgia's condition," Jerry and Will said almost in unison.

"Ah, then come this way. Mr. Mercer is in here," Dr. Fells said as he opened the door wider.

Joey talked with the detectives for a few minutes. He gave them all the information he had, but told them that they would have to wait for further details. Dr. Fells looked in and motioned for Joey. "They're ready for you, Joey, if you want to see her." Joey stepped into the hallway and scanned the crowd that had congregated. Joey saw Dr. Fells standing by the door of Treatment Room One and headed that way.

Dr. Fells pushed the door of Georgia's room just wide enough for Joey to go in as a group of reporters started in their direction. Joey looked into the room and hesitated long enough to take a deep breath and try to master his fear. The last thing he wanted to do was show Georgia that he was afraid. He wanted to show love, acceptance, and compassion, even concern, but he didn't want her to see fear.

Feeling a hand on his shoulder, Joey turned and looked into the tear-filled eyes of George and Lucinda. He could see their pain and concern. Dr. Fells motioned for them all to go in. "Go on, but be quiet. No crying, no hysterics, understand?"

"Yes, sir," they all said at once.

The people who loved Georgia the most looked down at her. She was unrecognizable. The bruising and swelling, the twisted nose, and battered lips and eyes made her look like something from a horror movie. There was no place on her that seemed safe to touch.

Joey eased the chair sitting alongside the bed closer and motioned for Lucinda to sit. She nodded and gratefully sank into the chair. Joey heard her sigh as she settled in and reached out to her daughter. Her small, plump hands were rough and worn, but Joey had never seen more gentleness. George walked to the other side of the bed, never taking his eyes off his daughter. He made his way to the head of the bed amidst IV poles and monitors. Ever so gently, he too reached out a hand to touch his only child. Joey saw the big hand shake, he heard the man sniffle and saw his shoulders shudder.

George leaned forward and kissed Georgia on the forehead. "I love you, Georgie. Come back to your momma and me. Nobody gonna hurt you no more." George Amando was desperately trying not to cry out loud. He and Georgia's mother started to pray. The words were Italian, but somehow words to the Lord transcend all language barriers.

Joey knelt by the bed. Suddenly he felt alive as he too spoke to God. His shoulders shook and he clenched his jaw and his fists. He leaned his forehead against the side of the bed and whispered his own prayer. "Lord, I've not been as good as I should have. I'm not the most holy man. But I know who You are, I know what You've done for me here and I thank You. I just need You to go a bit further and bring her all the way back to me, to us." He looked up as Georgia moved on the bed.

Georgia moaned softly as her eyes fluttered open. "Momma, Papa," she said.

"Georgie, oh my Georgia," Lucinda gasped as she made the sign of the cross over her chest. Tears welled up in Georgia's eyes. Her father and Joey both bent forward into her view. "Joey! Oh Joey," Georgia whispered.

"We're here, baby, be quiet and rest. The doctor says you'll be okay, but you need to be still."

Georgia could barely move, but slowly she slid her hand over her stomach. Joey saw the gesture and smiled. "We're okay, Georgia, we're still a family." Joey hoped that she could hear him well enough to figure out what he was saying without giving the situation away to her parents. Lucinda looked at Joey, then at Georgia, then she stared long and hard at her husband. She knew. In that moment Joey was sure of it, but he wondered if she would tell Georgia's father. Joey smiled down at her and gently touched her shoulder.

Georgia seemed to be struggling with words, and as her father bent over her to listen, she whispered, "A baby, Papa, Joey and I are going to have a baby. I want you to pray for our baby, Papa, please. God listens to you so much better than me."

George Amando looked up at Joey, who squared his shoulders and prepared to take it like a man. Everyone waited, including Dr. Fells. He knew how this conversation would go. George finally smiled a tight-lipped smile. He reached out to shake Joey's hand, as he said, with a stern look in his eye, "Welcome to the family."

Joey understood exactly what he was being told. He knew what Mr. Amando was saying to him, but he also saw the gleam in his eyes. Joey took the offered hand and shook it firmly. He smiled and looked down at Georgia, but she was out again. Joey reached into his pocket and pulled something out. He held the tiny object up to the light. The diamond twinkled like the brightest star. He laid the ring to his lips and kissed it as he showed it to her parents. "We wanted to wait to tell you until after the prom. Please don't be angry with us. I love Georgia so much, and I promise I'll take good care of her."

Mr. and Mrs. Amando smiled and nodded at Joey. He tucked the tiny ring back in his pocket and leaned in to whisper to Georgia, "I'll take care of it for you, baby, just until I can put it back on your finger."

Lucinda sat by her daughter's side and fingered her rosary. She was tired and relieved but still so scared. Her stoic expression, the firmness of her jaw spoke volumes when the nurse came by to tell them it was time to go.

"No, I'm not leaving. I'm staying right here with my daughter. I'll be quiet, but I stay!" The nurse looked at Dr. Fells, who smiled and nodded his head. Joey and George kissed Georgia and carefully worked their way around all the medical equipment to leave the room.

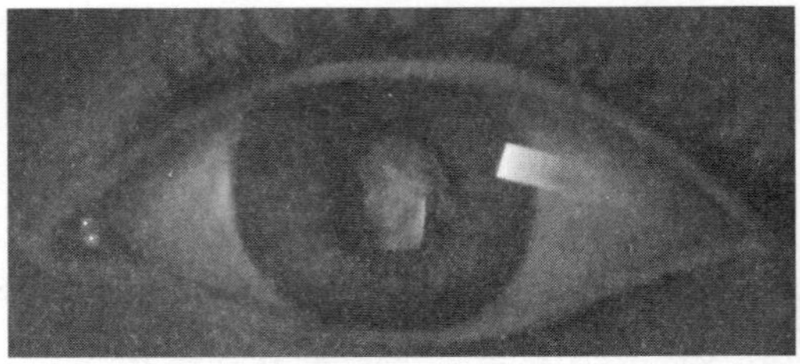

CHAPTER 29

As they left the room the two men heard the noise in the hallway just outside. Swinging the door open, they came face to face with reporters, Amy and Scott, and the two detectives who had wanted to question Georgia. Two other men stood with them, but they didn't look like police. Joey walked away from the reporters as quickly as he could, but they wouldn't be put off.

"Mr. Mercer, can you tell us how she's doing? Have you spoken with her yet? What is her prognosis? Does she know who took her? Was she raped?"

The questions flew at Joey one right after the other till he reached forward and grabbed the man who had asked the wrong question. Scott tried to stop him, but Joey's fist found the reporter's jaw. "You son of a bitch, I'll kill you, you heartless bastard. Get out of here," Joey screamed. Scott pulled Joey back and the other reporters swarmed in, staying a respectful distance from his fist. Jerry and Will motioned for Scott to bring Joey in their direction as they held a door open. Mr. Amando was already in the room, so Joey went willingly.

Inside the room, Joey, George, Scott, Amy, Hugh, and Marvin sat with Jerry and Will.

Joey stuck his bleeding knuckle in his mouth. "Are you okay? Joey, you know Detectives Jerry Leeme and Will Halpin, right?" Scott asked.

"Yeah, I'm all right. I met them the night Georgia disappeared." Joey stuck his knuckles back into his mouth. "That guy pissed me off. Can you believe those greedy bastards? She's lying in there fighting for her life and all they care about is getting the news, the dirty little details."

"Joey, they really do care. But this is big news after the Amanda Wiggins story. They want answers for a scared public."

"Bullshit—they want to scare the public, that's what sells newspapers." Joey's anger showed, but something else was there, some other emotion. Scott stood. "I'm gonna get us some coffee and sandwiches. Does anybody want anything particular?"

Joey's stomach grumbled at the mention of food. George stood and reached for his wallet.

"No sir," Scott said. "I got this."

"Joey, we need to give them a statement. We need to tell them something, so that we can have some control over what is printed about this. Otherwise the Brandt's farm is going to be overrun with reporters. You will have no peace at all, not to mention the Amandos. Someone needs to tell them something. Do you want me to do it?" Jerry said as he leaned across the table.

"No," Joey said. "I can do it. But first I want to know where you've been, what have you found out? Did you catch them?"

Jerry spoke. "No, we didn't catch them because when we got there they were gone. We figured they must have come back while the Brandts had Georgia, and when they found her gone, they grabbed what they could and hauled ass. Our forensic guys are up there now going over that area with a fine-tooth comb. They grabbed some of the guns, blankets, sleeping bags, and some supplies, but so much is still up there that it may take days to go through it all."

Will took over. "Everyone in this room must understand something. Don't share this information with anyone. Keep it to yourselves, because those guys may be reading the papers, listening to the radio—or they may even know someone that you know. There are a lot of strangers in town with the state fair here. There's also lots of construction going on. We have no idea who these guys are, and if they get wind that we know too much they may just leave this area all together. Keep this stuff confidential, okay?" Jerry and Will looked seriously at their listeners.

Everyone across from them nodded. "Now, who should make the statement about Georgia?" Will asked.

Joey looked at George. "No, Joey, my English isn't so good when I'm nervous. I get all tongue-tied and forget the English words. I don't want to look like a foreign fool. You do it."

Joey nodded, but he was struggling mentally. How would he tell the whole town that his fiancée had been beaten, raped, and left for dead? What words could he say that would tell the story without ruining Georgia's reputation? Joey decided to make a statement but not to take any questions. He felt better. Bracing himself, he stood and walked to the door.

"Joey, they won't blame her, if that's what you're struggling with," Jerry Leeme said.

"Are you sure?" Joey asked, not to be sarcastic, but because he really wanted to know.

"She's the victim here, sort of a Madonna figure. Of course, later on, when your baby gets here, there will be some raised eyebrows, some questions after the shock has worn off. But those are things you won't really have to address, since you and Georgia plan to leave for the University of Illinois as soon as graduation's over. You are still planning to do that, right?"

"Well, I don't know. Now there's so much more to consider. She needs her mother more now than ever before. I don't want to take the baby from them right away," Joey said, as he looked at the Amandos and smiled. Both of them nodded.

"We could go, too," George said tentatively.

Joey looked at him. "What, you would do that, leave here, leave everything that you have, for us? For me?"

"We only have our Georgia, now you and our grandchild. That's what we have. If you're gonna be a doctor you're gonna work long hours. Georgia is gonna need us. We could sell our dry-cleaning store and start over somewhere else."

It touched Joey's heart, but he wasn't going to run away. "I appreciate that. I love you both for it, but I'm not running from here. This is my home too, my parents are here, and my mom and dad went to the same high school that Georgia and I go to now. I'm not running. We are gonna hold our heads up high. You can come with us if you want to, but you need to know that I plan to practice medicine here when I finish school. Of course, that's eight years from now, but that's my plan. It has been all along."

Everyone in the room nodded, most seemed lost in thought. "Joey, let me make this statement for you. I think we should keep to legal matters and not make this a personal issue until we have to. What do you all think of that idea?" Will Halpin asked.

Joey nodded. "If you think that's best, I'm for it."

"Well, for now it may be the best idea. Georgia needs some time. And we really aren't sure what's going to happen. Let's wait till Georgia comes out of surgery before we make any other plans," Jerry said.

As he stood and headed for the door, Dr. Fells poked his head in. "We're going, and the hallway has been cleared so we can get her to surgery. She's going to be out in a minute, if you want to see her on the way by. We'll set the broken bones and do some repairs. She seems to be resting easy right now. It will be awhile, though, before you can see her again, so you might want to come now."

Everyone in the room stood up. They could see that Georgia's bed was being wheeled into the hallway. She looked like a bundle of white cloth with a red patch right where her face should be. She lay so still as she was jostled through the opening, she must have been unconscious again. Her mother and father hurried to one side and Joey to the other. The nurses stopped long enough for them to look at her. She never moved, but those who loved her touched her blankets, rubbed the sheet, anything to make contact without hurting her. "I love you," Joey whispered.

Her parents murmured something in Italian as she was wheeled away.

The night would be a long one, but less stressful than the night before. Joey walked back into the room and lay down on the couch. He was dog-tired. He felt a blanket being placed gently over him; someone offered him a pillow. Looking up he saw his own parents. "Mom, Dad!" Joey started to cry again, like the young man that he was—eighteen years usually isn't long enough to learn how to deal with such experiences.

"Shh, sleep, son, we'll be here when you wake up. How's Georgia?" his mother asked.

"She's gone to surgery. That's her parents, over there," Joey said, pointing in the direction of the Amandos. They were watching Joey's interaction with his parents. They'd never met them before. Joey's mom stood and walked toward Lucinda Amando. Holding her arms out to the other woman, she embraced her. Lucinda willingly took comfort from another mother, one who would share her grandchild someday, and who now shared this moment.

Phil Mercer took George Amando's hand in his and clasped it warmly. "I'm so sorry for your pain and suffering. But I'm so glad we got her back. I'm just sorry it took something like this for us to meet. I'm Phil Mercer, Joey's father."

"I'm George Amando, Georgia's father," George said, shaking hands.

All four parents turned to see Joey sound asleep on the couch, snoring softly. "Let's get some coffee and let him sleep. I know he hasn't had much since this happened, and it's going to be a while before she comes out. We can talk things over in the other lounge," Phil said.

"No, the reporters are everywhere. Let's sit in the far corner by the television. He won't hear us. You know how he is, Phil," said Bethany Mercer.

They all sat down across the room from Joey. The television showed images of detectives Jerry Leeme and Will Halpin talking about the day's latest events. No one in the room paid any attention to it. Joey slept. The Brandts had been escorted home by two police officers who would stay with them until the criminals were caught or they could be sure they weren't coming back. Scott was probably sleeping in his own bed. Georgia was in surgery.

CHAPTER 30

"Hey girl, come on in. Everyone else is here already," Susan said from the doorway under the carport. She stood there in the light from the porch, smiling and waving, a greeting that touched Lindsay's heart. Friendships were hard to cultivate—true friendships, that is. So many people were attracted to Lindsay, but true friends were really hard to come by, and Lindsay could feel the difference. The sight of Susan was like salve to her wounded soul. It had been a tough week, with her kids, her job, and the current guy who called himself her boyfriend.

"Gosh, how am I ever going to get rid of him?" Lindsay muttered to herself.

The door behind Susan opened wider as Debbie stepped up behind her. "Hey, Lindsay, come on. The wine's cold and the whiners have already started." Lindsay slung her overnight bag over her shoulder and locked the car door. She felt the weight of the world lifting from her shoulders. Taking a deep breath, she sighed, "Ahh, a good night, finally."

Inside, Dana, Wendy, and Laura were lounging on Susan's oversized, overstuffed sofa. The smiles on their faces told Lindsay they had been talking about their favorite subject, men. "Who is the flavor du jour, ladies?" She giggled as she set her stuff down and took the glass of wine offered to her. "Thanks, you have no idea how much I need this night."

Everyone hugged Lindsay, and Susan showed her to the room that they would be sharing with Wendy. "Dana, Debbie, and Laura are in Max's room. Put your stuff on the chaise and let's go join the others," Susan said.

Lindsay followed Susan down the hall. "Is this the new paint texture you were telling me about last week?"

"Yep, what do you think?" Susan said, as she stopped and turned the hall light on.

"I like it, the color is great. It feels warm and cozy to me." Lindsay stood and gazed at the walls.

"Are you okay, Lin?" Susan asked.

"Yeah, sorry, I've just had the strangest feeling all week. You know that feeling that something is coming. That feeling that someone is watching you?"

"Yeah, I know it. But I'm usually wrong, and it just sort of goes away—or I get my period." Susan laughed, and Lindsay joined her. "Come on, silly," Lindsay said as she wrapped her arm around Susan's waist.

"Okay, let's have it, what are you two laughing about?" Wendy demanded as they entered the living room.

"Susan and her permanent female problems!" Lindsay laughed.

"Oh, that. Well, I'm with her, it's a great excuse for my permanent behavioral problems, and it keeps everyone feeling sorry for me," Wendy quipped.

Everyone laughed and they settled into catching up on the events in each other's lives. They talked the night away. It was good for Lindsay to be among friends who could gather and share their lives, friends who loved her in spite of her clairvoyant ability and instead of it, as well. Lindsay and the gang all knew each other well, had shared difficulties and triumphs, had cried and laughed together. Their friendships were deep, even if not lifelong. They felt complete when they were together

"What are you working on, Lindsay?" Susan asked.

"Nothing right now other than the hospital and Jackie's baseball stuff and the girls and my car and laundry and . . ."

The others held their hands up. "Stop, you're killing us. We don't want normal, mundane issues. Thrill us, please," Laura said as she laughed.

"Sorry to let you down, girls. It's just life in the big city—single life, that is."

"Oh my gosh, how is that new guy you went out with?" Susan asked.

"Ekkk! Please don't mention him. I can't get rid of him. No matter what I do, he keeps calling. Last week I just told him that I really wasn't ready to have a serious relationship. Do you know what he said?" Lindsay looked around the room, loving the suspense she saw on their faces.

"Tell us!" they all said at the same time.

"He said, 'I'll wait.'"

"You're kidding! I thought he was gorgeous. I thought you really liked him. What happened?" Debbie asked.

"That was till he opened his mouth. Then pfft, forget it! His brains are on vacation and he thinks with his, uh, well, he just doesn't think. Let's leave it at that."

Wendy laughed and rolled over on her side as she drained her glass. "Well, that's why I like Head. He's always so understanding, just listens and goes along with everything that I want to do, never complains, and anything I make or don't make for dinner is fine with him." Wendy was giggling hysterically now.

Susan pushed her, toppling her over. "That's because he's a bust, nothing more than a lump of clay. He doesn't count as a date, silly. He's just a head." The rest of the room burst into laughter. Wendy stuck out her lower lip in mock disappointment and laid her hands on her heart in mock horror. Dana reached over and hugged her.

"It's okay, sweetie, some of the best men in the world could never be as well trained as Head. As long as you're happy, that's all that counts." Dana hugged her again. Giggles ran around the room as Wendy hugged Head.

Head really was just that, a molded bust of a man that had been adopted into Wendy's group years before. He had taken turns traveling with the other members of the group to places like Mardi Gras in New Orleans, Paris, and Austin, to name a few. He even had his own photo album. Head was a part of it all. Wendy laughed again as she tipped him back and dribbled wine on his lips.

“Hmmm, good, huh, Head?” Wendy put a pillow over Head’s face, “Don’t look, Head, don’t listen, we’re talking about men. Wait! Maybe you can explain men to us. Start talking, Head, or it’s the grinder for you,” Wendy said as she wrapped her hands around Head’s throat.

The night wore on, long and flavorful. The conversations went from serious to hilarious and then back again. Times like this kept Lindsay and her friends going through the hard times of being women, mothers, employees, and wives or girlfriends. This was sisterhood at its best.

The following afternoon, as they went their separate ways, they hugged each other and smiled, knowing that it would be some time before they all got together again. “Laura, I’ll see you in October for your birthday. I’ll see the rest of you soon,” Lindsay said as she backed her car out of the driveway. Laura, who had the longest drive, waved as she followed. Debbie and Dana stood with Wendy and Susan in the driveway and waved.

“See you soon, talk to you sooner. Hey let’s all get together on Friday for lunch! Be nice to that guy, you never know. He may be a prince in frog’s clothing,” Susan yelled.

“Rib-bitt,” Lindsay yelled back.

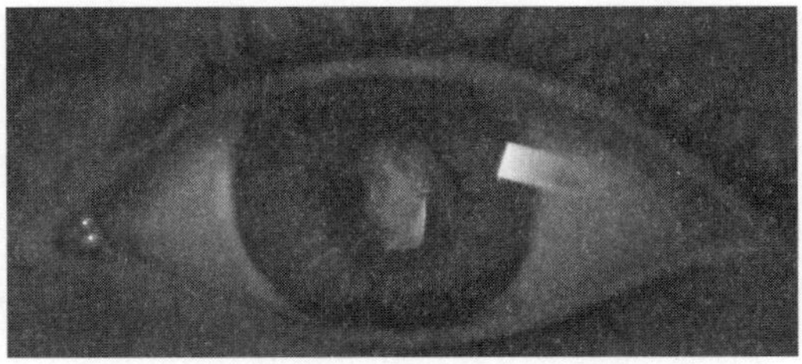

CHAPTER 31

Will and Jerry went back to the place where Georgia had been found. Uniformed officers and a very good forensic team were still there. The team walked around with rubber gloves and plastic bags, digging here and there, using pencils to push things around. Everything was evidence, nothing would be left behind. Large clear plastic bags were filled with all the things that Mike and Tony had abandoned. Some of it was trash and would have been left anyway.

Obviously, the guys who had been camping here weren't nature lovers, even though the site was beautiful. But it provided more than beauty. Jerry noticed how secluded and bountiful it was. The crystal clear lake edging the campsite provided water and fishing. The trees provided protection and seclusion. The sky sparkled through the treetops and created an illusion of perfection. Truly, this place was a perfect hiding spot. Jerry walked the perimeter again, slowing his steps as he looked into the inner circle. He could see the beauty, he could feel the magic of this place, and he longed to be here on a different mission, a vacation perhaps.

Jerry looked around for Will. Camping was more his thing, and Jerry knew he would see awed respect and desire in his partner's eyes. But when he spotted Will, Jerry saw something else—loathing, anger, misery, and fear. Looking in the direction of Will's gaze, Jerry saw the tree stump, some of Georgia's bloody clothing, and the horrible shackles. Will was staring at the items, his emotions plainly reflected on his face. Jerry let the moment pass and said nothing as he continued his inventory of the site.

"Let him stew in his own juices," he muttered. "For him, it's better that way."

Walking around the campsite, taking note of what was there and what wasn't that should have been, Jerry tried to mentally set up the campsite. He needed Will, since he had never been camping in his life.

"Will, hey, buddy, if you can pull your head out of your ass for a few minutes and get rid of that scowl, I need your help over here."

Will looked up and mentally shook himself. "What do you need? And watch your mouth. I don't have my head in my ass, by the way; that is biologically impossible, in case you didn't know it."

"Walk with me here, let's work this out together." Jerry motioned Will towards him. Will walked over and together they wandered the perimeter, talking as they went.

"Tell me what you see here, tell me what's missing," Jerry said.

Will looked at him and for a moment he thought of telling Jerry to kiss his ass, but something in Jerry's face made him smile and go along with the game.

"Okay, I see a beautiful campsite, one that shouldn't have this sort of history."

"Come on, Will," Jerry said.

"Okay, sorry." Will stopped walking and stood still. He turned slowly, staring at the site. Looking at Jerry, he said, "I got it, I see what you want me to see." Will had the same enthusiasm in his voice that Jerry felt in his heart.

"Okay, some of the possessions left behind are necessary items. Things they would have to have to set up camp somewhere else—like the tent, guns, fishing poles, and tackle box. It looks like they reacted in a state of panic and made foolish choices when they came back and found Georgia gone. But they did take some necessary things, so at least one of them is thinking. Look right here, see where this table is, see the grease stains, there should be a camp stove here, or something that made grease splatter."

Jerry looked at the makeshift table, the two branches cut short and laid on the ground with a piece of board obviously found somewhere other than here. He could see the grease outline of what must have been a camp stove, something along the line of his son's Coleman stove.

"Where do you think these outlines are from?" Jerry asked as he traced the greasy lines with his forefinger.

Will looked over his shoulder, "Utensils, fork, spatula, that sort of thing."

The two walked to the water's edge where the tent sat. Looking inside, Jerry and Will turned and looked around. Seeing a uniformed officer, Jerry said, "Has this site been secured?"

"Yes sir, the forensic guys have been done here for about an hour now. I've just been asked to stand by in case something or someone should turn up."

"Thank you, son, good job," Jerry said as he pulled the tent flap back and Will ducked his head and went inside. They stood there close together, "What do you see, Will?" Jerry asked.

"No blankets or sleeping bags, very little clothing scattered about, and no lantern. I don't see any matches or extra mantels. No shoes or personal items, but if you look in that corner, right there, you can see that they must have been here. See the outlines on the tent floor? These boys weren't part of the house beautiful team, no cleaning or keeping things neat. They would have just had things strewn around. But that area over there and this one here where beds should be is just bare canvas flooring." Will had gotten into it now and, he headed out of the tent again. "Jerry, see that ring of stones right there?"

"Yeah, I see it, what about it?"

"That ring of stones is the fireplace. There should be a stove grate, or something like it, on top of that fire. It's either gone or they didn't have one. See these oval shapes that have flattened the grass here by the tent? These look like the butt ends of rifles."

"They didn't take much, did they?" Jerry said, not really expecting a response, and Will didn't let him down. He seemed lost in thought. His eyes had that faraway look.

Suddenly Will looked up, "You know, I was just thinking. They might have been here watching us earlier. All this stuff is stuff they would need in the next campsite. I wonder if they were hiding in the woods, watching and waiting and hoping for a chance to come back and get the rest of this stuff. Something about the haphazard way they abandoned this site seems odd. I can see they took some of what they would need, but important things are still here. The tent, for Christ's sake, I can't see them leaving that."

Will was rubbing his chin as he looked at Jerry, who continued to move in a circle. "They left it because they really had no way of knowing how much time they had before we descended on them. We should have gotten here sooner. It's our fault they got away." Jerry was pissed and getting more so as he walked around.

Will walked in one direction, back toward the water's edge, while Jerry headed deeper into the wooded area. He approached the tree stump that Georgia had been tied to. In his mind he could hear Hugh and Marvin's words about how they'd found her, hog-tied and naked, stretched belly down over the tree stump. The stakes were still deeply imbedded in the hard earth. Jerry called to one of the men walking around with a large plastic bag in his hands.

"I want these, all four of them," he said, pointing to the shackles in the ground. "Be careful, there should be a ton of evidence on and around them." The detective pulled on a new pair of gloves and gently went to work. Slowly he placed plastic baggies over the shackles and pulled each rope into the bag. Then he taped it tightly. He then slowly unscrewed the stake from the ground and wrapped it in plastic. It was a slow, painstaking effort, but what they were hoping for might solve the largest crime this area had ever known.

Will called, "Jerry, over here." Stooping down he pulled a pair of tweezers from his pocket. As he unfolded a piece of white notebook paper with the tweezers and one gloved hand, Jerry ran in his direction.

"What have you got?" he asked.

"I'm not sure; maybe a letter of some sort. This area was too clean before those two assholes got here, so let's hope it gives us a name or something.

The paper lay spread out on a piece of clear plastic on the ground. Jerry and Will read the first few lines out loud. "Dear Tony, I hope this letter finds you well and you've left that asshole Mike behind. If you come this way look me up. I'm staying on the beach with some friends in a rented beach cabin…"

As the wind blew gently across the campsite, Jerry shifted and wrinkled his nose. "Shit, what is that smell?" he asked as he straightened and looked around.

Will laughed and said, "That's exactly what it is—shit." He pointed into the woods. "That's where they took a dump; see the toilet paper hanging off the branch?" Jerry noticed that the smell came from an area closer to where Georgia had been tied than he was standing now.

"Will, that poor girl had to be beaten, violated and humiliated, and held hostage in that smell? They walked over there, took a dump and left her this close to it. I can't wait to find them. I'm gonna wrap my hands around those pencil-dick necks and choke the shit out of them." A vein in his neck stood out as evidence of his frustration and anger.

"Man, you can't do that, but I don't blame you, I'd want to, too. I know if this were my daughter or fiancée I would kill these two for what they did to her."

Will grabbed the edge of the notebook paper with the tweezers and held it out, "Open the bag for me, Jerry." Will gently lowered the paper inside. He then sealed the bag shut and wrote on the front, "Amando Evidence."

Jerry stood looking down at the clear plastic bag in his hand. The white piece of notebook paper seemed dismally small compared to the task at hand. He stuffed it into his pocket and walked in the direction Will had taken.

For hours they combed through the mess. The tent was disassembled and stuffed into a large plastic bag. The trash that had been lying around went into a different bag. Everything had its own bag. Everything was labeled, everything was important.

Suddenly an investigator stood up and called to Jerry and Will, motioning them to come in his direction. They saw a look of concern on his face. "What have ya got, Adam?"

"I found something. I hope neither of you has eaten lately."

"What do you mean?"

"Well, this is sort of a collection. These guys are true sociopaths. Serial killers, is what I'm getting at." He held out a dark-colored backpack, the look on his face grim. Will and Jerry looked at each other.

"Where did you find this?"

"Over here, under the boughs of this tree by the trunk. There's a bunch of stuff here, but most of it's paper and food wrappers. This is something I know they didn't mean to leave behind for us to find."

Will and Jerry took the bag. While one held it open, the other held a flashlight and looked inside. "Oh, sweet Jesus," Will gasped as he looked away. "What the hell is all that?"

Jerry took the flashlight as he looked at his partner's stricken face.

"What? What's in there, let me see." He too looked in the bag. "Oh, shit, is that a dead animal, or what? I can't see it. Is that blood?"

Detective Adam Kent spread a piece of clear plastic on the ground and dumped the contents of the backpack. Inside, the bloody clothing had fermented. Outside, the odor quickly spread through the air. All three men held their handkerchiefs to their noses. As they bent over the bloody collection of clothing, each held a pointer of some sort. Will had a pencil, Jerry had a pen, and Adam had something long, silver, and pointed. They looked at each other as each formed his own thought.

"What kind of animals do we have here?" Jerry said shaking his head. "Damn it, are those Amanda Wiggins's jeans?" Will got the picture of Amanda out of his pocket, and on the back was a description of the clothing she had been wearing when she had been abducted.

"She had on Jordache blue jeans, size six, and a pink angora sweater, size small." Will said.

Adam turned the jeans over in his gloved hands. He read the Jordache label and found the size six tag on the inside back seam. "Bingo!" he said.

Jerry remembered the pink angora sweater that had been thrown out of the car at Jeremy. He could see it on Amanda and in his mind's eye he pictured her loving it, the softness and the color. He knew from her parents that pink was her favorite color. He could see her as she must have been, standing in front of a mirror in her room, getting ready to go out to meet her death.

"The guys threw the sweater at Jeremy Wright, remember? They tore it off her." The others turned their attention to the articles before them to give Jerry time to collect himself.

The other clothing cried out for recognition, but no one had a name to connect to it. The men stuffed it all back into the backpack, trying not to notice how the dried blood felt crusty even through their gloves.

"I'm gonna leave you with it, Adam," Will said. "I know I don't need to say it, but tag it, bag it, label it, and don't lose a damn thing. I want to catch these bastards."

Adam nodded and turned back to the task at hand. "Yeah, I wonder where those two bastards are." He looked around in the fading light. They could be out there in the woods just waiting to see what would be left after the officers had finished.

"I'm not leaving you a fucking thing," he said out loud. It sounded loud even in his ears, and he glanced up to see the other officers in the area looking at him. He went back to work, muttering softly under his breath.

CHAPTER 32

It took three days to sift through the campsite. In those three days Will and Jerry walked around the perimeter more than a dozen times, ducking under the yellow plastic tape so often they felt they knew it by heart.

Georgia fought infections, swelling, and her own nightmares. She struggled with pain as her parents, Joey, and his parents, sat by and waited, unable to help.

The investigation continued. Mandy's parents struggled with their grief and with the many curious onlookers who drove up and down their street, day in and day out. Life wasn't back to normal, far from it.

On day three Will and Jerry returned to Pine Ambly fishing hole, where Amanda's body had been found. It was hard to see the site now, so long after the beautiful, lifeless girl had been lifted from the water. It was back to the way it had been before she had been dumped there like so much garbage. They noticed a children's playground. A rope hung from a tree, and in his mind Will could hear the sounds of kids splashing into the water as they swung from the rope. A child's toy truck lay in the mud. The site seemed deserted now and both men were aware that the death of Amanda and the discovery of her body here had tainted the place. The kids probably didn't come here anymore.

Will and Jerry noted the contrast to where Amanda had been murdered and where Georgia had been found. While this place had its own special quality, it didn't have the beauty of the campsite. It seemed clear that the murderers didn't choose places for their victims. They just seemed to present themselves, with no rhyme or reason. For Will, this went against the grain. He liked order and reason, in fact his mind required it.

"Why do they do this, what's the pattern, and where the hell are they?"

Will and Jerry spread out and started walking the perimeter, trying to visualize the day of Amanda's murder.

They were sure that she hadn't been murdered where they'd found her. For one thing, it was too close to the house of the Michels family; one of them would have heard something. For another, it appeared that she had been killed at the campsite because of the skin and blood found on the shackles, that might or might not be hers, and the bloody clothes that were hers for sure. She did have the same marks around her wrists and ankles that Georgia had. Unfortunately, Amanda's abduction and torture had ended fatally.

Standing at the water's edge, Will looked around. "How do you think they got her here without being heard?"

Jerry looked up from the autopsy report that he had been studying. "They must have carried her. I mean, we know she wasn't killed here. We know those are her pants that we found at the campsite. She had no water in her lungs, so we know she wasn't drowned. They killed her there and then drove her here to dump her body."

Will nodded. "I guess you're right. I wanna know what happened, though. I want to be sure." He looked deeper into the water. Something pulled at him, something that just wouldn't let him go.

Straightening, he turned slowly in a circle. He took it all in, the reeds growing at the water's edge, the dirt that formed mud along the bank, and the minnows that swam close to shore for safety. The water wasn't deep here, it was more of a fishing hole than a lake or pond, and he came from the land of fishing holes—Texas was famous for them. The trees leaned into the water, their roots sunk deep in the earth, but their trunks swinging out over the waters edge.

Will walked along the bank, studying it intently, letting his mind look for something that he couldn't name. The water and mud sucked at his shoes as he let his hands trail along the tops of the tall grass. The sun was beating down on his neck, and he was reminded of another day, long ago, when he had fished a body out of the water. Shaking his head to rid his mind of that memory, he looked suddenly to the left. There before him was a small dirt road, rutted from tire tracks and with lots of standing water, tucked up in the tall grass. "Jerry, over here!" he shouted.

Jerry stuffed the autopsy report in his pocket and headed in the direction of Will's voice. He slipped and skidded in the mud. "Damn, I just bought these sneakers," he muttered. He caught sight of Will as he disappeared down what appeared to be a path. "Will, wait up."

Will watched as Jerry came closer. "I hate this mud," he was saying as he approached.

"Quit your bitchin', and come see what I found." Will and Jerry walked the rest of the way to the road. Looking back, they could see that it wasn't visible from the point where Amanda had been found. "It's a dirt road," Will said.

"I know it's a dirt road, I can see that," Jerry said. "I just don't want to go down it. Look at all that mud; shit!" Jerry was disgusted. He gritted his teeth and started walking forward. "Damn it, I hate this shit."

Will was laughing in spite of himself and the seriousness of the situation. "What's the matter, you can't handle a little mud?"

"No. You got a problem with that?" Jerry had a mean look in his eye. "I'm not a nature boy. I don't like nature, okay?"

Will laughed again. "Come on, you're gonna be okay. It's just a little mud." They stumbled on, slipping and sliding until they reached a fork in the dirt path. Stopping, they looked in both directions.

"What do you think, which way?" Jerry said. "'Cause I ain't doin' this twice."

Will pointed down the path to the left, "That way."

"How do you know?"

"See those tire tracks right there, the ones with the wide tread?"

"Yeah, so?" Jerry asked.

"Those are the only ones that go all the way to the water where we found Amanda. All the other ones start back there near that big oak tree," Will said, pointing at a huge oak.

"Whoa, Texas boy, is that something they teach you in school down south?"

Jerry was goading him, and Will knew it.

"No, Yankee, it's not, but I saw it right away. I could be wrong, but then again I might not be."

They headed to the left and were soon rewarded. On the path in front of them was an empty pack of cigarettes and an empty Tequila bottle, the same brands found at the campsite. Next to the bottle lay a pink ribbon, partially covered with mud.

"What do you think?" Will asked as he bent down to examine the things lying on the wet earth.

Jerry bent down too. "I think we found something, what I'm not sure, but the pink ribbon seems to scream out at me."

"Me too," Will said, as he took a plastic evidence bag from his pocket. He lifted the ribbon with a pair of tweezers he had taken from his pocket. As he did he saw it—tangled in the ribbon were a rubber band and several long blonde hairs. Jerry, too, pulled a plastic bag and a pair of tweezers out of his pocket.

"Our luck is just not this good," he whispered as he gently tucked the blonde hairs and rubber band into the plastic bag. He labeled it as Will was doing, "Wiggins's evidence" and a question mark. The cigarette package and the liquor bottle were also bagged. It would take weeks for the forensic guys to get back to them on DNA, but this was solid evidence if it panned out.

"Can we get out of here now?" Jerry said, looking down at his mud-covered sneakers.

"Yeah, ya weenie, if you quit your whining." Will laughed.

"I'll quit whining when we're out of here and I'm sending these sneakers home to your wife to wash. Mine would just throw them away, and I just bought the damn things."

They made their way out of Pine Ambly fishing hole and reached the car as the radio crackled. "Dispatch, go ahead," Jerry said into the mike.

"Detective Leeme, Joey Mercer called in and ask that you be informed that Georgia Amando is awake and is ready to speak with you."

"Ten-four, Dispatch, we're in route."

"Ahh, this might be a good day all the way around," Jerry said as he buckled his seatbelt.

The day was waning, and slowly the sky filled with a pink glow. "Red sky at night, sailor's delight," Will said softly.

Jerry smiled, "Another southern saying?"

"Actually no, a Yankee sailor made that saying up, I'll have you know."

"Yeah, right, let's go see Georgia."

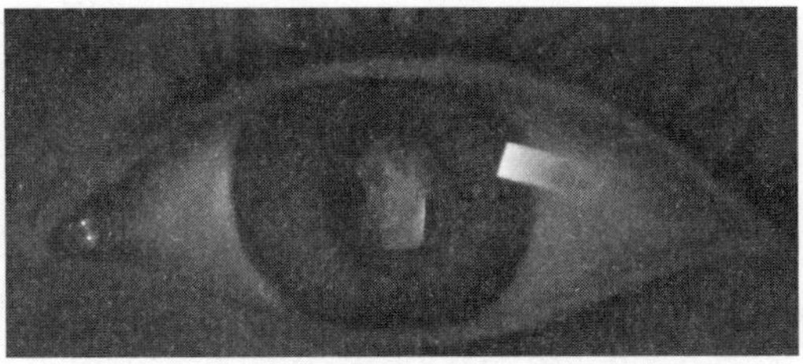

CHAPTER 33

Mike stomped around outside in front of the old house. He didn't like living indoors. Perhaps it was because it had been so long since he had done so, or maybe it made him feel hemmed in and controlled, like being in jail. And Mike knew what that feeling was like. He had been there often enough.

Walking to the edge of tree cover, Mike stepped into the brush and peered through it in the direction of the farmer's land. He could see signs of life over there even though the distance between the two houses was considerable, and he knew that everyone was up and about. His line of sight was obstructed by the house and a line of clean laundry hanging out to dry in the morning air.

"I hate farm people," he said. "Getting up with the chickens ain't normal."

"Me too," Tony said from behind him.

Mike spun around, and from the look on his face Tony could see that he'd scared the crap out of him. He snickered softly as he covered his mouth with his hand. "I scared ya, didn't I, Mike?"

Mike reached forward and grabbed Tony by the collar. "You asshole, yeah, you scared me. What if I had screamed out? Those farmers would have heard me, and you would be the reason again that we had to move. Do you want to move?"

"I ain't the reason we had to move. You left that girl there, you killed her. I didn't even get to do much of anything with her. It's your fault, not mine."

"Yeah, what about Philly, remember that time in Philly when you made so much noise we got caught and run off private property? We had to leave in the middle of the night. That was a fucking mess because you don't think. You just run through life in your merry little way, and you don't think. You don't use your noggin. You're stupid, and you could have scared me into making enough noise for them to hear us." Mike motioned with his thumb to the farm across the way.

Instead of being mad, Tony felt terrible. "I'm sorry, Mike. I wasn't thinking. I just wanted to have a little fun, that's all."

"Yeah, you never think. I have to do all the thinking for us."

"Well you ain't too good at it, or we wouldn't have lost most of our stuff," Tony whined.

"Yeah, and where would we be if I left everything to you?" Mike stood there looking at Tony.

Suddenly the smell of breakfast cooking worked its way across the warm, sunny countryside. Bacon. . .or was that ham? The smell was wonderful and both Mike and Tony sniffed the air.

"I'm hungry, let's eat," Tony said, immediately forgetting their disagreement.

Mike looked in the direction of the farmhouse. In back of the house was a smokehouse. He could see the chicken coop from where he stood. He formed a plan.

"Tony, if you be real good and don't make any noise today, all day, I'm going to get you bacon and eggs tomorrow morning. What do you think of that?"

Tony danced a bit as the excitement caught up with him. "I love bacon and eggs; where we gonna get 'em Mike?"

Mike again motioned with his thumb. "See that little house in back of the big house, that's a smokehouse. The chicken coop has eggs, and if we're real careful they won't even know we took anything."

"How we gonna do that, Mike? I got a powerful hunger when it comes to bacon and eggs."

"We're gonna take a little bit every day. No so much as they'd notice it gone, just what we need to have a nice breakfast, and we're gonna have breakfast when they do so they won't smell it cooking. Now you go get the house put to rights. I got planning to do."

"How come you always get to do all the planning and I always have to do all the work?" Tony stuck his chin out at Mike.

"Because I'm smarter than you, and I ain't as noisy," Mike said.

All Tony could do was nod; he knew Mike was right. He turned and started back to the house. Looking over his shoulder, he saw Mike stretch out on the ground with his forearm shading his eyes from the morning sun.

"Some planning," Tony said to himself. He continued, knowing arguing with Mike would only bring trouble.

He clenched his fists. "One of these days I'm going to get even with him, and he's going to do the work and I'm going to do the nap taking." The truth was, Tony wasn't tired. He'd slept well in the house. The cots weren't that bad, they were better than the ground, actually, but he knew Mike hadn't slept all that well. His cot was still covered with the sleeping bag, but it was a twisted mess; Tony knew Mike had fought sleep all night long. He knew Mike hated to be indoors. His nap would be long.

Tony set to putting things right, but only inside and in the back, where no one could see. Otherwise the changes might get noticed from the road.

His stomach grumbled noisily as he covered the hole in the roof with a piece of wood. His plan was to cover that wood with tree branches, but he was gonna eat first. Stuffing powdered-sugar-covered donuts in his mouth, he thought about all the things he could do to make the place more livable. He sat down at the rickety table and started forming plans while he ate.

It was well into the day before Mike returned. He was covered in dust from the ground and there were leaves in his hair.

"Feeling better?" Tony asked.

"Yeah, sorry I bitched at you earlier, Ton, you're my best friend. I was just tired. I didn't sleep good last night."

"It's okay Mike. Are ya hungry? There's some soup and chips or some powdered donuts left."

Mike nodded and sat down at the table. He looked around as he ate. Tony had done a lot in the time that he'd slept. "The place looks a lot better. What did you put on the roof?"

"Just an old piece of plywood that I found, and some tree branches. I tied 'em together nice and tight, so they shouldn't leak if it rains again." Tony was smiling. He loved it when Mike praised him.

"It looks real good, Tony, you did a fine job."

"Can we go for a ride Mike? I wanna go outside. What do you think; you wanna go back to the carnival? Maybe meet those chicks again? Aren't ya lonely yet, Mike?"

"Yeah, Tony, I was just thinking that I'm getting kinda lonely. As soon as the sun goes down we can sneak out of here and go to the carnival. Come on, I'll give you a hand with the rest of this." Mike stood and wiped his mouth on the sleeve of his shirt.

Together they finished making the abandoned cabin a home. Mike tested the cot he should have slept on last night. "I might make the night in here now, thanks to you, Tony."

Tony had dragged in a potted tree that he had found out back of the farmer's shed. He had put it near where Mike's head would rest on the bundled blanket pillow. Mike tested the leaves with his fingers. They were still soft and supple.

"Thanks, Tony, that was a real nice thing to do. Thanks." Mike could be nice when he wanted to, but never so nice as when he had treated Tony badly and knew it. Tony didn't care, he didn't seem to dwell on things. He just enjoyed the moment.

"Come on, let's get ready to go. There's a creek down the way a bit, we can get cleaned up there. 'Cause we ain't gonna get laid looking and smelling like this," Mike said as he ruffled Tony's hair. Tony laughed and followed Mike like a faithful puppy.

Later that night, after they had washed in the nearby creek, Tony and Mike walked silently to the back of the property they were on. Pulling back the branches that had hidden the car, they quietly pushed it to the road. Then they headed for the carnival, both of them hoping to have a good time. It had been far too long since they'd had a good time, especially Mike.

Pulling into the parking area, Mike spotted a familiar face. Getting out of the car and momentarily forgetting about Tony, Mike waved. The pretty girl standing all alone in tight jean cut-offs and red-and-white checkered top waved back.

"Hey, Mikey, what a stroke of luck, there's your girl. I wonder where her friend is." Tony said as he looked past her.

"Yeah, buddy, I see her, but don't worry. I've learned to share, and we're brothers, ain't we?"

Tony grinned, "Yeah, Mike, we're brothers, and brothers always share." Tony was grinning like a little kid in a candy store. He smoothed his unruly hair back and stuffed his shirt just a bit tighter into his jeans. Both men smiled and walked in the direction of the pretty girl standing by the entrance gate.

"We're gonna have us some fun tonight, Tony my man," Mike said.

CHAPTER 34

The familiar hospital smell greeted Will and Jerry as they cleared the big automatic swinging doors. They walked down the hallway toward the reception desk. Everyone they came in contact with knew in an instant they were policemen. They had the look.

Jerry looked at Will and said, "Ever get the feeling we could never go undercover?"

Will laughed, "Yeah, some of them look at us like we have the plague, and others seem to think we're gods. But no matter how we do it, people see us."

Jerry nodded as they arrived at the desk. The elderly woman sitting there smiled up at them. "Are you gentlemen here to see Ms. Amando?

Jerry looked at Will, "See, I told you."

"Yes ma'am, we are. Can you tell us what room she's in?" Will asked. They hadn't seen Georgia in two days. In that time she had been moved from the emergency room to the intensive care unit. She was still in serious condition.

"She's in room 106, down the hall and to your left." Will and Jerry could see the uniformed officer walking back and forth past the hall entrance.

"Thank you, ma'am," Will said. She smiled at him again and went back to her crossword puzzle.

Both Will and Jerry were feeling a little sick. "Gosh, I hate this, going to hear what I don't want to hear," said Will. "Knowing that someone somewhere is going to want me to say or do something that will make this all better."

"Yeah I know. Damn thing is, I don't know what to say half the time," Jerry said as he nervously brushed his suit off.

They looked in the door of the intensive care unit, watching doctors and nurses move purposefully as they went about their work. There was a large blackboard with the names of all the patients and the doctors and nurses assigned to their care.

Will and Jerry saw the name "Amando" about midway down the list. "Room 106," Jerry said.

Will looked at him, "Yeah, Einstein, that's what the lady at the front desk said."

"Very funny," Jerry said, flashing his badge at the woman sitting like a bulldog on guard behind the desk. "We're here to see Ms. Georgia Amando."

"Yes sir, I know. She's in room 106. Sign in here, and only stay fifteen minutes at a time. She's really tired, and she needs to rest. Don't upset her, and don't sit on the bed."

Jerry and Will could see her lying there in the bed. Bandages still engulfed her face, and she lay perfectly still. She was in a slightly inclined position, and her mother was sitting near the head of her bed. They slowly approached the glass room. Looking around as they entered, they could see the monitors that told the nurse's station at a glance how Georgia was doing. There was also a nurse in the room, adjusting the machines that pumped medications through clear plastic lines into Georgia.

As they approached the bed Will cleared his throat. Mrs. Amando looked up, and both men realized that she'd been napping sitting up. She stood as they got closer.

"You're here to see my daughter?" she asked.

"Yes ma'am, we are. We've met before, the other day when your daughter was brought in. We're the detectives investigating her kidnapping, and we received a call that she wanted to see us."

Lucinda Amando nodded. "I try to get her to rest but she won't. She wants you to catch the men that do this to her. She say she no can rest till you find them. My daughter is scared, she is afraid the men will come back for her." Lucinda Amando's Italian accent prompted the two men to listen closely. They could hear the emotion in her voice, they could see the love and, something else—the maternal instinct to protect her young.

"We understand, please let her know there's an officer outside her door all the time. He won't let anyone in unless they have clearance from you and her father." Will spoke in a hushed voice so as not to wake Georgia.

"I'm awake, detectives, you can talk to me," Georgia mumbled through a badly bruised jaw. She had two black eyes and she was terribly swollen. She looked even worse than the first time they'd seen her. The bandages wrapped around her face and across her forehead made her look almost mummified. One of her legs was in traction. Neither Will nor Jerry had realized she had a broken leg. Her hands were casted, with just her fingertips showing beneath the bandages—most of her fingers had been broken.

"Ms. Amando," Jerry started.

"It's Georgia, please," she mumbled.

"Okay, Georgia, can you tell us what happened to you? We need as much detail as you are able to give us. If at any time you feel too tired to go on, just say so, and we can pick up where we left off later. Do you understand?"

"I speak fluent English, gentlemen, I was born here. My parents are from Italy. To be honest I don't speak much Italian."

Jerry and Will looked at each other. This was a strong young woman who had been through the worst and somehow survived. But her speech was slow and difficult. They both looked around for chairs. Seeing two in the corner, they pulled them up and sat down. Both men had taken writing tablets from their inner pockets.

"Go ahead Georgia; we're ready when you are," Will said, trying to smile. She looked so tiny and broken lying there, it was hard to stay objective. He knew that in just a few minutes, if she faced this as she did everything else, it was going to get even harder.

Georgia seemed to go into a trance as she started speaking. Her mother reached out and took her bandaged, casted hand as gently as she could.

"I left work with my dress and shoes for prom slung over my shoulder. I had my keys in my hand, and I remember someone offered to walk me to my car. I had parked under the streetlight, so I said no. I heard them, but I didn't really feel there was any danger till they got closer. Somehow they got between me and my car, I think, or, oh gosh, some of this is still so fuzzy. I have trouble with names and things that I used to know. Bear with me, please." Georgia was softly crying. She shuddered and took a deep breath, as deep as her four cracked ribs would allow.

"The one man, Mike was his name, grabbed me from behind and shoved me up against my car. I dropped my dress on the ground and I could feel him pressing his hips into me. I heard the tires of a car squeal behind me, and I thought someone had come to help me. But the man Mike pulled me into the car. I hit my head and I could feel the blood running down my scalp later. Funny, how you think of those things. He grabbed my hair and turned my head so that I could see out the back window as the man in the front drove us away. Then he turned my head toward him and kissed me. His hands were all over me, and the man in the front wanted to watch him rape me. Oh God, he raped me in front of that other man. He pulled me down on the seat, and he raped me. I couldn't stop him. I tried, but he hit me so hard I felt numb all over. All I could think about was Joey and our baby, so I let him. I had to let him."

Painful sobs wracked Georgia's body. Her mother dabbed the tears streaming down her daughter's face. "Georgie, maybe we can wait some more, do this a little bit at a time."

"No," Georgia said firmly. "I want this done. I want those men caught before they do this to anyone else. They killed Amanda and they would have killed me if those men hadn't come to rescue me."

Georgia started again, and again the trancelike state seemed to take over. Jerry looked at Will as he saw the glazed look come over her face.

"They took my clothes, and all I had on were my socks. I was cold, but every time I asked for something, Mike would pinch me and ask me if I wanted some more. The man in the front seat, the driver, kept asking Mike if he could have a turn. It was more than an hour before Mike let him. Mike raped me again. Then he told, um, he told, Tony, that's his name, he told Tony to pull over. I was going to run away if I got the chance, even if I had to run naked. But Mike tied my hand to the seat bracket and pulled the top half of my body near to the floor before he got out. Tony came around to the back seat and raped me, and I never even saw his face. He punched my back and slapped me hard, and I never saw his face."

Through it all, Georgia let the tears slip unattended down her face. Every now and then her mother would wipe them away, but the narrative never stopped, like the narrative of a movie that no one would want to watch.

"Later, when we got to a real bumpy road," Georgia continued, "Tony climbed over the seat and sat with Mike. Mike asked him if he got enough. They were talking about me, a human being, like I was an object, a piece of furniture or a piece of pie. And they left me like that, tied to the seat bracket and naked in the back seat of that car. I managed to get my hand loose with my other hand and I waited till they came to a slow turn in the bumpy road. Then I opened the door and tried to jump out. But the light from the car door being opened caught their attention, and Tony grabbed me by my hair. I couldn't get all the way out the door and it kept banging on me as they drove to the camp site where I was rescued.

"Mike beat me terribly after that. He broke my fingers for untying myself. Then both of them dragged me over to a big tree stump. Mike had sent Tony for some light and he came back with a lantern, the kind you use when you camp. When the light shone on the tree stump I could see blood, oh my God, I could see Amanda's blood. I started to scream. No matter how hard Mike hit me, I couldn't stop it. He punched me in the mouth, and I guess I lost consciousness. When I woke up I was shackled to that tree stump. My legs and wrists were held to the ground, and I couldn't see anything; but Mike was raping me again. He didn't even care if I was awake or not. I threw up again and again. They were so drunk, and they would pour whatever it was they were drinking on me, or blow that awful smoke in my face. It seemed to make what they were doing to me more bearable somehow. I was out of it most of the time. When I wasn't, I wished I was. They wouldn't untie me so that I could use the bathroom or anything. I had to urinate right where I was, tied to that tree stump."

Georgia cried again, this time almost inconsolably. Her shoulders shook, and since one of them was broken, it hurt her to cry. Her trancelike state seemed to slip from time to time, and it was then Jerry and Will saw her pain. The trance seemed to buffer her but when it slipped, the tragedy she'd suffered and the proof of her youth and vulnerability came out.

Jerry and Will couldn't believe the strength of this woman. To them the saddest thing was that she wasn't even afforded the soothing comfort of a good cry; the pain was too great. They watched her grapple for the strength to control herself.

Her mother fussed over her and fingered the beads in her other hand. "Say the rosary, Georgie, say it with momma," she would whisper. And Georgia would. For five minutes or more the whispering would go on. It seemed to give both women strength, and the detectives gave them the time they needed.

"They talked about Amanda Wiggins. They danced wildly around the campfire and laughed about her crawling around on the ground begging for mercy. Tony would get on his hands and knees and imitate Amanda. It was horrible, but I know that Mike is the one who killed her and that Tony never did anything to her, because they fought about it. Mike is the stronger of the two and he's a bully, even to Tony. He treats Tony like a kid brother. Does that make sense?" Both detectives nodded.

"When they could tell I was awake, usually one of them would rape me again, sometimes both of them. I don't remember how many times, I lost count. I just lay there and prayed, and God heard my prayers. You know, I swear one time I felt the touch of an angel while I was lying there, tied to that tree in that humiliating way. Something touched me, soft and tender, and someone whispered in my ear, 'You will not die, little one. God has great plans for you. Be brave, pray and believe.' And I did, I stayed as still as I could, and I waited. Finally when it seemed as if the two of them couldn't go any further, they started talking about being hungry. But Mike came over to me again. He hit me, pulled my hair, and banged my head on the tree stump. All I ever thought about was being strong, strong for me, for my baby and for Joey, but also for Amanda. She suffered worse than I did, much worse, if that's possible."

Georgia's voiced trailed off, and for a moment Jerry and Will thought she had fallen asleep. Just as they were about to leave, she started talking again. "Mike thought I was dead, and something in me, some inner heavenly magic allowed me to still my breathing, to calm my nerves and to lie as still as possible even through all he did to me. They covered me with a plastic sheet of some kind. For that moment I felt safe. I saw the face of God, detectives; He was under that plastic sheet with me, holding my hand. Do you believe me?"

Will and Jerry seemed to be falling into Georgia's trance, too. They nodded, and as they did, the calm that settled over the room was warm and amazing. A horrific story was being told, and yet both men felt serene. Georgia's mother smiled as she wiped her daughter's eyes again.

"I felt so relieved, I just lay there and waited, and then I heard them drive off. Can you even imagine how I felt? It was over, and the thought that they would come back for me never entered my mind until after I had been rescued. I was afraid for a minute when the plastic was lifted, but then this wonderful soft voice spoke to me, just to me, and said, 'Fear not, you are safe.' And I was. The men who came for me gave me a blanket and carried me away. But then I remembered Mike and Tony and I was so afraid that we wouldn't get away before they came back. Do you know what that told me?"

The detectives shook their heads in unison. "It told me that God had let me go, let the situation go, that the men who had come had come at His command, but that now it was up to them. I felt Him go. I know it sounds so odd, but I swear I felt it all. I saw it all, I was there. My mom and dad believe me, Joey believes me. I can see by your faces that you feel it, too. You believe me, don't you?"

"I do, I believe you, because I have just listened to a brave young woman describe a terrible experience, and I feel so calm. But I've never felt this way before, in all my years as a policeman or detective. In my line of work you struggle with your faith. It's hard to keep believing when you face tragedy every day," Will said. "Thank you for sharing that with us."

Jerry just nodded. He felt overwhelmed and close to tears. "Is there anything else you want to tell us, Georgia, before we go?" Will asked.

"Yes, Mike is about five feet six inches tall. He has dirty blonde hair and has had very little education. He weighs about a hundred and sixty-five pounds, but he argued about that with Tony. I think he's from Illinois or Michigan because they talked about those places. Tony is taller, six feet, but skinny. I bet he weighs about a hundred and forty-five pounds. He eats all the time, and he's slow, mentally I mean. He isn't retarded, but he's really slow and he does everything Mike tells him to do. And he's terrified of the water. Also he has a brother he cares a great deal about. He gets letters from him."

Finally, Georgia's voice faded. She was done, God had seen her through it. She smiled ever so slightly as she drifted off to sleep. Her mother too had dozed off.

Both men felt as if they were intruding now. Quietly they stood and returned their chairs to the corner. Will turned at the door to look one more time at the sleeping Georgia. She looked like a wounded angel.

Jerry saw it too. "I wonder sometimes about things like this, people like them, people that God seems to love so much He reaches out a special hand."

"Me too, partner, me too," Will said as he closed the door.

The ride back to the station was a quiet one. Finally, Jerry looked at Will and said, "Did you hear the tone of her voice?"

"Yes, I did, why?" Will said.

"It's just that this girl—she is just a girl, you know—goes through this horrible ordeal, and it's only been three days, and she talks about it like it was years ago. Calm with some tears, but more like it was a memory, like she would talk to a therapy group." Jerry looked confused. "I have to tell ya, we've been in this business for a long time and I have never interviewed anyone that calm after a kidnapping and multiple rape. I couldn't have done it. No way in hell would I have lived through that."

"Yeah, I know. I was thinking that same thing while we were in there with her, but did you notice that feeling in the room? Almost like a religious thing. A few years ago, Betty and I went to the Cathedral in Washington D.C., and believe me when I tell you it's a religious experience. Something about that girl and her mom made me feel the same way I did when I was in that church. Do you believe in miracles, Jerry?"

"I never thought much about them, but after that last few days I have to say yes. What I really would like to know, however, is why her, why save her and not Amanda Wiggins? When I die, I'm gonna have a long, hard talk with God and get me some answers to some of life's little mysteries, and some of the not so little ones. I mean, how does He pick which ones will and which ones won't be saved?"

"I don't know buddy, but let's keep this between us. Somehow I don't think the guys in the station are going to believe us," Will said as he parked.

Jerry nodded as he got out. "I'll see ya tomorrow. I'm gonna go home and get rip-roaring drunk, if you don't mind."

"You wanna come over for dinner Friday? I'm supposed to ask, and I always forget," Will said as he slammed the door.

"Sure, Friday's good. See ya in the morning."

"Yeah, see ya," answered Will.

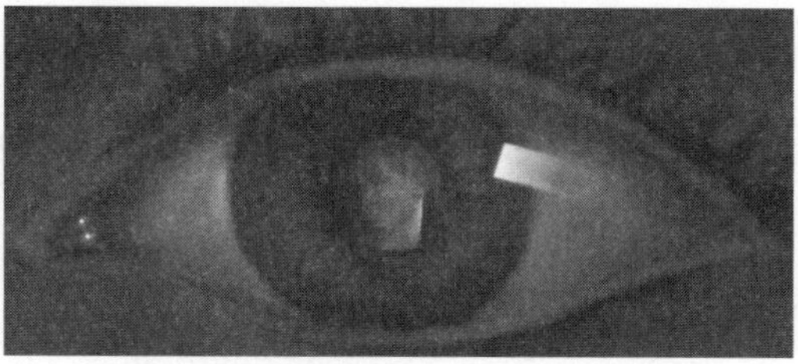

CHAPTER 35

In the police station near the mall, the end-of-day activity was taking place. Will and Jerry each had a Styrofoam cup of hot, stale coffee in one hand and a packet of papers in the other as they headed to the chief's office for the briefing they tried to attend at least once a week. Today they needed the input of other officers because they didn't have a damn thing, not one piece of solid information as to who these two perps were, where they'd come from, or where the hell they'd gone.

"Okay, everyone, let's settle down and come to order here," Captain Morris bellowed. He was a large man with a commanding presence. He'd been the captain of this police station for five years, and he had no intention of giving up his position. He liked his job, and he was only seven years away from retirement—not that he planned on retiring, but he wanted to retire from this position when he chose to. Damn thing was, right now his house was drawing a lot of unwanted attention from the higher-ups.

The media was camped outside and just this morning the mayor's secretary had called. It seemed the mayor wanted to meet with him sometime tomorrow. He had a little more than twelve hours before that meeting, and he intended to have answers. He needed some action. His ulcer was giving him a fit. He belched out loud and the smirks that went around the room drew a glare from him.

"I said, shut up!" he roared.

Will and Jerry slid into seats as he started talking. "Someone tell me something. Ah, I see our famous detectives have decided to join us this evening. Let's start with the two of you. What've ya got?"

Jerry and Will looked at one another. They cleared their throats, and the "ums" and "ahs" started.

"Well, I'm not hearing anything worth hearing. Do you have anything on these two wackos yet?" the captain wanted to know.

"Well, sir, we have a lot of stuff that went to the lab, and none of it's back yet. We do know that the perp in the Wiggins and Amando cases is the same guy, and from what eyewitnesses have told us we know there's two guys. Hugh Brandt and Marvin Hiller told us they saw two of them. From the findings at the campsite we are sure of a few things, but if you want to know where they are, we don't have a clue. That's why we're here today, we need help," Jerry said, returning to his seat. He'd stood through his speech and felt like the spotlight was on him. And in truth, it was—on him, on Will, on the whole forensic team.

Will and Jerry could see the captain winding up for a big blow, but just then the door to the room opened, and Sergeant Strider poked his head in, "Will, Jerry, we may have another one. I need you out here." Both felt they'd been saved from certain doom. But this wasn't the salvation they would have chosen.

As they exited the room, Sergeant Strider said, "I just got a call from a man, Don Corley, he's a hotshot lawyer. Seems his daughter is missing. She wasn't at school today, and she never made it home."

"What makes you think it's one of ours, Ray?" Will asked.

"Call it gut instinct. Call it a hunch. But this one reeks of trouble. The best friend hasn't seen her either, and to me that's the strangest thing of all. She leaves a note saying she's going to her best friend's late last night but never makes it. I just have a feeling, that's all."

Will and Jerry nodded. "Did she go to the mall? Both of our girls were taken from the mall. I would expect that to be the first hint of trouble." Jerry asked.

"No, nothing like that, but if you think about it, when's the last time we had a missing person?"

"Ray's right, Jerry," Will said. "We need to check this out. Besides, do you really wanna go back in there?" He was gesturing with his thumb in the direction of the field room.

Within twenty minutes Will and Jerry were pulling into the large circular driveway of the Corley home. As the car came to a stop, they were greeted by Phyllis and Don Corley. After introductions and an offer of something to drink, the Corleys sat and explained the story to Will and Jerry, the whole story. Starting with the divorce and ending with Wanda's disappearance. Phyllis sat quietly by Don's side. Neither of them answered the ringing phone while they were talking. Will and Jerry observed a friend or housekeeper answering the phone that rang every few minutes.

Finally, Jerry asked, "Sir, how do you know who's calling? I mean, if my daughter were missing I would sit on that phone."

"That sir, is my soon to be ex-girlfriend. I have been seeing Daphne Horstle. Yes, that is Judge Horstle's ex-wife. I will admit that I've made a few mistakes. Let's call it a midlife crisis and leave it at that. And no, my daughter didn't approve of her. But I don't think she would have run away from her mother because of that." Don was being as direct as he could be.

"I understand, sir," Jerry said. And in fact he did, all too well. His divorce was only a year old. His wife had found someone else in all the hours she spent alone. She had left him and taken the two boys with her. Jerry felt the loneliness, but he also felt the helplessness. He didn't know know what to do any more than Don Corley seemed to.

"Mr. Corley, you've been very candid. Thank you for that. Can we have Lilly Williams's phone number and address, please, and we'll get started looking for your daughter. If she comes home, please call us. Mrs. Corley, please keep going through that address book of your daughter's and calling all her friends, even those she seems to have lost contact with. We'll alert the police department and have them out looking for her as well. What kind of car does she drive?" Will was making notes as they stood to go. He shook hands with the Corleys and promised to call when he had some news.

The two detectives left with a photograph of Wanda Marie Corley and an address for Lilly Williams in their possession. As they got into the car they looked at one another.

"What do you think?" Will asked.

"I'm not sure. Something's fishy, but to be honest, it's just too different. I mean, we have no reason to believe she might have been abducted. This sounds like a spoiled little rich kid trying to get back at her parents to me." Jerry just didn't see the connection.

"I have to say I agree. Let's hand this one off to Sam Kent. He has a lighter load, and I think we really need to stay focused on our case. If something comes up in the meantime, we'll look into it," Will said.

Then the radio in their car crackled. Will drove while Jerry reached for the mike. "Go ahead, dispatch."

"Sir, the sketch artist is finished with Mr. Brandt and Mr. Hiller, and the sketch of your possible perpetrator is complete. He asked me to let you know."

Will and Jerry had totally forgotten that Hugh and Marvin were coming in this afternoon to help make a sketch of the two men they'd seen with Georgia Amando. It had taken a week for the sketch artist to get down their way. "Dispatch, we'll be right there. And dispatch, can you have Detective Sam Kent meet us in the conference room?" Jerry asked.

Jerry and Will felt excited for the first time in days. "Finally, a break; this should keep the captain off our asses for a bit and give patrol something to look for," Jerry said.

Will just nodded. His mind was back at the Corley house. "Hey, Jerry, let's at least visit with Lilly Williams before we pass this off to Sam. I want to give him something to work with so he won't feel like he's getting our castoffs."

"Okay, makes sense. You aren't considering taking this on full time, are you?" Jerry asked.

"No, I just wanna do some checking first, okay?"

"Yeah, okay," Jerry said.

They rode in silence to the station, where Sam Kent met them "Hey, what's up? I heard you wanted to talk to me. Also, it's almost seven o'clock. Don't the two of you ever go home?"

"Yeah, and my wife is gonna skin my hide. We have a missing girl, seventeen-year-old Wanda Marie Corley, from the west side. But it seems more like a kid trying to punish newly divorced parents to us. We were wondering if we could give this one to you." Will said.

"Sure, how long has she been missing?" Sam asked.

"Well, really since last night, but her parents just noticed this morning. She wasn't in her room when mom went to get her up for school. I have a feeling she's hanging out with this kid Lilly Williams. They've been palling around at school, and Mom and Dad Corley aren't too happy about it. Seems the Williams kid is a bit different, from the wrong side of the tracks, figuratively speaking." Jerry chuckled.

"Okay, I'll do a drive-by on my way home, and if the two of you fill out the paperwork I'll send some uniforms around to look into it. But I have to get home. Who's on for this evening?" Sam was already looking at his watch.

"We did the drive-by already. The paperwork is here," Jerry said as he handed the packet over to Sam. "Mark Handley is on for tonight. Maybe he can get started with this. Jerry and I will do the initial talk with Ms. Lilly, and we'll leave it on your desk for you first thing in the morning," Will said as he turned to go.

"Will, do you think this girl's a runaway?" Sam wanted to be sure before he dismissed this as just another runaway kid.

"Yeah, at this time I do. She's got it all and a loving set of parents who seem to have gotten off on the wrong foot. None of the circumstances are the same as the other two cases. But we still have to look into it. Handley can do it for tonight. We'll get some rest and start fresh first thing in the morning."

Will was reaching his hand out to the officer headed in his direction.

Taking the manila envelope, he mumbled thanks and turned it over to open it. Seeing the names Brandt and Hiller on the back of the envelope gave him a tremor. "The sketch artist has finished!" he said.

Sam and Jerry followed him into the conference room. All of the men present were silent. Sliding the drawing out of its wrapper was almost a religious experience. "Shit, they're scary looking even to me," Jerry said, as Will laid the two drawings face up on the table.

"Yeah," breathed Sam.

The sketches were actually very good. They had missed the mark on some things, but had done incredibly well on others. The likenesses of Tony Garrison and Mike Hennessey met their eyes.

"Hello, gentleman—and I use the term loosely," Will said.

"I wonder how accurate those are." Jerry pointed at the drawings.

"We'll know when we catch the bastards," Will said as he swept the drawings up and handed them to Jerry. "Ask the desk sergeant to make some copies of these and have them ready for distribution at a.m. roll call. It's been way too quiet lately. Something is fixin' to happen."

"Fixin', is that a Texas word?" Sam asked. Teasing Will was one of his favorite pastimes.

"Yes it is, smart ass. Don't you have a home to go to and a wife that will tear those ears off your head if you ain't there soon?"

"I'm as good as gone. See you two tomorrow. Make sure you go home some time tonight. I want you both fresh as daisies in the morning." Sam ducked out of the room as Will wadded up the envelope and threw it at his head.

"Will, something's wrong. I'm not sure what it is but something ain't quite right. Do you have the same feeling?" Jerry asked. He looked troubled.

"Yeah, I do. Let's go talk to Ms. Lilly Williams. I smell a rat. I'm gonna call home first, or I'm the one that won't have ears in the morning. Can you talk to Mark Handley and give those to Ray?" Will asked, motioning toward the sketches.

"Consider it done. I'll meet you at the car." Jerry went in one direction as Will went in the other.

CHAPTER 36

Lilly sat opposite Will and Jerry with a stone face.

"Ms. Williams do you realize that your friend Wanda could be in serious danger?" Will asked. He just couldn't believe what he was hearing.

"Yeah, but she's okay. I mean she just wants some time away from her mom. The bitch is always griping at her, making her clean her room or something like that. She takes Wanda's car all the time. She just needs a break. She'll be back."

"Do you know where Wanda is? Have you talked to her today?" Jerry asked.

"No, but I know she's okay." Lilly wouldn't budge. She sat on the sofa in her parent's apartment and pulled at a string that had come loose from the corner.

"Lilly stop that!" her mother said.

Lilly turned and glared at her mom. "Leave me alone or I'm going with Wanda. Would you like that, you bitch?"

Jerry jumped up and grabbed Lilly from the couch. Turning her around, he handcuffed her "You're going for a ride, missy."

"For what? You can't arrest me, I'm a minor and I ain't done nothing wrong." Lilly was struggling in his grasp. She raised her foot to kick him in the shins just as Will pushed her leg out of the way.

"Let's start with obstruction of justice. Harboring a runaway and talking back to your mother. Give me a few minutes more of wrestling with you and I'll add resisting arrest."

"It ain't against the law to talk back to your mother," Lilly said.

"Yeah? When did you graduate from law school?" Jerry was getting winded struggling with the girl.

"Leave me alone, pig," Lilly yelled.

"That's it. Open the door Will. Let's take her downtown for the night. We'll see if she's more cooperative in the morning."

Will knew this routine. They could take Lilly downtown, but she really hadn't done anything wrong other than mouth off and refuse to give information which she might or might not have. Jerry was playing bad cop. It was now Will's turn to play good cop.

"Lilly do you want to spend the night in lock-up? Have you ever been locked up before?" Will was looking down at the struggling girl. Her parents were shocked at the way their daughter was acting. She'd been difficult lately, but they had never seen her this bad.

"No and I ain't going tonight either. You can't take me unless my mom and dad say so. I know my rights." Lilly raised the foot again and this time Will let Jerry take it on the leg.

"Damn it!" Jerry yelled.

"Well now, Ms. Lilly, you have assaulted an officer. I guess you know that now you're going, no matter what!" Will grabbed her cuffed wrists and twisted them higher behind her back as Jerry rubbed his leg. He was glaring at Will who shrugged his shoulders and looked apologetic

Lilly's parents stood up, shock on their faces. "Do you really have to take her?"

"Yes ma'am we do. She's assaulted an officer and she's withholding information about a runaway. She'll go before the judge in the morning. You can be there at nine if you want to, but the wait could be a long one. I'd get there about one-thirty if I were you. She won't be processed before then anyway." Will was escorting Lilly to the door.

Lilly started crying then. Will and Jerry had expected it a little sooner but she'd held out. Now the tears flowed freely. "Okay I'll tell you where she might be. I don't want to go to jail," Lilly said through her tears.

Will stopped walking her in the direction of the door. Jerry reached around him and opened it for emphasis.

"We met a couple of guys at the carnival the other night. That was before I started dating Hickey. We were supposed to meet them last night. I didn't go because Hickey would have been mad. He's kind of jealous. I bet that's were she is." Lilly looked up through tear-drenched eyes. "Are you going to take me to jail?"

Will and Jerry felt the tremor again at the same time. "Shit!" Will said as he thrust Lilly into Jerry's arms. He ran out the door and jerked open his car door. He grabbed the copy of the sketches he had made before leaving the patrol barn.

"Please God, please let me be wrong," he whispered as he raced back into the house. Jerry had known all along what was going through his partner's mind. That's what happens when you work well with someone even for a short time. You can read your partner's mind. And what he was reading wasn't good.

Will held the sketches out to Lilly. "Are these the two men you met at the carnival?" Lilly looked at the sketches. As she studied them, Will and Jerry were praying for a negative response, but it didn't come.

"Yeah that's them. I mean it kind of looks like them. Why, what'd they do?" Lilly was shaking all of a sudden. Something in the demeanor of the two officers made her scared, not for herself this time but for Wanda.

"They kidnapped and raped a classmate of yours, Georgia Amando, and they may have kidnapped and murdered Amanda Wiggins," Will said slowly. He watched Lilly for a reaction.

"Oh my God," Lilly said as she sank back to the couch. She was crying softly now. "Wanda called my house late last night. She left a message on the answering machine telling me that she was going to the carnival to meet Tony and Mike. She wanted me to go, but I sneaked out to be with Hickey," she said, turning to look at her parents. "It was late and I had turned off the ringers in the house. It's what we do when we want to talk late at night. Then we pick up the phone every few minutes to see if anyone's there. I didn't get her message till this morning after I talked to her mom. Do you think she's okay? I mean they seemed so nice to us. I just can't believe they're the ones that did all that stuff to Georgia and Amanda." Lilly laid her head on her knees and sobbed.

Jerry reached over and removed the handcuffs that held her hands behind her back. As she rubbed her wrists she cried out loud. "It's all my fault. I'm the reason she's into all this. I kind of led her along. She was such a goody-goody. I like her and all but shit, I mean shoot," she said as she looked at her mom. But her mother wasn't looking at her. Her mom had her fist over her mouth. Lilly's father was glowering at his daughter.

Will and Jerry were thinking as quickly as they could. Standing between the father and his daughter Will said, "We need to get an investigation started, Lilly. It doesn't matter right now whose fault this is. We need your help to make these sketches as good as we can. Will you do that, will you come with us, not under arrest but as a witness to help our sketch artist make these more accurate?" Lilly nodded. Her parents stood to go with her. As her mom grabbed a sweater off the couch, her father stuffed a pack of cigarettes in his shirt pocket.

"Folks, we can bring her back in about an hour if you want to stay here. I mean you're certainly welcome to go, but you don't have to. She isn't under arrest," Jerry said.

"No we've done enough damage to this family. It's time we stood together," Mr. Williams said. "And when we get home some things are going to change around here, like no more Hickey."

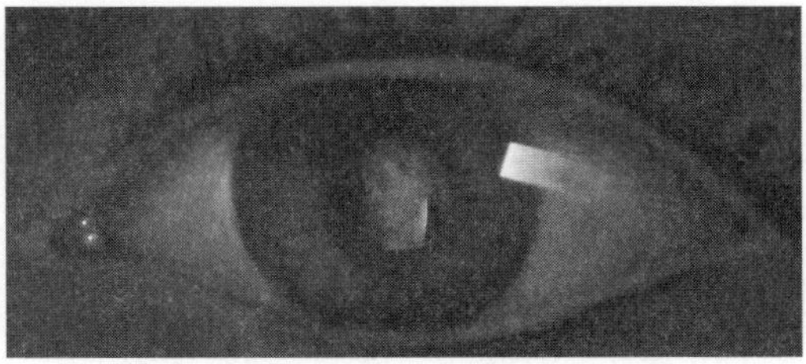

CHAPTER 37

Lindsay sat at the dinner table in silence. Marie and Jackie sat opposite her.

"Mom, are you okay?" Marie was just over for dinner. She lived a short distance away with her husband. But tonight he was working late.

"Yes, sweetie, I'm fine. I'm just tired. This shift at the hospital seems worse every year. I would love to retire, but Lord knows I'm years away from that. Jackie, chew with your mouth closed and sit up straight."

Lindsay did look tired. She wasn't sleeping well, and the hours at the hospital were taking their toll on her. Jackie seemed to be acting out as well. The overtime was nice in the paycheck, but bad for everything else.

"Are you off this weekend?" Marie asked.

"Yes, thank God. I'm going to sleep late and then take Jack to the beach. Do you want to go with us?"

"No, I can't, but I'm glad you're off. You look beat. Dinner's good. Can I take a plate home to Jerry?" Marie's husband Jerry worked hard. He always seemed emotionally distant, but he was good to her. Perhaps that's just his personality, Lindsay thought.

"Sure you can. There's plenty. I still cook like I'm cooking for a large family. It's a habit I haven't been able to break." Jack got up and went to the sink with his plate. He scraped the remains into the garbage disposal and then let the plate fall into the sink.

"Jackie, be careful," Marie said.

"My name is Jack; don't call me Jackie anymore. It's a baby's name." Jackie was getting older and he had started to exert his independence.

Marie smiled and raised her eyebrows as she glanced at her mother, "I'm sorry, Jack." But he'd run off already, heading to his room to play with his toys.

"He's growing up so fast. In no time at all I'll be alone in this big house, all my kids grown and gone." Lindsay seemed melancholy. Perhaps it was the fatigue she was feeling.

"Mom, gosh! We're not gone. Maybe grown, but not gone, and the grown part just depends on which of us you're talking about. Melissa will never grow up. Have you heard from her lately?" Marie asked, as she stood to help her mother clear the table.

"No, you know how she is. I worry about her but it seems there's nothing I can do. She has a mind of her own."

"Well, she better start getting it together. I need to get home. I'll give Jerry your love." Marie kissed her mom on the cheek and headed out the door with her care package. Jack hollered a goodnight from his bedroom. Marie hollered back. The door closed, and the melancholy Lindsay had been feeling settled in like a cloak.

She loaded the dishwasher and made herself a cup of tea. As she wrapped her hands around the warm mug, the feeling of depression seemed to lift some. Taking her tea, she wandered outside to sit in the swing under the huge oak. Jack came outside to sit with her. He climbed up in the swing and rested his head on her shoulder. She wrapped her arms around him. Sometimes he was still so young, still her baby. She breathed in the scent of him. He still smelled like a little boy, not great, just comforting. They sat there together and rocked long into the evening. The stars came out, and Lindsay took off her sweater and draped it over Jackie as he slept in her lap.

She shivered slightly as the chill settled around her, but she wasn't ready yet to go in. The beautiful night sky seemed like salve to her tired soul, as the stars and planets twinkled above. Lindsay tilted her head, first in one direction, then in the other.

"What was that? Is someone there?" Feeling the first tingles of alarm, she started to gather Jackie into her arms when she realized what it was. "Ah, something's coming. I hear it in the wind. Something bad is heading in our direction." Lindsay picked her son up and walked into the house. She pulled the covers on her bed back and tucked him in. "Let him sleep with me tonight," she thought, as she went to change into her pajamas.

She thought about her teacup and went back outside to retrieve it. As she turned to go back in, that feeling that someone was watching crept up her spine. It was all she could do to keep from running. As she cleared the doorway she hurriedly threw the lock into place. "Now I'm being silly," she thought out loud to herself. But she checked the lock again just to be sure. As she turned out the lights, she glanced at the telephone. "Are you going to ring soon or do I have to watch the news to find out what's coming?" she asked it. Needless to say, she got no reply. "Well, suit yourself. I know it's just a matter of time. Goodnight," Lindsay said as she clicked off the lamp.

CHAPTER 38

Rake and Aletha Wiggins stood to go, as Rake shook the man's hand. "Thank you, Mr. Breaux. We love the stone. Our daughter would appreciate all your hard work and how quickly you handled things."

"Mr. Wiggins, it's been nice to meet you. I'm just sorry it happened under these circumstances. My condolences to you and your family."

"Thank you, sir. I would love to tell you we're mending, but I'd be lying." Rake Wiggins had the look of a man in pain. His face bore the signs of extreme fatigue. His wife seemed to be covered in shadows. Her mouth smiled, but not her eyes.

"She's grieving," Matthew Breaux thought to himself. "Mr. Wiggins, if you don't mind sir, can I ask you something in private?"

"Sure you can. Aletha, I'll meet you by the car. Tell the boys I'll be right out." Rake waited for her to leave the office before turning to the man. "What can I do for you?" He was ready for the usual questions about his daughter. Most people didn't mean any harm. They just couldn't help themselves.

"Sir, I don't mean to pry. But are you and your family getting counseling? I mean, my wife is a licensed therapist. Maybe she could help you all deal with this terrible thing. I can't imagine going through anything this bad. I don't know what I would do. Perhaps you and your family feel the same way."

Tears filled Rake's eyes. He held his hand out again. "I think you're right, Matthew. I have to say we aren't doing very well. The boys aren't back in school yet. I can't seem to get back to my office, and Aletha has turned Mandy's room into a shrine. Can I have your wife's number?"

Matthew scribbled the number on a piece of paper. "She'll be glad to hear from you. I know she can help you."

Rake thanked the man and turned to go. As he joined his family, they held hands and walked across the cemetery. The flowers in their tall stands still graced the gravesite. They had lost their first bloom, and their edges were dried and cracked. They hung their pretty heads as if in grief, too.

It was a miracle to have received the headstone for Mandy's grave so soon. When Rake had contacted Matthew Breaux, his voice had cracked several times as he told the sympathetic ear on the other end of the phone what his family had been through.

"I want a pink granite stone with two angels carved into it. I want it to be beautiful, graceful, and pink, just like my daughter. She was seventeen years old when a madman took her life. We need closure, all of us. Maybe this will help." Rake wasn't even sure if the man at the other end was listening.

"I will do my best, Mr. Wiggins," he finally heard.

And now he stood and looked down at the marker that would represent his daughter in her final resting place. It was truly beautiful. The edges were scalloped, white and pink. The twin angels were on either side of her name and the dates of her birth and death. Rake, Aletha, and the boys stood and gazed at the beautiful marker.

The dirt was still showing on top of the gravesite. The flowers just covered the center. The grass hadn't packed down, and it was clear to everyone in the area what site the family of four now stood beside. Aletha knelt by the beautiful stone. She ran her hands over it, enjoying the coolness of it under her fingertips.

"She would love this, Rake. Gosh, it's beautiful," she said, as she started to cry.

The boys slipped to their knees beside her. "Mom, please don't cry anymore. I can't stand it. Mandy wouldn't want you to."

Aletha looked at her youngest son. "I have to, sweetie. I just can't seem to help myself. We all have to cry and get it out. That's part of the grieving process."

"Aletha," Rake said quietly. "We need help, we need professional help. Matthew Breaux's wife is a licensed therapist. I think we need to make an appointment to see her."

But Aletha wasn't listening to him. She had laid her head down on the new pink stone and started whispering to it. Rake knew she was talking to Mandy. But Mandy was dead and couldn't hear her.

"Aletha, come on honey. Please get up, do it for the boys." Rake looked at his sons. Tears were streaming down their faces. Then he heard an awful sound. His wife was moaning, getting louder and louder.

"Rake, oh God, I can hear her. She's begging me to get her out of the dark." Suddenly Aletha was on her knees digging furiously at Amanda's grave. Rake and the boys stared in horror.

Steven, the older boy, reacted first. "Mom, what are you doing? Stop it!" he screamed.

"No, no, I have to get her out of there. She's in the dark. Stevie, Rake, help me. You know Mandy's scared of the dark. Help me!" she screamed as she dug at the soft earth with her bare hands. Huge clumps of dirt were coming away fast. She was hysterical and her strength seemed almost superhuman. Rake looked around as Steven wrestled with his mother. He seemed lost and uncertain. He looked around for help.

Kyle, Steve, and Aletha were shocked out of their horror when Rake threw his head back and screamed, "Help!"

Kyle ran, screaming for help, toward the car. He got in and locked the door. Caretakers ran across the lawn to restrain Aletha Wiggins as she knelt by her daughter's grave. They could see the damage she'd done to the gravesite. Flowers were strewn about behind her. The dirt was torn away from the top layer. Rake stood there looking at her helplessly, and now Steve was sitting by her side, crying.

"I hate this family and what we've become. I loved Mandy, but she's gone, and what we're doing to ourselves is not going to bring her back. I'm taking Kyle and we're going to stay with Grandma and Grandpa until this is straightened out." Steve stood and brushed off his hands. "She's gone, mom, dad, she's gone." He turned and joined his brother in the car. At fifteen, he had matured suddenly and it seemed that now he was going to take charge of his life. Thank God he thought to include his younger brother.

The caretakers helped Rake get Aletha inside. She was a mess. Dirt clung to her hands and knees, and her hair was tangled. She looked wild and mentally unstable. The cemetery caretakers stayed with Rake while he waited for an ambulance.

It was clear to them all that she wouldn't be coming home that night. She held herself and rocked back and forth as she crooned, "Momma's gonna make it better, Manda Panda, Momma's gonna make it better." Tears marked fresh grooves down Rake's face.

A young couple who had been walking across the carefully tended lawn witnessed the drama from a distance. The young man stood still and leaned on his cane with one hand; with the other he clutched the hand of the girl with him. "This isn't a good idea. Let's wait, Cammy. I just can't go over there now. Not with the earth all torn up that way. Let's wait," Jeremy said as he wiped a tear away.

Cammy too was crying softly as she nodded. They turned to go and leaned on each other for support. They could be seen from a distance by anyone who cared to look. But lately, no one looked toward the cemetery. It was as if looking might bring bad luck to their family, as well.

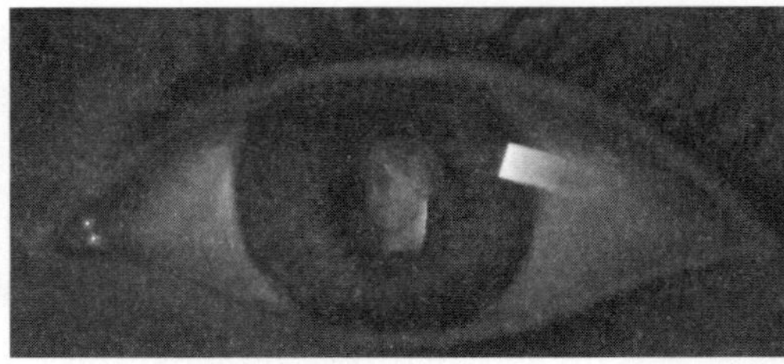

CHAPTER 39

Jerry and Will hurried back to the station, with Lilly and her family following in the family car. They radioed ahead to ask someone to call the sketch artist, Sam Kent, and Captain Morris and to have those three men ready for conference when they got there.

"Captain Morris isn't going to like being disturbed, sir," the dispatcher said.

"And I don't blame him, but he's going to dislike being left out of this even more. Call him!" Jerry yelled into the microphone.

"Gosh, Jer, bite her head off," Will said.

"We have another one. Do you realize that? Some time in the next few days we are going to have to knock at the door of some more parents and tell them that their daughter is dead. I don't want to do that, Will, do you?" Jerry was looking at him. Will could see the anger in his face and something else. He could see fear.

"I hate this case, Will. I really do. What the hell are we going to do? These guys seem to be one step ahead of us all the time."

"Jerry, don't take this personally. They aren't one step ahead of us, they aren't even aware we're the ones looking for them. They don't know who we are, they haven't seen us, and that gives us one up on them. Take a deep breath. We just got a huge break in this case, and Wanda Corley isn't dead yet. I hope." Will seemed calm as he drove to the station. In his mind he was going over what he would say to Captain Morris. He knew now that Wanda Corley was a victim. He knew he had to call her parents, but he just wasn't ready yet. He didn't know what to say. They really didn't know anything yet. Why ruin the last good night of sleep this couple would have for years to come? Let it rest until tomorrow, he thought to himself.

Jerry sat quietly, staring out the window at the city as it went to bed for the evening. As they pulled into the station the lights from the patrol barn brought him out of his thoughts. "Will, do you think we could wait until tomorrow morning to notify Wanda's parents?" Jerry seemed genuinely upset.

"My thoughts exactly, Jerry, since we don't really know anything anyway. Let's see what Lilly does to that sketch first. Then we'll make our plan."

Within two hours the sketch was revised considerably. The sketch artist wasn't happy when he'd been notified that he had to come back. But Lilly had done a remarkable job describing Tony Garrison and Mike Hennessey. She had brought them to life on paper, if that's possible, adding things here and there to the existing sketches. Somehow the images on paper now were scarier. Both men looked absolutely menacing.

Captain Morris agreed with Jerry and Will about contacting the Corleys. It just wasn't time yet, they all agreed. It was ten o'clock at night when they finally broke up.

"I'll see you all in the morning," Captain Morris said to Will, Jerry, and Sam.

The Williamses had already left and their moods collectively had been somber.

"Mom, do you think I should call Wanda's mother?"

"No, Lilly, let's just wait. Do you see what happens when you hang out with the wrong crowd? What the hell were the two of you thinking?"

"I'm sorry, Mom. I never thought about it. I mean... I'm sorry." Lilly was crying softly in the back seat. Her father was driving, and her mom was sitting in the passenger seat next to him. It had been years since they'd done anything together like this. Now here they were, all of them grieving, and finally acting like a family.

CHAPTER 40

Early the next morning, the phone on the sergeant's desk was ringing when Will walked past it. He gave a thumbs up to Ray Strider on his way by.

"Hey, hold up, buddy, I think this one's for you. A man says he thinks he saw a naked body on the side of the road as he was driving in this morning from Hill Valley. He says it's out on Highway 71 at the 298 marker." Will had stopped walking. Now he had a sick feeling in the pit of his stomach again.

"Get his name, Ray. I'll call him right back." Will continued toward his office. He needed coffee and some time to get himself together. He saw Jerry with his head down on the desk. "Hey man, what's up?" Will asked as he set his things down on his already overloaded desk.

"The damn phone hasn't quit ringing since I got here this morning. The Corley girl never made it home last night, needless to say. Her parents want information. They're asking questions like did we talk to Lilly Williams? What do you want to do, Will?" Jerry looked terrible.

"Did you go home last night? I could almost swear you smell like leftover bacon," Will teased.

"Yes, smart ass, I went home last night. But I couldn't sleep. This thing just kept running through my mind. We have to get to know these guys, Will. Somehow, some way, we have to get to know them so we can find them. They must be moving around like gypsies because even with all this manpower we haven't gotten one good lead on their whereabouts yet."

"Hey, man, hold on. We just got the picture of them out to the roll call. Someone is going to see them. I was thinking about going to the media with a copy of that sketch. My only problem with it is that every man out there who even slightly resembles them is going to be harassed, and our already overworked desk sergeant is going to be on our collective asses. Besides, we have something we have to go do. Things have a way of making themselves known."

Jerry looked up, "I don't wanna go do anything. I want some fresh coffee, and I want some sleep, and I want someone else to handle this damn case. It gives me the creeps. All night long I had the feeling that we were missing something." Jerry laid his head back down on his arms.

"Come on, sleepyhead. Sarge says we got a dead body out on the highway. A citizen called it in. Said he saw it near the 298-mile marker."

Will reached over and picked up his Styrofoam coffee cup. "What? You asshole! Why didn't you tell me? You just come in here all calm and acting like it's just gonna be another day. Damn it, Will, sometimes I think you have ice running in those veins of yours." Jerry was still fuming as they walked out the front door. Will made a slight detour and picked up the number of the man who had seen the possible D.B.

As he walked outside he could still hear Jerry bitchin'. "Damn you anyhow, Will Halpin. Sometimes you just flat-ass piss me off, do you know that?"

"Oh shut up. I told ya, didn't I? I mean it's not like I had you come out and get in the car and then tell ya. I gave you some warning—anyway, the drive is gonna take us twenty minutes. How much more time do you need to get ready for what we both know is coming?"

"What? You think this is Wanda Corley?" Jerry gaped at Will over the top of the car.

"Don't you?" Will asked.

"Shit, let's go. Damn it, what a fine day this is turning out to be." Today it was Jerry's turn to be in a mood. "Jer, my man, you know what you need?" Will asked as he backed out of his parking space. "You need to get laid, that's what you need."

"Up yours, Will. Leave me alone today, okay? I didn't sleep worth a damn. I'm tired, pissed off, and Marion called me last night. She wants more money. Now where, I ask you, am I supposed to get more money."

"Tell her to kiss it! The judge set the limit, the divorce is final, and it's time to let it go. You need to start having some fun, go out, meet new people, and remember that tonight is the night you're supposed to come for dinner. Dress nice, I think Betty wants you to meet someone." Will looked at Jerry. He did look terrible. "Are you coming down with something?"

"No, man, I'm sorry. Marion always makes me so damn mad. She's so greedy. She got the house, the car she wanted, and she got to keep all her stuff. What did I get?"

"It seems to me you got all the furniture, your truck, and the lake house," Will said.

"Yeah, I know I did. I'm just in a foul mood. Do you think Betty would mind if I passed on dinner tonight?" Jerry asked.

"Yeah, but let's leave it till the end of the day. I'll call her with an excuse if you really don't want to come. I can tell you, the girl's fine looking."

"What girl?" Jerry seemed slightly interested all of a sudden.

"The one Betty has invited to dinner tonight." Will was baiting him, and Jerry knew it.

"Yeah, what's she look like?" Jerry was definitely interested.

"She looks something like Betty, but she's younger. She's got brown hair and she's small, about five foot two."

"Does she have blue eyes?" Jerry asked.

"What? What difference does that make?"

"You know, that old song, 'Has Anybody Seen My Girl?' Five foot two, eyes of blue, coochey, coochey, coochey, coo, has anybody seen my girl?" Jerry was singing now.

"There it is," Will pointed suddenly. Jerry looked in the direction of Will's forefinger. Sure enough, there was a naked body lying on the side of the road. They parked across the street and got out. They got rubber boots, gloves, and overcoats out of the trunk. They took in the site, making mental notes of their surroundings. The body was lying on its side, more face down than right side up. There seemed to be multiple lacerations and abrasions. As they walked across the street they could tell that the body, female most likely, had been dragged for quite some time. The skin was missing in patterns that suggested a dragging death. As they got closer, they could see multiple puncture marks and then brown hair. Will walked back across the street and reached into his car. He called the station on his radio. After asking for backup he took out his recorder and started his narration. Jerry had his notepad out, and he was flipping through the pages.

"Will, what did Wanda Corley's parents say she had on when they last saw her?"

"They didn't say. Remember, no one saw her leave. Why?" Will asked as he got closer.

"Well this young woman, age approximately seventeen, has a red and white checkered something or other torn into what appears to be strips and tied around her head. I can see the brown hair but we really can't see much else." Will walked up behind him with the camera.

After taking several pictures of the body and the surroundings, Will and Jerry turned the young woman over. Taking the picture from his pocket, Jerry said, "We have a match. It's Wanda Marie Corley."

In the following hours Wanda's body was treated much like Amanda Wiggins's had been. She had been photographed, measured, and then moved. The site had been combed for clues. Baggies had been marked Corley rather than Wiggins. The day wore on, traffic backed up, and traffic cops tried to keep things moving. There had been numerous calls to the station that morning to report the D.B. on the side of the road. So Will and Jerry knew they couldn't keep this under wraps any longer. After filing away their findings in the trunk filing cabinet, Will and Jerry went to do what they hated most, tell the family that their child wouldn't be coming home tonight, or any other night, for that matter.

They drove in silence to the Corley home. All the money in the world wasn't going to help the Corleys take this. "You know they don't live together," Jerry said as they drove.

Will nodded. "I had the dispatcher call Mr. Corley's residence and ask for him. He said he would meet us at his ex-wife's."

"Do you think he knows?" Jerry inquired.

"Yeah, he didn't ask, but I would say he has to know. He just said he would meet us there." Will wiped a hand across his tired face.

It was two o'clock in the afternoon by the time Will and Jerry pulled into the Corley driveway. They could see Don's BMW parked in front. The couple stood waiting for them at the door. Will and Jerry ushered them back inside the house. The press would be right behind them. Personal grief triggered a feeding frenzy for the press, and this was the third victim.

"Mr. and Mrs. Corley, there's no easy way to say this." Will started.

Phyllis started crying, and Don took a deep breath. He instinctively put his arm around her and she laid her head on his shoulder. Gone was the animosity, replaced by grief. Given the choice, Jerry would have taken the anger any day. Will continued, "We found a young woman's body out on the highway about twenty miles from here. She matches the description of your daughter. We'll need you, Mr. Corley, to come with us to identify her if you will." Will was clasping his trembling hands together to still them.

"Of course I will. Are you sure it's her?" Don asked.

"No sir, not completely. That's why we need a positive I.D. Did your daughter have an appendectomy scar?" Will asked.

With those words, Phyllis Corley screamed out her pain. She had sat with Wanda for five days when she'd had her appendix out. Wanda had developed an infection and had to stay longer than the customary seventy-two hours. "Oh God, Oh God," she screamed as she sank to the floor. Don reached down and picked her up.

"Phyll, come on honey, be strong. I'm gonna call Elise to come and sit with you. Hang on to my neck, let me help you." Don picked her up easily. Setting her gently on the couch, he grabbed the phone. Dialing and waiting, he stroked her forehead; finally he said something into the phone and then hung up. "Detectives, my sister is on her way to sit with my wife. I'll meet you at the hospital in a few minutes, assuming that's where they've taken her."

"We'll wait and take you there. Then we'll bring you back, if that's okay with you, Mr. Corley," Jerry said. "It's customary."

"Fine, fine," Don mumbled. Phyllis was lying on the couch, holding Don's hand in a tight grip.

"Don't leave me, Don, please don't leave me," she moaned.

"I have to go see about Wanda, Phyll, but I'll be back. I'll call you if things change, but I will be back," he said, looking directly into her eyes.

The doorbell rang, and Don's sister Elise came into the room. "Barry's in the car, Don, he wants to go with you." Barry was Elise's husband of twenty-three years. They had married the year before Don and Phyllis and had stood up for each other. Elise sank onto the sofa and took Phyllis's hand.

Phyllis laid her head in Elise's lap and sobbed, "My baby, oh God, my beautiful child."

At the city morgue Jerry and Will watched as another father identified his child. They heard the cries of anguish and felt the sorrow in their own hearts. Don Corley laid his hand on his daughter's head. He kissed her cheek and then vowed to find the man or men who had done this and take what they had taken, life. Jerry looked over his bent head into Will's eyes. They both knew that if the time came, they would look the other way. Let him find his comfort any way he could. God knew they would want the chance.

Across town, Mike and Tony had passed out. The carnival had been a ball, but what they had shared later had been even better. Wanda had made the last mistake of her life when she agreed to meet Mike at the carnival. Now she knew it, but now it was too late. There was no way for anyone to know just how long she had been with them, but when Georgia saw the news on television, she knew what had led to Wanda Marie Corley's death.

They had known one another; in fact they had played together as children. As they'd matured, they'd gone their separate ways but had remained friendly. Georgia closed her eyes, wrapped what she could of her broken hand around Joey's and cried. Joey cried too, because a friend was dead, because it could have been Georgia, and because he felt so damn helpless.

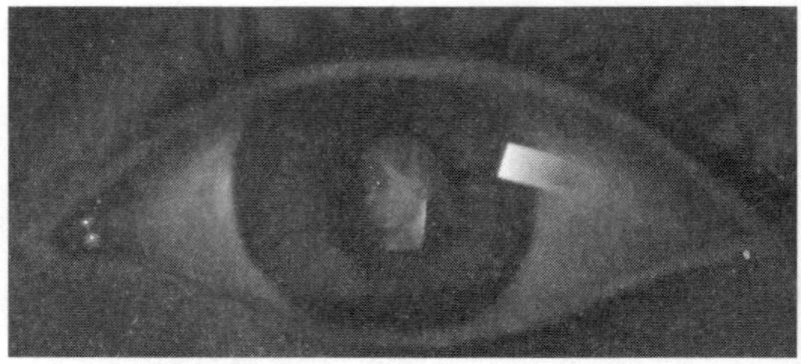

CHAPTER 41

The autopsy, release of the remains, and funeral of Wanda Marie Corley were almost identical to that of Amanda Wiggins. In fact, the timing, the funeral home, and the people in attendance were the same, except for members of the legal community, which Don belonged to. The only other differences were the color and the names of the family members. Wanda's favorite color was yellow, so yellow draped the coffin. Her favorite flower, the yellow tea rose, lay in a gorgeous blanket over her closed casket. Inside, her battered body was dressed in her mother's wedding gown. Phyllis had insisted, and Don didn't have the heart to tell her no.

"It was our dream, Don, hers and mine, that someday she would get to wear it. Now the only way that will ever happen is if she wears it today."

As the friends and distant family filed out of the funeral home, the director called the family to him. "Would you like a final viewing?" he asked. It was a common enough question. The Wigginses had silently viewed Amanda's body, most families did. Don nodded, and as the attendants closed the doors, the top of the casket was lifted. Inside lay Wanda Corley. She was beautifully gowned in her mother's wedding-day finery. If not for the bruises and the lack of oxygen to her alabaster skin she would have looked like a bride; instead, she looked like a grounded angel. Her mother and father bent and kissed her tenderly. Her aunts and uncles followed suit. Phyllis's and Don's parents waited until the last. The four of them held hands. They encircled the casket. The other family members joined in. The circle was complete when Don and Phyllis stood at the opening. They looked down on Wanda for the last time and sang "Amazing Grace." Tears flowed freely, and knuckles were gripped tense and white. As the service ended, Detectives Jerry Leeme and Will Halpin dried their eyes and followed the family out of the funeral home.

"As God is my witness," croaked Jerry, "I'm gonna get these bastards."

CHAPTER 42

Joey watched the televised film clips of Wanda's funeral. The media had attacked the grieving Corley family like hounds on a bone. Some said it was because her father was a well-known lawyer, but Joey felt it was because she was the third victim. Maybe it was a bit of both. He sat there watching Georgia sleep. Somehow she was enduring the pain without drugs for their baby's sake and finding peace at the end of the day, peace enough to sleep. She still cried out during the night, she still jumped in her sleep, but she was slowly becoming calmer.

She refused to be alone, however. And while she was awake, she still asked almost every hour to see the team of police officers stationed outside her door. They had come to love her. When she asked to see them, they would poke their heads in to say hi. It was a small gesture, but it was enough to calm her.

Joey watched television until the news was over. Then he slipped out the door of Georgia's room. He nodded to her mother as he went. She'd never left Georgia. She'd never gone home, to church, or to the market. Everything she needed was supplied by her ever-faithful husband, Georgia's father. Joey whispered to the officer outside Georgia's room. "I'm going to the chapel. I'll be back. You can call me if you need me."

The officer nodded and watched Joey go.

The chapel was the one place Joey could go that he didn't have to be strong. He could go and be the child of God that he was. He walked inside and was greeted by burning candles, a rare sight in the hospital.

Someone had been there just before him. Joey's head felt heavy, and he lowered it to his arms as he knelt there whispering the Catholic prayers of his youth. The words came naturally; he knew them because he'd heard them his whole life. Then suddenly he felt strangely comforted, more comforted than he'd ever been in his life. He felt whole, complete, and at total peace. It was as if the arms of God had reached down and wrapped around him.

"God help us," Joey whispered. They were simple words. But somehow they seemed to reach the ears of God.

Joey didn't know how long he had been sitting there. It could have been hours or minutes, but when the peace left him he simply stood and walked back toward Georgia's room. He strolled casually as if he had all the time in the world, stopping in the lounge area to pick up a new magazine. Joey felt good, relaxed for the first time in more than a week.

With his magazine tucked under his arm he stopped and bought some tea from the machine in the hallway. Brewing tea was a therapeutic ritual, his mother had told him. Something about its comforting aroma and the ritual itself had always brought a smile to her lips. Joey stood there smiling now. He stirred his tea and continued toward Georgia's room. As he passed the officer, he nodded and said, "Why don't you get some coffee or tea? I'll stand guard for a few minutes." The officer smiled and nodded. Joey knew he would only be gone a few minutes because that's how they all were. They took their job seriously. Anyone who didn't, anyone caught talking to the nurses or the candy-stripers in the hall, never came back. Guarding Georgia was serious business; one look at her battered body was enough to instill that in the hearts and minds of the officers.

While the officer was gone, Joey sipped the hot tea and thumbed through the magazine. The colorful ads and the bold type held his attention briefly, but one headline stood out among the others. It was an interview with a clairvoyant about crime solving, and how local law enforcement agencies had used his services. Joey almost flipped past it, but something inside him wouldn't let it go. He decided to read the article, to really give it a good look. He was interested, and something in his heart kept pulling him back to the story.

When the officer came back he thanked Joey and watched him disappear into Georgia's room. They were used to his comings and goings, and they knew who he was; but it still made this officer feel better to watch the door close behind him. He sat and sipped his coffee, imagining what it would be like for him if his sister or wife were lying in that room in that condition. Intense anger filled him, and he had to stand and walk it off. As he paced back and forth he clenched his fists a few times. Finally he was able to calm down some. He'd seen Georgia earlier that day when he'd come on duty. She did seem to be getting better; she'd actually smiled at him. As he took his seat in the chair outside her room, he promised himself that when he got home he would check the security of his own home as well as his mother's, where his sister lived. He'd never be able to forgive himself if something like this happened to them.

Joey sank into the chair in the corner of the room after speaking briefly with Georgia's mother. He asked how Georgia was doing. "She's sleeping like a lamb," Lucinda said and went back to her needlework. Joey wondered if Lucinda would have made either a huge blanket or several sweaters by the time Georgia was ready to go home.

He opened the magazine to the article that had so drawn his attention, rereading the headline, "Psychics and Law Enforcement." The article discussed several different psychics and the roles they had played in solving different crimes around the country. They all looked normal enough, Joey thought, as he gazed at their photographs. The last few lines focused on a clairvoyant who refused to be interviewed but who had been highly successful. Something about her, the way she hid her life and her dedication to who and what she was, touched his heart. "She seems more real," Joey thought to himself.

This particular clairvoyant was a single mother who was determined to protect her family. She had all the work she could handle and she was not available for comment. Joey scanned some of the pictures in the article to see if he could pick her out. Only one picture showed a light-haired woman holding one hand in front of her face while she tried to block the camera with her other. There was no name or information about the picture. Joey wondered why she was so camera-shy. "I wonder if she's hiding something or if she really just wants to be left alone."

He drifted off to sleep with the elusive clairvoyant on his mind. "I wonder if someone like her could help us.

As he whispered this softly in his sleep, Lucinda Amando looked over at him, "Did you say something, Joey?" she asked. But she received no reply.

Joey was asleep with something intense on his mind. When he woke, he was like a man with a mission. He told Georgia all about the article. She listened, but only half-heartedly. "My mom and dad will never allow it. You know how they are, Joey," Georgia said through still-swollen lips. Joey had noticed a change lately, though. Some of her normal color was returning, and the swelling seemed to be going down. Joey was pleased with her progress, and so were her doctors.

"Georgia, this is a chance to get all this horror behind us. The police tell us they have nothing to go on, some minor clues but no sightings. They've talked to all the neighboring police departments and started a statewide manhunt, but they're not finding them, Georgie. They've killed someone else, it could have been you. Oh God, Georgie it could have been you." Joey laid his head on the bed at her side. Georgia gently touched the top of his head with her bandaged hand.

"Joey, I survived, do you hear me? I survived because Hugh and Marvin noticed the lights and noise by the river. Someone else will report them, too."

Joey looked up at her. "Georgia, don't you see, these guys are smarter than the police are giving them credit for. They know we're looking for them, and now that we have you back, you're the only eyewitness. Don't you see that?"

"I do, Joey, really I do. But that's why the officer is outside the door. That's why we have around-the-clock protection."

"Baby, it's not enough. We have to find them before they kill another young woman. Can you even begin to imagine what I think every time I see something on the news about another one of our classmates missing or dead? I think of you, Georgia. I think I'm so selfish because all I can do is thank God I got you back." Joey wiped his eyes with his forearm. "I'm a selfish man, I admit it. But I hurt for friends and their families, too. Don't you see, honey, we've got to do something? We have to! It's up to us," Joey said passionately. Georgia could feel the intensity of what he was trying to say.

"Okay, read the article again. Let's think about it, and then call Detective Leeme and Halpin. Let's ask them before we do anything."

Georgia was getting tired. Even though her speech was better, it was difficult for her to talk. She briefly closed her eyes, and Joey felt like a jerk for pushing her so hard. He stood and kissed her forehead. Some of the bandages had come off, and more were scheduled to come off today. Joey wondered what she would look like, not that it mattered. He thought about their baby. How could something so tiny survive such a horrifying assault? He smiled as the answer came to him; she had been protected by her mother's body. Joey always thought of the baby as a girl. "What if it's a boy?" Georgia had asked him. Joey just smiled and shrugged his shoulders.

He watched her sleeping and formed his own plan. He agreed they should talk to the detectives about using a psychic, but if they didn't want to he was going to make contact on his own. Joey believed it was the answer. Georgia was going to be safe again. Joey had made the vow already in his heart and mind, but the only way that was going to happen was if the two killers were caught. Joey intended to see that they were.

He cut out the article and stuffed it in his pocket. He needed time at the library to do some research in the newspaper archives, as well as a phone to make some calls. Joey made a list of things to do and people to call. Three hours later, he was ready when the two detectives came by for a visit.

Joey and Georgia spoke openly. Her mother sat silently at her head, even though she didn't approve of what was being discussed. "This is of the devil," she warned. "You wait till your poppa hears about this."

But Joey didn't care. He'd done his homework and found out how law enforcement agencies had used clairvoyants. Some of them had been fakes, he'd found; but some of them, many of them, had been incredibly successful. Joey never did discover anything about the clairvoyant who refused to be interviewed. Something about her haunted him. Joey had all his findings laid out on the floor when the detectives came by. They smiled slightly as Georgia's mother crossed herself every time she looked over at the papers.

Joey pointed out one thing after another to the detectives. He showed case studies that he'd stapled together, with a photograph of each psychic or clairvoyant who had solved a case. Will looked at Joey and asked, "Son, are you serious?"

"Sir, I have never been more serious in my life. Tell me, detectives, have you found these guys; do you know where they are? Do you have any clues?" Joey studied their faces and knew the answer. "Admit it, guys, you need help. You need someone who might have this special talent, this extra edge. Will you at least think about it?"

The look on Joey's face told them he was not only serious but passionate about this. "We'll give it some thought," Jerry said.

"Can we take these?" Will asked.

"Sure you can," Joey said excitedly, as he gathered the pages together. Stuffing them all into one bundle, Joey handed them over. "I know you think this is silly, but if you would just take a look and then consider it, we might be able to find these guys before someone else dies."

Joey didn't mean it the way it sounded. He still had every faith in the police department. He was doing this as much for himself and Georgia as he was for them. This was the one thing Joey could do, his last stab at making things right. The detectives understood that Joey still felt guilty about Georgia's kidnapping.

"We'll take a look at this and get back to you both," Will said as he tucked the bundle under his arm. Joey smiled, Georgia nodded.

As Will and Jerry walked down the hospital corridor, Jerry took long studied glances at Will. Finally Will stopped walking and looked at him. "What?"

"Are you going to take all that horse crap seriously?" Jerry asked.

"I said I would take a look at it, and I will. I'm not gonna lie to that kid," Will said, his frustration showing.

"Okay, Will," Jerry said hesitantly. "Listen, I understand how you feel. Hell, I feel the same damn way. I know this case sucks. I know what we got and what we ain't got. I'm your damn partner, remember? But, Jerry, you can't really consider taking that crap seriously. We'd be laughed out of the station. The guys would never let us forget it."

"I know. That's why I'm not gonna say anything to anyone about it, and neither are you." Will had that look in his eye, the look Jerry called "the wild-eyed Texan" look.

"So, we're gonna look into this but not say anything. And we'll talk to a psychic, but not say anything. If this looks promising, we'll use a psychic, right?" Jerry asked.

"And not say anything!" Will emphasized with raised eyebrows.

"Right!" Jerry said.

Will was strangely quiet, Jerry noticed, but he didn't say anything. The strong Texan would speak when he was ready and not before. To ask would be an invasion of his privacy, one that Jerry had learned would not be welcomed. They had an appointment to meet with Lilly Williams and her family again that evening, and something from the county examiner had come in. The day would be a long one and Jerry didn't want to spend it bickering with his partner.

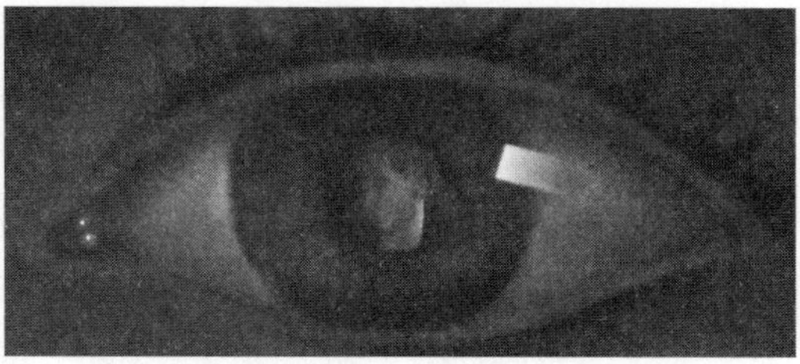

CHAPTER 43

Will was quiet and withdrawn, lost in thought. Jerry sat with the Williams family and asked most of the questions, until they got to the part about Tony and Mike and what Lilly knew about them. Suddenly Will stood up and said, "Thank you for your time. We'll be in touch again soon, and if you think of anything, please call us." He held out his business card. Jerry jumped up too, shocked.

The surprised Williams family promised to call if they remembered anything else. Jerry waited until he and Will were in the car. "What the hell was that all about? Have you lost your mind or something?"

"No, but all day something's been bothering me. I couldn't put my finger on it, but now I remember what it is. Jerry, do you remember the case about the missing seven-year-olds that happened down south about a year and a half ago?"

Jerry shook his head, "No, why, should I?"

"No reason, but I know one of the guys on that police force. When it was all over he told me something that's stuck with me all this time." Will pulled the car to the side of the road and put it in park. He turned to look at Jerry. "Tony Miller told me they used a psychic to help find those little girls." Will let it hang in the air.

Jerry stared at him for a moment and then looked down the road at the town and the people he loved. He felt a kinship with it all. To him what was happening here was personal. Will didn't have that. He wasn't from here, didn't know many people other than his close neighbors and the guys on the police force. But Will had passion, something that Jerry had thought he lacked in his character, and it was rare that he was wrong about things. Not that it didn't happen, it just didn't happen often. "We're going to open ourselves up to so much ridicule if we do this. Are you sure that's what you want to do?"

"No—but Jerry, what else do we have? We have more than half the police force out looking for these guys. They could be anywhere, and the only leads we have on them are the carnival and the mall. We have guys staked out there, and so far the only thing they've come up with is higher credit card bills. Jerry, I'm getting scared, I'm afraid we can't crack this one. I was thinking I might call Tony Miller and talk to him."

Finally, after a few long minutes, Jerry turned and looked at Will.

"Okay, I'm with you on this, but we have to use the same person, because you and I both know that some of these people are kooks. I mean have you seen some of those signs out on the highway? The flashing crystal ball and the neon palm sign aren't for me, I gotta tell ya." Jerry looked serious.

"Deal. I'll call him this evening. Hey, partner, I'm sorry about the way I acted back there at the Williams's. You know how I am when something's stuck in my craw."

Jerry nodded and laughed. "You should have seen their faces when you stood up so abruptly. I thought they were gonna freak out and run for cover."

Will chuckled. "Me too! Shit, I scared myself."

CHAPTER 44

Later that evening Will sat in his big easy chair with Betty on his lap. "To what do I owe the honor of this visit, sir?" she asked playfully.

"Visit? I live here; at least the last time I was here my clothes were still hanging in the closet. Did you move me out while I was sleeping?" Will asked as he patted her bottom. "You're getting a little plump back here, ain't ya?"

She grabbed his hand and slapped it. "No, I'm not. And yes, you still live here, but you haven't been home before dark for weeks. Did something break in the case? Did you catch those guys?" Betty was his pretty Yankee wife. He always referred to her that way, but she didn't seem to mind. "You're still the light of my life, do you know that? And I still think you're as pretty as a speckled pup." Will said as he nuzzled her neck.

"Okay, you're stalling. Come on, big guy, out with it. What's on your mind?" Betty also knew him better than anyone else in the world.

"Can't get nothing past you, can I?" Will asked.

"Nope, so don't try. Come on, babe, really, what's the matter?" She sat still in his lap and waited. He told her about his frustrations with the case, about his lack of information and leads. "I underestimated these guys right off the bat, and now I'm paying for it. I don't know where they are, and I'm scared shitless they're gonna grab someone else before I can find them." Will had tears in his eyes. He started to wipe them away, but Betty gently did it for him.

"I love you; I believe in you, I always have. You're the single smartest man I have ever met. I know you'll do the right thing when the time comes, and Will, you always get your man." She smiled at him and kissed his tear-stained cheeks.

"Betty, I'm thinking about calling Tony Miller. Do you remember him?" Will asked.

"Yes, I think so. Isn't he that friend of yours from the police academy who became a sergeant down south somewhere?"

"Yeah, but he's a captain now. Did I tell you about his case a year and a half ago, the one about the kidnapping in his town?"

"Yes, you told me. Will, what does this have to do with your case?" Betty was watching his face. She knew from his expression that he was struggling emotionally. And that usually meant that he wasn't one hundred percent sure of what he was about to say.

"Well, Tony Miller told me about this woman clairvoyant who helped him solve his case and bring those two little girls home. He told me he wouldn't have gotten them back alive if it weren't for her. He was sure the perp would have gotten another child," Will said, letting his last words trail off.

Betty remembered the case because her mother's heart wouldn't let her forget it. In those days she'd watched their youngest daughter closer, spent more time with her, and didn't let her walk anywhere alone. Now she was watching their son. He was the age of the kids killed at the mall. If they'd lived in the same district, he'd have gone to school with those girls. Betty shuddered, and Will knew why.

"Are you thinking of calling her?" Betty asked.

"Yes, what do you think? Do you think it's too far-fetched?" Will needed to hear what she had to say. He watched the skin on her forehead pucker. It was something that he loved about her. He knew she was "pondering," what his mother had called it the first time she'd seen Betty do it. "Are you saying you're going to call a psychic?"

"I'm thinking about it. I want to hear what you think. I want to talk to Tony Miller and hear what he has to say about her. I haven't made up my mind yet. Jerry's on my side, if that means anything to you."

"It does. Do what you think is best, sweetheart. I know you, you're no fool. We do have a madman or two out there killing, raping, and God only knows what else. I trust your judgment. Have you talked to your captain about this?"

"No, we haven't. Jerry and I want to talk to Tony Miller first. Then I want to talk to this woman and see if she is willing to help us. So many roads to take, so many things left to do, and in the meantime young women are dying. Betty," Will said. "I'm so damn scared." He buried his face in her neck. Betty wrapped her arms around him. She knew he had to work things out. She just let him ramble, cry, get it out of his system, and then he would find his own way.

"I love you," she whispered into his ear. "You'll do what's right."

Hours later Will woke in the same chair. Betty wasn't in his lap anymore, and a blanket had been lovingly placed over him. The scent of her still lingered in the air. Will held the blanket to his nose and took a deep breath. He remembered the first day he'd seen her, years ago, her long hair blowing in the wind at a picnic. She'd been dating a guy in her communications class, and Will had to work his butt off to get her. But in the end, he'd won; she'd agreed to marry him eight months later. He'd never been sorry, not even when they argued. He lay down on their bed next to her and was lulled back to sleep by her presence. She instinctively wrapped herself around him and breathed softly on his back. Will felt better than he had in days. Just lying there with her leg and arm draped over him brought comfort and a feeling of being loved.

In the morning he awoke, his decision made. He headed downstairs to the smell of coffee brewing. His kitchen was a madhouse on school and work days. The three kids were stuffing food in as fast as they could, kissing their parents good-bye and running for the bus. Betty ruffled Will's hair. "Good morning, sleepyhead. How are you this morning?"

"I'm better, thanks to you," Will said. She kissed him and set a cup of coffee in front of him. "Want some breakfast?"

"Yeah, are you cooking, on a weekday?" Betty usually didn't cook on these harried mornings.

"Yes, smarty pants. I'm willing to make you some breakfast if you will eat it and not just gulp it down and run out the door. Besides, I don't have an appointment until this afternoon." Betty was a very successful real estate agent.

"Okay, I'll have some eggs, if it's not too much trouble and some toast maybe…again if it's not too much trouble." Will's eyebrows were just about hair line level.

"Very funny! I'll have you know I had every intention of making you breakfast this morning. I'll make you eggs, dippin' eggs at that, and toast, of course, to dip in your eggs. You can even have orange juice and coffee. So there!" Betty said as she threw the dish towel at him. Will ducked and laughed. Betty was a great cook, but she wasn't a morning person. So, unless you were sick, dying, or delusional you didn't ask her for breakfast.

As she set about preparing Will's breakfast, he poured them both coffee and orange juice that he knew was fresh because he checked the date on the carton. "I saw that!" Betty said.

"Just checking, I know how hard you work. I'm not complaining, just checking."

"Will, what are you going to do?" Betty said with her back to him, as she spooned hot grease over the eggs.

"I'm gonna sit right here, have my breakfast, maybe read the newspaper if it doesn't depress me too much, and flirt with my wife. Why?"

"I meant about talking to Tony Miller and checking on that psychic," Betty said, looking over her shoulder.

"I knew what you meant, honey. I was just kidding. I'm gonna do it. I had made up my mind yesterday. I was just hoping you would talk me out of it." Will folded the paper in half to make it more manageable.

"I think you should, if that matters at all."

Will got up and wrapped his arms around her as she stood at the stove. "I love you, you know that don't you? You're the reason I live in Yankeeland when my heart longs to be in Texas. Everything about you matters to me, including what you think. Do you want to meet her if she agrees to come?"

"No, not really. I don't want to know what's coming. I like the mystery of life and I'm afraid I won't be able to keep from asking her."

"I have a feeling, honey, that she's very professional, if she is who Tony says she is. Of course I haven't talked to him about it in more than a year. But I'll call him right after breakfast."

Will sat back down at the table after kissing her neck. He reached for the newspaper again. As he did, something caught his eye. "Cops Can't Nab Killer," the headline said. The story went on to read like a bad bio. Officer Brandon, Jerry, Will, and Captain Morris were on the front page, looking like the bumbling cops the story made them out to be. "Shit, shit!" Will said as he stood up and crumbled the paper in his hand.

"What's the matter?" Betty asked as she set his plate on the table. He grabbed the paper and smoothed it out as he reached over her head for the phone to dial Jerry. They'd both agreed they would take some time off this morning because of all the hours they'd been putting in. It was 7:30. Jerry answered the phone on the second ring.

"Hello," he said through a mouthful of food.

"Have you seen the morning paper, partner?" Will asked sarcastically.

"Oh yeah, reading it now. We look like the Keystone Cops," Jerry laughed.

"I don't know about you, buddy, but I don't like looking like the Keystone Cops. In fact it pisses me off." Will said as he slammed his fist down on the table.

"Take it easy, Will. This is gonna blow over in no time at all. We'll catch this guy and the whole town will see us as heroes." Jerry was still laughing.

"Have you forgotten, you buffoon, that I intend to call Tony Miller today and talk to him about using that psychic?"

"Oops! I had forgotten that. I have a feeling that for now you better hold off. That and this headline aren't gonna sit good with the captain."

"No shit, Sherlock," Will said. "I'm gonna sit down, eat my breakfast, and shoot myself this afternoon. I'll call ya later." Will had started to hang up when he heard Jerry's voice.

"Uh, hey, did you forget we have that meeting with the forensic guys this afternoon?"

"Thanks for ruining my plans and reminding me. I'll see you at the station around nine unless you have any more bad news you want to tell me." Will was starting to calm down some as he hung up the phone. He finished his breakfast in silence as Betty puttered about cleaning the kitchen.

Finally she couldn't take it anymore. "Will, you need to call Tony. I want you to think about something before you lose your temper," she said as she held up her hand to block his objection. "Honey, you need to call him because it's been days now since the Corley girl was found dead. The pattern seems to be about three to four days. Can you really afford another dead girl?"

Betty was right, of course. Even though Will hadn't really seen it before, the pattern was about right. Three girls taken, two dead in the course of three weeks or less, that's one a week, Will thought to himself.

"What do you think I should do?"

"I can't tell you what to do. I'm not the one who's going to take the heat, as you say, from this; but I would rather be ridiculed than stand at a door and tell another parent they can go and pick out a coffin for their child."

Will drained the last of his juice, then his coffee, and without saying a word he walked into his study and closed the door. Betty knew he was making the inevitable decision, but she didn't envy him it at all. "God, if you're listening, please be with him."

"Dispatch!" Paula shouted into the phone. She grabbed it on the first ring, since whoever was calling was on the private line.

"Can I speak with Captain Tony Miller, please? This is Detective Will Halpin," Will said as he massaged his sore ear. "I'm gonna be deaf."

"Pardon me?" Paula had heard that and she wanted him to know it.

"I said, can I please speak to Captain Tony Miller?"

"You don't have to shout, detective, I can hear ya. Sure you can, hold on." Paula clicked the hold button without waiting for his response.

"Hey Tony, some guy, a detective Halpin somebody is on the phone for you. Line one," Paula said as she blew one more time on her wet fingernails. She'd had a manicure for the first time in her life and loved the look.

"Thanks Paula. Nice professional job," Tony said as he grabbed the phone.

"Tony Miller here," he said.

"Tony, Will Halpin here. How the hell are ya?"

"Hey, Will, my man, how are you? How's the fishing in Rayburn Country?" Tony and Will had gone to the academy together and later Tony had come down to Texas for a cops' convention.

"What fishing? I left Texas for that damn Yankee I married and now I'm up here with all the snowbirds. I have a problem, and something you said last year when we talked keeps bothering me. Do you have a minute to talk?" Will asked.

Tony got up and closed the door to his office, a movement that turned heads in his police station. He could see them all looking at him. He knew they were wondering what was up, since Tony never closed the door. "Okay, Will, sorry about that. I have a lot of nosy cops and an even nosier dispatcher."

"Paula—I met her briefly. She's a hoot," Will said.

"Buddy, you don't know the half of it. What can I do for you?" Tony was all ears.

"Tony, this is just between us, right?" Will asked.

"That's why I closed the door, buddy. Wait a minute, don't say anything. Paula?" Tony whispered into the phone, "If you don't want to work this weekend, hang up the phone," Tony and Will heard a decisive click. "Okay, now we have some privacy. What can I do for you?"

Will laughed out loud. "Gosh, I miss the south. Tony, I have a situation here. Two girls are dead and one has been kidnapped, raped, and then rescued in less than three weeks. I haven't got a clue as to the whereabouts of these assholes; and even though forensics has suitcase loads of stuff on them, we don't have names other than first ones. We don't have much, and to be honest with you, I've underestimated them. The girl we got back is a good witness. She's very candid and willing to work with us, but she's pretty messed up. They only had her for about twelve hours, but you should see the damage they did." Will took a breath. Tony just listened to him breathe and took a sip of his coffee.

"I thought we were dealing with amateurs, Tony, I wasn't thinking clearly. Now I'm paying for it. The sons of bitches have killed another young girl, and I don't know where to look for them. I need some help. I was thinking about what you did, with the psychic and all." Now Will was quiet. Tony took a deep breath himself.

"Will, first of all, and this is important—never, ever call her a psychic. She hates that word. Don't refer to turbans, and whatever you do, don't test her mentally. She'll make you feel about two inches tall. Remember Sergeant Connor in the academy? Remember how he could make you feel like a complete asshole?"

"Yeah, I remember," Will said. And he did. Visions of Connor came back to him.

"She'll make you feel worse. And she'll let you roll around in it for awhile trying to soothe your wounded pride. But she's good, I mean it man, she's really good. She won't play games with you, but she will point out your shortcomings if you make her. She's tired most of the time, and she's like a bloodhound. She doesn't take orders well when she's on the trail of something. One day, man, one day I let her go by herself, out to scout the neighborhood. She wanted to get a feel for it alone. I let her go. What do you think she does?" Tony asked.

"What?" Will asked.

"Damn if she didn't catch the perp in the middle of taking the third victim, a little girl, same age as the others. The kid was playing in her backyard in broad daylight and the perp drags the kid over the fence. Lindsay, that's her name, feels it or whatever people like her do, and takes off after the guy. We catch him, of course, but I could have wrung her neck. She's good at not following orders, and she's smart. You don't want to try to pull something over on her." Tony let Will digest all of that. Then he said, "Will, she can be a bit of a ballbuster, too."

"Great. So Tony, do you think she could help us? I mean would you use her again if you needed her?" Will asked.

Tony didn't need to think about it. "I sure would. Will, it makes you feel funny. It gives you the willies to be around her, but she's pretty normal. Wives like her, mothers like her, everyone likes her. She's a Christian, what's not to like? The creepy thing is she knows what you're feeling, or how you're feeling. I'm not really sure which one. It's all based on feeling. So she's not a mind reader and she doesn't even believe in all that; but let me tell you something, if you're doing anything you don't want her to know about, or if you have secrets, well, let's just say, tough luck, kiddo."

"Tony," Will said, "What should I do?"

"I'd call her, buddy. Hell, she may not be able to help you. But at least you can say you tried everything."

"Yeah, and the newspaper has my department looking like a bunch of idiots this morning. I'm afraid for them to find out I'm using a psychic. What do I call her if I don't call her that?"

"Call her a clairvoyant," Tony said.

"Okay, so this clairvoyant, does she have a name and a number?" Will asked.

Tony scrolled through his Rolodex. "Hold on," he said. Covering the mouthpiece, he opened his mouth to yell for Paula when she popped her head in the door. In her hand was a white piece of paper. On it was printed Lindsay Freeman's name and number.

"Thanks Paula," Tony said. "That woman worries me," Tony said into the phone.

"What woman?" Will asked.

"My dispatcher, never mind. The number is.... and Tony rattled it off. As he did he was looking out the window at Paula, who was sitting behind her desk, still blowing on her nails. She glanced up at him, smiled, and went back to whatever she was doing. Tony crooked his finger at her. She pointed at herself and raised her eyebrows. Tony nodded.

As Paula got up and headed in his direction Will thanked him and promised to keep him posted. "Thanks again, Tony," Will said as he hung up.

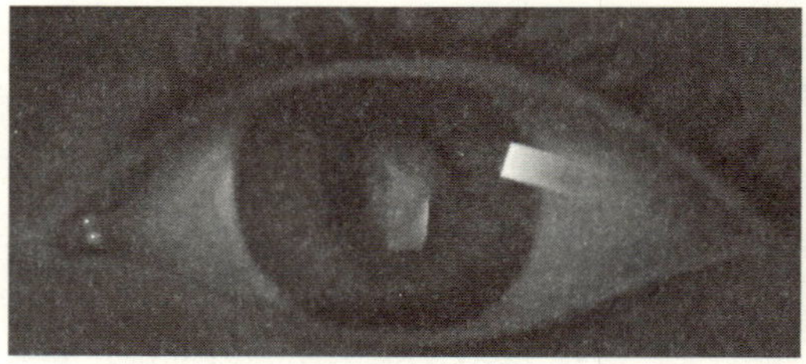

CHAPTER 45

Will sat there holding Lindsay's phone number after he finished talking to Tony. He thought about making the call and then thought about the newspaper headlines. "Damn it," he said out loud. He dialed the number slowly, willing someone to come in or call and interrupt him.

"Hello," said a soft feminine voice. "This is Lindsay."

"Hello, is this Lindsay Freeman?"

"Yes, this is she. Who's calling, please?"

"Ms. Freeman, you don't know me. My name is Detective Will Halpin. I got your name and number from Tony Miller. I hope you don't mind."

"Tony, how nice! How are Tony and Claire doing?" Lindsay wanted to see just how close this man was to Tony Miller.

"Tony's fine. He's the only one I know, but he didn't say anything about his wife, so I'm assuming she's fine also."

"Detective, are you from Texas or the south somewhere?" Lindsay asked. She was really just trying to keep him talking.

"Yes, ma'am, I am as a matter of fact; but I've been transplanted by my beautiful wife to the north where even in the summer time it's colder than a—well it's cold." Will said.

"Yes, Detective, I've heard the saying." Lindsay laughed, breaking the ice between them. "Detective, why don't you tell me why you're calling?" Lindsay said. And he did. For the next hour and a half Lindsay and Will talked. She asked questions, he asked questions, and together they put the story together.

"Can you help us?" Will asked finally.

"I hope so, but since you don't have much to go on, I'm not sure if I can get a handle on your perpetrators or not. I can get a handle on the victims, though, and that may be enough to help you find them. I do have one particular concern. The one you talked about—Mike, I believe you called him. He seems to have a sexual addiction. This worries me because I have a feeling that he's like clockwork. He does things without much thinking, and he's a criminal at heart. To me that means that he does whatever he wants, and then works out the consequences as they arise. That's why he's always a step ahead of you. I also feel a pattern, like a three-day, two-day pattern or something like that." Lindsay said.

Will nodded. "She's good," he thought.

"Detective?" Lindsay said.

"Yes, I'm still here. You're right, there is a pattern; but we haven't been able to figure it out yet. It's not two-day or three-day, but it happens and there seems to be something about it that's the same. I just can't put my finger on it," Will said.

"I'm willing to take a look at it for you if you want me to. However, I will need a place to stay and some of the paperwork and pictures. I'll also have to interview the girl who was rescued and the family who rescued her, as well as the other families involved. The more I get, the better, because these guys seem to fly by the seat of their pants," Lindsay said.

"Can I get back to you on that, Ms. Freeman?" Will asked.

"Sure you can, and, Detective, it's Lindsay."

"Okay, Lindsay. I need to clear this with my captain and find you a place to stay. I also want to talk to my partner. His name is Jerry Leeme; you'll like him. He's a Yankee, but he's a good guy."

"I'm a Yankee, Detective," Lindsay said.

"Damn," Will laughed. "I'm surrounded by 'em."

"And Detective?" Lindsay said.

"Yes?"

"You don't have much time. One of them seems to be afraid of water."

"Yes, we know that. Our rescued girl told us that. I'll get back to you by tomorrow. Thank you very much for your time, Ms., I mean, Lindsay."

"Have a good day, Detective," she said as she hung up.

Lindsay sat with the phone in her hand and her finger on the disconnect button for a few moments. She stared off into space as her mind replayed the conversation.

"Finally," she whispered. She'd known for some time that something was coming. Each time she moved her head, there was a hint of something floating in her peripheral vision. It was always a clear warning—never the answer, but a warning.

As she thought about what Detective Halpin had said, she could almost see the images of the young girls found murdered. She knew she could get something from them, their belongings, and their families, but it was the girl who'd been rescued who intrigued her the most. What was it about this girl that was so special? Lindsay grabbed a notepad from her desk and scribbled a few notes. Who were the girls? What did they have in common, above and beyond location? What was the timing issue, and which of the two perpetrators was the stronger character?

Lindsay knew the answer to that last question, but something about that answer didn't seem right. And the fear of water, what was that about? Lindsay tore the paper from the tablet and put it in her day planner.

"Food for thought," she said as she got up and prepared to start her day. "Coffee first, shower, and then off to the meat market." She was working the graveyard shift at the emergency room. "Ugh!" she said.

CHAPTER 46

Mike had been as good as his word. Each morning, miraculously, eggs and a two-inch slab of bacon had appeared on the kitchen table. Tony never knew how it got there, and Mike never said, but Tony was pretty sure that Mike had pilfered the food during his nighttime wanderings. Now Mike lay very still and stared at the ceiling. He'd heard something, he thought.

"Tony, Tony, wake the hell up. We have to get out of here," Mike said urgently.

"What's the matter, Mike?" Tony asked.

"I heard something. We gotta go. Come on, get up." Mike was already moving around in the dark, picking things up and stuffing them into his duffel bag. It was one of the few things he'd managed to take from the campsite.

Tony turned over and pulled the makeshift pillow over his head. "I don't wanna go, Mike. I'm tired and hung over and I'm hungry. I don't wanna go anywhere."

Suddenly the cot fell out from under him and he found himself face down on the floor. "Hey, you asshole. What'd you do that for?" Tony said as he sat up and rubbed his forehead.

"I said, we have to go, you dipshit," Mike hissed. "I heard something outside. Do you wanna be caught on private property? We could go to jail. Now get your shit and let's try to sneak out of here."

Tony suddenly came awake. He didn't want to get caught and he didn't want to go to jail. He'd never been there, and he wasn't ready to start now. Tony got to his feet and started moving quietly about, collecting the things he thought might be important.

They both heard it at the same time, a soft scratching at the back door of the long-abandoned cabin. Mike walked silently to the table, picked up a long knife and moved toward the door. Tony stood on the other side of it and waited. As Mike approached, Tony gently grasped the doorknob. On Mike's nod, Tony jerked the door open. To the surprise of all three involved—Mike, Tony, and the raccoon—the door fell in instead of swinging free. The raccoon ran, Tony screamed, and Mike swung the knife.

Nothing much had happened, but Tony burst into laughter. "Man, you're paranoid," he said as he bent low and grabbed his stomach. Mike laughed too.

"Did you see Rocky Raccoon take off? I scared the shit out of him. I bet there's a trail a mile long dragging behind his ass."

Slowly the guys settled down, and Tony replaced the door. "I gotta fix that," he said.

"Yeah, home sweet home," Mike chanted. Tony looked at him.

"What's the matter, Mike?"

"I gotta get movin', Tony. I can't sit like this. I get bored and I need to be outside. Remember we talked about headin' south when the weather turned?"

"Yeah, I remember." Tony sank into a chair as he listened. He knew what was coming. Mike never stayed in one place too long, a few days at the most.

"I was thinking we might start that way sooner. This place is boring, and there ain't no chicks around. We need to make some money, get a job or something, and maybe have some fun," Mike said as he tossed a wadded-up piece of paper in the air like a ball.

"Yeah, I know. We just had some fun, Mike, with Wanda, that girl from the carnival. Remember?" Tony was watching Mike's face for signs of anger. When Mike got like this, he always had a quick temper, and Tony didn't like being on the receiving end of it.

"That chick wasn't any fun. Did you see her face every time we talked about going somewhere else, maybe having a little bit of fun, one on one? She didn't want to. She didn't want to be with us, with me. She wanted us to spend our money, buy her things, and then she was gonna go home. I bet she would have laughed at us all the way home. You know how women are, they think they can get us poor saps to moon all over them, wait on them hand and foot and not have to put out. Hell, they think it's their right or something." Mike leapt to his feet now, grabbed the back of a chair, and swung it around the room, letting it go just in time to send it crashing into the upturned bed Tony had been sleeping in.

Tony jumped up himself. He was ready to run for the door if Mike moved in his direction. Time and again he had slept out in the open because Mike was having one of his fits, as he called them. Mike glared at him, and Tony stood poised for flight.

"Relax, I ain't gonna do nothing. I just wanna go outside, man, have some fun. Maybe meet some nice chicks who wanna party," Mike said in his whiniest voice.

"You kill the nice chicks, Mike, you party them till they die. Then we go through this again. You wanna go out, you wanna party and you wanna meet some nice chicks. Only thing is, no nice chicks are gonna wanna party the way we do. Nice chicks don't party with guys like us, they go to school, and they go to church. They hang out at the pizza parlor. They don't take their clothes off, and they don't smoke pot, and I ain't never met a nice chick who drank tequila," Tony said with a sneer on his face. "We need chicks that wanna party like we do, Mikey. Not the go-to-church kind of chicks, real party animal kind of chicks."

Tony knew right away that he had said the wrong thing. Mike's face was a mask of fury. He was just about ready to explode when Tony threw the shirt he'd been holding into Mike's face to temporarily blind him as he ran for the door.

"Mike, I mean it, man, if you hit me I'm going home. I mean it, Mike."

But Mike was past hearing, and he was way past reason. Tony ran down the dirt road and out onto the main road and kept on running. He knew Mike would never chase him out into the open. Mike was afraid of people he didn't know, mostly because he'd been to jail so many times. Mike's temper got him in trouble and usually kept him there. His fear of people was the only thing that controlled him. "Yeah, you better run, you chickenshit," Mike yelled.

An old pickup truck honked its horn at Tony as he ran for his life down the middle of the road. He didn't dare venture to one side or the other, Mike might be stockier, but he was just as fast as Tony, and he didn't have enough of a lead to feel sure that Mike couldn't catch him.

"I'll come back when you calm down," Tony yelled over his shoulder. The truck driver couldn't hear them, but it looked to him like the tall skinny one was running for his life.

"He looked plumb scared to death," he would later tell police. Mike had flipped the old man the finger as he ran behind the truck.

Finally, Mike gave up and headed back to the cabin. "What the hell were we thinking of, running outside in broad daylight like that? Dammit, now there's gonna be trouble," Mike mumbled to himself.

As the day wore on, he started to worry about Tony. He'd been gone a long time. "Fucking Tony, he's always acting like a kid. Now that old man's seen us and we're gonna be on the run again." Mike talked to himself, pacing back and forth. At least Tony had run out the back door of the cabin instead of the front. The front door would have taken him down a dirt road too, but right past the farmer's house.

Mike walked to the window. He pulled back the dark cover hanging over it and peered out into the approaching darkness. Tony had been gone all day. Mike had slept for a few hours, but then he had paced and stewed. "Shit, I wonder if that stupid asshole got himself caught?"

Mike grabbed his long-sleeved shirt and slipped silently out the front door. He stood in the shadows and whistled. It was a special whistle that he and Tony shared. They'd come up with it as kids long ago when they played hide-and-go-seek. Mike waited for a return whistle. Nothing came. "Shit, shit, where is that kid?"

Mike was really getting worried now, more worried than mad. He slipped into the trees and made his way to the main road. He could see the lights in the farmer's house. He wondered if the farmer had found out about his stolen station wagon. "I bet those license plates from that old van gave them a turn or two. Assholes! That should teach 'em to mess with me." Mike had taken the plates from the van he'd used in Amanda's kidnapping and switched them with the station wagon's plates. Then he'd found another car in a department store parking lot, late at night, and switched them again.

"The cops ain't never gonna find out whose plates are whose." Mike laughed to himself. He looked around for Tony and whistled again. This time he heard it, a soft whistle just like his. Tony was somewhere nearby. "Tony," Mike whispered as loud as he dared. But he didn't hear an answer. "Come on Tony. I'm not mad anymore. Come on out," Mike pleaded.

Tony inched out just enough for Mike to see him. "Come on, Tony. I said I wasn't mad at you anymore. I mean it man, I ain't mad. Come on out." Mike knew why Tony was being so cautious. Just last week he'd beaten Tony up pretty badly right after that Georgia chick had got away. But that was then and this was now. It was time to let bygones be bygones. Tony stepped up to see what Mike was looking at. He looked over Mike's shoulder and saw the house Mike had been staring at.

"What're ya gonna do, Mike?" Tony asked.

"I'm gonna go back in the cabin and get some rest. I need a bath and I was thinking about that campsite. Remember how nice we had it back then?"

Tony nodded. The campsite had been ideal. It had water, trees for coverage, and all the privacy you could want. The fishing had been good, and Mike and Tony had spent lazy days sleeping or getting high.

"I wanna find us a place like that again. Only I have a feeling it ain't safe for us to be wandering around in the daylight looking like we do." Tony thought Mike was referring to his unclean state. Mike was thinking that perhaps Georgia had provided a description of him and Tony. In fact, she hadn't been able to help much in that department. But Lilly had. Lilly had given them a description so good that anyone could have picked them out. But Mike didn't know that. He wasn't thinking about Lilly at all. If he had been, Lilly wouldn't have been safe anywhere.

Mike thought of Georgia all the time now. He hated the fact that she'd gotten away. "I wonder if that chick's alive." Mike said out loud. "Anyway, Tony, I was thinking about that farmer's garage and all that camping equipment he has in it. Since he obviously don't need it, I was wondering if maybe we could borrow it, you know, maybe leave him a note and tell him we'll bring it back in a year or two."

Tony laughed, "Yeah, we could just borrow it. Leave him a note and all and sign it Amanda, Wanda, and Georgia." Tony rolled forward and produced a belly laugh. He was being silly because he was scared, and Mike knew it.

"Yeah, we could do that, Tony," Mike said.

The plan had already formed in Mike's mind. He'd seen all that gear in the farmer's garage, but he hadn't been interested in it then because he had his own, and his was newer. Now he didn't have any because someone had come up on his private campsite and trespassed. Mike would just find some gear and make a new campsite. He'd known all along that Tony would go along with it. Tony never really had ideas of his own; he just followed Mike around and did what Mike told him to do. Now Mike was telling him to borrow some new camping gear. Tony would do it.

They waited until all the lights in the farmhouse had gone out. Then they gave it another hour and slipped across the lawn. The run from the main road to the farmer's barn took about eight minutes if you pushed it. Tony and Mike pushed it.

They reached the barn and flattened out along the far side of it. They inched toward the door that faced the main road. Carefully Mike worked the handle, but nothing happened. Turning around, he grabbed the handle with both hands and pulled, but still nothing happened. Mike thought, "The old bastard's installed a lock on the door."

Tony looked at him, "What's the matter? Open the door."

"I can't. It's locked or something. It won't open. Let's try the side door."

"Hell, no, that door faces the house. They can see us, if they hear us. I ain't into getting shot, Mike."

"We ain't gonna get shot, stupid. But we ain't gonna get in this way either."

"Okay, what are we gonna do?" Tony was getting nervous.

Mike stopped and thought for a moment. "Okay, you wait here, and I'll open the door and let you in." He ran silently around to the other side. The door facing the house opened without a hitch. Mike eased inside and stopped dead in his tracks.

"Son of a bitch!" he yelled and ran out the door. Right on his heels was the family dog, snapping and snarling at him. Tony laughed at first, and then, seeing that Mike wasn't kidding around, he took off and ran in the other direction. He slipped around the barn and inside. Since the dog was busy chasing Mike, he had some time to get what they'd come for. He grabbed as much camping gear as he could carry, and then for good measure he scooped up a duffel bag that was full of something, but he didn't take the time to look inside it. With his arms full and the duffel slung over his shoulder, Tony slipped back outside. He couldn't see Mike, but he was pretty sure Mike had made it back to the cabin. Now Tony had to get away before the dog came back—dogs always return home, he knew, no matter how far you haul them off. Tony never noticed the lights in the farmhouse come on. He ran for all he was worth with his heavy bundle.

Mike stood at the back door of the cabin waiting impatiently for him. "Where the hell did you go? That damn dog chased me all the way back here and almost tore the door down trying to get to me. Thanks for your help, asshole." Tony held his arms out and let the things he'd taken from the garage fall to the floor.

"While you were creating a diversion," he laughed, "I took what we needed." He wasn't looking for praise or even a pat on the back.

"Son of a bitch!" Mike said. He was astonished that Tony had done it. He figured Tony had run like a scared rabbit and would be hiding in the woods for hours. "You did it, Tony. You're fucking Al Capone. You did great!" Mike was proud of him, and Tony was beaming. Mike started going through the stuff Tony had stolen. "Tony, man, we have a tent, an extra cook stove, two lanterns now, and some cooking gear. You did great!" Mike said again.

As Mike opened the duffel bag he let out a whistle. Inside, wrapped in an old grey army blanket, was some fishing gear, a shotgun, and some ammunition. Deeper in the bag were two hunting knives, some oil to clean them with, and a sharpening stone. At the very bottom was a small tackle box. Mike looked up at Tony and smiled. "Tony, my man, you are incredible. What you did back there was great. I'm never gonna be mean to you again. That's a promise."

Tony was smiling from ear to ear. He always felt good when Mike was proud of him for something. "Tony, we got gear, baby, we got gear. We can go camping now. We can sleep outside and fish and swim in a lake again. And Tony, we can find us another stump!"

Tony grinned. He watched as Mike stuffed things back in the duffel bag and started collecting their belongings. "Mike, what are you doing?" Tony asked.

"I'm getting us ready. We gotta go now. We can't stay here now, Tony, you gotta see that. That dog is going to bring that farmer back here in the morning, if not before. And that old man in the truck, remember him? He saw us, Tony, and he's gonna tell someone. That someone might put what he says and this cabin together. We gotta get out of here and find us a new place." Mike never stopped moving while he talked to Tony. Tony could see the childlike animation in Mike's eyes. He was catching the fever, but it took him a little longer. He slowly picked up a shirt here and a blanket there. But Mike was moving at top speed. "Come on, Tony, get a move on. We're going camping, buddy."

He didn't know it, but it was a damn good thing he was hurrying. At that moment the farmer was dragging on his overalls and stuffing his feet into his work boots. The phone was in his wife's hand and she was dialing frantically. "Someone's breaking into our barn again," she screamed at the dispatcher. "This is Myrtle Lape, and someone's breaking into our barn."

If Tony and Mike had waited only another hour, things would have been different. As it was, the police and Mr. Lape had no idea who'd been staying at the abandoned cabin or how long they'd been there. It had taken the police time to get there, time to look over the barn, and then suddenly Mr. Lape had thought of the cabin. Driving there had taken only a few minutes, but the investigation once they got there took all night.

From the amount of trash, it was clear the men had been there for at least a few days. But what really attracted the attention of the law enforcement officers was Wanda Marie Corley's purse, containing her driver's license.

"Get Leeme and Halpin out of bed," the officer told his dispatcher. "We found Ms. Corley's clothes and her purse and a fair amount of her blood—not that she'll be needing it."

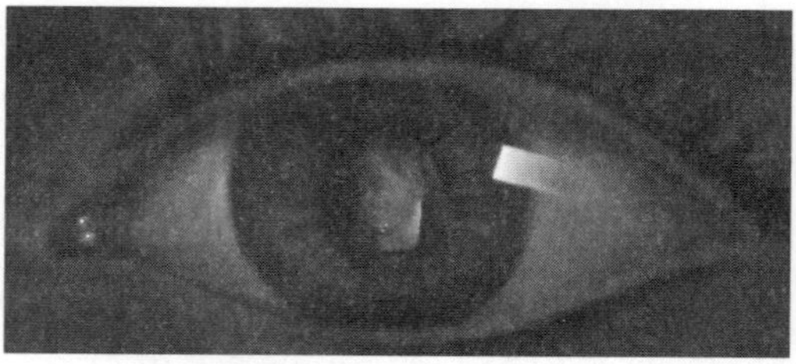

CHAPTER 47

Jerry and Will walked around the cabin, examining trash and debris. Wanda's purse lay open on the table, the contents spilling out. Sam Kent, who'd responded with them, was labeling and bagging things and marking the baggies with the name "Corley."

The forensic guys were as tired as the investigative team and they welcomed all the help they could get. Will talked with one of them as he looked carefully around the room from his corner vantage point. "I just don't get it," he said.

"What?" Dan Adams asked.

"We've been looking for these guys for weeks now. It's been all over the news and we've asked everyone to be on the lookout for these characters, to check out odd things, to make sure you know who you're talking to, not to go out alone, stay together. Right?" Will asked.

"Right, far as I know," Dan agreed.

"And this is the family who had their station wagon stolen, true? And their house is the same house that an officer came to, to take that report, true?"

"Far as I know, that's true," Dan said.

"Then tell me—why the fuck hasn't anyone found this little hiding place?" Will roared. He kicked the cot Tony had slept on, already damaged from Mike's abuse. Everyone in the room stopped what they were doing and looked at Will. Jerry hurried to his side and, placing a hand on his shoulder, led him outside. "Hey man, come on. There's no need to scare the shit out of the hired help. Take some deep breaths, get some air." Jerry led Will away from the house.

"Did you see it? Did you see all the blood that poor girl lost? I can't believe that someone could lose that much blood quietly, Jerry. I just don't believe it. And I can't believe that after all this community has been through, that these people, these Lapes, didn't check this place out. I can't believe that an officer who came to investigate a stolen car didn't drive around and check out an abandoned cabin that is visible from the damn road." Will's tirade continued. He paced back and forth. Jerry let him continue.

Then, quietly, he said, "Will, first thing is, we aren't in the same community. We're forty miles south of the mall. Second, this is old farm country. I bet these folks go days without looking at the news or listening to the radio. They may have read the newspaper; but forty miles, Will, that's a good stretch of land. My guess is they just didn't think it could happen to them.

"The police report on the stolen vehicle says they weren't even sure what day the car was taken. They gave a day of last use, but Mr. Lape clearly stated that sometimes a week or more goes by without his using the car or checking out that barn. Seems he uses the back barn more often. What got this man's attention, Will, was someone stealing eggs and a two-inch slab of bacon every day from his smokehouse. Without that, we might not have had this lucky break." Jerry waited for Will to take his customary deep breath and start speaking. Will didn't let him down.

"Okay, I understand all that. Why in God's name didn't the officer check this place out?"

"Because he came from the other way and he went back that way. This is sort of off the beaten path, you know," Jerry said.

Will nodded. "We got fingerprints, true?"

"Yeah—we have more fingerprints to go along with all the other ones we have." Jerry said.

"We have Wanda's purse. We have some hungry killers on our

hands, and now they're on the run again. What was taken from the barn? Do we have a list of missing things from the Lapes yet?" Will asked.

"He's working on it now. Do you want to go and talk to him and his wife?" Jerry asked. He was watching Will's face for another explosion.

Will looked at him. A thousand things went through his mind, but none of them would help. "Yeah, let's go talk to him."

Jerry went back inside and told Sam Kent where they were going. Sam held up the baggies in his hands that showed Wanda Corley's belongings. "I got these labeled, and forensics is just about ready to make a haul. The photo guys are done, and I need at least two hours of sleep before roll call in the morning. I know you guys want to be there. I'm sorry about this. I don't know what else to say, man."

"It's okay," said Jerry. "We'll see you in the morning."

Will and Jerry walked down the dirt road that Tony and Mike had walked down some twenty times. Suddenly Will stopped and turned around. What he saw made him feel a little better. Jerry turned around too. He saw what Will saw. The front of the cabin was completely untouched and the lights that he knew were burning inside didn't show from the dirt road because of the heavy oilcloth covering on the windows. "I feel better about our cops and worse about our perps," Will said.

"Yeah," Jerry said. "Shit, they're smart, smarter than we give them credit for. Either that or they do what comes naturally, and they're two of the luckiest sons of bitches in the world. But that luck is gonna run out. I wanna call her, Will. I wanna call her today and I wanna ask her to come. I want these bastards. I want them alone for just ten minutes. That's all it's gonna take me to wring the life out of those vicious necks of theirs."

Will and Jerry spent two hours with the Lape family. They ate breakfast with them and listened to the story of the last two weeks of their lives. It sounded so normal, nothing much out of the ordinary except for the stolen station wagon. Eggs and stuff came up missing from the farm all the time. "Kids," said Mr. Lape, "I think them little bastards do it just to rile me up," he said. Mrs. Lape threw a dishtowel at him.

"Stop that cussing, Henry, or you'll sleep in the barn with the other jackass." Will and Jerry snickered, and Henry glared over his shoulder.

"I didn't know anyone was in the old cabin. I certainly didn't know they had a young woman with them," Henry said.

"So you didn't hear anything, you didn't see anything, and you never got that funny feeling that someone was around?" Jerry asked.

"No, funny feelings is my wife's department. She gets 'em all the time. I call 'em hormones. She calls them feminine intuition. She's been reading that damn newspaper over there and saying she had a feeling about this and a feeling about that," Henry whispered as he looked over his shoulder.

"It would seem, Mr. Lape, that this time your wife was right. We'll be in touch. Please don't go in the cabin or out in back of it. Don't disturb anything till we get back with you," Will said and he and Jerry stood to go. He left a business card on the table with directions to call if something else happened or came to mind.

"Damn fine thing," Jerry said as he and Will made their way to the station for roll call. "Two women are murdered and one is raped and left for dead and these two go through life like nothing's happened. I can't believe it."

"Yeah, nothing like an informed citizen," Will quipped.

CHAPTER 48

Georgia lay very still. Her mother and father and, of course, Joey stood by her bed. She was sitting nearly upright, after lying flat for more than a week. She felt lightheaded, but it had taken her an hour to get this far. The bandages were slowly being peeled away from her face, and the pain was almost more than she could bear. "Georgia, are you sure you wouldn't like something a little stronger than Tylenol for pain?" Dr. Fells asked.

"Yes sir," Georgia said.

"You're a brave young woman. But I've told you time and again that we can give you something stronger."

"No, I don't want to hurt my baby. She didn't get such a great start, you understand, and with all she's been through already... well, I just want to protect her." Tears collected in the corners of her eyes.

"Not all medications for pain will harm the fetus, Georgia," Dr. Fells gently urged.

But Georgia knew better. She'd made it this far, and she wasn't going to back down now.

It was odd how freely they talked about the baby now. She had been such a secret in the beginning, such a source of emotional trauma, but now everyone in this room believed the only reason Georgia hadn't died at the hands of Tony and Mike was because of the tiny angel growing within her. Her parents would be married on September 27th if Georgia could make it by then. "I want to walk down the aisle on my poppa's arm," she'd stated. Her mother had raised an eyebrow, thinking of the swollen belly she would have by then. But her father had smiled, and that had been enough for her.

The bandages were gone. Dr. Fells had kept Georgia talking the whole time to calm her fears and take her mind off what would she would see. "There's still some swelling, Georgia, and your color hasn't returned. The yellow tinge will go, the swelling will go, and we still have to do something about your eyebrow. But, pretty girl, I have a feeling you're going to be happy." Georgia looked at Joey; he was smiling, really smiling, even his eyes. She reached for the mirror and brought it to her face with a steely resolve.

The fingertips of her bandaged hand came to her face. The tears that had collected in her eyes flowed freely. She smiled a tiny smile, but her eyes were sad. "I'm scarred," she whispered.

"No, Georgia, you're bruised. I told you that will pass and the swelling will go, too." Dr. Fells felt panic rising in his throat. The surgeons had worked so hard to restore her to what she had been. The fact that she wasn't permanently disfigured was a miracle. But this little lady had been difficult to work with. She wouldn't take pain medicine, and she wouldn't allow other doctors to talk to her. She had come to know Dr. Fells and his gentleness the day she came in, and something in her wouldn't release him. The fear that had shown in her face then was even stronger now.

"You don't understand, Dr. Fells. I meant my eyes; the shadow of sadness is in my eyes. My face looks fine, just like I knew it would. I look almost like me, I can see that coming in time—time I now have thanks to you and your team. But my eyes are scarred, like the women in Bosnia. Have you seen those documentaries on television? All those women have war-scarred eyes. It's like you can only see so much, and then a veil comes over your eyes to protect your soul." Georgia tried to look at her mother, but Lucinda was standing behind her, so she raised her hand. Her mother's hand slipped into hers, the olive skin contrasting with the white bandages. Lucinda laid her cheek on the cast.

"Georgie, you look beautiful," her mother whispered.

Dr. Fells had never met people like these. What sadness had they witnessed in their lives to prepare them for this moment? "You, my dear, are a remarkable young woman. That baby of yours is very fortunate indeed to be born to this family.

"Speaking of your baby, the obstetrician wants to stop by today. I have a feeling you will like her very much." Dr. Fells had chosen a woman for Georgia because of her fear of other doctors. As soon as he started to explain, Georgia was ready to voice her displeasure.

"Georgia, I want you to give her a chance. And I want to tell you something about this doctor. She does rape crisis counseling, Georgia, because she's been there. She was raped in college and she survived. She speaks openly about it now, but her road hasn't been an easy one. See her, please, for me." Georgia looked down at the sheet where her bandaged hands lay and nodded.

After Dr. Fells had gone Georgia's parents and Joey moved into her line of sight. "You look beautiful, Georgia," Joey whispered. He was relieved, and Georgia could see it and hear it in his voice. To her it was enough. If he could live with it, so could she. She looked into his eyes for the same shadows she saw, and they were there. Her mother and father had them, now she and Joey had them, too. Life might be the school of hard knocks, but love did soften the blows.

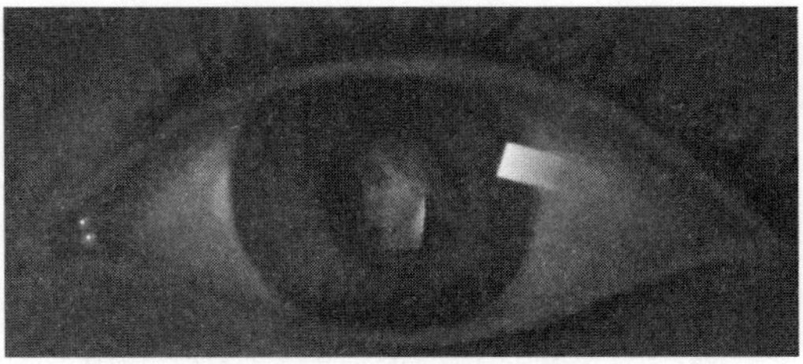

CHAPTER 49

Don Corley sat, half drunk, alone, and despondent, in his dark apartment. The scotch he was drinking had helped some, but he still couldn't get himself together. Daphne had called every day, sometimes ten times a day, leaving messages on his recorder that ate up the tape; but so far he hadn't called her back. She hadn't come to the funeral because Don had told her to stay away. She'd cried like a spoiled child and said the worst thing she could say, "What will the media think, darling, if I'm not by your side at a time like this?" Don had slammed the door in her face.

He hadn't shaved in days, or taken a shower. He just sat there thinking about Wanda and what a mess he'd made of her life. If he hadn't been so selfish, if he'd been a better father, if he'd spent more time with her, maybe she wouldn't have been looking for something at a fucking carnival.

The glass fell from his hand, spilling scotch onto the white carpet he'd been so proud of just a year ago. Great wracking sobs shook his body. "Wanda, I'm so sorry, baby. Daddy's so sorry." The soft knocking on the door finally registered.

"Daphne, go away," he yelled.

From the other side of the door the noise didn't really sound human. It was more of an animal croak or growl. She knocked again, softly. Again she heard, "Daphne, please, go away. Leave me alone."

"He thinks I'm Daphne," she whispered. "Don, it's me, it's Phyllis. Please let me in."

Don heard it, but somehow he didn't really believe it. If she was here she must have forgiven him. Again he heard the insistent tapping. "Don, please, please let me in," Phyllis begged. "Don, you're scaring me. Please—this isn't doing either of us any good. I need you. Please, Don," Phyllis's voice trailed off into sobs. Don staggered to his feet. He saw the golden brown stain on the carpet, and even that didn't really register.

"Don please," he heard again. This time the pain in the voice registered. "Please, Don, I need you," Phyllis wailed from the other side.

Don staggered to the door, ten steps from where he'd been sitting, but the simple act seemed to take forever. He grabbed the doorknob and pulled, but the chain caught and kept the door from opening all the way. He remembered that he'd put it on when Daphne had tried her key. It had kept her out then, but he didn't want to keep Phyllis out. Finally, as he jerked the chain free, she came into his unstable arms.

They fell together to their knees as their arms entwined and their tears mingled. It had been three days since they'd seen each other. They had stood at the gravesite after all the guests had left and watched as the dirt was thrown over their daughter's casket. The blanket of yellow tea roses had remained, at Don's insistence.

"Let her take it with her," he'd said. "Phyllis, oh God, Phyllis, our baby," Don moaned now. He'd known then she needed him, needed him to be strong; but he didn't have it in him, he just couldn't do it. He needed to be comforted and held, he needed to be forgiven.

"I know Don, I know. But you can't stay in here like this. You're still wearing your suit, Don. Haven't you eaten or showered?" Phyllis tried to smooth the hair back from his brow. It wasn't like him to neglect his hygiene. He had always been so fastidious. But he just knelt there in the doorway, weeping, with his arms draped over her. He couldn't be consoled, and Phyllis didn't have the strength to lift him alone.

The other doors in the hallway had opened, and many of the residents had witnessed Don's collapse. Of course, they all knew, everyone in town knew, because the media had covered the story relentlessly. A man came forward and looked at Phyllis tentatively, without saying a word.

"Yes, please," Phyllis said, and the man tried to help her lift the limp, weak Don to his feet. He was like a newborn baby with no strength. The neighbor looked down the hallway to see if someone else could help with this large broken man. Several men came then and together they managed to get him upright. Phyllis stood back with her clenched fist covering her mouth. She watched as the man who had shared her life was lifted like a baby and placed in his bed.

Other women came forward now to her aid. Some made coffee, and some brought food, cookies and pieces of cake. In Don's room, his neighbors helped him take his shoes off, and he rallied slightly. Eventually everyone left and Don and Phyllis were alone. It was temporary relief, and it was all they needed.

Phyllis sat on the edge of the bed and held Don's hand. "This isn't your fault, Don. I want you to know that I feel that way. Wanda got friendly with the wrong crowd, but ultimately it was her decision to go with those men. She knew better, we had told her time and again all her life. I hurt, too, but we have to stand together. I can't do it without you." Phyllis was crying softly now. She was spent.

"I let you both down, Phyllis. I can't tell you how sorry I am or how guilty I feel. I keep seeing her face the last time I spent time with her. She looked so disappointed in me. I was angry at her and I told her she was being selfish." Don hid his eyes behind his hands. Phyllis reached forward and took his hand in hers.

"Don, she wanted ten thousand dollars to go on a trip to Europe after graduation. Do you really think you were being selfish?"

"No, I didn't then, but now, Phyll, if I had only known it was the last thing I could give her, I would have done it gladly. But I lost that chance, I lost it," Don said, starting to cry again. He couldn't seem to control it. "I need a drink," he said.

"I think you've had enough. How about a shower and something to eat?" Phyllis asked, as she stood and walked to the kitchen.

"Phyll, why are you here?" Don asked.

"Because I can't get through this without you, and obviously you can't get through this without me. And because I'm not going to let that woman come between us anymore."

As if on cue the phone rang. "Don, this is Daphne. You had better answer this phone or I'm getting the super to open your door for me," Daphne screeched into the phone. Phyllis looked at him and raised an eyebrow. Don gave a slightly guilty smile. "You get in the shower and I'll handle this—if you're sure you want me to."

"I'm sure," Don said as he stumbled to the shower, wiping his eyes.

"Phyll," he said, as he watched her go.

"Yes," she said as she peeked around the doorjamb.

"Thank you."

"Go shower. I'll make us something to eat." The tears were still wet on her eyelashes, but for the first time in days she felt a little better. The phone rang again. "Don, I mean it," Daphne said.

"Hello, Daphne. This is Phyllis Corley. Stop calling here. That means don't call anymore. Don and I need to grieve over our daughter's death without your pestering."

"Don needs me," Daphne said defiantly.

"Like a sore throat," Phyllis answered.

"Tell Donald to call me," Daphne said as she hung up the phone.

"Right, when donkeys fly; hell, when elephants fly," Phyllis said as she placed the phone back in the cradle. Thinking better of it, she stuffed the receiver under a sofa cushion.

The Corleys spent the rest of the weekend together. Don packed a bag and they went home. He lounged in his favorite chair. Phyllis hadn't been able to bring herself to get rid of it when they'd divorced, and Don hadn't taken it with him to his new life. They ate at the table together and slept in each other's arms for the first time in eighteen months.

"Phyll?" Don whispered as he drifted off to sleep.

"Hmm," she'd responded.

"I'm sorry."

"Me too."

CHAPTER 50

Roll call at shift change wasn't a pleasant experience, no matter what, but today it was downright miserable. The end-of-the-day shift change was usually harder than morning roll call, but equally as important. Will, Sam, and Jerry sat in the back and waited. Captain Morris bellowed and hollered at the room full of officers for twenty minutes. Then he looked at the detectives, "What do you have to say for yourselves?" he demanded.

Will stood up first. "Our perpetrators are Tony Somebody and Mike Hennessey. We know that from fingerprints and from his having been in our wonderful penal system. Mike has a rap sheet as long as his arm. It seems that someone forgot to put the results of the print sheet on our desk, and I would like to personally thank whoever did that. Also, this guy has some health issues we should all be aware of. He's manic depressive, bi-polar. He's also been diagnosed with a sexual addiction."

Laughter met his ears; but he didn't laugh, and neither did Sam or Jerry. None of the investigative team did, for that matter. None of the men or women who had been at the old cabin could have brought themselves to laugh after seeing Wanda Corley's blood all over the sheets. Most of them had worked all night and through the day. Will continued, "The other man, Tony Somebody, doesn't have a record that we know of."

Will and Jerry had finally found the fingerprint results by demanding them from the records department. They had been filed without the detectives being notified. Now, standing in the field room listening to the Captain chew out the group only made them madder. Jerry and Will looked around the room at the faces that had stopped laughing. "Someone has made a serious mistake. And if this mistake has cost a life, the person who did it will have to live with that forever. You don't want that on your conscience, folks, believe you me," the Captain said.

Will waited until he was done. "Okay, we have to catch these two. They are smarter than we've given them credit for. So double your efforts and don't count anything out as a waste of time. An officer in the next county did, and these two wise-asses are still on the loose because of that. He didn't know about the cabin. Even though it was visible from the road, he didn't see it because he went in one way and came out the same way. He never passed the cabin. What I'm telling you is, check everything out, every doghouse, outhouse, henhouse, and cathouse, for that matter. These guys need shelter and we know they aren't afraid to move around."

Jerry had set up a blackboard and drawn a diagram of the area. He showed them the pattern the perps had taken so far. The campsite was there, as well as the cabin, even though they were more than forty miles apart. The sketch of Tony and Mike was tacked on the board. "These are our target kids," he said. "Make sure you study their faces. Show these sketches to everyone you see while you're out there. You don't want to make a mistake. You don't want the death of a young woman on your conscience, I promise you." As he sat down, the questions started.

They answered the questions they could, but "We don't know" was a common response. Finally someone asked the right question, and Will held his hands in the air. "Folks, please give me your attention. I need your input on something. You've asked what we're going to do—I have an idea, but I'm not sure if you're open-minded enough for it, and I will need your support if this is going to work."

All eyes were on him, and he felt like he was standing there naked. "I have a plan. A guy I know, a captain from another police force. told me about a tool that he used, more than a tool really, a person. This person was instrumental in solving a case, one where the lives of two seven-year-old girls were on the line, a kidnapping case where they had no leads."

Will was being elusive on purpose. He and Jerry wanted to watch the faces of the people in the room. He had everyone's attention, even the Captain's. "This person," he continued, "is clairvoyant." He waited for the murmurs to die down. "I want to know what everyone thinks of using this person to help us find these two guys."

"It wasn't as bad as you thought it would be," Jerry said an hour later as he and Will walked down the hallway.

"No, but it wasn't great either. Did you see the Captain's face? I thought we were going to have to do CPR on him," Will said.

"He always looks like that. Don't worry, give them some time to think it through, and they'll get behind you," Jerry promised, even though he wasn't sure it was true.

"We don't have time," Will argued.

"Will, Jerry, telephone," Millie shouted. Looking in her direction Will asked, "Why do secretaries shout?"

"Huh?" Jerry said.

"Nothing, just something I was thinking about," Will said as he headed in her direction.

"This is Will Halpin," he said into the receiver.

"Detective, this is Henry Lape. I figured out what was missing from the barn like you asked me to."

"That's great, Mr. Lape. What was it?"

"A duffle bag with a shotgun in it that needs some work. The trigger pin doesn't release like it should. Some old army blankets and some broken fishing gear. It's some stuff that I bought at a barn sale. Also, an old tarp or something, I never opened it, but that's what I think it was." Henry Lape couldn't have said anything worse. Will thanked him as he hung up the phone.

"We have bigger problems. Seems our perps may have a gun again. It's broken, but hey, these guys seem pretty resourceful," he said to Jerry. Jerry raised his eyebrows and opened his mouth to say something as they made their way to their office, but as they reached the desk they shared,

Jerry started laughing. There on the desk was a small clear marble stuck to the top of a bottle cap with a big wad of pink chewing gum. Will and Jerry knew right away what it was supposed to represent. "A crystal ball, someone's a real genius," Will said as he stuck his head back in the hallway and yelled, "You should spend more time working on this case and less time acting ridiculous."

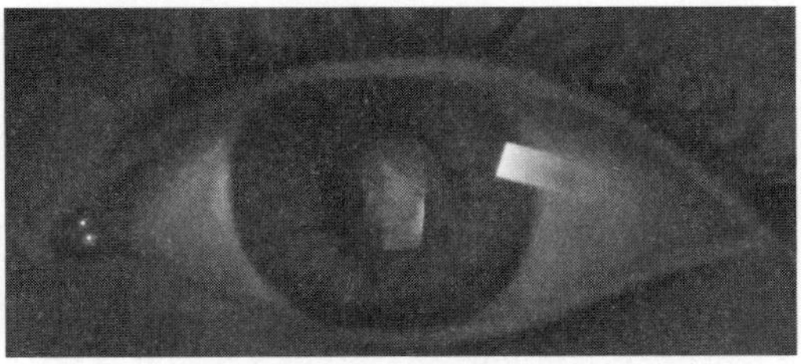

CHAPTER 51

Lindsay had been twisting and turning in a tangle of covers most of the night. She struggled in her sleep with the images playing themselves over and over again in her dreams. Varying degrees of black, white, and gray formed little squares for her mind to play with that slowly took shape. Initially she saw familiar things like the circular lines of a seashell or the outline of a box filled with things, but they were never in color. Then the images took different shapes, lines formed and crossed, becoming objects she didn't recognize. It was a seemingly endless mirage of shapes and shades.

Finally, Lindsay tossed the covers back and sat up. Rubbing her hands across her face she stood and went to the bathroom. She looked at the clock—two thirty a.m. Not nearly time to get up, and she needed all the sleep she could get to face the day ahead. "Leave me alone," she whispered into the night. "It's not my problem, it's not my problem."

But the images continued to come. Lindsay realized she had no choice and reached for her recorder on the bedside table. "Tonight is Wednesday, June first. Images coming to me after a conversation with Detective Halpin in regard to the murders and kidnappings he's investigating. This is rambling at best: a seashell with dramatic lines that curve in an ever-widening circle, the lines of a box in varying shades of gray, a man's goatee, I think, and then some trees in shadow as they blend together in the forest. I have no idea what these things mean, so I'm recording them to listen to later."

Lindsay laid the recorder back on the table and turned the light out. She stared at the ceiling, waiting. Slowly she started to drift off. Just as she let herself go, images of men moving through the shaded colors she'd seen came back to her. They were moving fast, then slowly, then not at all. Slowly one man turned and looked right at her. As he did, he pointed his finger at her like a gun. The other man was carrying something large draped over his shoulder, something that had long wisps of things hanging from it that moved in slow motion, in her mind. It looked like a body. Lindsay sat up with a start. She flipped on the light and looked around the room, breathing hard as she checked out the familiar surroundings. Slowly her breathing calmed and she sank once again on to the pillow. "Well, so be it," she whispered. "It might as well come."

The images let go of Lindsay, and once again she drifted into a troubled sleep.

That's the way it was. Once Lindsay picked something up or looked at something for someone, she had it until the job was done. So often she found herself a victim of the happenings around her or an open portal to those she knew. Lindsay struggled with crowded places where thoughts and emotions were flying. She often felt rather than heard someone crying. So many times she'd reached out to help a stranger, only to have that person feel as if she were intruding.

Then there were times when Lindsay would find herself hearing a stranger's life story—in fact, it happened all the time, and the other person never knew why they'd given so much information or to whom they'd given it. People didn't have to know Lindsay was clairvoyant in order to want to talk to her. She hid her life and her gift as much as she could. Lindsay's greatest dream was to go back to that dreadful day so many years ago and have it all taken back, before she had become "gifted," as people called it. But she couldn't go back—this was her life, this was her gift.

CHAPTER 52

Mike and Tony drove for hours, totally oblivious to the events taking place at the old cabin. Mike's excitement was contagious. Even though it had taken some time to get caught up in this moment, Tony was finally there.

"Come on, Mike, I'm ready to stop any time, now. This looks like a good place, and I ain't sure this car can go any further on this dirt road. These ruts are gonna hang us up." Tony was holding on to the door for dear life. The car wobbled over the huge, hardened ruts of the dirt road. The station wagon wasn't really made for this kind of off-road terrain.

"We're gonna make it, Tony. I have an idea. We have to ditch this car or find some way to camouflage it. We can't keep driving it cause someone is gonna recognize it. So I wanna find a place to hide so we can do some artwork to this car. Then we need to find us some new license plates and set up camp." He was rambling—something Lindsay, many miles away, had picked up on.

Tony smiled at him. "Yeah, and then we can get something to eat. I'm hungry and I'm tired. I wanna take a pee, too."

"Okay, it's just a little further up this road. I got a feeling, if you know what I mean, but I can stop right here and you can take a leak," Mike said. He was feeling very agreeable. Tony looked at him and knew it in a heartbeat. Now was the time to get whatever he wanted.

"Hey Mike, can we maybe find us a dog? I mean we wouldn't have to buy one, we could just find one. I really want a dog." Tony was looking at Mike with a look that told Mike he shouldn't say no.

"Tony, man, we have enough to take care of with feeding ourselves. A dog needs things, buddy, like shots and a collar and special food. You ain't supposed to feed dogs table scraps, you know?" Mike watched Tony's face fall.

"I know you ain't, but I really want a dog Mike. Maybe later? Do you think later when we head south for the winter we could get a dog?" Tony asked.

"Sure, buddy, we can get a dog then if you want to. How much money you got left?" Mike asked.

"I got about forty dollars. What about you?" Tony was instantly suspicious. Mike always wanted his money, too, even if he still had some of his own.

"I got about the same. Do you wanna get some party materials? Are ya hungry?" Mike asked, watching Tony's face carefully.

"Yeah!" Tony crowed.

"Cool. I'll drop our stuff off at that campsite just up the road and you can get set up while I go find us some new plates and get some grub." Mike knew just what he was doing, and Tony knew it too. Mike usually left the work up to Tony, and now he saw Tony look down at his hands as they drove.

To change the subject Mike said, "Tony, look." There to the left was a beautiful clearing in the thick wooded area they'd been driving through for more than an hour.

"Gosh, Mike its great," Tony said. And it was. Water flowed nearby in a small bend in the river, and the woods themselves had hollowed out the campsite. It was a totally natural area, hidden miles and miles away from anyone. Mike had stumbled upon it accidentally, but he let Tony believe he'd known the spot was there all along.

"Tony, just remember the water is part of a fast-moving river. Be careful, and don't go near the water unless I'm with you." Mike wanted Tony to hear the concern in his voice. He also wanted to keep Tony's mind off the fact that he was once again leaving all the work up to him.

They parked the car and got out. The two men walked around the clearing and looked for what they needed: water, trees, a place to build a campfire, and seclusion. Had any of those things been missing, they would have gotten back in the car and continued down the bumpy dirt road.

Mike smiled at Tony as he saw the look on his face. "It's good, huh? Don't ya think it's a good spot, Tony?" Mike was waiting for him to say yes. Tony always said yes, even when he didn't agree.

"It's fine, Mike, real fine. I'll start unloading the car," Tony said. Mike could tell something was bothering him, but he didn't really care. He would go to the store and get some tequila and some grub, and that would make everything right with the world. Mike helped Tony unpack the car, and the two of them trudged back and forth several times. As Tony hoisted the last load, the large duffle bag that had been stolen from the Lapes barn, Tony and Mike walked back to the site together. Mike gathered sticks for kindling.

"Tony, did you hear that?" Mike whispered. Tony turned, and as he did the duffle bag's drawstrings flapped in the night shadows, "What? I didn't hear anything."

"I thought I heard someone or something. Are you gonna be okay here by yourself?" Mike asked, as he turned slowly around looking into the shadows.

"Yeah, go on. I'll get this stuff put together and see you when you get back. Hey Mike, bring some tequila, would ya?" Tony asked.

"Yeah. I need some money, though, Tony. I'm just about out 'cause I bought the gas back there," Mike said. He watched the woods for signs of something to be afraid of. Nothing showed itself. Tony shook his outstretched hand in front of Mike's face.

"Mike, you okay? Here's the money." Tony was looking at him funny. "Hey Mike, you wanna stay here, and I'll go?" Tony asked.

"No man. I'm okay. I don't wanna stay here by myself. I'll be back as soon as I can. We'll get plates tomorrow." Tony saw Mike look around one more time as he got in the car. Tony laughed and started working on the campsite.

It never occurred to him that Mike had never been here before. He figured since Mike knew where it was, all was right with this place. Tony worked hard for about an hour. The camping area took shape. The new tent was new just to them. Actually, it was an old canvas tent, and it had a few holes in its floor. But Tony covered them with the tarp that had come with it. He put the sleeping bags out and built a fire close enough to the tent to provide light if they needed it. He grabbed the toilet paper from the pile of camp gear, and took off into the woods. About fifty feet back, Tony found the perfect spot. A felled tree would make a nice perch for doing your business, and a low-hanging tree would hold the paper up off the ground. Tony fitted the plastic bag over it in case of rain. He let some of it trail off.

As he walked out of the woods he realized that he'd created a place much like the one they'd had to leave. Tony missed that place. As he looked around he was pleased with the work he'd done. Walking the perimeter one more time, Tony came to the water's edge. He stood back and peered into the water.

The moon's reflected light seemed to form a path to where Tony stood on the bank. He leaned just a bit further and almost toppled in. Breathing hard, he grabbed the branches of the nearby bushes, then he moved away from the water's edge. Tony turned and hurried back to the tent. Crawling inside, he waited for his heart to calm down. Images of his youth came back to him, and tears filled his eyes.

Tony's fear of water had started at a picnic in the fourth grade. He'd been running around playing tag with some other kids and someone had pushed him in the water. He'd never learned to swim, and after that incident he never wanted to. Tony had gone under several times before anyone realized he was in trouble, and a teacher had jumped in to pull him out. Instead of being glad he was okay the teacher had punished him by making him sit out the rest of the day. Tony never forgot the incident or got over his fear of water.

"Tony, hey Tony, where are ya?" Mike yelled from the car window as he pulled back into the clearing. He'd been gone for a long time, and Tony had not only put the site together but he'd fallen asleep. Mike walked to the tent and shook it violently. "Tony, wanna party, buddy?"

Tony rubbed his eyes and climbed out of the tent. "Where ya been Mike? I was getting lonely here by myself."

"Tony, my man, you did a right fine job setting up camp," Mike said as he held up the bottle of tequila for Tony to see. Tony let out a whoop and grabbed the bottle.

"Tony, I did some scouting around and we are totally alone up here. There ain't another soul for miles and miles. I didn't even see no farmhouses. We can make all the noise we want up here," Mike said, smiling widely.

"Yeah? Cool. Do you like the way I have the camp set up, Mike?" Tony asked as he took a huge swig from the tequila bottle.

"Yeah, Tony. You did a fine job. It looks like our other one, 'cept the tent's old and we ain't got us a stump yet. But we'll get one," Mike said with a sneer on his face. "Yep, buddy, we'll get us a stump and get us some stump-broke bitches, too."

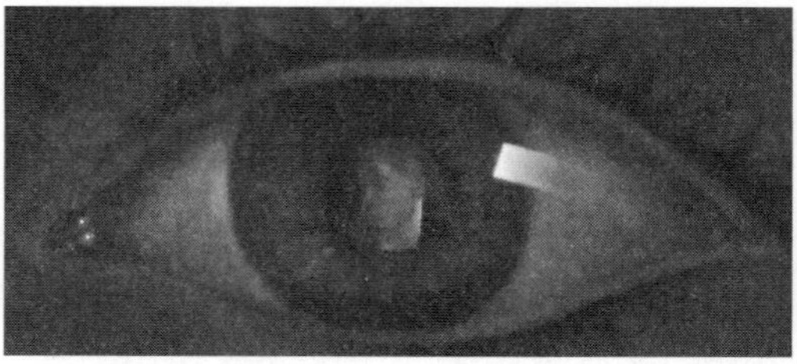

CHAPTER 53

"Okay, everyone, listen up," Captain Morris said. "Ripney High School's prom is less than two weeks away. All three of our victims went to school there, so it's safe to say that we're going to have hundreds of teenagers out there shopping, and on prom night it's gonna be a smorgasbord for these two perps. We've got to find these assholes. It's my job to tell you, and it's your job to do it. I don't want any more mistakes and I don't want any more jokes left on Halpin's desk. DO YOU ALL UNDERSTAND ME?" he bellowed. Heads nodded everywhere.

It had been a week of constant jokes about clairvoyants. Will and Jerry had taken it good-naturedly, but it was starting to wear thin. Forensics had come back with plenty of information, none of it unexpected, but none of it pointing to where Mike and Tony might have gone. They had fingerprints, sketches, blood samples, and clothing identified. All of the items collected at the various scenes were in baggies. Every baggy was labeled with the name of a victim, with "Mike," because they knew his name and had his fingerprints on file, or with "Tony" because he was the one missing link. They had fingerprints for all the victims, so Tony's were easy to pick out. The station had a field room set up just for this investigation, and Jerry and Will had moved desks into it temporarily.

Sam Kent sat at the table and processed the last bit of information that had come in that morning. "Roll call was a bitch this morning, and I don't look for this afternoon to be any better," he said. Jerry and Will nodded at him but said nothing. The trail was starting to get cold.

"Somebody tell me how the hell they just up and disappeared like a fart in the wind? Will somebody please tell me that," Jerry said.

"They didn't, we just can't find them. I've been thinking about it, and you know what I came up with?" Sam asked.

"No, Einstein, tell us. What did you come up with?" Will and Jerry said together.

"We live in an area that's pretty easy to cover. I mean, with the uniforms we have; the media, which, as you know, has been all over this like white on rice; and eyewitnesses, we should be able to cover this area. I believe our boys don't mind driving. I have a feeling they like it, and somehow they've figured out how to beat the law of averages." Sam sat there and waited for them to respond. Jerry went back to what he was doing. Will walked out of the room and headed to the john.

"What, you guys got a better idea?" Sam asked.

"Nope, we don't, but that one has been done a hundred times," Jerry said. Will came back into the room and set his coffee cup on the table. He plopped down in a chair and put his hands over his eyes.

"What are we gonna do? Does anyone have any fresh ideas?"

Jerry grabbed the sketch and laid it on the table. He was tired of working the evidence. "Suppose they've changed the way they look. Maybe that's why we can't get anyone out there in the general public to identify them," he said.

"Yeah, I thought of that," Will agreed.

"Suppose Sam's right. Maybe the area we're looking at isn't large enough. Suppose they don't mind driving, and suppose, just for good measure, they have a clean car. Something we aren't looking for." Jerry continued.

"Guys, we've been over all of this. It's been quiet. Way too quiet. I'm scared shitless because I don't know where they are or what they're planning. We don't have a clue to their whereabouts and no one is coming forward, and I'm tired," Will said. "We need some fresh meat in here. Someone that hasn't been through this like we have. Someone that can see what we're missing."

"Will Halpin, line one," Millie yelled from somewhere down the hall.

"Don't either of you go anywhere. Stay here and solve this damn thing while I'm gone." Will chuckled as he walked to the phone.

"Halpin here," he said and waited.

"Detective Halpin, this is Lindsay Freeman. I hope you don't mind my calling you at work, but I have some information that you may need. Hello, Detective? Are you there?" Lindsay asked, listening to a dead-silent phone.

But Will was busy, throwing a wad of paper at Jerry and Sam to get their attention. "Ms. Freeman, hello. Can I put you on speakerphone? I'm here with my partners and I'd like them to hear what you have to say."

"Yes, you can, and it's Lindsay, please."

"Okay, go ahead, Lindsay. In the room with me are Sam Kent and Jerry Leeme. You can speak freely in front of them."

"Hello, gentlemen. I hope you'll forgive my calling like this. When I spoke with Will last week I forgot to mention that once I start something I must see it through. That's one of the reasons I don't usually like to get involved unless a family member contacts me. I know they'll see it through. I have a tape I'd like you to hear if you don't mind."

"Sure, Lindsay, we'll listen to the tape. Can you tell us what it's about first?" Will asked.

"Yes—this tape is something I made in the middle of the night. I don't get the warm fuzzies about your interaction with clairvoyants so I'll assume none of you have ever worked with one of us before. The thing is, once I get some information on something or I meet someone, that person or situation is like an open portal of information for me. But I must have an outlet for it. I can't just ignore it. It's one of the pitfalls of the gift, if you ask me," Lindsay said.

"We understand," Will said and shrugged his shoulders as Sam and Jerry looked at him like he was nuts. They didn't understand. Neither did Will, for that matter.

Lindsay hit the play button on the recorder and the men in the room some thirteen hundred miles away sat and listened.

"Tonight is Wednesday, June first. Images coming to me after a conversation with Detective Halpin regarding the murders and kidnapping he's investigating. This is rambling at best: a seashell with dramatic lines that curve in an ever-widening circle, the lines of a box in varying shades of gray, a man's goatee I think, and then some trees in shadow as they blend together in the forest. I see two men, they were moving fast, then slow, then not at all. Slowly one man turned and looked right at me. As he did he pointed his finger at me like a gun. The other man was carrying something large draped over his shoulder, something that had long wisps of things hanging from it that moved in slow motion in my mind. It looked like a body.

"Tonight is Thursday, June second. Again my sleep is interrupted by the events I can't control. The images of the two men are back, and the shapes and images of prisms in square boxes. The varying shades of gray and the shapes are the same, but something is different. I see the two men moving around an area that feels largely open. I can see a fire, but it's small and controlled. There is a tent or some sort of a structure that provides safety for them. There is uncontrolled lust in the air; it makes me feel nervous. It's not like passion—it's more like lust, or a feeding frenzy. There are stars and water and pacing back and forth. I know this is disjointed, but I can only tell it as I see it without someone to help me find some structure for it.

"I see a car, larger than a sedan but smaller than a van, being moved back and forth. The images are changing and people with it, dirt, lots of dirt, water, trees, and safety from prying eyes. It is my opinion they have been quiet, but that is about to change because someone, one of these two men needs something that only activity can provide. Closing remark, the images have changed. What you were looking for has changed, again."

The detectives heard the machine click off. What they hadn't heard was Captain Morris coming to stand in the doorway. Behind him were several uniformed officers. They'd all stood silently and listened as Lindsay's tape had played.

"Ms. Freeman, I'm Captain Morris, the head of this unruly rabble. I want to ask you a question, if that's okay."

"Yes, sir. That's fine," Lindsay said.

"Has anyone, even our Detective Halpin here, told you anything about this case?"

"Yes sir. Detective Halpin and I spoke at length about this case last week. He told me some of the particulars of this case. I hope that's okay with you."

"So, Ms. Freeman, you haven't spoken with Detective Halpin since that initial conversation?" Captain Morris asked.

"No, sir. Can I ask why you're asking?" Lindsay inquired.

"Because, Ms. Freeman, that tells me a great deal about you. Our boys are on the move as you say, things around them are changing, and I believe they are ever changing. I understand the images you say you see because I see them too—only I don't know how they work." Captain Morris looked around the room as he spoke, daring anyone to make even the smallest noise.

"Sir, how do you know these men are on the move?" Lindsay asked.

"Because our team has been to a cabin in the woods where they were staying. They're one step ahead of us all the time. They were last seen driving a station wagon, and we know someone stole a station wagon from a neighboring farm where they also stole a duffle bag with a broken rifle and some army blankets in it," Captain Morris said.

The field room was quiet. In fact, you could have heard the proverbial pin drop. No one expected this out of their rough and tough Captain. They had never heard him speak so kindly before. Will and Jerry stared at him as if he'd dropped from outer space. Sam Kent was smiling like the cat that ate the canary. Morris was looking at them all, daring them with his eyes.

"Ms. Freeman," he said. "What do you need in order to come here?"

"I need a place to stay, some time to wrap up my affairs and get ready to travel. I need someone to work with when I get there and I need access to the victims and their families."

"If you have all that, can you help us?" Captain Morris asked.

"I believe I can. There is no guarantee, of course, but I will try. And Captain, absolutely no press. That is my only stipulation. Well, almost. I don't want to come there and be the target of jokes, and I don't want to have to prove myself the whole time I'm there. Can you give me that?" Lindsay asked.

"I believe I can. Of course, this is a police station and ribbing each other is our way of maintaining sanity around here. Ms. Freeman, if you don't mind my asking, what's the price of all this information?"

"Just my expenses, Captain. My airfare and someone to pick me up at the airport. That's all I need, and a place to sleep. I can take the ribbing, but I can't take being left out of the loop. I'll be at roll call, and I'll share all the information I get with you."

"You got it. I'll have my secretary make the arrangements for you. I'll give you twelve hours to get things in order, if that's okay."

"Yes sir, that's fine," Lindsay said.

The whole thing, the entire conversation between the Captain and Lindsay, had taken place on the speakerphone. The Captain had been candid and had shared his thoughts, doubts, and fears in front of everyone. Captain Morris's organization admired him for it. A man they feared had gotten down in the trenches with them. A round of applause went up when the phone line disconnected.

"Okay, okay, everyone back to work. We have a lot to do before this woman gets here. Don't embarrass me and don't waste her time. Get your t's crossed and your i's dotted. Let's show her what we're made of," Captain Morris said as he walked out of the room.

Millie made the reservations for Lindsay and called her with the information. "An officer will be at the airport to pick you up this evening, Ms. Freeman," she said.

"Millie, its Lindsay, if you don't mind. I really appreciate all your hard work. Thank you for taking such good care of me," Lindsay said.

"No problem. I'm glad I could help. We look forward to meeting you," Millie said. She felt terrible now. After hanging up she called the hotel back and changed the reservations. She'd gotten Lindsay the worst room available. She'd secretly been jealous. Something about the way everyone was talking about her had riled Millie up. It was as if everyone thought she was some kind of special weapon or something. Now Millie found herself liking the woman. "Damn it," she said, after talking to the hotel reservation clerk. She called the florist and had flowers delivered to the room in the station's name. "Now I feel better," she thought.

Thirteen hundred miles away Lindsay smiled to herself. "One mean bulldog disarmed with kindness," she said, and giggled. Lindsay could feel Millie's animosity and she knew it wasn't conducive to a good night's sleep to piss off the big dog. She reached into the hall closet for a clean set of sheets for the king-sized bed she knew she'd have at the hotel.

"Always take your own sheets," she whispered to herself, "or sleep with the maid and what she was thinking when she made the bed."

CHAPTER 54

As darkness fell, Tony built a fire. He'd been happy the last few days. Mike had stayed close to camp, and he seemed content. They fished in the cold river in the morning, lay around and dozed all day, and partied most of the night. The money was running out, and today that could be what Mike's sour mood was about. Or it could be loneliness. Mike usually had a powerful thirst for company, female company. The argument they'd had at the cabin about the kind of girls Mike could get hung in the air like a bad smell. No one talked about it but it was there.

Tony was determined to lift Mike's mood. He danced on spindly legs around the campfire, kicking up dust and dirt. Mike sat brooding near the tent while he smoked the last of his pot. Tony hadn't had any. His excuse was that he wanted to save it for Mike, but he really didn't care for it. Tony sang all the songs he knew, and all the nursery rhymes he could remember. He whirled and jumped in the air and clapped his hands.

Though he was trying to be funny, the shadows cast by the firelight and the dust flying through the air created an eerie picture. Mike was in the mood for eerie. It suited his temperament perfectly. He was bored, he wanted entertainment, and he wanted to get high. The getting high part was working out perfectly; the bored part was another matter all together.

"Come on Mike, come dance with me," Tony shouted. Mike waved, but he didn't get up. Tony went back to his singing and dancing. He waved his arms wildly in the air and kicked his feet as high as he could. Mike smiled and thought of all they'd been through.

"If we get caught it's going to be all my fault because he's just a stupid kid. He never thinks past the moment, but he sure is fun to be with." Finally Mike got up and went to join him. They danced around the fire together and sang the words to songs they knew, songs all the kids knew. Mike sucked on his joint while Tony drained his bottle. "Wake up, Maggie, I think I got something to say to you…" they sang as loud as they could. After all, who would hear them?

They talked about things that needed to be done, things that Mike needed. Mike wanted action, and for him action usually meant women or something illegal. He told Tony they needed money, and he started working on a plan as Tony nodded off.

Long after Tony had passed out, Mike stayed awake. If Tony had woken up, he would have found Mike and the car gone. Later that day a robbery many miles away would be front-page news in a small community newspaper, but it would take days for the central station to put it together with everything else that was going on.

Mike had pulled an all-nighter, but he wasn't one to sleep at night anyway. The nighttime was for partying and having fun. It was meant for wine, women, and song. He would sleep during the day, when he couldn't be out anyway. While he drove back from his escapades, he sang.

When he reached the campsite, he shook Tony awake. "Man, one of these days you're gonna roll in the fire. Why don't you go get in the sleeping bag? But before you do, feast your eyes on this," Mike said, as he waved the wad of cash in his hand under Tony's nose.

"Hey, man," Tony said as he rubbed his eyes. "Where'd you get that?"

"I got it from the guy at the store. The money store," Mike said, dancing around the fire himself. "Then I went to the liquor store and I got this!" he said as he held the bottle of tequila in the air. Tony could see that Mike was on a high. Not high on drugs or pot, but high on action. It happened all the time, Tony was used to it.

As he staggered to his feet, Tony drank from the bottle. The last thing he needed was something else to drink, but he did it for Mike.

Dawn was much like sundown for Tony and Mike. They drank and danced wildly around the fire, singing songs and kicking up the dust storm that had settled from their earlier rambunctious behavior.

From time to time, Mike gazed around the area. "Where are we gonna get a stump? And, Tony, my man, wait 'til you see what else I brought home!" Mike said. The party was on, and it lasted long into the morning.

They fell asleep there by the smoldering embers of the campfire. The morning dew settled on their scattered clothes. It was going to be a glorious day.

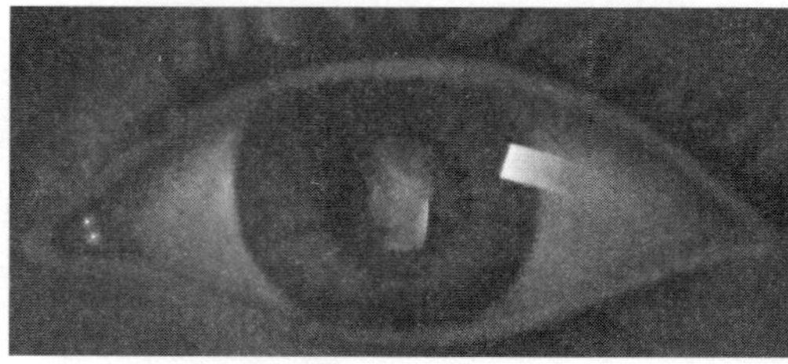

CHAPTER 55

For Lindsay the day had been a flurry of activity. She'd sat across from her supervisor and tried to explain.

"Lindsay, you really have got to stop taking these spur-of-the-moment vacations. I know you're entitled to the time, but could you please give me just a little more warning? It's hard to find someone to take your place on such short notice."

"Willa, you know I would give you more notice if I got it. But I just got word today. It's not like I plan this stuff, or even know it's coming. Well, I know it's coming, but I never know if they're going to need me, or want me, for that matter. I'm so sorry."

"Don't be sorry. I think Candy will cover for you, and I'll do what I have to. I know you're not going for a good time. I don't know how you do it. I couldn't, but then I'm not like you, am I?" Willa had known about Lindsay and her gift since Lindsay had transferred to her shift three years earlier. "Go, take care of yourself. And when you come back, if you make it back before two weeks are up, spend some time at home. I'll put in for your vacation pay for you. Any idea where you're gonna be?"

"Yes, the number's on that piece of paper. I'll call you, you're a doll," Lindsay said as she left Willa Dixon's office.

Willa shook her head. "I feel sorry for her; I wouldn't want it to be me."

Hours later, Lindsay stood in the doorway of the hotel room she'd been assigned to. It wasn't her old friend Tony Miller's house, there were no pink ruffles anywhere and there was no warm, bubbly Claire Miller fussing around, making sure everything was perfect. There was no precious five-year-old climbing around begging to be picked up or rubbing her eyes, looking for her daddy. It wasn't warm and inviting, but it was private.

Lindsay thought fondly of the Millers. Her time with them had been the last time she'd been away from home. Tonight she missed them, and she missed her family. But the flowers on the desk and the note from the station were lovely.

"Miss Freeman, is there anything else you need this evening?" the bellboy asked.

"No thank you, everything's fine. Have there been any messages for me?" Lindsay asked.

"I'll check, ma'am, and have them ring your room if there are any." Lindsay tipped the young man as he left. She stood in the room and looked around. As she put her things away and re-made her bed, she thought of home and her children. As usual, she hoped and prayed for their safety.

Climbing into bed an hour later, after some tea and a hot shower, Lindsay stared at the ceiling. "Oh great," she said in disgust. "Not tonight, please. I really need to sleep tonight." But it wasn't to be. The images came fast and furious—of a man standing with a knife in his hand, terrorizing someone behind a counter. She could hear singing and smell fire.

As the images faded sometime later, she realized she was gripping the sheets in her fist. "Wake up, Maggie, I think I got something to say to you…" Lindsay whispered into the night.

The day came way too early for Lindsay, but already there was activity at the front desk. A uniformed officer was waiting to escort her to the station. Roll call was at eight o'clock, and Lindsay wanted to be there. She'd had time for one cup of coffee, her limit normally, but not today. Today would be a two-cup day, unless of course the coffee at the station was left over from last night.

The officer in the hotel lobby looked her up and down. "Good Morning, Ms. Freeman. I'm Officer John Wilson, and I'm here to escort you to the station." Lindsay smiled at him as she followed him out to the car. They rode in complete silence.

"He's scared of me," Lindsay thought. "I don't bite, officer," Lindsay said as she got out at the station.

"Yes ma'am," John Wilson said.

Lindsay was shown into the field room and asked to wait. She walked around the room, looking at all the materials lying on the table. The jeans that had been Mandy's, a multicolored sweater caked with blood and mud, the letter from some unknown relative. The table held printed cards, sketches, and articles of clothing. Each thing was in its own plastic bag and marked with the last name of either a victim or a possible perpetrator. Lindsay felt total despair as she continued to walk in a circle. She longed to take the objects out of the plastic bags and run her fingers over them. She wanted to get familiar, but no one was available to give her permission.

Will and Jerry watched her from the doorway. They could see her trailing her fingers lightly over the tops of the articles lying on the table, never actually touching anything. She seemed to be lost in thought. She didn't know the detectives were there until she got to their side of the table, and then she turned and looked up.

"Detective Leeme, we meet at last," Lindsay said as she held her hand out to Jerry.

Jerry looked at Will and then at her hand and then back at Will. "How did you know?"

Lindsay laughed. It was the one thing she could do most of the time to get them off on the right foot. It unnerved them, but not as much as telling them about their families or eating habits. Jerry took her hand in his. He didn't know what he expected but nothing happened. Then she held her hand out to Will.

"Detective Halpin, it's nice to finally meet you in person." Will shook her hand. "It's nice to meet you too, Lindsay. I see you found your way to the field room."

"Well, actually, John Wilson brought me in here, and then he literally ran down the hallway," Lindsay said, laughing softly.

Jerry and Will laughed too. "Needless to say, everyone here is a bit nervous about your being here. We don't really know how to act around you yet."

"Just act normal," Lindsay said. Jerry and Will smiled. They looked at the table. The silence in the room was very uncomfortable. No one knew what to say. Finally, Lindsay said, "Can we get started? I hate to be the bearer of bad news, but there's a killer or two out there preying on young girls, and it's our job to stop them."

That seemed to do it. This was familiar ground for Will and Jerry. "Okay, yeah," Jerry said. "Where do you want to start?"

"I would like to start right here. I mean, you are both leaps and bounds ahead of me, and I need to catch up. I'll just sort of throw things out there as I get them, if that's okay with the two of you," Lindsay said.

Will and Jerry nodded. "But first, roll call," Will said.

They went down the long narrow hallway toward the room where Captain Morris was preparing for the morning briefing. Ray Strider poked his head out and said hi, in an offhand sort of way. As Lindsay followed Will and Jerry, she could feel everyone looking at her.

"Get your asses in this room!" a voice bellowed from the room at the end of the hall. Suddenly there seemed to be a bit of a stampede. Officers came from everywhere, and pushed and shoved past Will, Jerry, and Lindsay.

"Gosh, where'd they all come from?" Lindsay asked.

"They were hiding in the nooks and crannies of this old station to get a peek at you," Will said. He held the door open for Lindsay and then walked ahead of Jerry into the room.

"You're such a gentleman, asshole," Jerry growled.

Will snickered, and Lindsay laughed outright.

"Well, good morning. I hope roll call didn't rob any of you of your beauty sleep. It was nice of you all to meet me here, ten minutes late!" Captain Morris yelled.

"Okay, everyone settle down," Ray said. "We have a guest."

"Will, Jerry, would the two of you like to introduce our guest?" Captain Morris asked.

"Sure. Everyone, this is Ms. Lindsay Freeman. She's here to work on the Wiggins case with us. Please treat her as nice and normal as you can," Will said. Everyone greeted Lindsay warmly, but she could feel the tension in the room.

"Hello, I'm looking forward to working with you all—please treat me just as you would anyone else," Lindsay said. "Captain Morris, it's nice to meet you. Thank you for asking me to come."

"You're welcome, Ms. Freeman. Hopefully everyone here can conduct themselves like adults." Captain Morris raised an eyebrow as he surveyed the room before him. "Okay, does anyone have anything new to report?" Captain Morris asked.

The room was silent. No one said anything, because nothing much had happened. It was beginning to wear on everyone's nerves. "Okay, other business?" Captain Morris asked.

Lindsay, Jerry, and Will went back to the field room. Other officers came and went, but the three of them stayed in there most of the day. Lindsay organized the evidence by victims. Then what was left was put in a separate pile. Lindsay started with that.

As she looked at Will and Jerry she said, "A red cardigan sweater. I don't see a tag of ownership. Did it belong to either of the victims?"

"No. Not that we know of. To be honest, we've looked at that stuff a hundred times and compared it to the victim's sizes and what they were known to have been wearing when they disappeared. The only one we're not sure of is Wanda Corley, because no one saw her go. She did, however, have a red and white checkered piece of material wrapped around her wrists," Will said.

"Can I see it?" Lindsay asked. Jerry reached into the middle of the table where the area marked "Corley" was and sorted through the bags. He found the one he was looking for and handed it to Lindsay. She opened the bag, and seeing the blood, she grimaced. As her fingers touched the checked red and white cotton, she saw images of Wanda being tied up.

"She was dead when they tied her up. The red sweater belongs to her," Lindsay said as she put the cloth back in the bag. Will and Jerry felt a new respect for her. The name on the baggie was changed from "unknown" to "Corley."

"We need to verify that with her parents. They'll want the sweater back when this is all over," Jerry said as he wrote the sweater on the log sheet for Corley.

Next Lindsay picked up a bag containing the notebook paper. She had seen the letter on the table earlier. Pulling it out of the baggie, she let the images and feelings come.

"A man, no, a worried man. A man who is tied to one of these men. He feels hatred for one of them and great love and fear for the other. He's a family member or something like that. They have a history, all three of them have the same history."

"Lindsay, are you saying they're related?" Will asked.

"No. Just two of them are related. One is just a friend or an acquaintance."

"Wait, there's three of them?" Jerry said, getting to his feet.

"No, you're looking for two men. This letter is for one of those two. The third man isn't like these two. Well, actually, the one who's related to this letter isn't really like the other non-related one. Gosh, I know it's all so confusing. But the one that isn't related, he's the worst of the bunch. We're only looking for two of them. Sorry to have scared you," Lindsay said with a sheepish smile.

"Well, that's good." Jerry said as he sank back into his chair.

Lindsay reached for the backpack next. As her fingers moved over the olive green canvas she gasped, and the now-familiar grimace was back on her face. "It belongs to a girl. Originally, this was a girl's backpack." Will and Jerry looked at each other and smiled.

"What?" Lindsay asked.

"You're right. The name in it is Casey Harbor. We called the phone number on the bag, and a Casey answered. She said the backpack was stolen three months ago from her kitchen table in her parent's home. She was really upset about it because her whole paycheck was in it. She works at a blue jeans store in the mall. The same mall Amanda Wiggins and Georgia Amando were kidnapped from. At the same time someone took the backpack, they also stole her mother's purse from the counter. It had money, credit cards, and a checkbook in it. The house keys, car keys, and her mom's office keys were also in the purse. All three places were burglarized. Money was taken from each place as well as a few things that could have been sold. They filed a police report and we've checked it out," Will explained.

"Did you also tell Ms. Casey Harbor how lucky she and her mother were?" Lindsay asked.

"Yeah, we told them. Initially, we thought maybe Casey was a previous victim and then possibly part of the team. Like one of these guys was a boyfriend or something," Jerry said.

Lindsay went back to the table. She reached into the unlabeled pile and picked up a large plastic bag. Inside was a pair of jeans with holes in the knees. She opened the bag and reached inside. Stumbling backwards, Lindsay grappled for a handhold before she fell to her knees. Will and Jerry rushed to catch her, but they were too late. Lindsay sat there on the floor, with her head in her hands, taking great gulps of air.

"Lindsay, what, what's the matter? Are you okay?" Jerry and Will asked.

"I'm fine," Lindsay said, though she sounded breathless.

"What happened?" Will asked.

"Someone was terribly drunk or high or both. The person who wore those pants was wasted. He's tall and skinny and mentally slow. He cries easily, and he has anger in his heart most of the time."

"Shit," Will sighed.

"Yeah, shit," Jerry said.

"They party, gentleman, they party like I did in high school," Lindsay said with a grin. Jerry picked up the bag from the floor and extended a hand to Lindsay. Then he labeled the bag "Tony" and put it in the pile with the fingerprint cards that had the same title.

The afternoon continued much the same way. Lindsay held things, and Jerry labeled them. The organization the trio found later that same afternoon amazed them. They couldn't believe so much had been accomplished.

"Okay, what now?" Jerry asked.

"Well, the day is still young. Can we go to the mall and take a look around? I need to see the abduction sites," Lindsay explained.

"Sure, get your purse. We'll clear it with the Captain and meet you at the desk," Will said, as he and Jerry left the room. Lindsay grabbed her purse and turned one more time to look at the table. It was now better organized, but the load on it was still just as heavy. The blackboard was written on with bright white chalk, and they were still no closer to finding the criminals.

"But at least we have a plan," Lindsay said, as she closed the door behind her.

CHAPTER 56

Lindsay, Will, and Jerry rode around the mall parking area. Will and Jerry showed Lindsay where Amanda had been taken and described the events they had heard about.

"Everything we have in regard to this is secondhand information. The witnesses Cammy Burke and Jeremy Wright gave excellent descriptions of what happened that day, but they were emotionally distraught at the time. We've tried to talk to them again, but they are both pretty messed up. Aletha Wiggins is in the psychiatric ward at the hospital with a nervous breakdown. She swears she can hear Amanda calling to her from the grave," Jerry said.

Lindsay got out of the car and walked around the area. She looked back at the mall entrance and started walking again. As she moved across the pavement, she stopped in different places and turned to look back. "The kids got separated," she said. "That's how they got her. She turned to run back into the mall."

"Yes, that's what Cammy Burke said." Will was pointing to a spot in the parking area where a brown van was parked. "Cammy also said Amanda's mom's car was parked about right there. She didn't have far to go to safety. If she had run that way instead of back to the mall, she would have made it, if you consider where the eyewitnesses say the van came from. She just picked the wrong direction to run in," Will said.

Lindsay walked to where the van was parked. She turned and looked back at the mall again. Something in the wind whistled past her ears and she tried to hear it. But it wasn't time yet . . . nothing else came to her.

As she got back in the car, Lindsay asked Will and Jerry to take her to where Georgia had been kidnapped. They drove to the back of the mall.

"A totally different area," Lindsay whispered. Will and Jerry didn't say anything. As they pointed out the area under the lamp, Lindsay could see Georgia running. She had no idea what Georgia really looked like but in her mind's eye a young woman she assumed was Georgia ran to a car.

"Five more seconds and she would have made it."

"Yeah, that's what we hear. She told us she had her keys in her hand and she ran to the car. She was groped and molested and her head was cut when she fought to get away. The other man, the one driving, had dropped off his partner and came around to get them as Mike ran up behind her and grabbed her. He's the one who dragged her into the car. He's the one who raped her first," Will said.

The three of them were quiet for a moment. Lindsay finally broke the silence. "If it's any consolation, guys, she did all the right things. They were ready for her. I believe they watched the parking area and waited until the right one came out. When she did, they knew to get between her and the mall and then between her and her car. That's why they split up," Lindsay said.

"Lindsay, you said something just now. You said, 'the right one.' What did you mean by that?" Will asked.

Lindsay stood there, in almost the same spot where Georgia had stood when Mike had grabbed her. "I'm sorry, Will, I'm not sure. It could be that the right one is just the right one for that moment. But again, I'm not sure. I may get something later when I get other stuff to tie it to. I know that sounds vague, and I try never to be vague, but sometimes what I get comes in bits and pieces."

"It's okay, Lindsay. It was just an idea," Will said.

"I don't want to let you down. Please just give me some time to work it out in my mind. I'll get an answer for you," Lindsay said. They could tell that she meant it and wasn't purposely withholding information. She seemed to be working it out right in front of them.

"Lindsay, we don't expect miracles from you. We just want whatever help you can give, and since we've never worked with someone like you before we're not sure what to think," Jerry said. He looked at Will for reassurance. Will nodded.

"Okay, where to now?" Jerry asked.

"It's dinner time, and to be honest, I'm famished," Lindsay said.

"Oh shit, gosh, Lindsay we're sorry. Sometimes the whole day goes by and we forget to eat. You should have said something. We've been working such long hours we just sort of forget and the day gets away from us," Will said. He felt like crap.

"Yeah, good buddy, and worse crap than that is, today's Friday. Remember Friday?" Jerry said as he looked at Will and raised his eyebrows.

"Oh. crap." Will was going to be in hot water, and he felt terrible that he couldn't take Lindsay to dinner with him. What the hell was she going to do for the evening?

"Guys, go to dinner. Don't worry about me, I'll be fine. I'm looking forward to a long hot soak in a bubble bath and my book," Lindsay said. She was letting them off the hook and she knew it.

Will had never been transparent in his life. He looked at Lindsay and wondered. She smiled at him and masked her face with her best innocent facade.

"Uh, Lindsay—well, this evening was planned by my wife some time ago. If you're sure you don't mind," Will stammered.

"Go on, go, and Jerry, have a really nice time," Lindsay chuckled.

"We'll drop you off at the hotel first," Jerry said.

"Well, I'd rather have a car if that can be arranged." Lindsay suggested.

"Oh yeah, that would be a good idea, wouldn't it?" Will said. "There aren't many restaurants around that hotel and the food there isn't all that great."

"My thoughts exactly," Lindsay said as she laughed. "Hey, that's my job."

Will and Jerry laughed too. "You can use the blue sedan at the station. It's the detective car that we get if we need it," Jerry said.

Lindsay looked out the window as they drove the one mile to the station.

"You know, I was just thinking about something. These guys are really smart about some things and not so bright about others. I mean, they change where they meet women or abduct them from, but they pick someplace close to the police station to do it. That makes no sense to me. There's no logic in it," Lindsay said.

"Yeah, we've thought of that already. It's one of the stumpers we've been working on," Jerry said.

"I'll work on that this evening while you're gone," Lindsay said. That small, insignificant statement waved a huge red flag at Will.

"Oh, no, you don't. Lindsay, I'm responsible for you while you're here, and I don't want you tempting fate by cruising the streets looking for these guys on your own. These men are dangerous, and they have already killed two young women and severely damaged a third. You will not go looking for them, is that clear?" Will said.

"Ah, you do know Tony Miller, don't you? Don't worry. I'm not stupid, you know," Lindsay stated. Will looked in the rearview mirror at her, and Jerry looked at him. Something in her statement didn't ring quite true.

"Lindsay, I'm warning you. It's not that we think you're stupid. It's that we know from your past experiences that you can be a bit tenacious, let's say," Will said.

"Tenacious, hmm. Well, I've been called many things, but I think that's a first. You underestimate me, gentlemen, but you're not the first to do so. I can feel danger, I can feel these guys. They aren't going to sneak up on me, trust me. If I go to the mall, it's just to do some shopping. I always take something home for my kids. They love to get some flavor of the culture from the places I travel to," Lindsay said.

"Nope, forget the car. We're taking you with us for the evening.

I don't think you can be trusted with the car and free time. Shit, I feel like I'm talking to my son," Will said, as he spun the car in a different direction.

"No, I'm not, I'll be good. Scout's honor," Lindsay said as she held two fingers aloft.

"You promise?" Will asked.

"Yes, I said I did, didn't I? Now you're both going to be late, and this is the night of Jerry's big date, right? So go home! I'll be fine with a hot bath and a good book," Lindsay said.

Will and Jerry looked at each other and Jerry shrugged his shoulders. "Okay, but we trust you, Lindsay. You promised, and you said 'scout's honor,'" Will said as he turned one more time. Neither of the two men saw Lindsay's crossed fingers in her lap. She smiled sweetly, a sure sign that she was up to something.

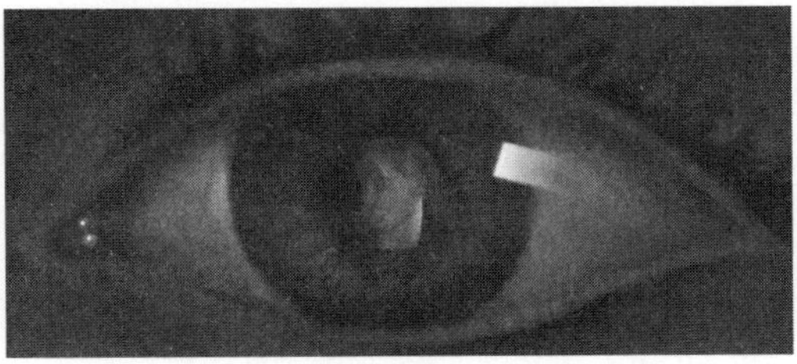

CHAPTER 57

Lindsay watched the two men pull away from the hotel. She walked into the lobby and asked to use the phone. The desk clerk smiled and said, "Sure, assuming it's local."

"Yes, ma'am," Lindsay said as she withdrew the card from her purse. Dialing the number, she asked for the person she knew would help her.

"Captain Morris, please," she said.

"This is Captain Morris."

"Captain Morris, this is Lindsay Freeman. I'm here at the hotel and I was wondering if you had a car I could use or if you know the name of a car rental agency close by?" Lindsay purred sweetly into the phone.

"A car?" Captain Morris was going to need more convincing than Lindsay had assumed.

"Yes sir. I'm here at the hotel, and—well, let's just say the restaurant here leaves something to be desired," Lindsay said. She smiled at the desk clerk and mouthed an apology.

"Oh, sure, we can get you a car. I didn't even think of that earlier. I bet you want to do some shopping, too, while you're here. I'll have someone bring a car to you and a rider for insurance will be in the glove box. The gas is your responsibility since you aren't official police personnel," Morris said.

"Thank you so much. Can you ask your person to ring my room when he gets here?" Lindsay asked.

"Sure will. Is there anything else I can do for you, Ms. Freeman?"

"You can call me Lindsay," she said.

"Okay then, Lindsay. Have a good evening."

Lindsay smiled, and the desk clerk smiled back. "That was better tap dancing than I've seen at my Wednesday afternoon tap class," the desk clerk said.

Lindsay smiled back and said, "Sometimes a girl's gotta do what a girl's gotta do."

Lindsay drove from the hotel to the mall after an officer had dropped off the car and the key and given her directions. He had no idea he was doing anything wrong, and neither did Captain Morris. They were being helpful and treating Lindsay as they had been asked to do—normally. But Lindsay wasn't a typical normal person. She didn't follow orders well, even when they had the best intentions, because she counted on her inside edge, that two-inch scar on the top of her head. When she was a teenager she had told everyone that God had put the direct line in there. Everyone laughed, and so did Lindsay, but she wasn't kidding.

Lindsay walked through the mall. She let her mind wander as she went from store to store. The image of the table in the field room came back to her. She'd seen the pink and white bag Amanda had been holding when she'd turned to run from the kidnappers. She could feel the panic Amanda felt. Lindsay stood still and let the feeling pass, and then turned and walked into the store just as Amanda and Cammy had done some weeks ago. She looked at all the lacy lingerie, and she giggled just as they had.

"Maybe I should have bought some of this stuff and actually worn it," she said. "I might still be married. Eww—what a thought." Lindsay wasn't actually opposed to marriage. In fact, she longed for it. But she wanted that perfect relationship. The one she and Mike had had in the beginning. Before she'd caught him in bed with his brother's fiancée, Annie.

"Maybe she wore that kind of stuff," Lindsay thought and then laughed right out loud. Other patrons of the store heard her and looked in her direction, finding her laugh infectious. A salesperson hurried over and offered assistance. Lindsay smiled nervously as she declined. Once outside, Lindsay thought of Annie. Nope, there was no way in the world she had worn anything quite so sexy. "She believes in being natural," Lindsay drawled to herself, imitating her ex-husband.

She continued through the mall, stopping occasionally to buy something for her kids. She bought Marie a beautiful sweater, and a cap for Jerry, something for Melissa and something for Jackie—or Jack, as he liked to be called now.

She found herself at the pizza parlor. Remembering that she was hungry, she went inside. As she sat there she thought about the case. Amanda Wiggins, Georgia Amando, and Wanda Corley, all three of them high school students, all getting ready for prom, all of them seventeen years old. Two of them, Amanda and Georgia, had been taken from the mall, and Wanda from the carnival. Wanda knew her kidnappers, but the other two girls didn't.

Amanda had blonde hair, Wanda and Georgia were both dark haired. Lindsay took a piece of paper and a pencil from her purse. She started a diagram of the case. The list of names, dates, and places took center stage but then Lindsay started working around it.

The waitress, a young girl about the same age as the three victims, came by and placed the slice of pizza Lindsay had ordered in front of her and set a coke down next to it. She glanced at the paper in front of Lindsay.

"Amanda Wiggins was in here just before she was kidnapped," she said.

"You're kidding," Lindsay said.

"Nope, she was in here with Cammy and Jeremy. They sat right there," she said, pointing at a table on the other side of the restaurant. Lindsay had avoided the table because it adjoined the mall hallway. The constant sound of mall shoppers through the open window wasn't conducive to thinking. Lindsay studied the table and then looked at the waitress.

"Did you know them?" she asked. The girl knew that Lindsay was referring to all three of them, Amanda, Georgia, and Wanda.

"Yeah, we went to school together. Our graduating class is doing a memorial to them during the ceremony. We don't expect Georgia to make it; but if she does—well, if she does, she's going to be the guest of honor. Her fiancé is our valedictorian, did you know that?"

"No, I didn't. What's his name?" Lindsay asked. She knew, but she was trying to keep the girl talking.

"Joey Mercer. He got an acceptance letter to the University of Illinois pre-med program. He got a scholarship for four years. We all pitched in and gave him money for books and stuff. Now I hear he and Georgia are engaged, and that she'll be going with him," the young girl said.

"What's your name?" Lindsay asked.

"Tammy Abrahms. I'm a senior at Ripney. Who are you?" Tammy asked.

Lindsay held out her hand, "I'm Lindsay Freeman. I'm from Illinois too."

"What are you doing here?" Tammy asked.

"Well, I'm working with the police to try to find out who did these terrible things." Lindsay watched the young girl for a reaction. None came, but she did say something that shocked Lindsay.

"Those two guys, the ones in the sketch . . . they were in here that same day. They sat right where you're sitting and they ordered a pizza and ate the whole thing. They drank cokes and laughed and got real rowdy, and the manager had to ask them to leave because they were giving me such a hard time. When we saw their pictures on the news a few days ago, I got real scared," Tammy said. Lindsay could feel the fear in her. "It could have been me," she said quietly.

"Did you call the police and tell them, Tammy?" Lindsay asked.

"I called, but no one ever came to talk to me about it. Besides, there wasn't much to tell. They came here, ate, and the manager kicked them out. They didn't even leave me a tip."

Lindsay looked at her and then squeezed her hand. "But they did leave you alive, Tammy."

Tammy nodded and wiped a tear from her eye. "Yes, ma'am, they did."

"I'll see that someone comes by to speak with you," Lindsay promised.

Tammy nodded and went back to work. Lindsay finished her pizza, made some more notes, and left the restaurant.

"I wonder how much other stuff is happening that Will and Jerry aren't aware of. Incompetence is not a good thing in a murder investigation."

As Lindsay headed to her car, she looked around the parking area. Fear crept up the back of her neck as she found herself hastening her footsteps. She felt foolish but she couldn't keep from looking around. As she did, she saw fear, fear in every group of people walking to their cars in the parking lot. Fear of what might happen to them or of what they might have to witness. "They're afraid that it might be them or they might have to take action," she thought. "They all just want it to go away."

Lindsay reached her car and turned one more time to look around the parking area. She forced herself to stand there in the light and look at the surrounding cars and people moving past her.

"No one is alone out here but me," she thought. "They're all moving around in couples or groups. Thinking they're safe. But Amanda was with a group. Wanda was at a crowded carnival; Georgia was kidnapped in the same parking area I'm standing in now. That means if they want you they'll take you. They have to be doing something or they have to know something we're not aware of," Lindsay thought as she scrambled inside the car and slammed the door lock into place.

The next morning, after Lindsay had given her information about Tammy Abrahms to Will and Jerry, she felt the chill. She looked at them across the table.

"What?" she asked.

"What do you mean, what, you know what. You did exactly as you damn well pleased. We asked you, no, we told you not to go to the mall alone. And what did you do? You did just what you were told not to do. Tony Miller warned me, he told me you were like this, but I didn't realize you would go this far. You could have been killed, those fucking madmen could have grabbed you, a woman walking alone, and killed you!" Will screamed.

Lindsay was seriously riled now, and she lunged to her feet and planted her hands on the table. "For your information, detective, I don't work for you. You can't tell me what to do. For another thing, I'm not seventeen, I wasn't with a group, and I don't have long hair!" Lindsay yelled right back at him.

The silence was incredible after the loud voices that had just reverberated across the room. But it wasn't the sound, it was the words—Lindsay's words. Will and Jerry looked at her and stood up. All three of them raced to the blackboard at the same time.

There in front of them was one of the missing pieces. The pictures of all three victims were taped up there in plain site. No one had seen it before because the picture of Wanda Corley showed her with her hair piled up high on her head. Amanda's hair had been in the ever-present ponytail, and only Georgia's long, flowing locks were obvious.

"I'll be damned," Jerry whispered. Will was still mad, but he looked at Lindsay. "How did you know that?"

"I don't know, it just came out. I never thought about it, I hadn't noticed it in the pictures before this moment," Lindsay said. The surprise in her voice validated her words.

Jerry looked at the pictures and then reached for the Ripney High School Year Book lying on the table. He looked through the senior pictures till he found each one of them. In all three pictures the girls had long hair. "Okay, so one of the missing pieces is that all the victims had long hair. But there has to be something else, I mean that's important, but what else does it tell us?" Jerry asked. He was walking around the table slowly just as Lindsay had done the day before.

Will snapped his fingers, "It tells us that one of them is in charge all the time and the other gives in, or just goes along with what that one dominant one wants to do. He makes no decisions of his own. Remember what Georgia said, Tony; the driver of the getaway car did what Mike, her kidnapper, told him to do. If we read over her statement I bet we'll see it now that we have this idea. But one other thing it tells us is that Mike is the more dangerous of the two. He's the one we have to subdue first when we catch them. Tony will be easy to confuse, I believe; and I think or I hope we'll be able to talk to him."

Lindsay thought about the words she'd said. "I'm sorry, just so you know. I didn't do it to disobey an order, but I had to get a feel for the mall. And look—I uncovered two very important things, the statement of Tammy Abrahms and the long hair thing."

"Lindsay, you also said something about the girls being seventeen and in a group. That part we do know. It amazes us that these girls could have been in groups and still taken against their will. Do you have any ideas about that?" Will asked.

Lindsay thought about it. "I think the cover of a large group and the noisy places they chose were camouflage. I guess what I mean is where else would you hear a young girl scream and not really pay much attention?"

Will and Jerry considered. "So it's your thought that these guys pick places like the mall and the carnival because girls scream there normally and it wouldn't be noticed?" Jerry asked.

"I didn't say that. What I think is their ages, the way they look, like if they're outgoing, laughing and cutting up, it makes them a target. Carnivals and mall shopping areas are prime targets for teenagers, and most teenage girls are noisy. It's a fact we all take for granted. They hit the mall twice because it was an easy target. It worked the first time, and then it worked the second time. The carnival was just there, Wanda knew them, she went up to them and in doing so she signed her own death warrant," Lindsay said.

Will and Jerry nodded. "Not that I disagree with you, Lindsay, but I want some more time with that one," Will said.

"Will, Jerry, prom's coming up. Have you thought of that yet?" Lindsay asked. She was calmer now, more subdued.

"Yes, we've thought of that. It's Friday, one week from yesterday. I don't know why, but I'm scared to death of that day. Teenagers, drinking, partying, all of them on the loose and milling around. Shit, yeah, I've thought about it," Will said.

"Are there plans for more police coverage Friday evening?" Lindsay asked.

"As far as I know. But you know what bothers me? It's been too darn quiet," Jerry said without waiting for a response from anyone.

Will agreed. "This is the longest period of time we've gone without something. Maybe they moved on after the cabin incident. I mean it's not unheard of for a perp to move away or look for another area after he's had a close call or a run-in with the law."

"It's a long shot, one I'm not willing to chance this coming Friday night, however. I'd rather have more men on anyway. These kids take chances I wouldn't normally take," Jerry said.

"I didn't want to say this until I was sure, but I just have a feeling something's coming. We're either going to catch them soon, or they're going to grab someone soon. I don't have enough information about them yet to say. I'd like to do some more traveling around today. I want to visit the cemetery, and Georgia Amando. I'd like to meet Joey Mercer and visit the Carson Pirie Scott's at the mall. Isn't that where Georgia worked?" Lindsay asked.

"Yes, she did. What about a visit with Lilly? She's met these two guys," Jerry said.

"You're kidding. You have an eyewitness?" Lindsay asked. She was shocked.

"Well, not an eyewitness exactly. I mean she's a friend; she was a friend of Wanda Corley's. Wanda and Lilly met Tony and Mike at the carnival the first time they went. Lilly didn't go with Wanda the night she was kidnapped, raped, and murdered, however. She had a date with a guy named Hickey, of all names," Will said.

"Okay, wait a minute. You have someone who has talked to Tony and Mike and you didn't tell me?" Lindsay was stunned.

"Yeah, why?" Jerry asked.

"Okay, let me see if I can explain this to you. I work based on people's emotions. I get lots of information based on what they saw and how they felt about it at the time. Lilly would be an incredible source of information to me. I need to see her because she has no idea just how much information she may really have," Lindsay stated.

"You're kidding, right?" Will asked, surprised. He had no idea how clairvoyants worked, but he was learning.

"Nope, not even one little bit. Our most valuable source of information almost slipped through the cracks again," Lindsay said. Standing, she grabbed her purse. "Are you guys coming?"

"I'm coming, are you coming, Will?" Jerry asked, as he scrambled to his feet.

"I'm coming," Will said.

CHAPTER 58

Lindsay, Will, and Jerry sat across from Lilly Williams. She sobbed into her tissue as she told the story of her date with Tony one more time.

"Wanda and I went to the carnival in her car. We parked by some bushes and changed our clothes in them. Her mom and dad were always freaking out about the stuff I wear, so Wanda never left the house dressed in anything cool. She has a whole wardrobe in her trunk. Then we went to the carnival. We'd been there about an hour before we met them. They looked rough even to me, and for some reason Wanda was so attracted to Mike. He was funny, and he was real touchy-feely, if you know what I mean. We rode all the rides; Mike liked every one of them and he and Wanda had a great time. When we saw them on the roller coaster they were making out pretty heavy.

"Tony's different; he's sort of quiet and shy and sweet. I liked him but he's not that cute. Besides, I wanted Hickey. That's a guy I go to school with. Hickey's not his real name. It's a nickname." Lindsay could see where he got the name. "My mom and dad won't let me see him anymore. My whole life's changed because of what Wanda did. At first I was pretty upset about it, but now I kind of think it was her fault. She knew Mike was trouble, but she did it just to get back at her mom and dad. Mike's mean, not when you first meet him but later that night when everyone was going home, Wanda and I tried to leave them. Mike grabbed Wanda's arm and twisted it up behind her back. She had to give him her phone number to make him let her go. I was real scared, Tony too. I could see it in his eyes," Lilly said. She was crying again and sniffling through her tears. "Mike kissed Wanda real hard and made her lip bleed. When we got in the car, she started crying and she wiped her lip on her sleeve."

"Lilly, where is that sleeve now. I mean the shirt that she was wearing, where is it?" Lindsay asked as excitement boiled in her.

"It's in her car, in the trunk I guess, unless her mom and dad cleaned it out."

"Lilly, is there anything else you can tell me about your encounter with Mike and Tony?" Lindsay asked.

"Well, I kissed Tony goodnight and gave him my phone number, and other than one time I haven't heard from him. Mike only called Wanda that one time too that I know of. She never mentioned it if he did. But Wanda was going to go all the way with Mike if she got the chance. For some reason she wasn't scared of him. She just said he was manly and that gave her a thrill. I don't know why she did it, but my guess is she tried to change her mind after she got there and that's why they killed her." Lilly was crying inconsolably now.

Her mother never moved in her direction. She just sat on the other end of the couch and listened. Finally she looked in the direction of the visitors in her home and at her daughter. "It could have been you, Lilly. With the things you've done recently it should have been you."

Lindsay stood to go, but something in her wouldn't let her leave it like that. She looked at Lilly's mother and said, "Our children learn by example. I don't have to wonder what role you played in your daughter's upbringing." The comment was wasted on Lilly's mom but not on Lilly. "There's still time for you, Lilly," Lindsay said as she squeezed the girl's hands. "Make something of yourself and learn from your mom's mistakes, be a better mother and set a better example for your daughter when you have her."

As they got back in the car, Will looked at Lindsay. "Well, what did you get besides a case of the red ass?" Lindsay laughed. "You really do know Tony Miller, don't you?"

"Yep, I sure do. Now tell me what you got?"

"We need the clothes in Wanda Corley's car. Lilly was very direct. She's not really holding anything back. There are nuances to her words, but what I see is pretty much what she says. She wasn't holding back even though her story is disjointed. She's telling it like she remembers it. I need to see what Wanda thought of the whole thing."

They rode in silence to the Corley residence. Lindsay replayed the conversation with Lilly in her mind. Something Lilly knew but wasn't aware that she knew was brewing just below the surface. Lindsay wondered to herself if the articles of clothing in the trunk of Wanda's car would give her what she was looking for. If they were still there and hadn't been touched by anyone other than Wanda and Lilly, and maybe even Tony and Mike, the chances were she would get lots of information.

"I need my recorder and absolute quiet when we get those articles of clothing. I'm going to tape what I get, and then we can go over it. If that's okay with the two of you," Lindsay said. Her mood was solemn.

Will looked in the rearview mirror at her and nodded his head. "I don't mind giving you that. One thing, however, how do we describe you? Who do we tell people you are?"

Jerry had been thinking the same thing since meeting with Lilly, and he knew they were going to Georgia Amanda's hospital room after this. Sooner or later they were going to have to tell someone who she was.

"I would be honest with the Corley family, or with any of the victim's families for that matter. They have a right to know you're doing everything you can to help find the person who killed their child. When it comes to the press I would prefer that you not mention me or what I do. It never sits well and it just creates a circus, not to mention that I don't want my family terrorized by what I do," Lindsay said. They all agreed it was the best thing to do, for the families, for the station, and definitely for Lindsay.

As they pulled into the Corley driveway, Don Corley came outside. In his hand was a bucket of soapy water and a sponge. He saw them stop the car and as he recognized who it was, his face fell just a little. Lindsay saw it and knew that he was suffering terribly.

"Mr. Corley, we'd like to speak with you for a few minutes if we can," Will said as he shook the man's hand.

"Sure, Detective, what can I do for you?"

"This is Ms. Lindsay Freeman. She's working with us to solve this case and hopefully catch the men who murdered your daughter. I know this is a difficult time for you," Will said.

"That, detective, is an understatement. I haven't been back to work yet, and my wife is trying to find the strength to clean out Wanda's closet. Have you ever buried a child, detective?" Don asked.

"No sir I haven't. But I've been to the funerals of many. I know that can never compare to what you're feeling and there's nothing that I can do about that. But I can find the persons responsible for your daughter's death and see that they are punished."

Don nodded. "Ms. Freeman, please forgive my manners. They aren't what they should be lately," Don said.

"I understand, sir, really I do," Lindsay grasped his hand in hers. It shook slightly. Visions of intense pain and suffering passed through Lindsay, causing her to take a step back. Tears came to her eyes as she looked at Don Corley.

"You feel responsible for your daughter's death. You shouldn't, really. Many parents divorce and many children are told no about things they think they want," Lindsay said as warmly as she could.

Don took a step back and looked at Lindsay. "Who are you?" he asked. His voice shook as he whispered the words.

Will and Jerry stepped forward, but Lindsay held her hand out to stop them. "I'm a clairvoyant, Mr. Corley. I'm here to help solve this case if I can."

Don looked at her one more time, long and hard. "I've never believed in people who say they can do what you do. I never have wanted to believe it. It scares me, to be honest, and my logical mind won't admit that someone can do what you claim to do, but I've just witnessed it first-hand. I do feel terribly guilty. My daughter asked me for ten thousand dollars for a graduation trip to Europe just three days before she died. I said no.

You can imagine my pain at this moment. Can you help find whoever did this to my only child?"

"I can try. That's why we're here. Lilly told us about something that may be in the trunk of your daughter's car. Do you mind if we look?" Lindsay asked. For some reason it was his believability factor. As long as she was willing to look him in the eye, he seemed to believe her.

They walked into the garage to see Wanda's car, a sleek, shiny, blood-red 1975 Camero. It had been recovered from a parking area not far from the carnival site the day after her body had been found. Now it sat there alone and almost forlorn looking. Don went inside to get the keys as he trailed his fingers down the rear quarter panel of the smooth red body. Wanda's purse had not been recovered with her body, but Don and Phyllis both had a set of keys to the car. Don came out and tossed the keys to Jerry, who opened the trunk. Behind him Phyllis Corley held onto the back of her ex-husband's arm and peered over his shoulder as she stood on the step behind him. Don introduced her to Lindsay, but she remembered Will and Jerry whom she'd met before.

She shook Lindsay's hand and Lindsay felt her pain. She was being strong for her husband. Well, her ex-husband, Lindsay conceded, but in time that would fix itself.

"How do you do, Mrs. Corley?" Lindsay asked.

"I would love to say I'm fine, but why lie? I'm hanging in there is the best I can say right now," Phyllis said. "Don tells me you're here to look in Wanda's car."

"Yes ma'am. Lilly told us of a shirt that might be in your daughter's trunk, that may have some very important information on it. I hope you don't mind," Lindsay said as she looked into Phyllis's eyes.

"No, I don't mind. I want the men who did this to my daughter caught and hanged, or whatever it is they do nowadays."

Don took Phyllis's arm and led her around to the trunk of Wanda's car. "This should have been done already. I'm sorry to put you through it here," Jerry said. He had no idea why this car hadn't been impounded and searched.

"I had the car brought here, Detective. The police didn't find it, I did. When we spoke with Lilly I knew where the car would be. I went and got it. No one said not to, and I didn't think anything about it," Don said. But the look in his face was troubled.

"Mr. Corley, if you want, you can go ahead with washing your car. We don't need you for this, and from the look on your face I would say you're not ready to handle it yet," Lindsay whispered in his ear. Don nodded and went outside. Phyllis watched him go and looked suspiciously at Lindsay, who smiled at her.

The recorder in her hand, Lindsay approached the open trunk. As she pressed the record button, she saw Phyllis in her peripheral vision. She was crying softly, probably thinking of the day Wanda had received this car.

"A white off-the-shoulder top, clearly altered but not sewn in the front, long sleeves. A pair of short blue jean shorts, button ups. A purple lace bra and panty set. A green silk shirt with long sleeves, ah here it is—the one we're looking for. There's blood on the sleeve in the shape of a diamond. Looks like a corner-of-the-mouth mark."

Lindsay looked over her shoulder at Phyllis. She felt uncomfortable doing this in front of her. As she looked at Will and Jerry, they seemed to know what she needed.

"Mrs. Corley, could we see Wanda's room, please?" Jerry asked.

As they left, Lindsay continued. "He kissed her hard. She expected the kiss but thought it would be soft. Instead she was shocked by his aggressive behavior. He pinched her roughly in the lower back. Her arm hurt for two days at least. There is pain throughout her body that thrilled her." Lindsay looked at Will. "She liked it," Lindsay said incredulously. "I will never understand women who love that kind of treatment. What happens in the female mind that draws women to this?" Lindsay wiped tears from her eyes.

"Lindsay, we found a mark, a bruise, red and purple, on her lower back. Now we know where it came from, not that it matters much. Do we know anything about the men who killed her?" Will asked. He stood with his hands braced on the quarter panel as he stared into the trunk.

The clothing was spread all over the trunk, and it was clear an alternative lifestyle had been hidden here.

Lindsay picked up a package wrapped in tin foil. As she opened it, pills and green clumps of dried grass spilled out. "She was getting high," Lindsay said.

"The guys, Lindsay, the guys," Will said as he took the foil pouch and picked up the spilled pot. Lindsay held up a condom, still in the wrapper. She raised an eyebrow as she looked at Will. He shook his head and gestured to the open trunk with his chin. Lindsay went back to work, discussing what she felt. As she emptied the bag, a yellow ticket stub fell out. On it was scribbled, "I love you," in a crabby sort of scrawl. Lindsay picked it up and looked at Will.

"I got 'em!" she said.

"What, tell me," Will said excitedly.

"He has a fear of people and a desire to be free and outside. This person doesn't sleep indoors well. He's not much of a sleeper at any point. He's a pacer with an irrational temper. He has to be in control all the time, and when he's not, things get severely out of hand. This man is a killer at his deepest level. On the surface he's wild, to say the least. He wants to be normal and he likes being crazy. Will, he's nuts, he's the epitome of a psychopath. He believed he loved this girl until she did what he didn't like. She said no, and tried to be in control of her own life. Then love turned to rage, and he killed her before she even knew what happened. She didn't suffer, but her body was brutalized long after her death." Lindsay said in a rush.

"So you're telling me Mike killed her alone?" Will asked.

"No, I'm telling you Mike killed her, but he didn't do it alone. Tony was part of it. Wanda knew sex with Tony before she died. But in all that time she never thought Mike would kill her. Her death happened so suddenly, so severely, she had no idea," Lindsay said as she cried. "She was scared, Will. She was so scared, but she didn't think she would die. She thought she'd found love with the wrong guy. Is that punishable by death?" Lindsay sobbed. Will put his arm around her and stuffed a tissue into her hand.

"Lindsay, I know you're hurting; but you have to get yourself together. You can't let her parents see you like this." Lindsay pulled herself upright and scrubbed at her eyes. She breathed in deeply as she struggled to compose herself.

"This isn't professional," she whispered.

"I'm not asking for professionalism, Lindsay," Will said. "I'm asking you for something much harder than that. I want you to mask your emotions, and I want it right now because Don Corley is coming our way."

Lindsay leaned forward and held her hand out, palm up. With the other hand she opened her eye as wide as she could and blinked.

"Is everything okay?" Don asked.

Lindsay dug at her eye and blinked furiously. Will caught on and said, "She lost her contact lens in her eye somewhere. It must hurt like hell."

Don offered her a tissue and patted her on the back. "I've used that one myself, recently. Thanks for caring about my daughter," he said as he walked away.

Lindsay turned and looked at him as she dabbed her eyes with the tissue. "Now who's clairvoyant?" she said. Will chuckled as he wiped his own eyes. Life with this clairvoyant woman must be difficult. Will tucked the recorder in his pocket as Lindsay walked back to the car. He called inside for Jerry who had been successfully keeping Mrs. Corley occupied.

They drove toward the hospital as Will played the tape for Jerry. Lindsay sat quietly in the back seat. Suddenly she said, "They're camping."

Jerry turned in the seat and looked at her. "Are you sure? They were in a cabin last time we knew anything concrete about them."

"Yes, I'm sure. They're camping and there's water and trees and something, wait—a tent of sorts, but huge. There's trash everywhere, burning things, and clothes lying around." Lindsay was breathing heavily.

"Are you okay, Lindsay?" Jerry asked.

"Yes, I'm fine. The water seems rough near them but not right in front of them. Does that make sense to you?" Lindsay asked as she leaned forward and gripped the seat in front of her.

"Maybe it's an inlet of some sort. That would help but we need to narrow it down some. Lindsay give me an area," Will said. He waited to hear something, ready to turn the wheel as soon as she said anything. But Lindsay couldn't feel them, she couldn't tell Will and Jerry where to go.

"I don't know. I'm sorry I don't know the area well enough and there's no sign. I can't tell you, I'm sorry," Lindsay said.

Jerry and Will exchanged glances. "Lindsay, we know the area and we can't find them. This isn't you're fault," Jerry said. But his words fell on deaf ears.

"I can't see everything. It doesn't work that way," Lindsay said. Will and Jerry just sat there. "I mean, it's not like I'm a mind reader or anything like that. I can feel emotion and smell things sometimes. I see in black and white unless it's real close to me, then I can see it in color."

"Lindsay it's okay. Really, don't worry about it. It happens to us all the time and we're detectives. Shit, I know how you feel. That helpless feeling is really bad. It makes you feel like a failure," Will said.

"But we don't blame you," Jerry added. "You know, their first home was a campsite. That's where Georgia Amando was rescued from," Jerry said. "Could that be what you're getting?"

"No, it's current, they're camping. They're camping right now, right this minute," Lindsay insisted.

Will drove into the hospital parking area, and they went inside. Lindsay hadn't met Georgia Amando, and Jerry and Will were anxious for her to do so. "She's a remarkable young woman. Wait until you meet her," Jerry said. Lindsay smiled.

As they walked down the hall to the intensive care unit Lindsay replayed the narrative of Wanda's trunk in her mind. Will and Jerry stopped short as Lindsay did when she realized she'd overstepped them. "What?" she asked as she saw the look on their faces.

Will and Jerry felt the adrenaline rush instantly. Pulling Lindsay to the side, they both loosened the straps on their weapons. As they pushed open the door to the room Georgia had been in, they expected to see the officer inside, since he wasn't where he was supposed to be, standing guard outside the room. The only reason he was allowed to leave was if something happened and he was in the room guarding Georgia. But the room was empty. No guard, no Georgia, and no ever-present monitors or Lucinda.

Will and Jerry turned around, fearing the worst. A nurse hurrying by saw them. "They've been moved to step-down," she said, never missing a step. Will and Jerry followed her, but she held her hand up as she opened the door. "You can't come in here," she said.

"What's step-down?" Jerry asked.

"It's where they go when they leave here. It's like a step down from ICU. It's graduation, a good thing," she said as she raised her eyebrows.

"Where is it?" Jerry asked.

The nurse pointed down the hall. Will, Jerry, and Lindsay started in that direction. As they turned the corner at the end of the hall, Lindsay saw the officer at the same time Will and Tony did. They re-strapped their gun holsters and walked in his direction.

"I see you found us," he said.

Lindsay saw it right away. This man had intense anger in his heart. The feeling was so strong she gasped. As she walked past him she paused and looked into his eyes as she touched his shoulder. It was a small gesture, but it was her way of getting inside someone without their being aware. She could feel the anger in him, but it was directed. He wasn't an abuser, he was angry at the damage that had been done to someone he cared about. She patted his shoulder and continued walking into the room. He watched her go, not knowing who she was.

As the door closed, Officer Tim Dunesbury leaned against it.

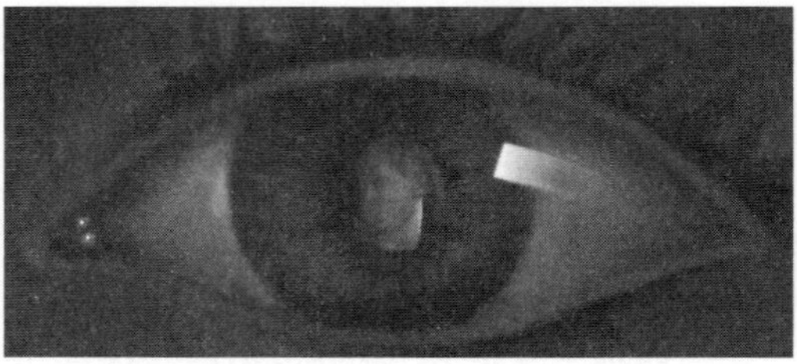

CHAPTER 59

The change in Georgia was remarkable. She hardly looked like the same person. Two weeks, give or take a few days, had given her back her color, and only the slightest swelling remained. Her bones were healing, and some of her large casts had been replaced by smaller ones. There was color in her face, and the gauze of the bandages had been replaced with colorful strips of cloth brought from home by Lucinda. She had some light makeup on and actually smiled when Will and Jerry came in.

The transformation was almost intoxicating. Georgia Amando was beautiful with her lightly tinged cheeks and softly glazed lips and that hair, that beautiful hair that flowed down around her shoulders in soft chocolate-brown curls.

She was able to sit up more than before, but she still looked small in the large hospital bed, like a porcelain doll, sitting there fragile and beautiful but strong, stronger than anyone had given her credit for being. Now the truth was out; Georgia Amando had grit.

Joey was napping on a cot in the corner of the room, a textbook spread across his chest. It was clear he'd fallen asleep while studying. Will smiled at him, thinking of his own son who did that all the time.

Lucinda, as always, was sitting at the head of Georgia's bed. George Amando was at the foot, signing Georgia's new leg cast in bright red magic marker.

"Good afternoon," Georgia said as Will and Jerry got closer. "I'm doing much better, as you can see."

"Yes we can see that. Congratulations, it's wonderful," Jerry said.

Will introduced Lindsay, "Georgia, this is Lindsay Freeman. She'll be working with us on your case and so far she's been very helpful."

Georgia reached out her lightly casted arm to shake Lindsay's hand. "It's nice to meet you, Ms. Freeman," Georgia said. But there was something in her voice that didn't ring quite true.

"Please call me Lindsay, everyone does."

"Okay, Lindsay." Lindsay was watching Georgia watch her. Something in her eyes told Lindsay that she knew. There were to be no surprises here.

"You're the clairvoyant, aren't you?" Georgia asked.

Bingo, Lindsay thought. "Yes I am, do you mind?"

"No, not now that I've seen you. I don't know what I expected, but you're not it. Are you a Christian, Lindsay?" Georgia studied her face.

"Yes, I am, Georgia. I wouldn't have made it this far otherwise. I need constant guidance and peace, and I need forgiveness every day for some of the things I think," Lindsay chuckled.

"Do you believe in miracles?" Georgia asked. Lindsay wondered about all the questions, but thought she should answer them as honestly as she could. "Yes, I do. There are many things about me that most people don't know. I have a feeling that in the time it takes for you and me to work through your trauma, we will come to know each other quite well. In that time I may tell you things I wouldn't normally tell anyone. Can I trust you not to share those things?" Now it was Lindsay's turn to watch Georgia.

Georgia's expression shifted several times as she thought Lindsay's statement through. "I didn't throw you for a minute, did I, Lindsay?" Georgia asked. "Forgive me; I just wanted to size you up. This is all Joey's idea. The investigation wasn't going as well or moving as quickly as he would like. He found an article in a magazine about clairvoyants and their use in law enforcement. After that he was like a dog with a bone. He just couldn't leave it alone." Lindsay looked at Will.

"I thought you said Tony Miller directed you to me?" Lindsay was visibly upset.

"Wait, Lindsay, before you get mad, let me say it was Joey's idea first. But your name wasn't in the article. I called Tony because he told me about his case and your work with him. We agreed to go with you because you've done this sort of thing before, and Tony trusted you," Will said solemnly. The sincerity in his voice was very real. "I wasn't trying to mislead you. I didn't think it was such a big deal."

"Forgive me, it isn't. I tend to be a little oversensitive," Lindsay said.

Georgia looked at her father, "Poppa, can you wake Joey up? I can't believe he can sleep with all this noise. He's been really tired lately—coming here to be with me, working, and going to school. And he has entrance exams coming up soon, right after prom." Georgia's face fell at the mention of the prom.

"It's this Friday, and Joey and I won't be there. We've waited all our high school years for this day, and now we won't be there," Georgia said, tears coming to her eyes. She fought them off as Joey came to her bedside. He took her hand in his and kissed her forehead. "Joey, this is Lindsay Freeman," Georgia said.

Joey looked at her. The name meant nothing, but one glance at her face told him all he needed to know. "You're the one, you're the person in the article who wouldn't be interviewed," Joey gasped.

Lindsay smiled at him. "I don't like to be interviewed. What I do is very private, Joey. I can't work effectively with the press all over me, and I don't like my personal life disrupted."

"I read the article, and if you manage to help us it would be a good thing that I did. Doesn't that mean anything to you?" Joey asked.

"It does. But Joey, so many people honor my privacy that I don't worry about that. I have children, and I hope I'll have grandchildren someday. Do you think I would put them at risk of some lunatic who's out to prove me wrong so that I could have my name in print? It could happen, you know. Someone I've helped put behind bars could get paroled, they could escape, and they could come after my family. Or someone who has the desire to prove a point could target my family and me. To be honest, I'd rather not go there," Lindsay said. Joey looked at her and nodded. Will and Jerry understood how she felt. They knew their families were at risk as well.

Lucinda and George watched Lindsay rather suspiciously. Their religion didn't allow for such things. But they'd watched the exchange between Georgia and Lindsay and now between Joey and Lindsay. She seemed to be a good person, but what she did was of the devil. That's what the Bible said. But still . . . something in her demeanor reached their hearts. They had sat quietly and listened, and they were silent still.

Lindsay smiled at them and reached out to squeeze Lucinda's hand. The two mothers exchanged glances, and each saw love for her children reflected in the other's eyes.

"I hate to be rude, but we do have an investigation to get back to," Will said. The exchange had only taken minutes, but it felt like most of the day was gone. "Georgia, could you tell Lindsay what you experienced, as candidly as you told us?" Will asked.

Georgia looked at Will and nodded. Lindsay said, "Folks, could we have some privacy, please? If everyone is in here I'll get information based on your emotions and that might impede my ability. I would like to talk to Georgia alone, if that's possible." Everyone nodded and left, everyone but Lucinda.

As the room emptied, Georgia tried to get her mother to go, but she wouldn't budge. "I stay," she said, and just sat there. Lindsay smiled at the look on Georgia's face. "It's okay, really," Georgia said. "She's heard it all before. And she's my momma."

So the story began again. Georgia poured out the tale of all that she had been through. She described Mike and Tony as best she could, but they'd always been behind her. When she did finally see their faces, her vision was blurry. She let her emotions boil out of her.

Lindsay, Lucinda, and Georgia cried and held hands, while Will and

Jerry stood with Joey and George in the hallway. "Let's get something to drink. I know this story and it's gonna be awhile," Joey said. He was sympathetic, but he was in survival mode. Will and Jerry knew it, they'd seen it before.

"Georgia," Lindsay said. "I need you to look past the stump and the toilet facilities, or lack of them. I need you to see your surroundings, so that I can see them. I need to feel what happened through you," Lindsay said.

Georgia looked at her. "But I've already told you what happened. I've told you all that I remember. I can't see it anymore." Georgia was still crying softly.

"Can I take you back there? Not physically, but can I ask you some questions that might trigger a memory?" Lindsay asked. Absolute panic crossed Georgia's face, and Lindsay knew what was going on. "That's how you're able to tell the story so well, isn't it? You've rehearsed this with your mother maybe a hundred times and you tell it like you're telling it about someone else," Lindsay said gently. "That is the smartest thing I have ever heard. I'm so proud of you, Georgia."

Georgia smiled. "You found me out. I'm impressed, too. I'm willing to work with you. What do I do?" Georgia asked.

"Okay, when you were in the camp area, Tony and Mike must have talked some. What did they say?"

"They said a lot of things. They talked about Amanda a lot. They talked about Tony's brother, the fact that he didn't like Mike much. His brother lives in Wisconsin!" Georgia sniffled and rubbed her nose with a tissue. "Oh my God, I remember, Tony's from Michigan, but his brother lives in Wisconsin. Mike and Tony grew up in Michigan."

"That's good, Georgia. Where in Wisconsin, did you ever get a last name or something that we can find Tony's brother with?"

Georgia thought. "No, I never heard a last name. Wait, there's an island in Texas with the same name, somewhere on the Gulf Coast," Georgia said.

"Is there anything else you can think of?" Lindsay asked.

"I don't know, I didn't know I knew this," Georgia said, amazed at herself.

"Okay, this may get you thinking; but it's going to require quiet time, time alone, and you're going to have to go through it step by step. If you heard that last name would you remember it?" Lindsay asked.

"I think so," Georgia said.

The guys waiting outside the room were called in. Lindsay told Will and Jerry about Tony's last name being the same as some island in Texas on the coast.

Jerry looked at Georgia, "Could it be Galveston?" Jerry asked.

"I don't know, I've never been there, but one of my uncles has. He told me all about it. I thought about it then, and it gave me strength. Isn't that funny? My uncle's memories of his travels gave me strength?" Georgia chuckled, but she didn't sound amused.

It was a sad sound, broken by George Amando saying something. "Garrison's Ridge, that's where Carlo went in Texas."

Will and Jerry looked at Georgia, "Is that it? Is his name Tony Garrison or Tony Ridge?"

Georgia just nodded. "Tony Garrison," she gasped. Something about hearing his name made him real again in her mind. All the tricks she'd come up with to save herself the mental anguish of reliving the moment didn't work now.

"Tony Garrison, that's his name," Georgia said.

"Thank you Georgia," Lindsay said as she squeezed her forearm. "Thank you."

Will, Jerry and Lindsay left shortly after that. Georgia had seemed quiet and withdrawn after her discussion with Lindsay. It was as if old demons had come back to haunt her. She smiled and said goodbye as they left, however, promising to call if she remembered anything else. Lindsay knew that Georgia would begin to remember more and more now. She would be calling.

As they rode in silence, lost in their own thoughts, Lindsay doodled with a pencil and paper. The black and white prism image formed in her mind again. Lindsay relaxed deeper into the seat and let it come. She saw images of kids, teenagers really, laughing as they moved in a single direction. Great doors were behind them as they moved toward her in her mind. The smiling faces seemed to float past her as she stood in their midst. She didn't know what she was waiting for, something seemed to be coming. Lindsay let her mind stand still and watch the sea of black and white faces move past her. The images were coming faster and faster and slowly color was coming to them. To Lindsay that meant that whatever the images were trying to tell her was coming closer, either in time or distance.

She didn't wrestle with the images; there was no need to fight. It was best to just let it flow. Suddenly she saw it, a small vacancy where only a few moments before smiling faces had been. The rest of the scene stayed the same, the crowd kept on coming—just that one small change, and it could have been overlooked if the picture had been still. But images that come to clairvoyants are never still. The constant changing, floating images move like the colors of light on a prism.

"Something's coming," Lindsay said.

"What?" Jerry said, turning in his seat to look at her.

"Something's coming. I can feel it. Someone's going to be missing from a large crowd, during the day when it should be safe to mill about. Something's coming," Panic started rising in Lindsay's voice.

"Lindsay, calm down. Tell us what you see," Will said as he pulled the car gently to the side of the road and turned in his own seat.

Lindsay told Will and Jerry what she'd seen. It was hard for them to understand, to comprehend what the clairvoyant mind saw or how it worked. She described the scene that had flashed through her mind.

"Lindsay, can you see the building?"

Lindsay searched her memory. "It's tall, and I think it's some kind of dark brick. There are a lot of kids. They all seem to be moving in one direction, all moving toward me as if I were standing right in front of them. What I'm trying to say is that no one is moving away from me. They're all coming in my direction," Lindsay said.

"Lindsay, is it like kids coming out of a school?" Jerry asked.

Will looked at him, "Oh, shit, is that it, Lindsay? Are they going to take someone from the high school in broad daylight?" Will asked.

"I don't know. I can't tell, because I don't know this area well enough. That's why I want to drive around. I have to see it in real time, so when I see an image of it I'll know what it is. It's a downside to being clairvoyant and traveling with it."

Will looked at Jerry again, "What do we do?"

"I don't know. It's not much to go on. Why don't we drive over to the high school so Lindsay can see it? If something's going on, we'll be there. If not, well, then at least she'll have seen it," Jerry offered.

"Good idea." Will turned the car in the direction of the high school.

CHAPTER 60

As they drove the five miles to the high school, Lindsay went over what she'd seen in her mind. The color that had come to the images toward the end scared her.

"Guys, do you remember earlier when we were going to the Corley's and I had the same feeling?" Lindsay asked.

"Yeah," Will and Jerry said, as they waited for her to explain.

"When I had that feeling and saw those images, all of that was in black and white. It looked like images running through a movie projector slowly. But today when I got that feeling and saw those images, it was much clearer, and some of it was in color." Lindsay nodded for emphasis.

"So, what does it mean?" Jerry asked.

"For me, it means the situation is getting closer. It's going to happen soon, that's what it means." Lindsay said.

"Oh, shit," Jerry said sheepishly.

Will agreed, but he was glad he'd kept his mouth shut. Jerry looked and felt foolish.

"It's okay, guys, working with someone like me is a bit different, to say the least," Lindsay said.

They pulled onto Ripney Drive and slowed down, watching the faces of the kids as they flowed like a river into the high school parking area. "Can you believe this many kids have their own cars?" Jerry asked.

"Yeah, I can believe it. My son wants his own car. To be honest, we're thinking of getting him one for graduation. It's too hard to share our cars with him; his hours are similar to ours. When he's home, usually one of us doesn't have a car," Will said.

Lindsay and Jerry laughed in sympathy.

They drove along the rows of cars. "Everything here seems normal, Lindsay," Will said.

"I know, but I can't help feeling that we're missing it. Or maybe we're too early."

"Lindsay, it could be the wrong day, the wrong time. It could be the wrong school for all we know. We need something more to work with," Jerry said.

"I'm sorry. Drive around some more, please," Lindsay said, looking out the window.

The crowd had dwindled as the kids dispersed. They drove to the front of the high school and as Lindsay looked out the window she saw it. "It's here!" she exclaimed.

"What, what's here?" Jerry asked her.

"This is the building I saw. Those are the doors, and other than the kids moving through it, it's the same." Lindsay said. Will pulled the car over to the curb and Lindsay got out. She walked up the stairs and put her hands on the doors as Will and Jerry watched.

"What are you doing?" Will asked.

Lindsay held her hand up as if to ask for quiet. "It's called psychometry. It's the ability to lay your hands on something and feel energy through it. It helps to define what I get," Lindsay said. She could see the kids moving through the door. They headed to the sidewalk and then they dispersed in different directions, some to the east, and some to the west. "Are there two parking areas to this school?" Lindsay asked, as she ran back to the car.

"Yeah, I think so," Will said, pulling away from the curb.

Lindsay was used to moving suddenly, based on what she felt or saw. The two men weren't "Lindsay, do you mind filling us in?" Jerry asked.

"I'm sorry, I have this feeling that something's coming, and it's about this case. Another teenager is going to be missing, but it feels worse than that."

"Worse than a teenager missing? What could be worse?" Jerry asked.

Lindsay started to answer, but a high-pitched scream pierced the air. It wasn't a giggling, schoolgirl scream. It was a cry for help. Will and Jerry jumped from the car with their guns drawn and ran through the parking area. The scream bounced around in Lindsay's head as she ran after them.

A young girl was bent forward, screaming, her books in a heap at her feet, her mouth open. There was absolute terror on her face. Will and Jerry ran in her direction. Lindsay was right behind them. She ran to the girl and shook her, trying to get her attention. Grabbing her shoulders, she turned the hysterical girl in her direction and the images came back with the sudden contact.

Spinning around, she looked at the ground. "There," she screamed, as Will and Jerry turned. They looked, and they saw what the girl was screaming about.

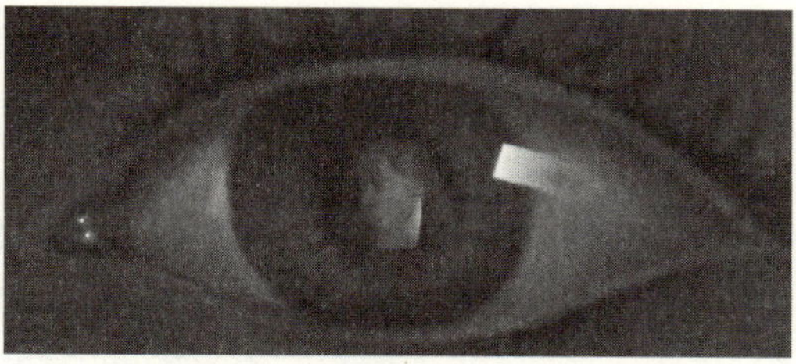

CHAPTER 61

"Hey Cat, are you coming over this evening?" Melissa Wells yelled to her best friend as she ran down the front steps of Ripney High.

"Yeah, after dinner. My dad's gonna drop me off so we can wrap up. I'll see ya around six o'clock," Catrina Vincent called back. Miles waited at the bottom of the steps and smiled as Cat ran towards him. She kissed him lightly and looped her arm in his as they walked to the parking area.

"You're late," Miles said.

"Yeah, the decorations are taking more time than I thought they would, and the planning committee meeting ran over. How was baseball practice?" Cat asked.

"It was good. I'm starving. Let's go get a burger before we go home," Miles said as he wrapped his arm around Cat's shoulders.

"I can't. We eat every day after school and then when I get home I'm not hungry, and my mom's starting to freak out about it. I gotta go home. I've got homework, my room's a wreck, and if we want this weekend together I have to get it all done. Remember, your mom and dad are going out of town and we have the house to ourselves," Cat said as she tickled Miles.

"Killjoy. I'll go eat by myself," Miles said, patting her on the bottom.

They walked slowly towards the parking lot, taking their time because they both knew it was all the time they would get today. They'd been going together for three months, and already the relationship was developing into something closer. Miles was a jock; Cat worked on the school newspaper and wanted to go to college to study journalism, eventually to become an investigative reporter. They'd talked about attending the same college in New York.

"Kiss me 'bye, I gotta go," Cat said as they parted ways in the parking lot. Miles leaned in for a quick peck and Cat pulled him close. She turned to walk across the parking area to her car, tossing her long, dark brown ponytail. Miles waved and jogged on toward his car.

Screeching tires and a scream from Cat brought his attention back to her. "Cat," he yelled as he watched her dragged into a fast-moving car. Her upper body was being pulled inside, just as a sock is sucked into a vacuum cleaner. Miles screamed again as he tossed his books aside and took off running. He could see Cat trying to fight off her assailant as her legs swung back and forth outside the window.

"Cat, no!" Miles screamed, as he ran in front of the car to stop it from taking Cat. The driver slowed down, momentarily confused, but as Miles tried to find a way to get to Catrina, Mike stomped on Tony's foot and the car lurched forward. Mike never let up, even when the car sent Miles' body hurtling into the air. The car swerved several more times as it left the parking area, taking Catrina Vincent from sight. Miles Handley's body lay where it landed, tucked up under the rear bumper, just behind the back tire on the driver's side of Alisha Wellington's car.

Alisha was on the planning committee with Cat and had left the building at the same time. But she'd run back in long enough to grab something from her locker and talk to a friend on the steps. Then she walked back to her car. It couldn't have been more than ten minutes. "It's Miles Handley; oh, God, is he dead? I saw him and his girlfriend Catrina Vincent walking together just a few minutes ago," Alisha was crying. Lindsay held her close and turned her so she couldn't see Will and Jerry turn Miles over.

He was clearly dead, his chest crushed and a large gash in his head. Jerry grabbed his radio from his holster and yelled into it for backup and an ambulance to Ripney High School, south parking area. There was blood on the rear fender and bumper of Alisha's car. Miles Handley's blood, no doubt, but they had to be sure.

Will and Jerry looked around from their squatting position. They could see a pile of books and a purse less than twenty feet from where Miles' body lay. An eerie feeling crept up their spines. Will looked around and saw another set of books.

"Those must be Miles's books over there. Okay, then, whose books are those?" Jerry asked. Will got up and moved toward them, his gun drawn.

"Lindsay come here, stay by us. They could still be in the area," Will said. But Lindsay continued walking, taking Alisha further away from the scene.

"They're not here," Lindsay said as she held Alisha close to her, her head resting on top of the girl's head.

"Lindsay, we have to talk to her, don't take her anywhere," Will said. "She's a material witness."

"I'm not, but she's in shock. She's not gonna be able to tell you much of anything until she calms down. We need an ambulance, where's the damn ambulance?"

"It's coming, but Lindsay, we have to know whose purse and books those are. Whose car is this? A girl may be missing, and we have to know who it is," Will said as he moved closer to them.

"The car is mine, and the books are Cat's," a soft broken voice whispered.

"Cat who, miss?" Will prodded.

"Catrina Vincent, those are her books. The white car is mine. The one Miles is under," Alisha said as she starting crying hard again. "The car over there, the red one, is Cat's." Alisha sobbed as she pointed out the red Mustang in the parking lot. There weren't many cars left in the parking area. Most of the kids had gone home for the day. "We stayed to work on the graduation celebration. We had a planning committee meeting. Cat and I are on the board," Alisha sobbed out. Lindsay looked over her head at Will. She could see panic in his eyes.

Jerry was waving his arms in the air for the ambulance as the sirens split the air. Several police officers arrived at the same time. Alisha was taken into the school office, where she tearfully called her parents.

Alisha's car and the area where Miles Handley had fallen were cordoned off and marked with yellow tape. The black tire marks from a car that had apparently been going very fast were photographed repeatedly. Will and Jerry worked diligently, quickly trying to gather all the information they could from the scene.

"We have to leave it to them, Will," Jerry said. "We don't have much time to find her. Lindsay has to come through for us, or we'll be standing at another teenager's front door telling her parents to pick out a coffin for their child."

Will stood as he broke a pencil in his hand. He'd been bending over the body of Miles while he was photographed and prepared to be taken away.

"Who's gonna tell his parents?" Will asked.

"I don't think anyone's gonna have to go," Jerry said, as he gestured to the woman running in their direction.

"Miles, Miles!" the woman screamed. She was fighting her way through the ever-growing crowd. Will grabbed her just as she broke through the people standing around Miles's body, lying covered on the stretcher.

"Mrs. Handley?" Will asked.

"Yes, I'm Mrs. Handley," she said as she stared at the body covered with the white sheet. "Is that my son?" she whispered.

"Yes ma'am. I'm afraid it is. I'm terribly sorry," Will said. He felt like shit. Lorraine Handley pushed Will away from her and ran to the stretcher. Jerking back the sheet, she grabbed the body of her son and cried violently on his battered chest. "Miles, Miles, please don't leave me. I can't do it alone. Miles!" she screamed.

Will motioned for a policewoman to take care of her. Gently,

Stephanie Lissard lifted Lorraine from Miles' body. Blood streaked her white shirt as Stephanie led her away. She was taken to a patrol car where she sat down inside. Miles's body was wheeled to a waiting ambulance. Will and Jerry stood there boiling with rage as they watched the emotional scene before them.

"I hate this case, and I'm gonna find those bastards, and when I do, I'm gonna kill them. Will, we don't know what they're driving or even what to look for. I feel like a damn fool standing around like this, but we don't even know which way to go after we leave the parking area. Let's get on the radio, make sure all police cars keep their eyes open for anything suspicious. Until Lindsay's ready, I think that's the best we can do," Jerry said as he wiped his hand down his face. Will nodded in silence.

Lindsay came from the school office. She'd left the Wellingtons with their daughter. "She didn't see anything. She ran back inside to get her keys from her locker. When she came out everyone was gone, and she walked to her car while she fiddled with her key ring. When she looked up, she saw the blood first, then his legs sticking out like we saw them. She says she didn't touch him, she just started screaming," Lindsay said when she was close enough to Will and Jerry. She could feel the intense anger within them.

"Lindsay, this is all on you, now. You have to find this girl, and we don't have much time. If they follow their usual pattern, she'll be dead in twenty-four hours or less. What do you need?" Jerry asked.

"I need something of the girl's and a picture of her. I need common stuff from all the victims, and I need a place to work where it's quiet. We need to be sure she's not at home or something like that, so that I don't waste my time and energy looking for her. I need to hold her stuff in my hand along with something from Amanda, Wanda, and Georgia," Lindsay said.

"Okay that's easy. Jerry, can you go to the girl's house? Talk to her parents. Show them her things, make sure they give you a positive ID, and then bring them back with you. See if by any chance she's there and maybe they've had an argument, or she got away and took off running. I mean, anything's a possibility," Will said. Jerry nodded.

"Lindsay, you come with me. We're going to the field room and round up the things you need, and we're going to set something up that works for you. Jerry, meet us there when you get what we need," Will said.

"Jerry, will you get a current picture of her for me?" Lindsay asked. "And I need her car keys."

"I will, and I'll meet the two of you at the station in about an hour. Call me on the radio if you get anything," Jerry said as he took off.

He ran to the car they'd been driving all day. Lindsay and Will would get a ride back to the station with a uniformed officer. As Jerry turned the car around in the middle of Ripney Road, he let the anger run freely through him. It wouldn't be the first time either he or Will had taken out their anger on a perp. They'd always kept each other from going too far. But this time Jerry wondered who would stop them from killing these bastards. Jerry gripped the steering wheel in a white-knuckled grasp. He had the girl's address from the school secretary clutched in his fist, and he drove with his jaw tight.

Lindsay and Will jumped in the patrol car Will had commandeered to take them to the station. Lindsay again sat in the back and Will in the front. They didn't talk because there wasn't anything left to say. She'd seen the event, but they'd been too late. Lindsay felt horrible as her mind replayed the day's events. Why hadn't they caught them? Lindsay struggled with it over and over again. She had police support; they were willing to help. She had a firm grasp on the situation and she knew what to do, how to interpret what she saw. She had acted as soon as she'd gotten the information. They all had.

"Why can't we catch them?" Lindsay whispered to herself.

"Did you say something, Lindsay?" Will asked.

"I'm sorry, that's all. I let you down and I don't know how or why."

"You didn't let me down. I've thought about this over and over. There is nothing we could have done, there is no way we could have acted any faster. I can't say what went wrong, but I can say that now we have another dead body on our hands. And I'm sick to death of this case already, and it's far from over." Will wiped his hands over his face.

"Will, don't give up yet, please," Lindsay said. Will could tell she was crying. He didn't say anything. He just sat there and waited until he needed to be active again. "Hurry up, this isn't a parade, you know," Will growled at the officer driving.

Jerry pulled his sedan into the driveway on Slema Lane. He sat there staring at the red brick house. He didn't want to go in there. "Damn," he said as he got out. He straightened his tie and tucked his shirt in. As he looked down he realized there was blood on his white shirt and his tie. "Damn," he said again as he buttoned his jacket over his shirt. Jerry touched the doorbell and heard it echo inside the house. He waited as he heard someone coming to the door. A woman in white slacks, a red shirt, and red heels opened the door. She stood there looking at Jerry with a tissue in her hand.

"Can I help you?" she said through her sniffles.

"Mrs. Vincent?" Jerry asked.

"Yes, I'm Tonya Vincent. Can I help you?"

"Mrs. Vincent, I'm Detective Leeme with Central. Can I speak with you?" Jerry was obviously uncomfortable with crying women, and he didn't know how much she knew already.

"Yes, come in. If you're here about my daughter, we already know. The school secretary called us about Miles. Have you found my daughter yet?" Tonya said in a shaky voice.

"No ma'am. That's why I'm here. So you haven't heard from her?" Jerry asked.

"No, I haven't heard anything from her yet. Did anyone see what happened? My daughter must be terrified. I want to go look for her, but

I'm afraid that I won't be here when she comes home." Tonya wiped her eyes again.

"Mrs. Vincent, is your husband home?" Jerry asked.

"Yes he's walking the neighborhood. He came home as soon as I called him. Cat usually comes right home. I guess I don't have to tell you we're both really scared," Tonya said, her shaking hand proof of her words. Jerry watched her. She doesn't know, she has no idea, and she hasn't put things together yet, he thought to himself.

"Can I have a recent picture of your daughter, Mrs. Vincent? Also, can I ask you to look at these things and identify them for me as your daughter's?" Jerry held out the books, purse, and sweater they'd found in the school parking area.

"They're Cat's. We bought the purse together at the mall last weekend." She flipped through the books and nodded her head. "Yes, these are Cat's as well. The sweater belongs to her sister." Tonya reached for a frame on the table. It held a picture of a beautiful girl with long chestnut hair. She was smiling sweetly as she held what appeared to be a diploma under her chin and to one side. The girl was beautiful, but it was the long hair that caught Jerry's eye. He removed the picture from the frame and tucked it into his inside jacket pocket, momentarily forgetting the blood on his shirt. When he looked back at Tonya, he realized she'd seen it.

"Is that Miles's blood?" she asked as she started to cry again.

"Yes ma'am. I'm sorry. I didn't mean for you to see it. We want to find your daughter just as soon as we can. We're worried about her, too," Jerry said as he covered his shirt self-consciously.

Tonya reached a hand out to touch the red spot on Jerry's tie. "Miles was such a nice boy," she said with a far-away sound in her voice.

"Mrs. Vincent, can I take Cat's purse with me to the police station?" Jerry was hoping to keep her talking until someone, her husband or her other daughter, came home. He didn't want to leave her like this.

"Sure you can, detective. I'm sorry. This has been such a horrible day. When Cat comes home, I'll have her call you," Tonya said politely.

Jerry looked out the window in the living room where they were sitting. He saw a neighbor in her backyard pruning roses. He stood and walked out the door, calling to her as he motioned her over. She came slowly and then a little faster as she recognized his badge. Jerry felt better about leaving now. The neighbor promised to sit as long as needed. "When her husband and daughter come home, have them call us, please," Jerry said as he handed the woman his business card.

Jerry grabbed the mike in his car when he was backing out of the driveway. He could see a tall man wearing a tan shirt and dark brown slacks hurrying in his direction.

"Dispatch, put me through to Will Halpin," Jerry said.

"Go ahead Jerry, this is Will," Jerry heard in a matter of seconds.

"Will, the girl's not home; but she has long brown hair and she's a looker."

"Are you sure about the long hair? You can't see it in the yearbook."

"Yeah, I have a picture of her that must have been taken for graduation. She's got a head full of reddish brown hair," Jerry said.

"No word to her parents?" Will asked.

"Nope, Mom's sort of out of it. She seems lost and confused. I have a neighbor sitting with her now till the husband gets home. He and the older daughter are out doing the once-around-the-block thing. I'm in route to your location. Anything on your end?" Jerry asked.

"Yeah, we got lots. You better step it up," Will said as they were disconnected.

Lindsay sat alone in the field room. A room divider was between her and the door. She had the pictures of all the girls laid out on the table and was waiting for the new one to arrive. Lindsay started with the picture of Amanda Wiggins that had been provided by her mother.

"This is Amanda Wiggins. She's seventeen years old, blonde hair, long, about mid-back. She's the first victim," Lindsay said as she looked down at the picture of the pretty, blue-eyed blonde. Lindsay reached forward and picked up the picture. "I see a black and white image of her standing in front of a mirror. She's not alone, she's talking to someone, and she's working on her hair. I see her in a picture now, it's black and white; and it has one of those white borders around it. There is something moving fast at it, I can't quite make it out. Wait, I can see it now. It's a teardrop; I can see the teardrop falling slowly toward the picture. Now I see the huge splash it makes as it hits the picture and washes away the image of Amanda." Lindsay put the picture down.

She picked up the picture of Georgia and started speaking again. "I see Georgia smiling as she runs down what appear to be stairs. The sun is shining, or there is a very bright light shining above her. She seems happy. Now I see a black and white picture of her and just like the one of Amanda, it too is framed in the white border. I see the tear coming now, slowly. Okay, it has splashed on the image but, wait . . . Will, Jerry, it didn't wash away her image."

Will had been sitting on the other side of the divider taking notes as Lindsay spoke. Jerry slid quietly in beside him and read the notes he'd taken already. Reaching in his front pocket, he pulled the picture out and held it up for Will to see.

"Hi, Jerry," Lindsay said. They looked at one another as Will raised his eyebrows. "Lindsay, don't do that," Jerry said. Lindsay chuckled softly on the other side of the screen.

Jerry slid the picture of Cat under the divider. "Thank you," Lindsay said as she reached to pick it up. Thinking better of it, she let it lie where it was. "Oh, Jerry, I saw your shadow, by the way," Lindsay giggled.

She knew better than to pick up the picture from the floor. If she did, the images would come and she had something to do before she got to that. Picking up Wanda's picture, she instantly saw something in the shadows.

"A man is crying; he's bent over and crying very hard. There's someone with him—he's not alone. He's young, with dark brown hair. He's crying, but he feels sick to his stomach too. There's an image of a young woman in black and white. She's hanging her hair over in front of her, like women do when they dry it with a blow dryer. No, wait, she's not moving, but she's crying—her tears are falling onto a photo page, and there are many photos this time. Hundreds, and the tears are falling on them, washing out the images," Lindsay said.

"Lindsay," Will said from behind the screen, "does that mean these guys have killed hundreds?"

"I don't think so, but I'm not sure. I have a feeling we don't understand the way these guys think yet, they're different. There's a lack of remorse in them about the people they kill or leave behind. That's what I think that means," Lindsay said.

Lindsay laid the photo back on the table. She reached forward and picked up the photo of Catrina Vincent. Instantly, she dropped it and jumped to her feet. Will and Jerry heard her moving suddenly and ran around the divider. Lindsay was on her feet, backing into a corner of the room. She looked horrified.

"Oh my God! Oh my God, no," she cried. "They have her. She's being driven somewhere far from here. She's so scared, and she's hurt. Terribly hurt. There's blood on her. I can smell and see it," Lindsay said.

"Lindsay, listen to me now. You're okay, we're here with you, and you're fine. Lindsay, can you see where they are or where they're going?" Will asked.

Lindsay shook her head. "I can't stand it. I can see what they're doing to her and I don't want to," Lindsay cried. She was in panic mode, as if she were an unwilling passenger in the car that held Catrina Vincent hostage. She could see the images in color and in slow motion. Lindsay held her hands over her ears and shook her head as she moaned.

"No, no please."

"Lindsay, let it go. We can't help her if you don't help us. This is your job, for Christ's sake. Let it go," Will yelled.

Lindsay shook her head. "No, I can't do this, I can't. They have her, Will, they're going to kill her with no remorse whatsoever. You don't understand." Lindsay cried.

Jerry pushed Will to the side and reached out and held her. He pulled her close even though she fought him and wrapped his arms around her and held her. Crooning softly, he whispered in her ear, "I've got you, you're safe now. I have you. It's okay."

Slowly, Lindsay let it go. She hung onto Jerry's large shoulders and cried.

"Oh, my God," she whispered. "This is too much for me. I can't do this anymore," Lindsay said shaking her head. She was calmer now, slowly calming down while she sobbed. Lindsay let Jerry lead her to a chair. She sank into it gratefully. "I'm so sorry," she cried.

Jerry knew what had happened. Will looked at him and said, "What the hell was that?"

"She's not a cop, Will," Jerry explained. "That's what the hell that was. She's a civilian, she's not a cop, but she's in here dealing with cop shit, seeing things that civilians should never see. Shit, she's seeing things cops shouldn't ever have to see."

Lindsay sat and looked at Jerry. "Thank you. I'm sorry, and Will's right. This is my job. It's what I do. No, it's more than what I do, it's who I am. But that doesn't mean it doesn't hurt me."

"We're gonna get you something to drink. Take a few deep breaths and calm down, and we'll be right back," Jerry said.

As Jerry led Will out of the room he said, "We need to send her home, Will. She can't help us. Shit, I don't think anyone can help us now. But this isn't her thing, she's not a cop. Will, I couldn't handle this if I could see what she sees," Jerry said.

Will looked at him. Images of the camp scene flooded his mind. He saw the blood-crusted clothing in the backpack and remembered how he'd felt that day, the horror in his gut. He nodded, and they walked back into the field room.

But what met their eyes wasn't what they expected. Lindsay was seated at the table with the pictures arranged in a circle. She had her recorder and her notepad and was taking notes. The sketches of Tony and Mike Hennessey were propped up against the blackboard. As they watched her from the doorway, they saw her reach down and turn the pictures of all the girls over. Then she picked up Catrina's picture and propped it up with Tony's and Mike's.

She dusted her hands as she reached for the pictures. "Lindsay, what are you doing?" Jerry demanded.

"I'm working; where's my coffee?" she asked.

Will and Jerry looked at each other and walked slowly to the table. "Lindsay, it's not going to get any easier," Will said.

"I know. I don't expect it to. But that girl is going to die unless we find her and even if we find her right now, the best we can hope for is another Georgia Amando—a victim in need of healing and therapy for years to come, but she'll be alive. That's something," Lindsay said. "I had a shock, and I lost it. But I'm okay now, and I want to see this through. Now, are the two of you going to help me or not?"

"We'll help," Jerry and Will said together as they sat down, slightly confused. Somehow Lindsay had collected herself and mustered some strength while they were gone.

"Okay, this is what I get about these two now. We know them, they're in the system, at least one of them is." Lindsay said.

"We know that, already. Mike Hennessey's rap sheet is as long as my arm," Will said. "His final paperwork came back right after we got his name and confirmation from Georgia. He's been in and out since he was eleven."

"Did you know that he doesn't like to sleep indoors? Did you know he has a fear of people? I think he's manic, or schizophrenic, or something along those lines. He stays on the run all the time. He's sexually addicted and his thought process is constant. It keeps him awake for hours on end. He's a night stalker. And the most important thing is that he thinks best on his feet. What I'm trying to tell you is that's why we can't catch him. He doesn't plan his attacks, he just attacks randomly. Sort of like flying by the seat of his pants, and he takes this other guy with him." Lindsay took a deep breath as she finished. "Will, Jerry, the only way to catch him is to find him now while this girl is still alive. I can't connect with Tony and Mike because we don't have anything of theirs," Lindsay said.

Will and Jerry looked at her. "Well, actually we do. We found a tent, some camping equipment, and some other stuff," Jerry said.

"We have some clothing, too," Will said.

Lindsay stood up. "Okay, let's go look at it. It's been two-and-a-half hours since we've started this. I don't feel like we've gotten anywhere."

CHAPTER 62

Mike sat on an old tree that he and Tony had retrieved from the nearby woods. "Stop your damn caterwauling," Mike said as he threw a tin can at Tony. Tony sniffed and rubbed his nose on his shirtsleeve. He gave Mike a dirty look as the can hit the dirt right in front of him. "I got you that chick from the school, didn't I? I even let you have a go at her first this time," Mike said emphatically.

Tony nodded, "Yeah, but Mike, you killed Wanda. I liked her, she was nice to me. You scared her, Mike, that was mean," Tony said.

"I don't give a shit! You think what we did to those other girls wasn't mean? Bitches deserve it. Leave me alone about it. I've been trying to make it up to you all week. We even broke our own rules and went into town to get you some. Still you're bitchin'. I've had enough. Shut up!" Mike screamed at Tony as he kicked dirt at him.

Tony jumped up. Mike stood up slowly, looking at Tony as if he were daring him to do something. Tony clenched his fists and stormed off into the woods. His long lean frame barely cast a shadow over the body of Catrina Vincent as she lay strapped to the tree trunk. Head trauma had caused her to slip in and out of consciousness, with Miles's name on her lips.

Mike walked over to where she lay. He looked down at her, thinking that she hadn't been much fun. Mike had a plan. He untied her and lifted her easily enough. Stuffing her into the backseat of the car, he propped her up against the window, then ran around to the other side and got in. Tony heard the car start, and peered out from his hiding place in the woods. He saw Mike drive off. He could see the girl sitting upright in the backseat, but he didn't think she was alive. Mike had told him a few hours ago she wasn't worth messing with any more. Tony knew what that meant.

Mike drove through the now dark countryside with Cat in the back seat. He'd heard her moan from time to time, but he knew she wasn't going to be any more fun. She hadn't been any fun in the beginning, and Mike could tell that wasn't going to change. He pulled into a gas station and asked the attendant for the key to the rest room. As he waited, another car pulled in. A kid got out of the car and glanced in at Cat.

"Hey, buddy, looks like your chick's had it for the night. It might be time to take her home," the kid said.

"It might at that," Mike agreed, smiling. "She puked all over my car and then she fell and hit her head. I don't know what I'm gonna tell her parents," Mike said, as his brain started working.

"Put her on the porch swing, ring the doorbell, and run like crazy," the guy said.

Mike laughed, "That's a good idea. Thanks, dude," Mike said, putting his hand out.

The kid shook his hand, "Don't mention it. We guys gotta stick together."

Mike used the bathroom. It had been his plan to leave Cat's body in the restroom, but now he had another idea. Anyway, there were too many witnesses at the gas station now. Mike got back in his car and drove to the first farmhouse with a porch swing that he could find and that wasn't too far from the road. He carried Cat's body silently through the woods. Creeping up to the porch, he listened for sounds coming from inside. He laid Cat's body down in the bushes and stood on the porch outside the railing so that he could look through the windows. No one was in the living room. He went back to where he'd left Cat and picked her up. As quietly as he could, he set her upright on the porch swing. Then Mike simply walked away. He never looked back.

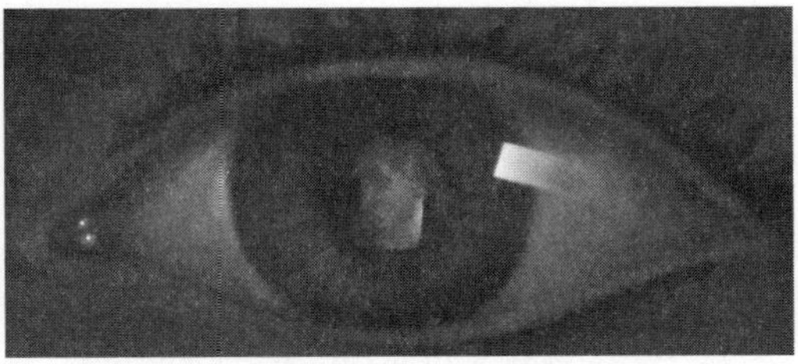

CHAPTER 63

Tony sat near the campfire. He was sad. He had liked Wanda, and now he missed her. The carnival had closed, and they would never see Lilly again. Tony wanted to call her, but Mike said it wouldn't be a good idea. Tony laid his head in his hands and cried as he thought about Wanda's face as Mike had tied her to the tree. Mike had said she'd like it, but she didn't. She'd screamed and screamed until Mike punched her in the mouth. Then she'd just cried.

Tony didn't want to party with her like Mike did, so he'd left them alone. He could hear her crying as he walked around in circles in the woods. His nerves were tense, and he wanted her to stop crying. Finally, after Tony had fallen asleep, crying himself, Wanda had stopped crying. When he'd come back to the camp hours later, Mike said she'd gone home. "Yeah, she was mad at me, so I made her walk home," Mike had laughed. But Tony knew better; he had challenged Mike, who finally admitted that he'd killed her.

"What'd you do with her?" Tony had asked.

"I left her not too far from where we found her, and I don't want to talk about it no more. Forget about it, Tony, we'll find someone else," Mike had said that day. It was the same thing he'd said every day since then.

But Tony didn't want to forget about Wanda. He stood up and kicked dirt on the campfire. Then he turned and walked back into the woods. He nimbly climbed the tree where he'd built a lookout tower for himself while Mike was away. He didn't like this campsite as much as the other one, because he was always here alone. Mike was always taking off with the car, leaving Tony to fend for himself. He would come back later with stuff he found or lifted from farmhouses. Sometimes it was a pie, sometimes a car, and sometimes it was a purse or wallet.

Mike was a pretty good provider, but he was meaner than anyone Tony had ever known. Tony sat down in the tower and looked out through the trees. He loved it up here where the air seemed cleaner and he didn't feel so alone. The stars were easier to see up here, and Tony could see the dirt road that led to the campsite. No one, not even Mike, could sneak up on him when he was up here. He'd never told Mike about the tower. It was his own place, a place he didn't have to share with anyone. He sat there and thought about Wanda, poor Wanda who was so nice to him. But he never gave a thought to Catrina Vincent; Mike was taking care of her.

CHAPTER 64

"Lindsay, let's go home. It's late, and you've been working on this for hours. We need a road sign. All you've given us tonight is great, but it's not going to help us find her until we get a direction or a road sign or something like that," Will said. They were all dog-tired.

"No, I won't sleep anyway," said Lindsay. You two go, I can nap later and take the other car back to the hotel when I'm ready. But you should go, since you have roll call in less than ten hours. Go, get some sleep," Lindsay said.

"We can't leave you here alone. You have to be supervised," Jerry said.

Just then the door to the field room opened and an officer stuck his head in. "I don't know if this will mean anything to you or not, but Albert Cummings from East called and said they've had a series of small-time robberies over that way."

Will and Jerry looked at him. "Why should that mean anything to us?" Jerry asked.

"The guy the store clerk described looks like your guy," the officer said. Will, Jerry, and Lindsay stood up. "Thanks, man. We'll get back to Albert," Will said as they left the field room.

It was a good tip, a lucky break. Too bad it would take them in the opposite direction, because Mike didn't mind driving. He knew he had to keep moving, and he'd recently learned never to hit the same place twice.

The shitty events at the cabin had taught him that. "That damn farmer was ready for me," Mike said out loud.

Now he turned the car back toward the other side of town and got on the freeway. He hummed a tune as he drove and then turned on the radio and sang along as it played "Uneasy Rider" by the Charlie Daniels Band. Mike kept time with the radio on the steering wheel as he drove. He thought of Tony and wondered why he was being so sentimental all of a sudden. It would take him forty-five minutes to get back to where Tony was; in that time Mike would rehearse telling Tony he was sorry about Wanda. Mike would mean it, of course, at the time.

The young man at the gas station had watched Mike drive away. He waved goodbye to him, then turned and started talking to the attendant. "Lock the door, hurry." The attendant, thinking it was a robbery, panicked and tried to reach under his counter for a gun. But the kid grabbed his arm and said, "That girl in the car was dead. We need to call the police. Lock the door in case he comes back."

The attendant looked at him and decided he was serious. He locked the door and turned out the outside lights for good measure. Then he motioned for the kid to come in the back with him. "I saw that blood on her head and on the window, too. She looked pretty beat up," the attendant said.

They called the police from the office located in the back off the mechanics' workroom. The smell of old grease and oil hung heavy in the air as they waited for someone to connect them with an officer.

"This is Officer Cole. Can I help you?"

"My name is Carl Boren. I own the service station out here on Highway 13. A guy just came through here with a dead body in his car. It was a girl."

"How do you know she was dead?" Officer Cole asked.

Carl looked at the kid standing there waiting with him. "He wants to know how we knew she was dead."

Jake grabbed the phone, "Officer, my name is Jake Lloyd. I saw her, too. The guy pulled in here just before me and when he went into the bathroom I tapped on the window. The girl never woke up, and there was blood all over her head and the window. When the guy left he shook my hand, and now there's blood on my hand."

"I'll have someone out there right away. Don't be a hero if he comes back. Did you get his license plate number, by any chance?" Cole asked.

"Only the first three letters, they are B as in boy, R as in Robert and L as in love."

"Okay, Jake, you two stay right there and stay inside. Lock the doors and don't answer them for anyone but the police. Do you understand?"

"Yes, sir. We'll be here," Jake hung up the phone and he and Carl sat and waited.

Lindsay sat in the back seat and thought about what she held in her hand. It was either Mike's or Tony's, and she was getting something from it, but so many people had handled it since it had been found, it was hard to say who belonged to what. In frustration she put it down on the seat next to her. She'd never liked knives, not even pocketknives.

They were headed in the direction of East station to talk with Detective Albert Cummings. The radio crackled and the dispatcher called out Will's name. Will grabbed the mike and said, "Go ahead."

"Sir, we have something for you. A guy called in from over on Highway 13. He says a man came through there with a dead girl in his car. Says there was blood on the window, on the victim, and now he has blood on his hands from shaking the guy's hand."

"Why was he shaking the guy's hand?" Will asked.

"I don't know, sir. Do you want me to give it to someone else, or do you want it? I have uniforms in route now," the dispatcher said.

"No, we'll take it," Will said. "What's the address again?"

After getting the address, Will turned the car around. "Damn, these guys are all over the place."

"Do you think it's connected, Will?" Jerry asked.

"Don't you?" Will stated, rather than asked. Jerry nodded.

"Lindsay, is it connected?" Jerry asked.

Lindsay sat quiet for a moment, then nodded her head. "It feels connected. And I have a feeling that sometime tomorrow, probably at first light, we'll get a call to come back this way for a dead body found on the side of the road or something like that."

Will and Jerry knew it was true. And they were right; only the timing was off by a few hours. Just as they crossed the county line, the dispatcher called again. "Detective Halpin."

"Go ahead," Will said as he pressed the button on the microphone.

"I just got a call from a Mr. Hank Gibbons. He says he has a badly wounded girl sitting on his front porch swing. He says his dog found her," the dispatcher said. Will and Jerry could hear nothing but professionalism in her voice.

"Did you get an address, and have you sent an ambulance?" Will asked.

"Yes sir, he's at 995 Highway 13. And an ambulance is in route."

"Let the uniforms at the service station know. Send someone out there to take a statement for us. We're in route to the Gibbons residence."

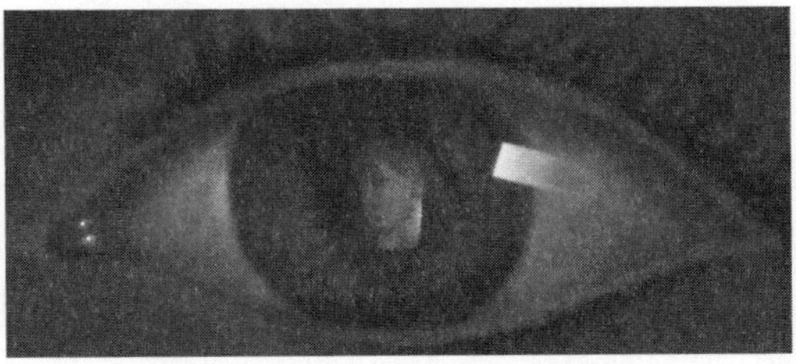

CHAPTER 65

Hank Gibbons sat on the front porch with his big flashlight. His wife had covered the poor girl, and together they had laid her down on the swing. When he heard the siren, Hank got up and walked to the road. He let the beam of light from his flashlight shine across the road. The ambulance driver saw it and turned in. The dust flew up everywhere as they came to a screeching halt.

"You don't need all that noise now, guys. She's dead. My wife is sitting with her on the porch. She died about five minutes ago."

"Sir, we'll meet you at the house."

Hank walked ahead as the ambulance drove past him. This was the worst damn thing that had ever happened to them, he thought. The girl wasn't any more than fifteen or sixteen years old. Her blood had congealed on the porch beneath the swing. They had been inside cleaning up the dinner dishes when the dog had created such a stir that they'd come outside to see what all the fuss was about. The dog had run to the road, so they knew that someone had been there, but they had no way of knowing who it had been. As they'd walked back to the house, they'd seen someone sitting on the porch. Duke had run up to her and then run to the front door. Hank knew in that moment that something was wrong.

As Hank reached the porch, he saw the ambulance attendants getting the stretcher from the back. They pulled it out and lowered the legs and started running toward the girl. The lights from the road caught their attention and all three turned to see Will's car pull into the driveway.

Hank flashed the light again, and he could hear the engine roar as it came toward them.

Will and Jerry showed their badges as Lindsay went to the porch. She looked at Catrina Vincent lying there, almost as if she had just gone to sleep. The attendant was starting to move her when Will and Jerry stopped him.

"We need to preserve the scene," Will said.

"Do you mind if I make sure she's dead, detective?" the ambulance attendant asked snidely.

"No, not at all," Will said, as he backed up, raising his eyebrows.

Then there was a flurry of activity as the attendant yelled, "I've got a pulse."

The other attendant ran to his side with an orange bag in his hand. "There's no time," the first one said, gathering Catrina in his arms. "She's a load-and-go. Get the stretcher."

Will and Jerry ran to help. Lindsay laid her hand on the ambulance attendant's arm and said, "I'm a nurse. Can I help?"

"Sure, if you wanna ride with us we can use all the help we can get."

Lindsay ran to the ambulance with the stretcher. As she climbed into the back Will said, "I'll meet you at the hospital." She nodded as the doors slammed shut and she was alone with the paramedic and Catrina.

They worked on her during the ride back. The paramedic was talking with the hospital via radio, getting orders while Lindsay was dressing a puncture wound in Catrina's abdomen.

"She's lost a lot of blood," Lindsay said as the heart monitor beeped, setting off a flurry of activity. Catrina's body was shocked repeatedly with a defibrillator, and drugs were pushed through the I.V., but as the ambulance rolled into the hospital emergency area, Lindsay knew it was a loss. The girl had just been too far gone when she'd been found. Even if the hospital had been closer, she never would have made it.

Lindsay tore off her bloody rubber gloves as the doors closed behind the stretcher wheeling Catrina's body away. The emergency room doctors would work on her for a while, but in the end Lindsay knew there would be two more funerals.

She turned and watched Will and Jerry screech to a halt in the parking area designated for police vehicles. She shook her head as they got out and ran her way. "Son of a bitch," Will said angrily. Jerry turned back to the car and laid his head on the landau roof.

They walked to the hospital emergency room desk together. There really wasn't anything left to do but wait until Catrina's parents got there. "Do you want to get something to eat?" Jerry asked. Will and Lindsay looked at him as if he'd suddenly grown two heads. "It was just a thought. We haven't eaten all day."

"Who could eat?" Will asked. Lindsay knew just how he felt.

They sat together in the waiting room reserved for them. All police personnel used this room to write reports while they waited for the doctors to finish doing what they could do and then call for them. Will and Jerry didn't have to wait long. The door opened and a young doctor came in wearing the typical hospital scrubs. He pulled an eye shield off his face as he looked at them. "The young girl," he said. But it was really more of a question.

"That's us," Jerry said as he stood up. Will and Lindsay followed suit.

"She's gone. There wasn't anything we could do for her. I'm sorry. We'll need some information from you, like next of kin and her name," the doctor said. Will and Jerry nodded.

"Well, should we go visit the parents?" Lindsay asked.

"It's our job, Lindsay. We have to do it. We'll drop you off at the hotel. Get some sleep. This isn't over yet. There are two psychopaths out there, and a lot more teenagers to choose from than cops to protect them."

As they opened the door, the reporters and broadcasters swarmed into the room. Will and Jerry held their hands up and pushed Lindsay through the crowd. Questions were fired at them rapidly as the media hounded them on their way to the car. But one question stuck, one they heard over and over again. "Is this another Mall Murder?"

CHAPTER 66

"Mr. and Mrs. Vincent, my name is Detective Halpin. I believe you've met my partner, Detective Leeme," Will said.

"Yes, we've met," Tonya Vincent said. "This is my husband, Tom."

The detectives shook hands with the Vincents. "We realize it's late but we need to speak with you about your daughter, Catrina," Will said.

Tom Vincent opened the door wider to allow the two men to come in. Will and Jerry saw the pajamas, slippers, and the dark circles under the eyes. Tom reached behind him and turned on the light in the foyer. Will thought momentarily about how many times he'd been in people's homes and only seen the foyer.

"We're here about your daughter, like I said. I'm sorry to say that a young girl's been found who matches the description of your daughter, and we need someone to come with us to identify her," Will said. Jerry stood there feeling as bad as he looked.

"I don't understand. Why don't you just ask her what her name is?" Tom Vincent asked.

"Um, sir, the young woman is deceased," Jerry stammered, looking at Will, who suddenly wasn't saying anything.

Tonya and Tom Vincent each took a step back as if that alone would separate them from the truth. "Oh my God, no!" Tonya wailed. Her husband put his arm around her.

From the stairs behind Will and Jerry, a young woman screamed out. Will and Jerry spun around in surprise and fright. There on the stairs was a girl who looked so much like Catrina Vincent that both men took a sudden breath.

"Catrina Vincent?" Will asked, stunned by her appearance. But the young woman was beyond answer.

"That's our daughter Candace," Tom said as he went to her. Tonya just stood there with tears running down her face, a faraway look in her eyes.

"Mr. Vincent, we need someone to come with us, please," Jerry said. He couldn't stand any more pain and suffering, not on top of his own.

Tom Vincent sat his wife and daughter together on the sofa. He dialed a number, just as Rake Wiggins and Don Corley had done. It was becoming a far too frequent scene for Will and Jerry. But sympathy was an emotion they couldn't afford.

They rode in silence, each lost in thought as the miles ticked by. Tom Vincent was thinking about his daughters and about his desire to leave his marriage. Will was thinking he'd had enough of this damn case and they needed help, help above and beyond what they had. Jerry was thinking about changing careers.

As Tom Vincent stared down at the battered and broken body of his youngest daughter, tears slipped down his face and splashed on the cold metal table. Anger boiled within him. "Who did this to my daughter?" he growled.

"We won't lie to you; we think it's the same men that killed Amanda Wiggins and Wanda Corley, who were in your daughter's graduating class. I'm assuming you've either read about it in the paper or heard about it on television," Jerry said.

"I've heard about it. You haven't caught them yet?" Tom asked.

"No sir, not yet. We're close, but so far we haven't been able to catch them.

"Are you saying my daughter is one of the Mall Murder victims, and her boyfriend too?" Tom Vincent asked.

Will and Jerry hated that title. "Yes sir, all signs point to it, but we're not absolutely sure. The investigation has begun and will continue. We'll catch them, Mr. Vincent, I give you my word on that," Will said. And he meant it.

"Is there any way you can turn back the hands of time so you can catch them before they kill my daughter?" Tom Vincent asked, as he walked past them.

"No," Will and Jerry whispered together to the retreating back of Catrina Vincent's father.

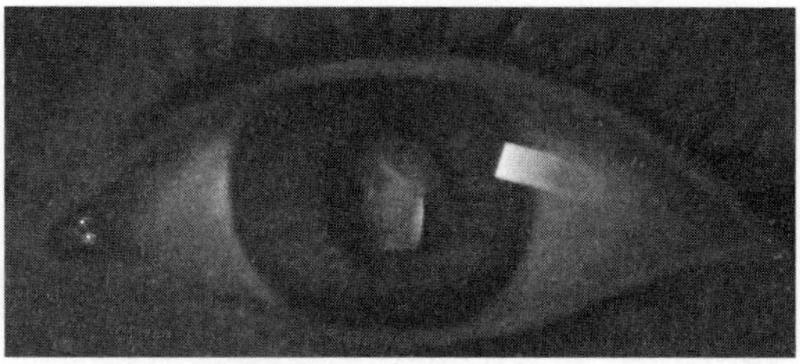

CHAPTER 67

Mike and Tony were not speaking. Tony had spent the night in the tower, and Mike had had no idea where he was when he'd returned from his "errand." Mike had yelled into the woods for thirty minutes before he gave up.

"Fine, stay out there, I don't give a rat's ass. I hope the wolves eat you," he yelled one more time. But Mike did care. What if Tony had been caught while he was gone, what if he'd fallen in the river and drowned? Mike got up and walked around the campfire. He was getting nervous as his mind went over the possibilities.

At sun-up he awoke to the smell of coffee brewing over the campfire. He lifted his head from the folded blanket he'd slept in under the makeshift table. His clothes were damp from the morning dew. Mike wasn't a morning person, but Tony was. He looked in the direction of the campfire and saw Tony walking around.

"Hey, where have you been?" Mike asked as he lifted himself on one elbow.

"I've been around," Tony said sullenly.

"Yeah. Why didn't you come when I called you?" Mike asked.

"Cause I ain't a dog and I didn't want to," Tony said as he walked away.

Mike staggered to his feet. "Come on Tony, I'm sorry about Wanda. Come on—can't we get past this and be friends again?"

"No!" Tony screamed at him suddenly. "You killed my friend because you want to be my only friend. You killed her, you butcher!" Tony ran back into the woods.

Mike ran after him, but Tony was quicker and more nimble, and he hadn't stayed up more than half the night drinking. "Fine, run away, you coward. And she wasn't your friend. She was a whore, they're all whores. Just like the others, Wanda was a whore," Mike screamed into the trees.

Tony heard him, but he kept running. Wanda wasn't a whore and somehow that managed to stick in Tony's mind. He scrambled up the tree, shoving branches aside as he climbed through the leaves. Tony worked his way out on the limb to the tower box he'd constructed. He climbed inside and sat rocking himself with his knees drawn tightly to his chest. Every time he came up here, he had to take time to still his breathing and calm himself. Not from anger, but because he had to climb across that limb, a limb that hung out over the river. Tony was terrified of the water, but the benefits to sitting up here, so high above everyone else, far outweighed his terror. All he had to do was be careful and grab large handfuls of leaves and limb on his way by. It was the best spot in the woods. It was the most peaceful spot in the woods and Tony felt safe and protected here.

The only problem with the tower was he could still hear Mike screaming down below. He knew Mike couldn't see him, but he could hear him if he made a sound. So Tony sat quietly and just let Mike scream.

"Tony!" Mike screamed. "Tony you come back here right now. Tony, she was a whore. Are you going to let a whore come between us? We're brothers. We're best friends Tony; we've been through thick and thin together. Come on, man!" Mike yelled as he walked through the woods, peeking around large tree trunks. He was ready for Tony. Not ready for him to jump out and attack him, since he knew Tony didn't have the balls to do that; but ready for him to jump out of hiding and take off running.

But Tony had him fooled, because Mike never looked up. Tony could hear him directly below him, even though he couldn't see through the thick foliage of the tree.

"She was trash, Tony. Forget her, we'll find someone else just like her if you want to, only she'll be a nice chick. Come on, man," Mike yelled.

"She wasn't trash. She was a nice chick and she'd been nice to me," Tony whispered in his tower in the tree.

"Tony, come out, come out, wherever you are," Mike chanted.

"No!" Tony yelled from his tower. Then he quickly put his hand over his mouth. But it was too late. Mike had heard him and he knew where Tony was.

He looked at the base of the tree. The great trunk grew straight up and then branched out in all its majestic glory. Mike followed the direction of the branches as he looked up. Most of them swung out over the water and he knew Tony would never go that way. He walked to the next tree and studied those branches as well. Since he couldn't see into the foliage, Mike could only guess which tree Tony was in.

"Oh, well, if you aren't hungry," Mike baited. He turned and walked back to the campfire. Tony could hear him messing with tin cans and things around the campsite. His stomach growled terribly. He'd come down originally to get some coffee. He knew Mike was there, since he'd heard him through the night calling him, but he thought he could make some coffee and then make it back to his hideaway before Mike woke up. He'd been wrong then, but he wouldn't make that same mistake again. Tony turned to his private stash there in the tower.

He opened the package of powdered sugar donuts and ate them at his leisure, missing his coffee. "Asshole," Tony grumbled.

Mike sat down below missing Tony. He was hungry, but he didn't want to fix anything for himself. He wanted Tony to do it. "You're pissing me off, Tony," he yelled into the trees as he rummaged for the powdered sugar donuts he knew were here somewhere.

Tony never said a word; he just flipped Mike off and smiled.

CHAPTER 68

"Come out, come out, wherever you are," Lindsay chanted as she sat in her hotel room sipping coffee and working on the case at her desk. Lindsay chuckled at her own silliness. But the saying stayed with her. She was pushing herself today, trying to find a link to the killers of the four teenagers. "Come out, come out, wherever you are," she chanted again. She embraced it now and let the anger come with it. Anger and frustration seethed through her. "They're fighting," she whispered.

Lindsay knew that when criminals fight among themselves, it's the beginning of their end. It weakens the bond between them. While she couldn't tell what they were fighting about, she could feel the animosity between them. She took a pencil and a piece of paper from the drawer and began to make a list of the things that she was sure of about Tony and Mike.

1. Tony is afraid of the water.
2. Mike likes to drive.
3. Tony follows Mike's lead no matter what.
4. Tony is afraid of Mike.
5. Mike has a history of violence and aggressive behavior.
6. All the victims are the same age, within months of each other.
7. All the victims are Ripney High School students.
8. All the victims but Miles Handley are girls and have long hair that they usually wear in ponytails.

Lindsay put the tip of the pencil in her mouth as she thought.

Something else rolled around her in mind. She reached for the coffee cup and took a sip. Suddenly, she put the cup down and picked up her pencil again.

9. There has been an increased number of robberies in all areas other than the Ripney High School area.
10. Mike likes to camp or sleep outdoors.
11. Mike isn't afraid of being seen or caught.

"That's it, I've got it!" Lindsay exclaimed as she jumped up. She grabbed the phone and dialed the station for Will and Jerry.

"This is Jerry Leeme," he said, after they'd been connected.

"Jerry, this is Lindsay. I've made a list of things we know for sure about this case, and something is sticking in my mind, other than a jingle."

"Okay, what is it?" Jerry asked. He and Will had just been wondering where she was. Will thought maybe she'd had enough and had gone home during the long night.

"The robberies are a clue. We haven't looked at that yet, but the robberies are a map of their location. We need a map and some pins so we can figure out where they are," Lindsay said breathlessly into the phone.

Jerry liked the idea, even though he wasn't exactly sure what she was talking about. "Okay, we can do that. Are you coming here today?"

"Yes, I'll be there shortly. Can you round up a map and some pins?"

"We have the victim recovery map. That should do, don't you think?" Jerry asked as he scribbled a note to Will. Will turned the blackboard around and studied the map himself while Jerry finished talking to Lindsay.

"That'll do nicely. I'll see you in ten minutes," Lindsay said as she hung up.

Will and Jerry were studying the map when Lindsay arrived at the station. Handing her a Styrofoam cup of coffee made just the way she liked it, they pointed out the locations where each of the bodies had been found. They added two new pins for Miles and Catrina.

Lindsay grabbed her notes from her bag and pointed to the heading "Robberies." "See this, something about those robberies makes me think they're a clue. They're a map for us, only not one the killer intended to leave. Do we have reports on those so that we can put pins in for the addresses?" Lindsay asked. Her excitement was infectious. Will ran for the desk sergeant's desk to retrieve the list Ray Strider had been working on. Jerry called investigations and asked Sam Kent to come into the field room.

Within minutes all the information was assembled. Lindsay had kept the red pins for the locations of the victim's bodies, but she had placed white pins at the robbery locations and two blue pins for each of the places where Mike and Tony had been seen. She stood back and looked.

A pattern had emerged. Will, Jerry, and Sam were amazed at what they saw. The map's pattern now showed that all the robberies were on the outside perimeters of the case. All the victims but Miles Handley had been found in the same area. Miles's death had resulted from his getting in the way of Catrina's kidnapping, so they didn't include him as a kidnapping victim. Mike and Jerry hadn't intended to take Miles; he was an unfortunate byproduct of the event.

Will and Jerry looked at Sam. "What do you think?" they asked him.

"Before you say anything, I want to show you something else, gentlemen," Lindsay said as she looked from the dates on the pages in her hands to the pins on the board.

"What?" Jerry asked.

"Look at this. Robbery number one is located here, where a witness says the sketch of Mike looks like the man who held him up," Lindsay said as she touched a pin. "Then the next robbery, according to dates, took place here," she said as she touched a pin on the opposite side on the map. "Then number three takes place here, another sighting of our sketched character is noted, and four is directly across from it. Again a witness identifies the sketch as the person who held him up. There are four more sightings at various robberies, but all around the state's perimeters."

"Lindsay, you're a genius," Will said. "Okay, so what can we expect?"

Sam looked at him. "What I think is we have about a week before they make another attempt. Lindsay, how long have you been here now?"

"Not even a week yet. Why?" Lindsay asked.

"It's escalating. Their actions are escalating, and we don't have much to go on. The map is great, but what does it prove?" Sam asked as he looked at it again.

"What it proves is that these guys don't mind driving to do what they have to, but it also proves that true to sociopath form, Mike goes back and forth in patterns. If he robs a place on the west side, then later in the week he robs a place on the east. If he camps out on the north side, then the next time we can count on him camping on the south side. Don't you see?" Lindsay said as she pointed to the map.

Will, Jerry, and Sam nodded. They did see it. "Okay so where are they?" Will asked.

"No, that's not the question. The question is, where will they be next. That's what we have to figure out," Lindsay said.

"Okay, Lindsay, where will they be?" Jerry asked.

"I don't know." Lindsay felt somewhat defeated but not totally and neither did Will or Jerry. Sleep had revitalized them all and this new pattern analysis helped

Will looked at the map; he walked back and forth in front of it and rubbed his chin. Jerry sat down with a pencil in his hand and absent-mindedly started to doodle. Lindsay walked over to the field table and ran her hands over the objects lying there. Sam sat and watched them. He looked at Will, and suddenly he knew that Will knew. He'd seen the light go on in his mind, if that was possible.

"I've got it. They go back and forth from east to west and north to south. That's the pattern," he said excitedly.

"Okay," Jerry said.

"So, the cabin is northeast of here. Then the campsite was south of here. My guess would be they've gone north or northwest this time," Will said, as he grabbed Jerry's pencil and pointed out the pattern on the map.

Sam caught on and took the pencil from Will. "If you look at this, you can see that they've never stayed inside the circle of where a body was found. I bet they did go northwest and almost to the edge of the state. Will and Jerry followed the pencil on the map.

"That's all woods," Jerry said. "We'll never find them in there. We'd need a bloodhound to do that."

"We have one," Will said, as he turned to look at Lindsay.

But she hadn't been paying attention. She was walking around the table with her hand suspended over it, chanting, "Come out, come out, wherever you are."

"Lindsay," Will said, "Are you okay?"

She didn't hear him; she was lost in thought. Will turned and looked at Jerry and Sam.

"Lindsay," Will said, as he touched her shoulder.

"Oh gosh, I'm sorry. I was a million miles away." Lindsay looked spaced out.

"It's okay. What were you thinking?" Jerry asked her as he turned a chair around and sat in it.

"They're fighting. Something has happened to ruin the relationship between them. I'm not sure what it is, but they aren't getting along well."

They all knew that was a good sign. "Lindsay, we think they're in the upper northwest quadrant of the state. That's about 45 miles from here. We want to go up that way, but we need you to go with us. Are you willing to do that?" Will asked her.

"Sure I am. When do we leave?"

"In about an hour. I want to arrange some things with the Captain first. We need to gas up the car and get a map. We should be ready in less than an hour."

True to his word, in an hour the four of them were in the car traveling northwest. They talked easily as they drove, and eventually stopped for takeout food. The trip took about an hour. As they approached the area, they could all see that Jerry was right—it was heavily wooded. Will turned into the sheriff's station and shut the car off.

"We're out of our jurisdiction, so I think we should get some local help."

They spent more than an hour talking to the sheriff and filling him in on what had happened. "We've had some robberies too, but it's been pretty quiet for a while now. We got the faxed sketch of the two guys you're looking for, but so far we haven't seen them. We've been putting them on our high alert list every morning at roll call, but there haven't been any sightings. I can give you two officers who know the forest preserves up that way pretty well, but that's all I can afford," the sheriff said.

"Thanks, Bill, I appreciate it," Will said.

"No problem, but there is just one thing. That's all forest preserves up that way. You have to have a permit to camp up there."

"Is the camping community gated?" Jerry asked.

"No, but we have it patrolled pretty well. There's a fine if you get caught camping without a permit," Bill said.

"Bill, they've killed four kids. I don't think they're worried about a fine," Jerry said.

"No, I guess not. But it would shine some light on 'em, wouldn't it?"

"That it would," Will said as they walked out the door.

The other officers were waiting for them when they got outside. "We'll be on Channel 16 if you need us," they said as one of them handed a radio to Jerry.

Jerry nodded as Sam planned a path for each car to cover. Lindsay just stood back and watched. She couldn't feel them here. There was no tingle of recognition in her at all. But she let it happen. "I've been wrong before," she muttered under her breath.

The two police cars went their separate ways. Several hours later it was clear they'd made a mistake. As the sun started going down, Will looked at Jerry, disgusted. "It was a long shot. I'm sorry we wasted the day. Anybody got any other ideas?"

Lindsay and Jerry sat there and thought. "Shit no," Jerry said.

"Hey, Jerry, pull into that area, will ya? I have to take a leak," Sam said. They all got out and walked around, stretching their legs, backs, and shoulders. The air was tense even outside the car and frustration showed on every face.

As Sam came out of the outhouse, he thought about the day. He could see the map in his own mind and tried to recall exactly where each of the pushpins was located. He hadn't studied it as well as he should have. As they all got back into the car, Sam said, "Will, where did you say the last location for Mike and Tony was?"

Will pulled the map from the glove box and studied it.

"Right here," Will said as he put the tip of his pencil down. Jerry looked at it.

"Will, that's southwest from the cabin."

"What? No it's not," Will argued.

"Yes it is. Technically, it's southwest. We need to go northeast if we're going to find them and if this plan of ours is right."

Will turned the map around. He took out his flashlight and studied the roads. "Oh God, you're right. It's south, southwest. Why did that map in the station show it being south?"

"I don't know. Different maps are made by different companies, but they're usually pretty accurate. The only thing I can think of is that map's older than this one. The new highway wasn't on that map," Jerry said.

"Damn it," Will said as he flicked off the light.

"I'm sorry, everyone. Not being from here puts me at the same disadvantage as you, Lindsay," Will said.

Lindsay smiled at him. "I know what you mean. It's frustrating. But I haven't been able to feel them all day. I don't think this is going to work, even though I had such high hopes for it early this morning."

"I still think it will work. Maps can be deceiving. We need to keep trying," Jerry said. He smiled at his partner. "It's okay, man, it was a shot. We would have had to check this out anyway, so now it's done."

They drove home in the dark after notifying the other officers that they were leaving and dropping the radio off at the station. The only light on this lonely highway came from the full moon. "It's beautiful," Lindsay said.

"Yeah, it really is," Jerry agreed. "It's hard to believe that somewhere out there two killers are enjoying the same moon, isn't it?"

"Yes, it is. But you know we'll catch them, don't you?" Lindsay asked.

"You think?" Jerry asked, and from the tone of his voice Lindsay could tell he wasn't sure.

"We will. I can feel it coming. It feels bad, but we'll catch them."

"I hope you're right."

There was silence until the radio crackled.

"Go ahead," Will said, as he grabbed the mike. The adrenaline was pumping through his veins. Every time the radio crackled that day, all four of them had jumped. Most of the time it had only been radio traffic for others, but this time Will heard his name. He could almost feel bad news coming.

"Sir, Georgia Amando has been trying to reach you all day. I asked her if it was important, and she said yes."

"Can you put her through to us," Will asked.

"No sir, she just asked that I keep trying to reach you. She wants you and detective Leeme to stop by as soon as you can."

Will looked at Jerry, who nodded. "I'm not the one with a wife. I don't have to be home anytime soon."

"Call her back. Tell her we're on our way."

The trip to the hospital took another ten minutes. As they walked into the room all of them were surprised to see Lilly Williams, Cammy Burke, and Jeremy Wright sitting with Joey and Georgia. As always, Lucinda was at her place by Georgia's head.

"We're the survivors," Cammy said as they entered. Lindsay was introduced to everyone she didn't know.

"What were you saying, Cammy?" Lindsay asked.

"I said we're the survivors. We're the ones left to put the pieces back together for our friends who have died. Jeremy and I witnessed Mandy's abduction. She was my best friend. We'd spent that morning together. I watched my best friend put her hair up in a ponytail and then die. It was horrible." Jeremy took her hand.

"I chased the van that took her till my heart gave out. I saw that man raping her. My name was the last thing she said to me. I couldn't save her," Jeremy said, beginning to cry softly. Cammy wrapped her arm around his waist.

"Wanda would still be here if not for her friendship with me," Lilly said. "I talked her into going to the carnival. She didn't want to because her parents had told her she had to wait till the weekend and then she could only go if her room was clean. It would never have happened except for me."

It was Joey's turn. He held Georgia's hand as he spoke. "I'm the lucky one. I got Georgia back, but the whole thing never would have happened if I had made her listen to me. I knew Mandy's killer was still out there, but instead of getting up and going to get her, I let her drive herself home. They wouldn't have gotten her if I had been there," Joey whispered. Will, Jerry, Sam, and Lindsay just let them talk.

When it was clear they were finished, Will and Jerry started talking at the same time. Will smiled and let Jerry continue.

"I agree with you all that this has been a terrible experience, but you aren't seeing it clearly. Jeremy, you and Cammy did all you were physically capable of doing. You were surprised and then out-motored. No one could have caught that van on foot; even if you had, there were two of them to your one. Lilly, Wanda had her own mind. She had all the same information you all had, and she made the choice to go out on her own. And Joey, you didn't know they would target Georgia. She'd been offered an escort to her car and turned it down. Who was to know this wasn't a random thing? At the time Georgia was taken, even we had no idea. But you're all overlooking one thing: Miles Handley is dead because he tried to interfere. Jeremy, they could have and would have killed you, and Cammy too, for that matter. Lilly, what if you had gone with Wanda again that night—you wouldn't have stopped them, but you would have died too. That's what you're all not seeing. These aren't normal people we're looking for. They're vicious criminals and for some reason they've targeted our community," Jerry said. He watched the faces of the young adults before him. He knew they would never be the same as they had been before this happened.

"You can't blame yourselves because you're still alive," Lindsay said. "But you can celebrate their lives. Be all that you can be for them as well as for yourselves. Don't let their lives or their deaths be in vain."

"Georgia, you called the station and said you wanted to talk to us," Will said

"Yes sir, I'm remembering more and more. The therapist has been helping me work through some of the things that I've remembered. Mike and Tony both have tattoos on their arms. They have the same thing, like a cross with an X over it. Mike's mom is gone; she has been since he was a little kid. Tony is his only friend," Georgia said. Cammy and Joey held her hands as she talked.

"But the most important thing I've remembered is that Mike is obsessive-compulsive and he is driven to use patterns. Tony teases him about it."

"We've figured that out, Georgia, but thank you for confirming it," Will said.

"It's been a long day and we're tired. I hope you'll understand if we leave," Jerry said as he and Will stood up. Lindsay and Sam did the same.

They said their goodbyes, and Georgia promised to call if she remembered anything else. What she had remembered in such a short time was really incredible. Will and Jerry had the feeling she was healing faster now with the therapist's help.

They dropped Lindsay off at her hotel with a promise to pick her up in the morning, to go northeast this time. As she walked inside, Lindsay got the feeling that someone was watching her. She looked behind her and saw only the door, but the creepy feeling continued. She stepped off the elevator and turned to walk down the hallway when the images started. "Oh God, no, not again."

Turning around quickly, she started to go back inside the elevator and down into the lobby, hoping to catch Will and Jerry, but she thought better of it. Racing to her room, she fumbled with her key. As the door opened she saw the image clearly. A young girl was being pulled out of her car as someone grabbed her feet. She was being forced into another car. Her hair was long and put up in a ponytail.

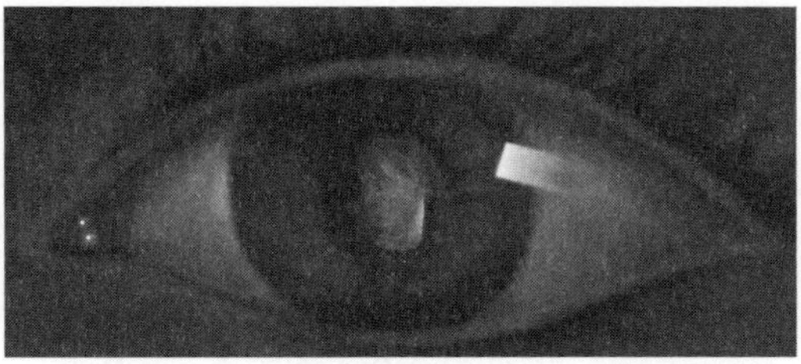

CHAPTER 69

Mike and Tony sat talking, Mike on the ground and Tony in the tower. "I ain't coming down till you say you're sorry about Wanda," Tony said. He sounded like a bratty kid.

"Okay, I'm sorry about Wanda," Mike said. He didn't sound much older. But it worked, and he watched Tony climb slowly out of the thick foliage.

"Damn, Tony, where'd you come from?"

"Up there. I made a tower in the trees. It's hidden real good, huh, Mike?"

"Shit, yeah, it's hidden real good. I would've never found you up there. How'd you do that?"

"Well, I spend a lot of time here by myself. I found some old wooden planks about a mile from here and used some rope to haul 'em up there. The hardest part is climbing over the branch that hangs over the water. You wanna come up and see it, Mike?"

Mike thought about it. This could be a great hiding place, because he'd been honest when he told Tony he couldn't see him from the ground.

"Yeah, Tony, I wanna see."

He followed Tony back up the tree. Mike hadn't seen the handholds and foot braces Tony used. If he had, he would have followed him up the tree when he realized that was where Tony had gone earlier that day.

"Watch that branch," Tony said as he deftly climbed over it. Mike followed him, and as Tony's hand parted the brush, Mike saw the tower.

He looked down and thought it was a damn fine thing he couldn't see the ground.

"How high up are we, Tony?" he asked.

"I don't know. You can't see the ground from up here. But Mike, no one can see us, either. And look at this, look at all the stuff I have up here."

Mike couldn't believe it. "You dragged all this stuff up here by yourself?"

"Yeah, it wasn't that hard."

"Hey, that's our food and my blanket. And that's my shirt," Mike said as he reached for his things.

"I was thinking you'd wanna come up here sooner or later, Mike," Tony said as he sat down in the corner.

The tower wasn't large, only about three-and-a-half feet wide and five feet long. But it had a canopy of leaves woven together for a roof and rope sides with branches tangled in them. Mike shook the branches.

"It's really stout, Tony. Man, you did a great job. We could hide up here if Johnny Law comes by looking for us, providing we could get up here quick enough."

Tony smiled and pulled the branch closest to him aside. He pointed with his free hand, and Mike leaned forward to look. "We can see the dirt road from here, Mike. No one could ever sneak up on us."

Mike saw it too. He also knew there was no other way out but that road. "You've made us a safe haven, Tony. Damn fine thing you did here. Come on, let's get cleaned up and go out and celebrate. We can go find us some chicks, too, if you want."

Tony looked down and an expression of pain crossed his face. "Mike, are you really sorry about Wanda?"

"Sure I am. I said it, didn't I? She just pissed me off real bad when she wouldn't give us what she promised to. I'm sorry I hurt her, Tony. I liked her too." Mike meant it. Tony could see that, but he didn't want to go through it again.

"I wanna go have some fun and celebrate, Mike. That sounds like fun. Can we get something to drink too?"

"You betcha we can. Come on, I'll race ya down," Mike said as he scrambled over the branches. Tony was hot on his heels.

As they bathed in the shallow river inlet, Mike realized how rapidly the water was moving. He looked over at Tony and saw the rope that he kept tied around his waist whenever he was in the water. He saw Tony's grip on the line. "You okay?" Mike asked. Tony looked at him and nodded as he held his fist and the rope in the air. The river must be rising, he thought.

"Hey Tony, come on, we better get out." They climbed out and dried off. Then, laughing and joking, they dressed in the clean clothes Tony had washed in that same place earlier and left on the rocks to dry. As they stuffed their shirts into their jeans, Tony looked over at Mike.

"Hey Mike, what'd you do with that other chick?"

"Oh, Tony, man, I left her sitting on the front porch swing. You should have been there, it was so cool. I bet those old folks were surprised at their early-morning visitor." Mike burst into peals of laughter. Tony laughed too and slapped Mike's upturned palm.

"Tony, why didn't you care about that chick or the others, but you care about Wanda?" Mike asked.

"I didn't know the others."

They drove into the neighboring town and cruised the drag strip. They were in a new car, one that Mike had stolen from a house some sixty miles away. The newspapers had been piled up on the lawn, so he felt pretty safe sneaking into the garage and taking his time hotwiring the car. "Thanks for the car, vacationers," he'd said as he drove off that night. No one would know about the car until they got home, and who knew when that would be?

Tony ran into the liquor store and bought each of them a bottle. Mike drank vodka straight when he didn't have any pot. Tony had his bottle of tequila tucked under his arm as he climbed in. "Ready to party?" he asked. Mike nodded and burned the tires as he left the parking area.

The clerk inside the store thought Tony looked familiar. Something about him made her wrack her brain trying to place him, but then he'd been so sweet to her, smiling and joking around, that she put it out of her mind. She opened the newspaper to her favorite section and started reading again. Pictures of all the models in the latest fashions graced the pages. As she turned from one article to another, the continued story from page one kept interrupting the flow. The caption read, "Mall Murders cont'd." But she didn't want to read any more about it. She'd seen enough on television and heard it on the radio every day for more than a week. Those guys were more than sixty miles away from her.

If only she'd turned to the front page when she'd seen Tony, since the sketch of his face was plastered on the front page.

Mike and Tony drove down the winding country highway, whooping and hollering out the window. "Woohoo!" yelled Mike, as he beat on the side of the car, his hair blowing in the wind.

"Yahoo!" yelled Tony. He looked over at Mike. "Where we gonna find some chicks, Mike?"

Mike thought about it for a moment, and then said, "What about that mall? We've always had good luck at the mall." Tony nodded.

They drove along, singing the songs on the radio they knew until Tony said something about moving south soon. Mike looked at him. "You really wanna do that?"

"Sure, I was thinking about Texas or maybe Louisiana, down on the bayou." Mike starting singing, "Born on the Bayou," as loud as he could. Tony joined in as the miles ticked away.

It didn't take them long to get to the mall. It sat right on the highway, with an access road to the right, if you were facing the great doors in the front. Mike pulled into the mall parking area and drove around slowly. They could see the shoppers walking quickly to their cars with their packages slung over their arms. All of them had their keys ready, and they looked nervous, especially when they saw Mike and Tony.

"Act like the law, Tony," Mike said.

"How do I do that?" Tony asked. He had a buzz. The tequila had taken its toll on him, and his speech was slurring already.

"Look out the window right in their faces and nod your head. Don't smile," Mike said.

Tony did it, thinking of it more as a game than anything threatening.

"There ain't any good-looking chicks here, Mike," Tony said after a few minutes.

"Let's make one more loop around the mall," Mike said. He really wanted to party and was hoping he wouldn't have to go somewhere else to find some babes. He was getting anxious as he thought about the fun to be had. He reached over and lightly punched Tony in the shoulder. "Keep your eyes open, man."

"Yeah, Mike, I'm watching. I want a girl with long brown hair, just like Wanda's," Tony said excitedly.

"Okay, buddy, we'll get you one if we can find one. I don't care what color hair she has, just so it's long like a horse's tail so I can hang on to it and ride like Roy Rogers."

Tony laughed at Mike's joke. "Ride 'em, cowboy," he hollered.

They drove on through the darkness, circling the mall like vultures looking for prey. The parking area covered almost two miles, and if you took your time and traveled up and down the aisles, a complete circuit could take a while. The light from the street lamps in the parking area shone down on nearby cars. The night was much like the night Georgia had been taken. But there was one big difference.

CHAPTER 70

"Get me Will Halpin or Jerry Leeme. Hurry!" Lindsay said into the receiver.

The dispatcher patched her through to Will, who was on his way home. Jerry tied into the same channel on the radio.

"Lindsay, this is Will. What's the matter?"

"Will, oh God, come back and get me. Where are you?"

"Lindsay, calm down and tell me what's wrong."

"Lindsay, this is Jerry. I'm closer than Will. Are you okay? Are you in danger?"

"No, but they're gonna take someone. I can feel them moving. They're on the move!" Lindsay shouted.

Will spun his car around, and reached under his seat to grab his mars light. Lights and sirens split the air as Jerry turned in the direction of the hotel. Jerry got there first, and as he was running into the hotel, he could hear Will's siren.

Jerry had called Sam Kent while he'd been in route, and Sam was on his way too. Will screeched to a halt and jumped from his car, as Jerry disappeared into the hotel. Lindsay was running down the stairs while they were in the lobby waiting for the elevator. Sam came running through the door as Lindsay reached the lobby.

"My car's in front. I hope you're right and I hope we can find them in time." Lindsay was running through the doors as she said, "They're close!"

Will, Lindsay, Jerry, and Sam jumped into Will's car and pulled out onto the main road.

"Lindsay, tell me where to go," Will said.

"The mall, go to the mall, and hurry! I saw it when I got on the elevator. That's when it started. It was all in color this time. As I got off on my floor, I could see the mall entrance and a young girl being pulled into the car. I think she's in her own car, but I'm not sure. The one thing I can tell you is that she is around a bunch of cars and she has long dark brown hair in a ponytail."

Across town, Mike and Tony had exhausted any possibilities the mall might have offered. People were being too careful now. Tony was making too much noise, and Mike was getting too excited.

"Hey, Mike, I'm hungry. Let's go over there and get us something to eat at the drive-in," Tony said, pointing to the Frost Top across the road. It was a busy road that intersected with the highway just half a block down. All the stores that lined it were still open, and people were coming and going even though it was getting near closing time.

Mike looked at it. When he saw the girls on roller skates carrying the trays of food to the cars, a plan formed in his mind. As they drove in that direction, Mike filled Tony in on his idea.

"When she comes up to the window to take our order, I'll drop my money. When I open the door to get it and she bends down to help me, grab her," Mike said. Tony gave him a funny look.

"What about getting something to eat? Can we get our food first? That way while you're busy with the chick, I can eat. I'm hungry," Tony complained.

Mike laughed at him. "Sure we can. One appetite has to be satisfied before the other, I guess," Mike said.

Mike headed toward the road. As he waited his turn to cross, he watched the girls. Suddenly he saw her. A very pretty, tall girl with long, dark brown hair pulled back into a ponytail. She had a pretty blue ribbon tied around it and her skates were polished to a nice shine. Fuzzy blue balls tied to her skate laces jingled as she moved. Mike smiled as he crossed the road and pulled into a parking spot in her station. Tony was busy reading the menu as Mike watched the girl.

She skated to the car next to them and took their order. As she left them, she smiled. It was an electric smile, and Mike couldn't wait to feel it shine on him. She turned in the order, holding up one finger to signal to Mike that she would be there momentarily. Mike smiled at her.

"I want a hamburger, fries, and a coke," Tony said. "But I don't want no onions on it. Make sure you tell her that I don't want no onions, Mike."

Mike nodded as the girl skated his way. He ordered their food and smiled flirtatiously at her, winking as she left to place their order. Mike watched her go.

"Ain't she got a cute butt?" Mike asked Tony. Tony looked at her. His eyes lit up as he saw her dark brown ponytail swinging back and forth in the lower part of her back.

Tony said, "Yeah, she's got a great butt. Are you gonna ask her out?"

Mike looked at him. "Tony, we're gonna do what we said we were gonna do. Remember?"

"Yeah, Mike, that's right, I forgot," Tony said. He smiled at the girl as she skated her way back to their car. She smiled at Tony as she worked her way over to Mike, and Mike was in love. "She's beautiful," Mike said.

It was over in the blink of an eye. Becky Torman had handed the food to Mike, and he had handed it to Tony. As he went to pay her, he dropped the money. Laughing, he opened the door and bent over, trying to pick it up from the road. As Becky bent down to help him, Mike grabbed the back of her shirt while Tony reached across him and grabbed her ponytail. Both of them pulled her in. Now she was three-quarters of the way in the car with her feet hanging out and her hair firmly caught in Tony's fist. She was also screaming her lungs out. Mike backed the car up and sped down one of the aisles of the drive-in with Becky's feet hanging outside the car door. Tony struggled to pull her in so Mike could close the door.

Most of the people there weren't sure what had happened. They stared and pointed, but the woman in the car next to Mike and Tony's had seen the entire thing and started screaming. She could see Mike weaving in and out of the cars in the drive-in, with Becky's feet hanging out of his door. Tony was munching on a hamburger and sipping a coke as he tried to hold her head down. But every few minutes Becky's head could be seen as she screamed.

A young man who worked at the drive-in saw what the woman was screaming about and took off after them. Mike saw him running after them in the rearview mirror and tried to go faster. Dave Clorey tried to catch them, but he knew he couldn't. He picked up the biggest rock he could find and hit the car with it. It didn't make much of an impact, but it did break the taillight on the passenger's side as Dave scribbled down the license number on his order pad.

Becky's screaming could still be heard as Mike drove onto the main road toward the highway. He made the turn at the corner and sped off, taking Becky Torman with him.

The reality was that Becky's kidnapping had taken only a matter of minutes. Will's car had sped across town to the mall. As they turned off the highway and onto the mall road, Mike and Tony were speeding down the feeder road that was taking Becky out of town.

The radio crackled, and Will and Jerry heard the dispatcher send all units to the Frost Top. "See the man about an abduction," the dispatcher said.

Will looked at Jerry as he turned the car. Jerry hit the sirens again, and Sam studied the road. As Will drove across the road, a young man ran toward his car.

"They took her. Two guys in a car grabbed Becky Torman and drove off with her. I tried to chase them, but I couldn't catch them. I did manage to break the taillight on the passenger's side, and I got the license number," Dave Clorey said excitedly. He ripped the page off his order pad and handed it to Will. "They turned right at the highway."

"Go, go!" Lindsay screamed. "There's still time, go, please."

Will spun the car around and drove quickly to the highway. As he climbed onto it Jerry grabbed the mike. "All units in the vicinity of Mall Road and Highway 73, be on the lookout for a car with a missing taillight and license plate number BL7-148. Possible abduction of Becky Torman from the Frost Top Drive In."

They were doing eighty miles an hour, scanning the road in front of them for a car with a missing taillight and the right plate number. Lindsay reached out with her ability, trying to find some trace of them. She'd never been able to do it before, but she had to try now.

"Look!" Sam yelled as he saw the car in the distance. The darkness seemed to wrap itself around the missing taillight.

Mike and Tony had the advantage of a large lead and would have used it if they'd known they were being followed. But the only thing they were aware of was Becky's continued struggling and screaming. Tony was doing all he could to hold her head down while he ate his food. Mike struggled with the steering wheel, but something stronger drove him. He ran his hand up Becky's bare leg, and she kicked him in the chest with her skates. But they were heavy and hard to maneuver, so Mike had no trouble shoving them away. Tony laughed, as the car jerked suddenly to the left. But he screamed in pain as her teeth sank into his thigh.

Becky was fortunate that Mike was driving, or the punch to her back that took her breath away would have been to her jaw. She cried out in pain and tried to suck in deep gasps of air. Tony twisted her hair in his hand and turned her head forcibly toward the glove box. With her body bent toward them and her head twisted away, Becky found herself not only in severe pain but also helpless. Mike laughed as she struggled to find some relief from her position.

"Are you gonna help me here or just sit there and eat that damn hamburger?" Mike asked as he looked disgustedly at Tony.

Tony wiped his mouth with his sleeve as he said, "I got her. Don't get pissy."

"Yeah, but I don't," Mike said as he raised his eyebrows and motioned with his chin to the back seat.

"Oh, sorry. Can't you wait till we get to the campsite?" Tony asked. He wanted to finish his fries before he had to drive.

"I can, but I don't want to," Mike said again and raised his eyebrows for emphasis.

"Please, please, let me go. I won't tell anyone if you let me go," Becky cried.

"You ain't gonna tell anyone, anyway, no matter what," Mike laughed.

Becky lashed out at Tony with her nails. She raked her hand along his shin, causing him to yell in pain again.

Mike punched her again, this time higher in the back than last time, taking her breath away. Tony rubbed his shin as he punched the side of her face. Becky lay there, stunned and scared. She cried quietly, trying to lift her head to wipe her eyes and catch her breath. She thought of Amanda Wiggins, Georgia Amando, Wanda Corley, Miles Handley, and Catrina Vincent. "Oh God, please help me," she cried softly.

Mike rubbed her leg again. Letting his hands travel freely over her backside as he drove down the highway. "Come on, Tony, you drive while I take our little friend here on the ride of her life," Mike whined.

At that, Becky struggled even more. She screamed and fought until Tony punched her in the back of the head. Then for a short time she neither did nor said anything. In fact, no sound came from her at all.

"Well, hurry, then. Cause she ain't playing right. She won't be still and I'm tired of fighting her already. Dump her on the side of the road, 'cause I ain't going through this shit so you can get laid first," Tony yelled.

"Is that what this is all about, me getting laid first? What, you wanna go first? Is that it? Well, I'll pull over buddy, and you can help me get her in the back seat, and you can go first," Mike said. Tony looked at him.

"Okay, wait till I finish my burger, and we'll do that," Tony said sarcastically.

The people in the car behind them watched the steadily disappearing taillight in the distance.

"Will, drive faster. Go faster, please, they're getting away," Lindsay cried. Jerry never said a word, and neither did Sam. They knew what Will was doing.

Jerry looked at her as he squeezed her hand, "Lindsay, we're letting them stay ahead of us on purpose. We don't want a hostage situation. We want them to get where they're going with us behind them, and we don't want them to notice that we're back here. That way we can sneak up on them. It's the best way, really."

"If they pull over, you catch up to them! You have to, or they're going to rape that girl. She's terrified, and she's hurt. And it's our job to save her," Lindsay said emphatically.

"We're gonna save her, Lindsay. It's not gonna happen this time," Will said. He never took his eyes off the car with the single taillight.

Darkness closed in around them as they sped down Highway 73, each sunk inside his or her own feelings. Lindsay was suffering with the things she knew; the mother in her wanted to save the child, the clairvoyant in her saw the suffering of the poor girl, who had no idea how close help really was. Will felt the pressure from those with him in the car—his driving abilities were on the line. Jerry couldn't bring himself to think he might have to stand in the foyer of another family's home and tell them their child was dead. Sam wanted to wrap his hands around Tony's and Mike's throats and squeeze.

"Where the hell are they going?" Will asked suddenly.

Mike slowed down as he looked for the turnoff road. It was a narrow dirt road full of ruts and holes. The car behind him slowed down as well, but only because they saw the brake lights on the driver's side. They watched the car turn right.

"Watch for that road," Will yelled. "Don't miss it, it's our only chance; we're gonna have to turn off the lights once we turn."

Lindsay grabbed the back of Will's seat. "I can feel them. The road out here is vacant enough for me to feel them."

Mike bumped over the dirt road. He went several miles, blowing up dust and dirt behind him. His mind was on Becky and her incredible hair. Tony was stuffing french fries in his mouth as they bumped over the road. Becky moaned softly and Tony smoothed her hair back.

Sam pointed over Will's shoulder, "There, see 'em?"

"I see them. Okay, people, let's be real quiet out here. Sound travels for miles," Will said.

Jerry and Sam watched the light in front of them. As it weaved and bobbed around the potholes in the road, it created a dust storm that made following it in the dark very hard, but it also hid their pursuers from Mike and Tony.

"I can't see them," Lindsay said.

"They're right there, don't anybody panic," Will hissed.

Suddenly the single taillight in front of them came to a halt. Will eased the car to a stop. But it was too late, Mike had seen them.

"Tony, jump out and run," Mike yelled.

"What's the matter?" Tony said, as he licked his fingers.

"Run, Tony, run to the tower. Leave the bitch and run!" Mike yelled as he jumped from the car. "Johnny Law's behind us. Run!" Mike jumped from the car and ran through the woods into the campsite clearing. He had pushed Becky's legs off his lap, so she was half on the floor and half in Tony's lap. In shock, Tony watched him go. He looked behind him and saw the police car, too. He opened his door and shoved Becky's head from his lap. As he jumped out of the car and took off running, he yelled for Mike.

"Over here," Mike hissed. Tony ran to him.

"The tower!" Tony whispered.

"I don't know the way," Mike said.

"I do, this way," Tony said.

Tony led the way to the tower. As he climbed the huge oak tree, Mike followed. They could hear the cops below them talking in hushed tones as they worked their way across the branches and into the box. Tony and Mike sat still and quiet and waited.

The complete darkness of the country road and the flying dirt had hidden the car containing the detectives, but not the glow of light from the brakes. It glowed bright red behind them and lit up the night.

"They're running!" Will shouted, as he opened his door and jumped out. He took off through the woods with Jerry and Sam right behind him, their guns drawn.

Lindsay ran to the car in front of them. She bent down to cradle Becky Torman's head in her hands. "Becky, come on, sweetie. We have to get up now. Come on," she said as she patted the girl's face. When she'd first seen the girl lying there at that odd angle, she'd feared the worst. But when she'd felt her carotid artery, she found the pulse strong and rapid.

"Come on, Becky, we have to get out of here," Lindsay said one more time as the girl started coming around. Lindsay could hear the men in the background and knew they hadn't caught Mike and Tony yet. "We have to get in the car, just in case they come back. Come on, Becky, you have to help me here," Lindsay said, as she pulled the young girl to her feet.

They staggered along, stumbling a few times because of Becky's skates, as they made their way to the car. Lindsay helped a sobbing Becky into the back seat, then got in herself and slammed the locks in place. There was a knot on Becky's head, and her face was starting to turn black and blue. The cut on her knee bled onto Lindsay's pants as she wrapped her arms around Becky and let her sob out her story.

Will, Sam, and Jerry found the lanterns Mike and Tony had left in the campsite and lit them. They stood with their backs to each other, their guns drawn. They were several feet apart, surveying the area, taking in the now familiar carnage these two men could create. Garbage littered the ground and the makeshift table. Clothing was strewn all over the place, and a tent sat near the water's edge. Will approached it slowly, expecting Mike or Tony to jump out at them or take off running.

But Mike and Tony were hidden in Tony's tree tower. They sat huddled together, shaking as they heard the voices below.

"Jerry, get on the radio, if it works up here, and get some backup for us. Sam, shine that light in the woods, see if you can force them to cast a shadow," Will said.

Turning around, he suddenly realized that Lindsay was nowhere to be seen. Jerry saw him looking and realized the same thing at almost the same time. They ran back to the car. Inside, huddled close together with the doors locked, were Lindsay and Becky Torman. They could see that Becky was crying and that Lindsay had her. Jerry tapped on the window, and Lindsay leaned forward to unlock the door. But Becky started screaming, "No! No don't open the door. They're gonna get me, don't open the door."

Lindsay held her and rocked back and forth. "Those men are with me, Becky. They're policemen, and they need to get in the car so they can take us out of here. I'm going to open the door now, okay?" Lindsay said as she slowly lifted the lock.

Jerry pulled the door gently open. "Hi, Miss Torman, I'm Jerry Leeme. I'm a detective and I just need to use the radio so I can get an ambulance for you and some help for us. Okay?"

Becky nodded but clung to Lindsay. "The radio can't reach a tower back here, Will. We're gonna have to drive out," Jerry said.

"We can't leave the site. We know they're here somewhere. I want to catch them," Will said.

"I want to catch them too, but we need backup and this girl needs an ambulance," Jerry argued.

"Okay, Sam, you take Lindsay and Becky back to the main road. Radio for help, and then wait till someone comes," Will said. Sam nodded as he got in the car. Will and Jerry watched the taillights as the car moved down the dirt road.

Will and Jerry returned to the campsite, but something was different. Tony and Mike had been there and taken a few things. Blankets were missing, along with the cook stove and some utensils, and the green duffle bag was gone from inside the tent.

"They've been here," Will shouted as he ran from place to place. Jerry looked at him and nodded. "That means they're close. Be careful."

But they weren't close. While Will, Sam, and Jerry had been at the car, Mike and Tony had climbed down. They took off, after making a quick grab from the tree house and the tent. Running through the woods, Mike motioned for Tony to be quiet as he heard Will in the distance.

"We have to get out of here before this place is full of cops," Mike said.

Tony nodded and silently laid his hand on Mike's arm. "This way," he whispered. He led Mike through the woods, down one trail after another. Tony knew the woods better than Mike because he'd spent so much time there alone. For an hour, they continued running. Finally, Mike stopped, breathing hard, and leaned against a tree.

"It's just a little further, Mike. Come on," Tony said as he grabbed the duffle bag Mike had been carrying and tossed it over his shoulder.

"Where are we going? We're gonna get caught if we don't hide, Tony," Mike said. He sounded weak and whiny. Tony looked at him, confused.

"I know a place where we can hide. We can see them, but they can't see us. It ain't far, now come on." Tony started walking. Mike followed.

In two hours' time, floodlights had been installed and the sound of generators could be heard. Policemen were everywhere, climbing in and out of hollows in the woods and shining their lights up into the trees. Becky Torman had been taken, with Lindsay, to the hospital where her parents waited. Suddenly a shout went up from somewhere in the woods. Will and Jerry ran in that direction. They could hear someone shouting for them, but they couldn't see anyone.

"Where are you?" Will shouted.

"Up here," the voice said.

Jerry saw a white cloth object lying on the ground at the base of the tree. Then he saw something fall out of the tree. It was another white object that looked like a sock with something stuffed in the toe for weight. Walking slowly to the tree, Will and Jerry looked up. "Are you up in that tree?" Will shouted.

"Yep, come on up. All the evidence in the world is up here. Clothes, food, trash, and some blankets," the voice said. Will and Jerry looked around the base of the tree. They tried several hand- and footholds and finally made their way up. As they climbed inside the thick foliage, they realized where the officer had been sitting.

"How did you find this?" they both asked incredulously.

"I saw that sock on the ground at the base of the tree. I just figured it was an idea, so I climbed up. They must have been here while you were in the campsite. Once you left to get help, they climbed down, grabbed what they could, and hauled ass." The young officer sat there with a smug look on his face.

"Smartass," Jerry whispered under his breath. The officer smiled.

"They're here, they can't have gotten far. We have to find them this time. I can't go through this again," Will said as he climbed down from the tree. "We're not going home without them, gentlemen, so I suggest you find them," Jerry shouted to the officers walking around, as he jumped to the ground from the lowest branch.

"Detective Leeme, the forensic guys are here," Officer Baker yelled. "Hey guys, welcome to the party," Jerry said, as he shook hands with Dave Matthews.

Dave smiled, "Yeah, it's been awhile, what—a week, maybe?" Dave said. "Catch 'em yet?" he added.

"No, but we're close," Will said as he came up behind them. "Jerry, the dogs are here."

They walked off to meet the man with the dogs. Dave knew how they felt, because he felt the same way. Whipped, tired, and disgusted, just like everyone else.

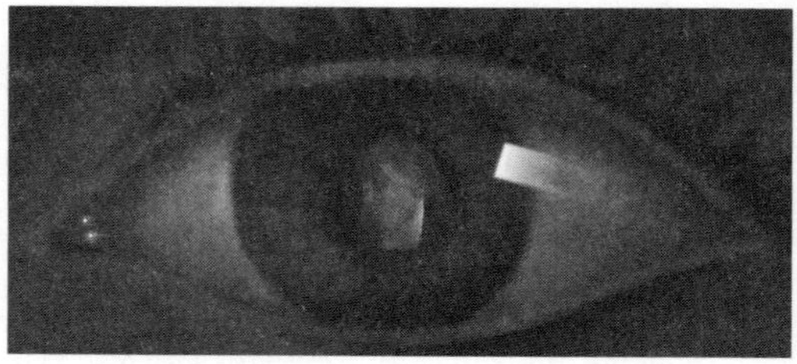

CHAPTER 71

Lindsay sat in the emergency treatment room with Becky. The doctors were putting stitches in her knee and ice on her head. Lindsay held her hand until she heard the commotion outside the room.

"Becky, Becky!" someone was screaming. The door to her room flew open as her parents rushed in. "Oh my God, Becky, what happened?"

"They had me, Mom, Dad. They had me, and they were going to rape me," Becky cried into her stepfather's arms. Katherine and Walter Bell stood in the treatment room and held on to their daughter. Walter Bell had married Becky's mother when he returned from Vietnam. Becky's father hadn't made it back. The two men had enlisted together and served until both of them were injured by enemy fire. Charles Torman hadn't come home, but he made Walter promise to take care of his wife and daughter. "Treat them like they're yours," he'd said. As Becky told them all that had happened, Walter mouthed over Becky's head, "Thank you." Lindsay nodded and left them alone. She squeezed Becky's hand as she left.

She didn't know what to do, or where to go. She wanted to find Will and Jerry, but she didn't know whether or not they'd come back. As she wandered around the hospital, she thought of the day and all that had happened. She was suddenly very tired. It was well after one o'clock in the morning. Lindsay considered going back to the hotel, but thought better of it. What if Will and Jerry showed up at the hospital? She wanted to be there if they did.

Walking back into the emergency room, Lindsay looked for a phone. As she dialed the police station, she was bombarded with images of two men running. Sinking into a chair by the phone, she embraced the emotions and images she was feeling and seeing.

"Hello, hello, is anyone there?" Lindsay heard.

"Oh yes, I'm here. I'm looking for Detectives Will Halpin and Jerry Leeme. Can you reach them for me?"

"Can I say who's calling?"

"Yes, this is Lindsay Freeman. I'm at the hospital emergency room. They can reach me here."

Lindsay hung up and walked into the police waiting room. She felt familiar and comfortable with it, almost like being at home. As she sank into the chair, Lindsay tried to conjure up the feelings of Mike and Tony. Her association with Becky must have sharpened her senses where they were concerned. The image of an overpass came to her. She wasn't sure at first what it was, since she was getting more sound than image; as the picture in her mind cleared, she could see the large concrete columns and the area surrounding them.

"Cardboard and cloth," Lindsay said out loud. "Climb, Mike," she whispered. "Keep your head low." Lindsay thought about the things she was hearing. She thought about Will and Jerry being out there in the woods looking for Mike and Tony, and then she knew. They weren't in the woods anymore. They had found a new home on the highway, under an overpass. The numbers on the highway sign glowed in her mind. Lindsay stood up and raced to a phone.

Mike and Tony climbed up under the overpass and settled in for the night.

"We can't stay here forever, but for tonight this should work," Mike said. He had gotten control of his emotions and was feeling much better.

Tony, however, had lost his. He was scared and crying because as he climbed all he could see was water rushing by him. "We're by the river,

Mike. I don't want to be by the river, and I don't want to go to jail. What are we gonna do?"

Mike looked at him. He'd always taken care of Tony, but now he felt scared himself. Scared that he couldn't keep them out of jail and scared he couldn't provide for them. "How much money you got, Tony?" he asked.

"I got about twenty dollars. How about you?"

"I got a little more than that. In the morning we head south. 'Cause this place ain't safe no more."

"Okay, Mike, that sounds good," Tony said. The confident sound of Mike's voice had eased his mind, and with a plan Tony felt safe. He lay down on the cardboard they'd dragged up with them and tried to sleep. He listened to the sound of the cars overhead. He lifted his head to check and make sure Mike was still there. Tony could see him sitting there, tucked up under the overpass just as far as he was, holding his knees and rocking. He knew Mike was working things out in his mind. Tony drifted off to sleep, for the last time.

Mike sat there in the dark, tired, frustrated, and feeling really low. The evening hadn't gone the way he'd hoped it would. As he thought about what to do, he looked over at Tony. He was sleeping soundly, letting Mike take care of everything, as usual. For some reason, this time it pissed Mike off. He got up and thought of going for a walk, but there really wasn't anyplace to go. The overpass sloped downward dangerously, and on one side was the rushing water of the Hudson River. The other side was concrete and grass—the road that ran along the waterway, and the grass that climbed the slope to the bridge overhead. Mike looked down at it and thought of all the fun they'd had. "It's been good for a laugh," he said into the night air. He couldn't sleep, so he stared out into the night at the highway sign below.

Sometime during the early morning hours, Mike realized they weren't going to make it out of this. He thought of Tony and his promise to keep him safe and out of jail. He knew in his heart that Tony wouldn't make it. And he knew that Tony's simplemindedness would only slow him down. If he were going to escape, he had to be on his own. He climbed down the slope and walked along the highway looking for something. Finding what he was looking for, he climbed back up the slope of the overpass. He stood there, looking down at Tony's sleeping form. Then he raised the large club in his hand and swung it downward with all his strength.

Lindsay drove down the same highway Will had driven earlier. She'd gotten the same sedan she'd used earlier in the week from the police station and followed the directions Will gave her over the radio as the dispatcher had put her through to him. She parked her car in the parking lot of the restaurant where Will had directed her and got into the police car with Will and Jerry. They'd come to meet her, leaving Sam running the investigation with Dave Matthews and his team. Lindsay filled them in on the information she'd gotten while waiting in the emergency room.

"Damn, I hope no one ever asks us to explain this," Will said, as he followed Lindsay's directions. Lindsay smiled as she sat next to Will in the front seat. Jerry was lounging in the back seat.

"Lindsay, are you sure of that number?" he asked.

"Yes, why?"

"Because that's a very small farm road off the main highway, according to this map," Jerry said.

"I can't help that. I can only tell you what I get. This is your neck of the woods. Not mine," Lindsay said.

"Okay I need to know what's going on with them now. You've told us about Mike and what he's doing, but what about Tony? Where's he?" Will asked.

Lindsay sat still, thinking. Will and Jerry could almost feel her reaching out to Tony. Suddenly Lindsay gasped. "Oh, my God, he's dead, or dying!" she said. Will and Jerry were just as shocked as she was.

"What! What do you mean he's dead or dying?" Will demanded.

"Just what I said. I can't feel him, but I can feel Mike's emotions about it. I really think he's dead."

They all sat quietly in the car as Will drove. They were looking for the turnoff from the highway.

Mike stood there, looking down at Tony's body. He saw the large gash in his head and the blood oozing from it. He watched the life leave him in the form of dark red blood. It stained the concrete and the cardboard where he lay. Mike lifted one foot and pushed Tony with all his strength down the slope of the overpass, into the water.

Just as Tony's body splashed into the cold rushing water, Mike heard him cry out. Mike scrambled down the side of the slope. "Mike!" Tony cried, as he sank beneath the surface. Mike panicked and tried to run alongside the river. He saw Tony come to the surface and heard him scream out his name again. Mike's heart was beating faster and faster as he ran into a chain link fence, designed to keep people out of the dangerous area. He remembered that he and Tony had climbed over it earlier.

"Tony!" Mike screamed as he saw him surface again.

"Mike!" Tony screamed back.

An incredible calm came over Mike as he halted his climb over the fence and watched the rushing water take Tony from him. He knew he couldn't save him, no matter what he did now. It was better to let the river have him. He hadn't killed his best friend after all. Mike walked back to the overpass and climbed back up to the top. He lay down on the bloody cardboard that Tony had vacated just a few minutes before. Pulling the blanket up over him, he fell asleep. He looked like any other bum sleeping under an overpass.

"Okay, you're telling me you can't find him now. Why?" Will asked sarcastically.

"I told you, I think Tony's dead. Mike seems to be alone, but he has to wake up or I can't get anything other than a normal sleep pattern from him," Lindsay said.

"Will, just go to the farm road. Let's see if we can find them without Lindsay this time." Jerry felt sorry for her. Will was tired and cranky. He knew nothing could be accomplished by yelling at each other.

Will sat fuming and staring out the window. If the sun would come up, it would be so much easier. "How much longer to sun-up?"

"About two hours," Jerry said.

"Will, I'm sorry," Lindsay said.

"It's okay. I'm tired, you're tired. We'll find them."

They drove on for another ten minutes when Jerry spotted the farm road sign on the right. Will slowed the car and turned off the headlights. He could see an overpass as he turned onto the farm road. It was more of a bridge over the river, but it had a feeder road and grass.

They almost didn't see him. If fact, if he hadn't run, they would have driven right past him. But Mike had been awakened by the sound of the tires crunching over the gravel. He jumped to his feet and started down the slope of concrete, stumbling as he went. His arms were flying wildly at his sides and he looked like a great awkward bird trying to take off.

Jerry jumped from the moving car as Will slammed on the brakes, yelling Mike's name. Mike only turned and looked in recognition, then ran on. Will jumped from the car, screaming at Lindsay as he went, "You stay in here!" he shouted.

They tackled him less than a hundred yards away. He'd been held up once again by the fence, and he tried desperately to climb over, screaming, "I didn't kill her, I didn't kill anyone," when Jerry grabbed him. Mike spun around and took a swing at Jerry, who ducked efficiently. Will lunged at Mike and took him to the ground. As he pounded Mike's head into the gravel at the base of the fence, Jerry kicked at him a few times, trying to dislodge the knife in his hand. Will gained control of his emotions as the knife finally clattered away due to a well-aimed foot to the wrist from Jerry. They flipped Mike over and cuffed him.

"Mike Hennessey?" Will asked.

Mike nodded. "Where's your partner?" Jerry asked.

"In the river, he went for a little swim. Don't you guys have anything else to do but pick on people?" Mike asked.

"That depends, scumbag. Don't you have anything better to do than murder defenseless young woman?" Will asked.

Mike laughed, "They liked it," he said sarcastically.

"Read this trash his Miranda rights, will you, Jerry, before I forget myself and send him for a little swim in the river with his friend. I'm going to see if he's a liar," Will said, as he shoved Mike from him and struggled to catch his breath. Will climbed the concrete embankment. It wasn't that he didn't believe Lindsay, actually he was amazed by her. But the cop in him had to be sure.

He squatted down by the bloody cardboard and pushed the blanket around with a pencil. "Jerry, he may or may not be dead, but he's not here. But there's enough blood to start a blood bank. I'm gonna look around." Jerry reached into his pocket for his sketch of Mike and Tony. It had actually been very good, remarkably accurate.

"Michael Hennessey, you have the right to remain silent . . ." Jerry said as they marched him back to the car.

Will joined them again after a fruitless search, shaking his head no at Jerry's inquiry.

Only a few things remained to be done. First, process this jerk, then arrange a lineup with Georgia Amando and Dave Clorey. And then, the funerals of Mike's and Tony's latest victims, Catrina Vincent and Miles Handley. Just a few little things.

EPILOGUE

Lindsay waved good-bye as she walked down the runway to the plane. Her job was done, and she was going home. The wounds from this tragedy would take years to heal, but the scars would be there forever. This was the first time Lindsay had felt the trauma of a victim. She shuddered as the stewardess greeted her.

"Cold already?"

Lindsay smiled at her. "This chill runs a little deeper," she said as she worked her way to her seat. She looked out the window of the plane. She could see Will, Jerry, and Sam standing there waving at her. She blew them a kiss as she thought about the three of them. Professional, compassionate, and hard core. She'd miss them.

As they turned to walk away, Will punched Jerry in the arm. "Do you have a thing for Lindsay?" he asked.

"No, could you imagine loving a woman like that? A woman who knew if you were lying to her or if you were slipping around hiding money or something like that? She would need a perfect guy, a guy with a name like Bob or something," Jerry said, blushing. "Besides, I have a date with Carla tonight."

"You snake in the grass," Will said. He was surprised. He knew they'd had a nice dinner, but Jerry had never given any indication he'd thought even once about Carla.

Jerry laughed, "You think I tell you everything? Shit, no. You would have told Betty, and she would have told Carla, and then my butt would have been on the line. I can hear it now, 'Carla wants to know why Jerry hasn't called her.' Sorry, partner, some things are better kept private."

Sam laughed as they approached the parking area. Will stopped and looked at Jerry. "I have something else to ask you, now that I think about it."

Jerry looked at him. "What?"

"How did you know to hold Lindsay the other day when we were in the field room, and she was freaking out?"

"She's a woman, she was scared, and you were making it worse by screaming at her. That's all women need—to be held, and comforted, and reassured," Jerry said with a shrug of his shoulders.

"And you're divorced. I'll never understand women as long as I live. I've given up trying, and I'm still married. And here you are, divorced, and you understand them better than they understand themselves," Will laughed.

"Guys, can we go now?" Sam asked as he climbed into the car.

As the doors closed the radio crackled. Will and Jerry looked at it. Sam felt the hairs on the back of his neck stand up. "Go ahead, dispatch," Jerry said.

"We have a D.B. over on the east end near the Hudson Bay Marina. See the man in charge at the boat launch."

"We're on it." Jerry said.

Within twenty minutes they were looking down at a man who had died suddenly and violently. As they turned him over, Will let out a whistle. The huge gash in his head was the apparent cause of death. The scrapes and abrasions only added to the trauma. The body was badly swollen and had started to decompose. Jerry reached in his jacket pocket and pulled out a piece of paper. Then he took the wallet that was being handed to him by the uniformed officer.

"Gentlemen, meet Tony Wiley Garrison."

"I'll be damned, he really is dead." Sam said.

"Yep, apparently so. Looks deader than a doornail to me," Will said.

"Bag him, tag him, and send him to the morgue, Todd," Jerry said to the uniformed officer standing with the men on the dock.

"Yes, sir," the officer said.

"Here's another one we can take off the M.I.A. list," Will said.

Mike was sitting in the corner of his cell when Will and Jerry walked up to the bars. "We thought you might like to know your buddy washed up this afternoon," Will said, as he stuck his hands in the pockets of his jacket.

Mike didn't say anything. He just sat there looking down at his hands folded across a newspaper in his lap.

"Well, have a nice life. We hope you find your accommodations satisfactory," Jerry chuckled.

They turned to go as Mike said, "I'll get out, you know. Someday I'll get out. And when I do, I'm coming for you, you and this chick here in the paper." Mike leapt at the bars, waving the morning newspaper in his hand. Will and Jerry jumped back, momentarily surprised.

A picture of Will, Jerry, Sam, and Lindsay was on the front page. Lindsay, as usual, had her hand in front of her face. "You forget; I've seen her up close. Hell, I rode in the car with her. I smelled her perfume. I bet she's real fun to party with, ain't she?" Mike taunted.

Will's hand shot out suddenly and he reached through the bars and grabbed the back of Mike's head, slamming his forehead into the bars in front of him. "You do that, you scumbag; you come to my house, or any of our houses, for that matter. But before you do, you should know that I'm from the South. Do you know what we do to guys like you in the South? We take 'em out back of the barn and we castrate them. Yep, that's right, we cut their balls off and shove 'em down their throats," Will said, pushing Mike away.

Mike staggered back, looking scared for the first time. One hand went to his forehead, the other instinctively went to his crotch. Someone had finally gotten to him where he lived.

Will straightened his jacket as he and Jerry walked out. "You think he means it?" Jerry asked.

"Yeah, I do. But I also think he'll never get out. Come on, I'll buy you a cup of the worst coffee in the world," Will said.

"I can hardly wait," Jerry laughed.

Lindsay walked back from the mailbox on a cold, crisp sunny day. As she did she flipped through the mail in her hand. The New Year had dawned bright and clear, and Lindsay shivered as a chill wind swirled under her light coat. A pastel pink envelope caught her attention. Lindsay flipped it over and read the address in the top left-hand corner. "Mr. & Mrs. Joseph Mercer." Lindsay opened the envelope and grabbed for a tiny picture of the beautiful dark-haired baby as it tumbled free.

It was a birth announcement for Hope Lindsay Mercer, five pounds, four ounces, nineteen inches long. "Dear Lindsay," the card read. "We just wanted to send you a picture of our precious gift from God. Our beautiful Hope was born two weeks early, but healthy in every way. Much love, Joey, Georgia and Hope Mercer."

The author's e-mail address is **DJAdams@aol.com**.
See her web site at www.GetEnlightened.com

If you enjoyed *Running Crazy*, try D. J. Adams's previous book, *Scenting Evil*, also published by Capital Books.

An excerpt from *Scenting Evil* …

A Note from the Author

Like Lindsay Freeman, the heroine of this book, I am a clairvoyant who works with law enforcement agencies to find missing children. Lindsay's involvement in this case is much like my own in a very similar case almost twenty years ago.

Then, as in the story told here, terror struck the heart and soul of a small southern town. Then, as in the story told here, two very brave little girls were kidnapped from their homes and brutalized by a psychopath very much like Roman Marsh. In that case, I was the clairvoyant who brought the children home. In this fictional account, Lindsay Freeman does the job.

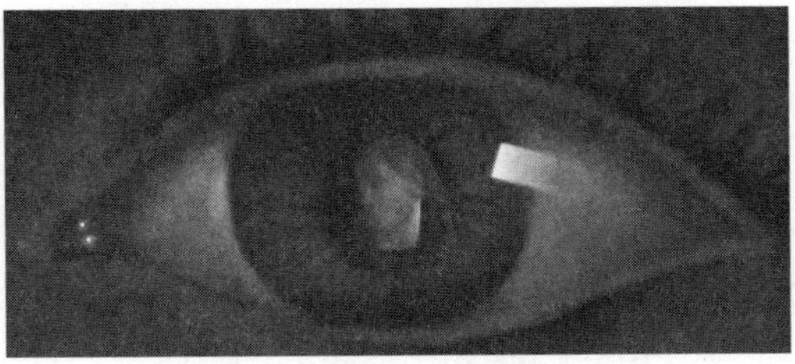

CHAPTER 1

Roman Marsh raised his head from sleep. What was it that woke him this time? He always wondered about that. Was it the things that go bump in the night or the sounds that stir your conscience as you sleep? Groggily he tried to focus his eyes as well as his mind. He let his head hit the pillow again and lay looking up at the ceiling. He growled long and deep in his throat. The kind of low rumbling you hear that makes the hairs on the back of your neck stand up and makes your skin tingle with a fear of danger. He had practiced this until he had it right, and now it was second nature to him. It was one of the things that gave him pleasure.

Roman lay there with his body slowly coming to life and the comfort of relaxation leaving him as the tension slowly eased its way back in. The hand resting above his head clenched tightly into a fist. His mind wandered through the avenues of his desire, searching for the things that gave him pleasure until the thought hit him like a bolt out of the blue. The adrenaline started racing through his body, waking him up completely.

"It's out there," he said out loud to no one but himself.

Or could it be that the tiny being on the floor heard him? Rolling over quickly, he pulled the mini blinds roughly away from the window. The sweat that covered his body glistened in the light of the full moon. He forced the muscles in his arm to work the window up. Raising his face to the warm moist June breeze that came through the opening, he inhaled deeply. As his senses came alive he started to tingle all over. He let the feeling run through him from the roots of his hair to the tips of his toes.

His throat constricted and his chest tightened. He wanted it to be tonight, he needed it, he even prayed for it, to whatever beast it is that a man like him prays. The scent that he needed was in the air. Blessed Be, there it was! He let the rumble in his narrow chest continue and enjoyed the vibration as it tingled within him. He glanced at the clock—1:38.

He let his head fall back to the pillow, letting the feeling continue to caress him. The night breeze blew in the window, and the coolness of it made his body erect. His mind wandered over the past to the day he'd had and what was in store for him tonight.

"Oh, you are crafty," he whispered to himself.

"Run, run, as fast as you can, you can't catch me, I'm the gingerbread man." He giggled in the darkness as his hands went to work on his body.

Feeling the rushing sensation overtake him, he surrendered to it and the sweet ecstasy only he could bring to himself. His stomach grumbled as he worked his body into a frenzy of sensation. He was hungry, but food was not his desire. In his mind he could see and smell his prey. His flames danced with desire as little Marcie Anderson lay perfectly still in the corner on a pallet of dirty blankets under the rocking chair, pretending to be asleep. She dared not lift her head.